WHATEVER IT TAKES

A GREY JUSTICE NOVEL

BY CHRISTY REECE

Whatever It Takes

A Grey Justice Novel

Published by Christy Reece

Cover Art by Patricia Schmitt/Pickyme

Copyright 2016 by Christy Reece

ISBN: 978-0-9916584-9-7

To obtain permission to excerpt portions of the text, please contact the author at Christy@christyreece.com.

PROLOGUE

Chicago, Illinois

"I want to see my sister."

The cool, abrupt statement had Frank Braden looking up from his desk. The girl in front of him was beautiful in a way so few chicks were these days. She had a fresh, innocent air about her. Laughable, considering her occupation.

"What makes you think your sister wants to see you? You're not exactly on speaking terms, are you?"

She flinched slightly, knowing he spoke the truth. "She's my sister. We may have our disagreements, but we still love each other."

"You saw her a few months ago." Frank didn't bother hiding his smirk.

"That was more than a year and a half ago, and it was a recording. I want to see her in person."

The fire in Alice's light blue eyes intrigued him. The last few months she'd been acting like a whipped puppy, and while he needed her obedient, he didn't want her to completely lose her spirit. Part of the fun in controlling his girls was the battle. Even though he would always win, he still liked a challenge.

"Maybe when I'm sure I can trust you again, I'll consider it."

"How much longer do you intend to keep using me as a…a…"

She trailed off, apparently uncomfortable describing her role. Frank had no such problem as he finished for her. "Whore?"

She flinched but then jerkily nodded. Yeah, she knew what she was.

"How old are you, Alice?"

"Almost twenty-two."

His eyes slid up and down her body, taking in the short skirt, halter top, and mile-high stilettos. The girls didn't like wearing the shoes, said they hurt their ankles and feet. Like he actually gave a damn.

After enjoying the scenery, he moved his gaze back to her face and saw icy hatred in her expression. No, she was most definitely not broken.

"I'd say you have a good five or six years left before you start to look like a used-up hag."

The color bleached from her face. "You told me I could pay you back in a year. It's been almost two. And I—"

"Changed my mind. I'm not tired of you yet."

Truth was, when he was through with her, he'd sell her to make a little more money off her. Or, if she lost her looks, he'd just get rid of her altogether.

"Besides, after that stunt you pulled, you're lucky I didn't kill you. Cost me money to find you."

"I've learned my lesson. I won't run off like that again. I promise."

Yeah, she'd learned her lesson, and the funny part was, he hadn't even had to lift a finger. Not that she would ever know.

He narrowed his eyes, seared her with one of his 'I mean business' looks. "Good to know. Do something like that again and it won't have as good an outcome."

"Just, please, let me see Kathleen. I won't tell her anything about…our arrangement. I just want to see her."

Frank considered her for a few seconds. He didn't like giving in to any of his girls' requests. Give 'em one thing, next thing you know, they're asking for something else. However, if he dangled seeing her sister in front of her like some kind of carrot reward, he could manipulate the situation to his liking.

"I'll consider it. We'll talk about it when you get back."

"Get back?"

He picked up his iPhone from his desk. "Noon tomorrow, Finley Hotel, Room 2002. He's paid for twenty-four hours. Wants the full treatment."

She flinched again, but this time Frank hid his grin. No use pissing her off. She was going to need all her energy and stamina for tomorrow.

He glanced at the wall clock behind her head. "Probably be a good idea to get some sleep. You need to look your best for this client. He's paying top dollar for you."

Without a word, she started for the door.

"Wait. Before you go, bring me a brandy."

Shooting him a withering look, she stomped to the bar, poured him a drink, came back, and slammed the glass onto his desk.

Frank grabbed her wrist, squeezed tight. "There's a fine line between spirited and ill-mannered, baby. When you return from your overnighter, perhaps we should explore that line."

Fear leaped into her eyes, and Frank let her go. She knew full well the words were not a mere warning. She would pay for her attitude with blood and tears.

He leaned back in his chair and took a swallow of the finest, most expensive brandy a man could get.

"If you don't get out of here, I'll assume you'll want the lessons to begin tonight."

She backed away and turned to the door.

Frank took another sip of his brandy and then grimaced. Hmm. Taste was a little off, wasn't it?

Agony seized his throat, as if gripped in a vise. He dropped the drink and grabbed his neck. Couldn't breathe. Breath pumped from his lungs but couldn't make it out an airway. What was wrong? What...what? He was smothering. Pressure built in his chest. His entire body stiffened with fear... Adrenaline shot through his veins as he gasped and heaved, desperate for air he could not release.

He looked up at the woman standing a few feet from him. Had she done this to him? Poisoned him? Her eyes were wide with surprise...but did they gleam with triumph, too?

Frank tried to speak...to beg her to call for help. He reached for her, and she jumped out of his way. His face slammed onto his desk. He lay there, helpless and in agony, while air rattled in his body, looking for escape.

Less than a minute later, he made one long last wheezing effort while the sound of mocking, sultry, female laughter followed him into death.

CHAPTER ONE

Slater House Hotel
Chicago

"Did you sleep well last night, Sophia?"

"Yes, Daddy," Sophia said with an emphatic nod. "I went to sleep right after story time. Slept all night long."

Not to be outdone, four-year-old Violet chimed in, "Me, too, Daddy. I slept-ed all night long, too."

"Good for you both. I know Miss Teresa appreciates what good girls you're being while Daddy's away."

"What are you eating for breakfast, Daddy?" Sophia moved closer to the screen to see what was on Eli's table. "We're eating strawberry pancakes."

"I wish I could have something that yummy. I'm just eating plain old boring cereal."

"When are you coming home?"

"Soon, I promise, Violet."

"Miss you, Daddy."

Eli's heart clutched, as it always did at the sheer sweetness of his daughters. There was no artifice, no hiding. Talking to them after a day of negotiating, dealing with fake smiles and hidden agendas was as refreshing as diving into a pool of cool water on a hot Texas day. This was the reason he continued despite all the worries and problems he had taken on. If not for Violet and Sophia, he wasn't sure he would have retained his sanity.

"It's time to get ready for school, girls," Teresa said. "Say good-bye to your daddy."

In between smooching sounds and "I love you's," he watched his daughters leave the kitchen table.

As soon as they'd left the room, Teresa Longview, nanny, housekeeper, cook, and all-around lifesaver, came on the screen. "They miss you, Mr. Eli, but they're doing just fine."

"Thank you for taking such good care of them."

"They're a pleasure, sir. You know that."

"Anything I need to know about?"

"No, sir. It's been amazingly quiet. Seems like everything is settling into place...finally getting back to normal."

Eli hoped that was true but didn't count on anything these days. "No odd incidents? Phone calls?"

"No, sir. I've been very careful with everything, just like you warned me."

That was a relief. It'd taken almost a year, but the Slaters were finally back on the right track. But just because he'd worked his ass off to clean up the mess didn't mean everyone was happy. No doubt there were still plenty of people who would love to see the Slaters completely decimated.

"Thanks for being vigilant, Teresa. I don't expect any problems but can't let my guard down."

"I understand, Mr. Eli."

"I'll call back tonight at bedtime."

"We'll look forward to it. Have a good day."

"You, too, Teresa."

Eli closed his laptop, now ready to start his day. A few minutes spent with his daughters were better than any vitamin ever created.

So far, having Slater as a last name hadn't impacted his children. The girls were just babies, much too young to comprehend. They still believed they lived in a safe, sane world. His daughters had no idea that it was all a lie—a lie he would willingly tell for as long as he could get away with it. He would do whatever he had to do to protect them from the family they'd had the misfortune to be born into and the world they would eventually have to face.

He had learned that hell the hard way. In one seemingly endless nightmare, his life had imploded. It had begun with the murder of his wife, Shelley—although he hadn't known it was a murder at the time. Eli had believed, as he was meant to, that she had taken her own life. Unintentionally, yes. Mixing booze and drugs was always a bad idea. And for Shelley, who'd been both an alcoholic and a drug addict, it had been a lethal combination.

After Shelley's death, he'd been hanging on, barely, but he'd been surviving. Then the clouds had gathered above them, the storm had settled in, and the shit had come down in torrents.

All of that was behind them now, but not without loss...not without major consequences.

Mathias, his father, was dead. And after an excruciatingly long and painful trial, his brother Adam was in prison, where the bastard would spend the rest of his miserable life.

Eli had worked like a demon to repair the damage the two had created. He had bartered, badgered, apologized, and pleaded, then scrubbed and scoured, doing everything he could to erase what Mathias had spent a lifetime creating. Businesses had been sold, stocks and bonds liquidated and contracts demolished. All the records found, in both Adam's and Mathias's offices, had been examined with a fine-tooth comb with one intent—to remove the scourge his father and brother had perpetrated.

Eli had succeeded. And while the Slater name still had a black cloud hanging over it, and the family's wealth had been cut in half, at least they could all sleep at night. Perhaps by the time his daughters were grown, being a Slater would be something to be proud of again.

His mother and sister were in France, as far away from this mess as he could get them. And Jonah, his youngest brother, understandably bitter, was on a personal mission of vengeance. Eli worried for him but understood. Jonah had yet to come to terms with everything that had happened...everything he had lost.

He and Jonah were like two survivors of the same catastrophe. So far neither of them had been able to discuss that night, or the events that had led up to it.

Eli leaned back in his chair, wishing once again that he hadn't had to come to Chicago. He didn't like being away from home, but traveling was sometimes an unavoidable burden. Whenever he did travel, he had breakfast via webcam with the girls each morning, and each night at bedtime, he called and read them a story. It wasn't as good as being there in person, but the girls seemed to enjoy the uniqueness of talking to their daddy via video.

Standing, Eli went to the bedroom and started dressing for the day. He clicked on the television, more for noise than to listen to the news. His mind on the myriad items he needed to accomplish, he didn't catch the beginning of the news story that was now on. It wasn't until he heard a husky, feminine voice thick with emotion that he paid attention. He turned to see the owner of that voice and froze in place, mesmerized.

"I have nothing to say to you people. You've gotten all you're getting from my family."

"Miss Callahan, do you feel shame for your sister? Not only for being a prostitute but for being accused of so cold-bloodedly killing Frank Braden?"

Fire burned in extraordinary eyes of aqua blue. "Do you feel shame for your stupid questions?" she sneered.

Undeterred, the reporter continued, "You're testifying today. What will you tell the court?"

Shoulders straight, expression resolute, she said fiercely, "That my sister was taken advantage of. She was not a prostitute. And that she most definitely did not kill Frank Braden."

She turned her back to the camera and strode rapidly away.

A smug smile tugged at the reporter's mouth. "To recap, the trial of Alice Callahan, who is accused of murdering local businessman Frank Braden, will resume this morning at ten o'clock. And as we just heard, today's testimony will include Kathleen Callahan, the accused's sister. Considering what we've learned so far, one can only speculate what today's revelations will be. Reporting from Cook County Courthouse, this is April Majune."

Eli clicked off the television, but it didn't matter. The image of Kathleen Callahan's captivating face stayed etched in his mind. The husky, musical tone of her voice was a sound he knew he'd never forget.

Returning to the kitchen table where he'd left his laptop, Eli opened it and entered the names Callahan and Braden into a search engine. He had heard nothing about the trial. Dallas and Chicago were hundreds of miles from each other. And having no love for the media and their shenanigans, he usually avoided the news, local and national, as much as possible.

A lengthy list of hits appeared. Eli clicked on one and skimmed the information. The more he read, the more intrigued he became. Exiting out of one site, he scrolled down until he came to the name Kathleen Callahan. Clicking on that one, Eli stared hard at the photograph of one of the most striking women he'd ever seen. This shot had been taken at a happier time in Kathleen's life. Though still not smiling, there were no tension lines around her mouth, no shadows beneath her eyes.

His gaze moved to the text, and once again he became immersed, unaccountably fascinated, so deeply engrossed that when his cellphone rang, it took him several seconds to identify the sound.

He headed back to the bedroom and grabbed his phone. When he saw the caller's name on the screen, and then the time, he winced. Dammit, he was never late.

"Hugh?"

"Eli, everything okay?"

"Yes. Sorry. I know we were supposed to meet downstairs. I—" Making a split decision, Eli said, "Listen, there's been a change of plans. Come up to my room and let's talk. I need to move some appointments around."

Thankful that his assistant wasn't one to ask needless questions, Eli ended the call and then immediately pressed a speed-dial number to one of his most trusted friends.

"Justice. Eli. You have any information on a case in Chicago involving the murder of a Frank Braden?"

Grey Justice wasn't often taken by surprise, but Eli could hear it in the man's voice—his British accent always became a little crisper. "Frank Braden? Chicago? Not that I recall. Is it something I should check out?"

"Yes. I'd—" He'd what? What was he going to say? That he'd seen a beautiful woman on television, looked her up on the Internet, and was now obsessed with knowing more? Hell.

"The case sounds like something you'd be interested in." Eli winced at the lameness of his answer.

"Is that right?" The slight amusement in Justice's tone told Eli that he hadn't fooled his friend in the least.

Eli relayed the basic facts. Grey Justice and his people could find out everything about the case within a matter of a few clicks. And even though Eli's interest in Kathleen was definitely personal, what he'd told Justice was true. This case sounded perfect for the Grey Justice Group.

"Let me look into it," Justice said. "I'll get back to you."

Eli returned the phone to the desk and stared out at the Chicago skyline. He had no explanation for what he was about to do. Impulsiveness had been beaten out of him long ago, and damned if he could begin to formulate a reason for his actions. Never in his life had he had such a visceral reaction to a woman. Something about Kathleen Callahan called to him, compelled him to know more. Despite all the scheduling problems, the headaches he was about to cause, Eli refused to not see this out.

CHAPTER TWO

Cook County Courthouse
Chicago

Kathleen Callahan sat in the courtroom on the front row, directly behind the defense table. It was as close to her sister, Alice, as she could get. Every day for two weeks, she'd sat in the same spot, alternating between cursing beneath her breath and biting her tongue.

Alice's attorney, Tony Burton, was young but had a solid reputation and was known for his ferociousness in the courtroom. Though he had come at a premium price, Kathleen had recognized early that to win, Alice would need the best defense money could buy.

This whole ordeal was wearing her sister down. Strawberry-blond hair, once lustrous and thick, was now dull, lifeless. Blue eyes the color of a cool, crisp October sky had lost their light. Though the Callahans were naturally pale, Alice's color was an unhealthy pallor. She looked the complete opposite of the bubbly, outgoing young woman Kathleen remembered.

"The prosecution rests, Your Honor."

She jerked her eyes away from Alice and concentrated on the proceedings. By the smug glint in the DA's eyes, he believed he had proven his case beyond a shadow of a doubt.

It did look bad—no one would deny that. Alice's fingerprints had been on the brandy decanter and glass. The poison that had killed Frank Braden had come from the decanter. If that had been the only thing, perhaps the crime wouldn't have looked so heinous, so intentionally vile. Not by anyone's standards had Frank Braden been a good man, and many people, including Kathleen, believed he'd gotten what he deserved. But the post-mortem throat slicing, eye gouging, and severed penis looked like the act of a psychopath.

Alice swore she had done none of those things, including poisoning the brandy. She'd admitted to pouring Frank the drink and watching him collapse, but she claimed she'd run out of the house right after and had done nothing more.

Kathleen believed her. Unfortunately, no one else did.

There had been no sign of forced entry, and to add to her appearance of guilt, instead of calling the police, Alice had stolen one of Frank's cars and left.

Driving for fifteen hours straight, she had shown up at Kathleen's door in Denver, Colorado, with nothing more than her purse. Those were the actions of a vulnerable, panicked person, not a cold-blooded murderer.

Kathleen knew her sister. Yes, Alice had made mistakes. She trusted too easily and too often took the easy way out, but she wasn't a bad person, and she was most definitely not a killer.

Because she believed in her sister, Kathleen had persuaded Alice to call the police and turn herself in. She had been sure it was the right thing to do—that justice would prevail. But now, Kathleen couldn't stop the doubt, the nagging suspicion that maybe she should have just grabbed Alice and headed out of the country. Had she made the wrong decision once again?

If only Frank Braden had never entered Alice's life. The man had been older and much too worldly for her innocent sister. He had charmed, wined and dined her, bought her pretty things, and made promises he never intended to keep. Alice had been dazzled by the money and gifts, and by the time she'd wanted out, it had been too late. He had used her in the worst way possible.

Now that the prosecution had rested, the real truth could be revealed. Tony would be calling expert witnesses, a psychologist who specialized in Stockholm syndrome, other women whom Braden had used and abused, as well as a former high school friend of Alice. All of them would cast doubt on the prosecution's claim. That no way in hell had Alice Callahan murdered Frank Braden.

But it would start with the one person who knew Alice better than anyone else. Believed in her above all others.

"The defense calls Kathleen Callahan."

Kathleen stood. Head held high, posture perfect but relaxed, she gave no indication that she was the least bit worried. Her heart, soul, her very being, was certain of her sister's innocence. She just had to convince twelve strangers of that fact.

Even though she walked slowly, calmly, she knew her slight limp was noticeable. The accident had been eighteen months ago, and she had completely recovered. However, when she was tired, her ankle had a tendency to ache. Her low-heeled shoes were not only for a serious and competent appearance, but also gave her the additional support she needed. Unfortunately, exhaustion was winning out, and her ankle ached like a sore tooth.

She stepped up onto the stand, and as she took the oath to tell the truth, Kathleen let her eyes roam the jury. They looked average and ordinary. Did they realize they held the fate of two lives in their hands? She and her sister only had each other. She would not, could not, fail.

Kathleen made her voice strong and true as she vowed "To tell the truth and nothing but the truth, so help me God."

Tony started slow, lobbing softball questions at her, giving her a chance to overcome her nervousness.

This wasn't new territory for Kathleen. As a security specialist, she had testified in court several times. The legalese was familiar, the procedure no mystery. A trial had a rhythm all its own, the courtroom held an ambience she'd always found comforting. Here, justice was served. Here, life and death decisions were made. She believed in the law, in the right and wrong of things. She had to trust that the justice system would not fail her sister.

Tony asked about her relationship to Alice, where Kathleen lived, what she did for a living. Tense muscles loosened, and she felt herself settle into a confident and comfortable rhythm. She could do this.

The questions became more intimate…personal. Kathleen valued her privacy—sharing details about her life, past or present, was most definitely not in her comfort zone. Alice was the outgoing, cheerful one. Kathleen was the serious, responsible one. But for Alice, she would gladly reveal everything, down to her unimpressive bra size, if that would help.

The questions became even more personal and direct, but Kathleen hung in there. No, she and her sister hadn't always lived together growing up. Explaining why wasn't easy, but hopefully she managed well enough that the jury understood that their father had been a loving man but had made some mistakes. Because of that, he'd served time in prison, and she and Alice had lived separately in various foster homes.

Kathleen was grateful that Tony didn't ask specific questions about those dark days. They weren't pertinent to what was happening now, but when any kind of reference was made, her stomach always twisted into knots.

When he moved on to asking questions about their father, the tight muscles in her body loosened. Even though Tony didn't ask outright, she was glad she was allowed the opportunity to explain that their father was given an early release from prison in exchange for working for the government as a security consultant. Because of that, Daniel Callahan had been able to be reunited with his family.

Kathleen appreciated the way Tony maneuvered the questions to show both she and Alice in the best light. What she liked even more was that the prosecutor hadn't made the slightest objection to any of the questions or Kathleen's answers.

The instant Tony said he was finished with his questions, she tensed up again. The prosecutor, Arnold Sims, stood, his long thin body unwinding from his chair like the uncoiling of a snake. The pitiless look in his eyes was a clear indicator that the soft, easy questioning had ended.

"Miss Callahan, how old were you when your sister was born?"

"Nine."

"And what happened to your mother?"

"She died giving birth to Alice."

"So your father had a nine-year-old and an infant to raise by himself?"

"Yes."

"Miss Callahan, isn't it true that your father placed much of the responsibility of raising your sister on you?"

"I helped a lot. Yes."

"That's not what I'm asking. Isn't it true that you basically raised Alice?"

Thankfully, Tony interrupted. "Your Honor, I fail to see what relevance this has on the case."

"Mr. Sims?" the judge said.

"Goes to the instability of the accused, Your Honor. Prosecution will show the defendant's unstable home life led to her poor choices as an adult."

"Very well. I'll allow it but tread lightly, Mr. Sims. Answer the question, Miss Callahan."

Satisfaction gleaming in his eyes, Sims turned his attention back to Kathleen.

Though the term *unstable home life* carved a wound in her heart, Kathleen answered honestly. "Much of the responsibility for Alice's care was left to me."

"Why is that, Miss Callahan?"

"My father needed the help."

"Isn't it true that you handled your sister's care because your father was too busy breaking into businesses and homes, being a thief? A criminal?"

Tony's voice rang out. "Your Honor, we've already established that Daniel Callahan broke the law and served time in prison. Not only did he pay his debt to society, but he served his country by working for the government."

"I agree, Mr. Burton. Objection sustained. Move on, Mr. Sims."

"Very well, Your Honor."

But the satisfaction was still there. The seed of doubt had been planted in the jury's mind. A father who'd broken the law, served time in prison. A child raised by another child. An unstable childhood had produced a cold-blooded, murdering adult.

"Miss Callahan," Sims said, "is it true that you and your sister, Alice, are estranged?"

Grateful to move on, Kathleen said, "No, sir, that is not true."

"Let me phrase my question a little better. Isn't it true that until she murdered Frank Braden, you had not spoken to your sister in years?"

That was an impossible question to answer. If she said yes, it would appear that she believed Alice had killed Frank. If she said no, then she would be lying. When Alice had shown up at her door that night, almost seven months ago, it was the first time in over two years that she had seen or spoken to her sister.

Thankfully, Tony jumped up and objected to the question. The prosecutor's smug smile when he asked again, rephrasing the question, fooled no one. Again, he'd gotten exactly what he wanted. More doubts had been sown.

Kathleen answered the rephrased question. "Alice and I drifted away from each other, as families sometimes do. It doesn't mean I stopped loving her or thinking about her often."

"But isn't it true that you and she had a rift?"

"We've had our share of arguments. All sisters do."

"But I want to know about the last argument you had with her. Where she told you to stay out of her life, and you told her that you were through with her reckless, irresponsible ways."

Sims glanced down at a piece of paper as if reading from it. "You said, and I quote, 'Don't come crying to me when your life turns to shit, and you screw up beyond all hope.'"

No need to wonder how he could recite the statement verbatim. When she'd hurled those ugly words at her sister, they'd been in a crowded room, at Alice's twentieth birthday party. Alice had just informed her she was dropping out of college. Kathleen had been stunned.

After working so hard to get Alice into a decent college that would take her with her unimpressive GPA, Kathleen, for once, hadn't bothered to soften her words. Dozens of people had heard her. Every word condemned Kathleen, and she wanted to crawl under her chair in both regret and embarrassment. It didn't matter that Alice had messed up time and again. She was her sister. Kathleen should never have abandoned her.

"I spoke rashly, without thought."

"Yet isn't it true that you hadn't talked to your sister in years? Until she showed up on your doorstep, after, using your own words, 'screwing up beyond hope'?"

"Objection, Your Honor. Mr. Sims is leading the witness."

"Since the witness has admitted that those were indeed her words, I'll allow it. Overruled."

"My sister came to me because she was scared. She knows I will always be there for her. No matter what."

"Even when she screws up beyond all hope?"

"Your Honor, this is getting ridiculous," Tony snapped.

"Continue with your questioning, Mr. Sims, and cease the editorializing."

"My apologies, Your Honor." The DA pinned her with those mean eyes again. "What caused the rift between you and your sister in the first place?"

This was the question she had dreaded. She had known she'd have to address it, but that didn't make it any easier to answer.

"Alice and I had different interests."

"And that caused you to become angry? What exactly were your sister's interests that you didn't share?"

"I was too focused on myself. On my career. I—"

"And what was your sister focused on? Selling herself to the highest bidder?"

Tony jumped to his feet and sputtered, "Your Honor, that's… that's outrageous."

"Overruled. Sit down, Mr. Burton. Since it's been established that the defendant was indeed a prostitute, the question is a fair one."

"No. My sister was not selling herself, and she most certainly was not a prostitute," Kathleen spat the words. "Alice was a victim of a man who took advantage of her."

"Yet she lived in his mansion. Wore designer clothes and expensive jewelry. Had her own website to show off her…um, wares, shall we say? Doesn't sound like a victim to me. In fact, it sounds exactly like a high-priced call girl."

"Then you're an idiot," Kathleen snapped.

"Mr. Sims, you're editorializing again," the judge said. "And I'll remind the witness to answer the questions asked, not give her opinion on the prosecution's intelligence."

"Everything that happened to Alice is my fault," Kathleen said. "She's young and naïve. Braden took advantage of her innocence. I should have been there for her. I'm responsible."

"*You're* responsible? It's your fault?"

"Yes."

"I see. So you gave your sister the poison that killed Mr. Braden? Did you also provide the knife she used to slice his throat, gouge out his eyeballs, and sever his genitals from his body?"

Her stomach heaved. "Of course not. I—"

"Or are you confessing to the murder yourself? Are we about to have a real-life Perry Mason moment? A confession on the stand? Did you, Kathleen Callahan, kill Frank Braden?"

"Don't be ridiculous. Of course not."

Sims nodded knowingly, his face revealing he'd led Kathleen exactly where he wanted her to go. "Of course you aren't confessing to murder, Miss Callahan." He twisted round, causing all eyes, including the jurors', to follow him as he pinned his accusing gaze on Alice. "Because we know exactly who killed Frank Braden, don't we?"

CHAPTER THREE

Cook County Jail
Chicago

"Thanks for the cookies. They'll go over well with my new cellmate."

"You have a new roommate? When did that happen?"

Alice's eyes flickered with sadness, but she didn't bother to correct Kathleen's terminology.

"Came back from the trial yesterday to find her sleeping... in my bed. Not that it matters. One cot is just as uncomfortable as the other. So far we've gotten along fine. She snores a lot, but other than that, we stay out of each other's way." Alice scrunched her nose in distaste. "As much as you can stay out of someone's way when they're within two feet of you at all times."

"What is she in for?"

"What else but murder? Don't you know they put all the badasses together?"

"Who did she murder?"

"We haven't exactly gotten that close."

The knowledge that her little sister had to share a cell with a murderer sent shudders through her. Even though Kathleen knew that Alice was no longer the innocent girl she'd once been, she was no hardened criminal either.

Wanting to give her sister some hope, Kathleen said, "I talked to Tony. He says the trial's going well and he's really optimistic."

Alice gave another tired little smile, and Kathleen wanted to cry because she knew she hadn't convinced her sister of anything. The hope that had once been in Alice's eyes was gone. All that remained was grim acceptance.

"We'll get you out of here. I promise."

"Oh, Kathleen, I wish you'd go live your life. Forget about me."

"Forget about you? Hell and damnation, Alice. How am I supposed to go about my life and forget that my baby sister—my only family—is on trial for a crime she didn't commit? No way in hell, Alice. No. Way. In. Hell."

"Your loyalty is one of the many reasons I love you." Tears glistened in her sister's eyes. "Have I ever thanked you for taking care of me?"

"No thanks are necessary. You know that. The moment Daddy brought you home, you were my baby doll."

A small smile tugged at Alice's mouth. "You did love to dress me up."

"That's because you were so tiny all of my doll clothes fit you perfectly."

A wistful look appeared on her face. "We did have some good times, didn't we? Before—"

Alice broke off, unwilling to add the obvious, but Kathleen knew exactly what she hadn't said. Before it had all gone so horribly wrong. Before their father had been convicted and imprisoned. Before she and Alice had been separated. Before the nightmare had begun.

It was useless to dwell on the past. It got you nowhere fast. The future was all that mattered.

"We'll have good times again, Alice. I promise." She took the small notebook from her pocket, picked up the pitiful excuse for a pen attached to the table. "Okay. Let's get to work."

"What's the point? We've gone over it and over it. I've told you everything."

"Then you'll tell me one more time. Dammit, Alice. I need you to fight. You can't give up. You understand me?"

Alice laughed softly. "Okay, Wildcat."

Kathleen grinned at the nickname their father had given her when she refused to give up on something she believed was right.

"Damn straight I'm a wildcat. Especially for people I believe in. I believe in you, Alice Callahan. Always have."

Grateful tears shimmered in her sister's eyes. Refusing to allow her own tears to gather, Kathleen said determinedly, "Now, tell me again about Braden. You met him at a party."

Even though they'd gone through the story numerous times before, Alice answered, "Yes. I was sharing an apartment with Renee Stokes at the time. She told me about this party. Said all sorts of sophisticated, wealthy men would be there."

Alice went on to describe how Frank had charmed her, bought her pretty things, romanced her. Her sister thought she'd found her knight in shining armor and had met the devil instead.

Kathleen blamed herself for her sister's naïveté. She had protected Alice from the harsher parts of life. Though they'd never had much money, if Alice had wanted something and it had been within Kathleen's ability, she'd done her best to see that her sister got it. She hadn't prepared Alice for how to cope with disappointment or rejection. Hadn't sufficiently warned her about the people who would take advantage of her innocence.

"And then you moved in with him a few weeks later?"

"No...I..." Alice trailed off, and Kathleen realized once again that there were more secrets yet to be revealed.

"What, Alice?" Kathleen leaned forward, whispered, "Sweetie, you can't keep things from me if we're going to prove your innocence. What haven't you told me?"

"Before I moved in with him...I was at his mansion for a party. I walked into a bedroom...saw him with a couple of women." She grimaced her disgust. "They were...you know... doing things. Anyway, it pissed me off. I was going to leave and never see him again. But I was so mad. So I—"

"What? What did you do?"

"Well...I had seen him in his study a few times before, when he'd gotten money out of his safe to give me for shopping and stuff."

"Oh, Alice," Kathleen whispered.

"It was only ten thousand dollars, Kathleen. After the way he'd treated me, lying and telling me I was the only woman in his life, I figured I deserved it."

"And you got caught?"

"No, not then. About a week later, he showed up at my apartment with a cop who arrested me for theft."

Kathleen shook her head, confused. "There's no record of an arrest."

"That's because it wasn't really an arrest. Frank had one of his friends dress up like a cop. I thought it was the real thing... I didn't find out until later that it was just another lie.

"Anyway, instead of taking me to jail, they took me back to Frank's house. The fake cop left, and Frank gave me a choice. Said I could stay with him, work for him to pay him back, or he'd call the cops, for real this time. He said he'd see to it that I served time in prison. I believed him. I'd already spent most of the money on rent and food and stuff. So I agreed to work for him. I didn't know what kind of work he was talking about until later."

Berating her sister for her choices would be pointless. Serving time in jail for theft would have been a walk in the park compared to what Braden had made her do. Alice had learned her lesson in the harshest way possible.

"So you moved in with him then. And you lived with him for how long before he brought in the first man?"

"A week or so." Alice closed her eyes as she described what happened next and the numerous men Frank had forced her to have sex with, all in the guise of paying a debt.

Kathleen made herself listen to each one. Though she knew the details by heart, and they sickened her every time she heard them, she was convinced that in this mass of horrific events, something would stand out that would reveal Braden's killer.

Even now, after having heard the horror stories of each encounter, Kathleen wished with all her might that Braden were alive so she could take care of him herself. Whoever had killed the bastard deserved a medal for the deed, but damned if she'd allow Alice to take the blame.

"Wait." Kathleen held up her hand, looking down at the notepad. "That's the first time you've mentioned Edward."

Her brow furrowed. "Are you sure?"

"Yes. Tell me about him."

"He was different than the others."

"Different, how?"

"All the others were forceful, sometimes to the point of cruelty. But Edward…I don't know. He seemed more amused than anything. And he didn't want to do anything other than talk."

"No sex?"

"No. He was in a wheelchair, so I'm not sure exactly if he was impaired sexually or not. We didn't talk about that. We might've kissed a little. I don't know, you kind of lose count after a while. But I do remember that we mostly just talked."

"About what?"

"About me. He wanted to know where I grew up. If I had family. Where they were. Why I stayed with Frank. Things like that."

"He didn't talk about himself?"

"No. I learned early not to ask questions."

"But you didn't get his last name either?"

"No. Last names were strictly forbidden. I'm not even sure any of them used their real first names."

That was one of the biggest problems. Frank Braden's records were as sketchy as his life. He used first names only and sometimes only descriptions or certain acts to describe the business transactions between the women and their "clients."

"Did you ever see Edward again?"

"No. Just that one time."

"Okay. Let's talk about the other women that Frank used this way."

"Kathleen, I promise. I've told you about them. He didn't let me associate with them other than a few times when he had parties. But even then, we didn't get to talk. We were there for only one reason. I don't even know where he kept them."

Refusing to back down, Kathleen forged on. "You've told me about five of them." She glanced down at her list, reciting the names of the girls Alice had given her.

Alice gave a weary nod. "Those are the only names I know."

"But there were others?"

"Yes, but I don't know their names. What do you want me to do, Kathleen? Draw their pictures? You think that's going to help you find them? I only know the first names of any of them. And even if you do find them, do you really think any of them would admit to killing Frank? Face it. I'm screwed."

"No, you're not. But we have to keep trying, Alice. We can't just give up. I won't give up."

Alice looked down at her hands, picked nervously at her nails. "You need to know something," she whispered. "It's not something I ever planned to tell you, but I think, for both of us to move forward, face what we have to face, you need to know the truth."

A chill swept down Kathleen's spine. "What?"

"First, before I tell you, I want you to know I never thought his threats were real. I—" She shook her head. "I just never believed he'd do it."

"What threats? Do what? What are you talking about?"

"Your hit-and-run accident. It wasn't an accident."

Her throat was so tight Kathleen was surprised she could get the words out. "What are you saying?"

"I think Frank was responsible. Oh, I'm not saying he did it himself, but I think he paid someone to do it. He told me about what happened, showed me pictures of you. He had a video. Someone came into your hospital room while you were unconscious and recorded you.

"You looked so battered, so hurt. I wanted to be with you. He laughed when I told him I had to go to you, and he said something like, 'See what happens when you don't do what you're told?'"

Kathleen mumbled through numb lips, "But why would he do that?"

Alice eyes dropped to her hands again. "I ran away from him… He caught me within a couple of days. I was surprised that he didn't do much more than yell at me, smack me around a little. It was a few days after that when he told me you'd been injured."

Kathleen had to grip the edge of the small table in front of her to keep from sliding out of the chair onto the floor. She remembered that day as vividly as if it had happened yesterday and not a year and a half ago—the horror, the pain, and the incredible, gnawing guilt.

She'd awakened in the hospital days later with an ankle so shattered it was almost demolished, a broken shoulder, fractured pelvis, a broken hand, and a severe concussion. Recovery had been slow, rehab had been hell. But to her mind, that hadn't been the worst of it. A child had almost died on her watch.

As a security specialist for Bankhead Security in Denver, Kathleen's job included myriad duties. One of her most frequent was protecting children. Dignitaries and wealthy, influential families who visited Denver often sought out bodyguard services for their families. Kathleen hadn't set out to be a children's bodyguard, but when her employer realized she had a special affinity for kids, she'd gotten many of those assignments.

Twelve-year-old Emily Van Hauer had been one of those children. Emily's father, a wealthy financier from Germany, was in the States for several months. No threats had been made against the family, but Lawrence Van Hauer was determined that his family stay safe. While others in the security company were assigned to protect Van Hauer's wife and son, Kathleen had been charged with protecting Emily. And she had failed.

The incident had done more than almost kill Emily, it had destroyed Kathleen's confidence in her ability to protect. Even after recovering her health and returning to work, she had refused all bodyguard assignments.

She saw the guilt in Alice's eyes. The knowledge that if she'd made a different decision, stayed away from Frank Braden, so much could have been prevented.

Forcing her mouth to form words, Kathleen said, "It wasn't your fault, Alice. I'm glad you ran from Braden, and I'm sorry he caught you. But you had no idea he would do something like that. He was the fiend, not you."

"But you and that little girl almost died."

Kathleen raised her hand, dimly pleased that it wasn't shaking the way her insides seemed to be. "It doesn't matter now. It's over. We both fully recovered. The most important thing is to concentrate on the here and now. We'll get you out of here, and you can start a new life. Put all of this behind you."

The last part came out a little shakier than she'd intended, telling her she needed to get the hell out before she lost the control that had been her mainstay for most of her life. Letting Alice see how this revelation had upset her would only make both of them feel worse.

"I'd better get going and see if I can run down any more leads. See you tomorrow. Okay?"

Without waiting for a reply, Kathleen returned the notebook to her purse and stood. She had to go...couldn't be there any longer, sure that she'd be screaming within the next seconds. Turning her back on her sister, she walked out the door.

CHAPTER FOUR

Kathleen didn't remember walking out of the jail or getting into her car. She barely remembered the drive to her apartment. When she came back to herself, she was parked at the apartment complex she now called home. A rat-infested hovel, with drug dealers and vermin competing for the top spot in repulsiveness.

She'd sold her house in Denver to pay for Alice's defense fees. Unfortunately, the money had dwindled quickly and was almost gone. This apartment, with its broken windows and cockroaches the size of small mice, was all she felt she could afford. It wasn't home. Just where she showered and slept a few hours at night. Most of her waking hours were spent at the library reading law books or talking to people who had known Frank Braden. Not that either one of those activities had done any good yet.

Tired in both body and spirit, Kathleen got out of her car and headed to her third-floor apartment. She paid no attention to her surroundings, and if she'd been in her right mind, she would've been cursing herself for her carelessness.

They came at her from both sides. Two men in their early twenties, knives glinting, smiles slick, confident they'd found easy prey. Just for an instant, she didn't care. The pull of self-pity was strong. Why fight? She'd lost so much. Did she even care anymore?

The horror of that thought jerked her back into the moment, out of her pity party. Hell, she was no quitter, nor was she weak. These young men with their cocky attitudes and lack of respect for life offended her on so many levels. They had underestimated her—they wouldn't be the first. At a little under average height, about five-four, with a slender, delicate-looking physique, she was often mistaken for fragile. Those who underestimated her soon discovered differently, as these idiots were about to learn.

Adrenaline replaced the wash of depression she'd been feeling. Now back in control, she found herself looking forward to this challenge.

She led them out into the open parking lot to give herself more room to maneuver. They didn't realize that, though. They would assume she was scared, trying to figure out how to escape. Little did these men know that escaping was the last thing on her mind.

She dropped her purse on the pavement. It held a weapon, but she had no plan to use it. She had faced these types of opponents before. Stupid arrogance was always a delight to take down.

Even though she knew it was pointless, she felt obliged to give them fair warning. "Okay, guys. No one's gotten hurt yet. Back away right now, and no one has to."

One of the men, the smaller of the two, grinned. "I like 'em feisty. We're going to have fun with you."

The larger one surprised her by saying, "I don't know, man, she don't look scared. Maybe she's right. Maybe we should—"

"If you're too chickenshit to handle this, that means I got her all to myself...and all the money, too."

"I ain't chickenshit, asshole," the big guy growled and then decided to show his lack of cowardice by lunging toward her.

Thankful she was wearing sneakers, Kathleen sprang nimbly away from her attacker, landing a couple of feet beside him.

Confused, he turned, and that's when she kicked the knife from his hand, followed by a one-two punch to his face then his soft belly.

Stumbling back, the guy bent over double. Knowing it would take him a minute or so to recover, she turned to the other guy, who was staring at her as if she were some kind of freak.

"You're a ninja."

Laughter bubbled up inside her, and for the first time in months, she felt lighthearted. If she'd thought these guys would cooperate, she'd thank them for the entertainment and let them walk away.

"Not a ninja. Just a woman who's going to beat your ass to a bloody pulp if you don't get out of here now."

She heard a noise behind her and glanced over her shoulder. The big guy had recovered quicker than she'd counted on and was now back on his feet.

She turned back to the smaller man, noting that with his friend's recovery, confidence had returned to his face. "Like hell, bitch. You're gonna pay for that."

They double-teamed her this time, and she went high with a split air kick. With the difference in their heights, one kick landed at the base of the taller guy's throat. The other kick was intended for the shorter guy's nose, but he shifted at the last second. Her foot missed his nose, bounced off his shoulder, jamming her weak ankle.

Damn, that hurt.

She dropped back to the pavement, hobbled backward, and landed flat on her ass. Cursing her weakness, she scrambled to get to her feet. She knew how to fight through the pain. Seeing their chance, they laughed as they came at her again. Unable to get to her feet in time, Kathleen scooted backward on her butt and then braced herself for the assault. It didn't come.

In her peripheral vision, she spotted a tall, broad-shouldered shadow. Startled, she turned in time to see a man with impressive speed and strength sweep one of the guys backward with a lightning strike fist to his face. Stunned from the blow, the guy wobbled on his feet, looking dazed. The stranger slammed his fist into the guy's nose and then his mouth. He fell backward onto the pavement, either unconscious or too stupefied to move.

Growling like a feral cat, the smaller guy ran toward the man, who merely met him with multiple fist strikes. Blood spurted, and the thug fell to the ground.

"Are you all right?"

The hand that appeared before her was large and, despite the bleeding knuckles, surprisingly elegant. She grabbed hold and allowed him to help her to her feet. "Thanks for your help. Where did you come from?"

"I was driving by, saw what was happening."

He didn't belong in this neighborhood. His clothes, though casual, were expensive, his shoes Gucci. His sunglasses alone could probably pay her rent for the year. She noted the sleek, late-model sports car a few feet away, the front door standing open, indicating he'd jumped out quickly.

No, he was most definitely not from around here. But he was trained, with the kind of moves that weren't learned in expensive spas or gyms. Military? Private security? Didn't really matter. She was just grateful for the help.

"You've got some impressive moves."

He lifted a shoulder in a shrug. "I've run into a lot of bullies in my life. Pays to be prepared."

"I really appreciate the help, Mr....?"

A scrambling sound behind them put them both on alert. Turning, they watched the two men hobble off at a run and then jump into an ancient black van that appeared to be waiting for them. It took off with a screech.

"Guess they didn't want to stick around for introductions," Kathleen said.

"You want me to call the police?"

She shook her head. The last thing she wanted was more publicity. "Thanks, but there's no point. No license plate, and every other person within five blocks has a van similar to that one. Hopefully, they learned their lesson."

His frown showed his doubt, and then he glanced down at her ankle. "You'd better get some ice on that."

In that instant, she felt the pain come and noted it was already swelling. If she didn't get ice on it soon, she'd be hobbling into the courtroom tomorrow.

He picked up her purse and handed it to her. "You need help getting to your apartment?"

No matter how handsome or elegantly dressed this man was, or how helpful he'd been, he was a stranger. Plus, she was surprised to find that she apparently still had a little pride left, because the thought of him seeing her hideous apartment made her cringe.

"No, thanks. I'll be fine. Thank you again for your help."

Hitching the strap onto her shoulder, she gave him a nod and then hobbled toward the apartment building. The elevator hadn't worked since she'd moved in, so she didn't bother to try it. Wincing with every step, she finally reached the third floor. Curious to see if her rescuer was still around, she stopped at a broken window and peered down at the parking lot. He had disappeared. If not for the throbbing pain in her ankle and the memory of warm brown eyes in an extraordinarily handsome face, she could almost believe she'd imagined the whole thing.

Shaking her head at the unexpectedness of life, she let herself into her apartment and went straight to the almost nonexistent kitchen. Thankful she'd remembered to fill the ice trays, she set about making an ice pack.

Easing onto the sofa, she propped her ankle onto the arm and placed the makeshift ice pack onto her ankle, hissing at the sting.

The adrenaline rush now gone, she leaned back against the cushion and allowed her thoughts to return to what Alice had told her. The horrendous truth couldn't be pushed away. Her sister had indirectly been responsible for what had happened in Denver. A child had almost died. And Kathleen had…well, she'd almost lost everything, too.

After working so hard for it, she'd finally achieved the security and life she wanted. A successful career, a home of her own, and what she'd thought was a mature and responsible man to share her life with. All the things she had dreamed of as a kid had been hers.

She still remembered the moment when it had all been destroyed. She and Emily had been walking across the street, heading to a large department store for a day of shopping. She had been hyperalert as usual, had been so damn careful of any possible threats. The next thing she knew, she and Emily were flying through the air.

Kathleen remembered little of what happened next, but thankfully, instinct and training had taken over. She vaguely remembered landing on the sidewalk with a terrifying crunch, several feet away from where they'd been. She was thankful she hadn't passed out and had been able to crawl to Emily, who had been lying in a pool of blood. The young girl had been bleeding profusely from a puncture in an artery in her arm. Kathleen had stanched the flow of blood until help arrived. Though she had been credited with saving Emily's life, Kathleen had felt responsible. The girl had been under her protection, and she had failed.

The driver had sped off. The vague descriptions from eyewitnesses had been no help.

Though Emily's injury had been life threatening, she had been on her feet within a few days and had left the hospital with only a broken arm and a few stitches.

Kathleen hadn't been so lucky. After weeks in the hospital, multiple surgeries, and months of extensive physical therapy, she had returned home. Though the recovery was painful, her confidence had suffered the most serious damage.

And then there was Stan.

Stan Dempsey, her weasel of a fiancé, had stuck with her for a few weeks, but his devotion and patience began to wane. He had most certainly not wanted to be stuck with a wife who had a ton of medical bills, months of physical therapy, and a possible limp.

Not that he'd used that particular reason for their break-up. The "we've grown apart" excuse worked so well with so many different scenarios. She'd just looked at him blankly when he'd uttered those words and had barely shed a tear when he'd walked away.

Learning his true nature before she'd made the ultimate mistake of marrying him was a blessing.

And now she was left with this awful, painful truth. She took a deep breath, let it out, then another one for good measure. Okay, yes, knowing who was behind the hit-and-run and what had precipitated the event, infuriated her and hurt her in a way she hadn't believed she could still be hurt, but what was the point in crying about it, dwelling on it? It was done. She had moved on…or at least she was still moving.

Truth was, if she'd reached out to Alice, all of this might have been prevented. Pride, and maybe sheer selfishness on her part, had kept her away from her sister. What would have happened if, instead of arguing and telling her sister how very immature she was acting, she had stayed close to her? Instead, Kathleen, with her self-righteous anger and arrogant pride, had stayed in Denver and concentrated on her own life. Now, Alice was in more trouble than either of them could have ever fathomed.

She had to find a way to prove Alice's innocence. The thought of her baby sister going to prison wasn't something she could begin to contemplate. Prison had changed their fun-loving, good-humored father into a grim-faced stranger. Daniel Callahan had been scarred by his experience. So much so that a large part of Kathleen believed he had jumped into the river instead of falling, as the authorities claimed. If prison had done that to him, what would it do to Alice? No matter what she had to do, Kathleen couldn't allow that to happen.

Cook County Courthouse
Chicago

The moment she had been both dreading and anticipating had finally arrived. The jury had been deliberating for three days. She believed, and Tony agreed, that the length of time was a good thing. If it took that long to make a decision, then there was obviously doubt in the jury's mind.

Kathleen had been living one day at a time, but she'd been making plans. First, her sister would be freed from that hellhole she'd been living in for the past few months. Then, she and Alice would move back to Denver. They would find an apartment together. Kathleen was sure she could get her old job back. And Alice was still so young. She could go back to college. Or, if she didn't want to do that, she could find a job she enjoyed. She could have a fulfilling, successful life. Soon, this would all be behind them and they could both start living again.

She sat in the front row, behind Alice, just as she had every hour of the trial. Tony had called twenty-five minutes ago and told her to get to the courthouse, pronto, that the jury had reached a decision. Her body was a mangled knot of nerves, every muscle clenched, as she recited a mantra over and over in her head: *not guilty, not guilty, not guilty.*

The courtroom was full. Frank Braden had been a wealthy man, and the way he was killed brought out both the curious and the morbid. Since neither the judge nor the jury had come into the room, people chatted with each other as if it were a social gathering. Kathleen was one of the few who sat quiet and still. Outwardly, she knew she appeared stoic and confident, a façade she'd perfected years ago. Her mind, however, felt as though it would facture into a thousand different pieces if she dared to breathe the wrong way.

A door swung open, and the jury marched out. Kathleen tried to read their faces, but either she'd lost her touch or they'd been told to maintain blank expressions. Not one of them gave her any idea what to expect.

When a jury looked at the defendant as they made their way to their seats, it often meant good things for the defense. Not one of them even glanced toward Alice as they walked to the jury box. Kathleen told herself it meant nothing. That thinking wasn't scientific fact. There was no way her sister would be found guilty. Justice would be served today. She believed in the process and was sure it wouldn't let them down.

A painful, rhythmic pattern pounded in her chest. She swung her gaze over to Alice and almost cried out loud when she saw her sister visibly shaking in her chair. Dammit, she was only twenty-two years old. On trial for a crime she didn't commit. This was so damn unfair. The jury had to see that. They had to!

The judge walked in, and at the "All rise" from the bailiff, the courtroom rose as one.

Looking both stern and pompous, the judge strode to his bench and seated himself. Everyone followed suit. Several long seconds passed, and Kathleen got the idea the judge was enjoying the anticipatory feeling of the crowd. It was like a football game with only a few seconds left in the fourth quarter, fourth down and only inches to go to make a touchdown. One team would have all their hopes realized, the other would have all their hopes dashed.

But, dammit, this was no game. Her sister's life was hanging in the balance. She was at the point of standing and yelling at the judge to get on with it when he intoned, "Has the jury reached a verdict?"

Kathleen heard nothing more after that. The roaring in her ears was a steady thrum of white noise. The only words she wanted to hear, prayed to hear, were "not guilty." Anything else would be unacceptable.

She watched as her sister stood, barely noting that Tony had to hold her elbow to steady her.

And still they waited. Kathleen's eyes kept going to the judge, then the jury, back to her sister. Back and forth, and then again.

Why didn't they just say it? Why all this pomp and circumstance? Why all this drama? Didn't they realize what was at stake? Didn't they see what this was doing to Alice?

"We find the defendant, Alice Callahan, guilty."

Kathleen jerked. No...it couldn't be. Everything around her darkened as her world narrowed to a pinpoint of light.

"Breathe."

The deep voice broke through the fog of panic, but her brain refused to comprehend. He said it again, this time with more force. "Breathe, Kathleen. Dammit. Breathe."

Numb, she turned to the man beside her—barely comprehending that he was familiar. The stranger who'd helped her in the parking lot. Why was he here? What had he said?

She took in the warm, compassionate brown eyes but couldn't comprehend the message they seemed to be sending her. She was so confused. Couldn't think what to say. Could not even fathom why he was here.

Her dazed attention moved back to the proceedings in front of her. The judge was polling the jury. Why did they keep saying the same word over and over again?

The man beside her took her hand, squeezed it gently, and said gruffly, "Stay strong."

Before she could react, he stood and walked away.

Stay strong. Strong? How was that possible? The only person she had left in the world, the only person she loved, had just been found guilty of a crime she didn't commit. Her sweet baby sister would be going to prison...possibly for the rest of her life. How could this possibly be happening? How could this get any worse?

Kathleen shook her head rapidly to clear it. No. She would fall apart later, on her own time. For right now, Alice needed her. She had let her down too much already. She wouldn't fail her again.

As if she knew what her sister was feeling, Alice turned around and gave Kathleen a brave, tremulous smile. Her eyes told a different story—she was terrified.

Kathleen mouthed the words, *Don't worry. We'll get through this. I love you.*

Alice's smile widened. Shoulders straight, she bravely turned back to face the judge.

Kathleen's thoughts whirled with all that needed to be done. Of course this wasn't over. They would appeal. They would fight this and win. She didn't care what she had to do, who she had to beg and plead for help, this was not over.

Odd noises erupted to the left, behind her. Screams and shouts. Kathleen looked over her shoulder. A woman stood at a side door. In seconds, Kathleen took in her appearance. Mid-twenties, long blond hair, pale, distressed face. Her mouth crimped with emotion, a crazed, desperate look in her eyes.

Kathleen stood, automatically recognizing a threat but unsure of the target.

"This is for Frank!" the woman shouted. Then, as if in slow motion, she lifted her arm and pointed a gun directly at Alice.

"Alice! Get down!" Kathleen dove across the railing.

Pop. Pop. Pop.

A split second too late, one second too slow.

They fell to the floor together with Kathleen's body covering Alice. Turning, she looked over to where the woman stood. The gun was still raised, still pointing at them. She was going to fire again! Why didn't somebody stop her?

Pop. Pop.

The sound was different. Kathleen dimly registered the shot had come from a different weapon. She eased off Alice and whispered harshly, "Alice? Are you okay? Alice? Sweetie?"

Kathleen knelt on the floor beside her sister. Alice lay face-down, while blood pooled around her fragile, lifeless body.

CHAPTER FIVE

Grande Lakes Hospital
Chicago

Dressed in a white nurse's uniform, the beautiful woman swayed her shapely hips in a sexy, swinging rhythm even as her steps were brisk, determined. She knew how to emulate, mostly by practice. This particular role was easier than most. She'd spent plenty of time in hospitals to know how medical professionals behaved and acted. This was an easy gig.

So what if the job hadn't been completely successful? Hadn't her friend, mentor, and trainer taught her the all-important mantra for an assassin? *If at first you don't succeed, you damn well better the second time.*

Sending in an amateur to make the kill was always a risk. Most times it worked like a charm. She had learned from the best. Her mentor had been the king of murder by proxy. She could only hope that someday she could be half as good as he had been. It would be a tribute to the man who had given her so much.

She shook off the melancholy. Not only was she the least sentimental person to ever exist, she had a role to play, a job to get done, a contract to fulfill.

A caring and compassionate demeanor firmly in place, she stopped at the door to Room 3242, assigned to Alice Callahan.

"I need to see some ID."

Her smile never wavered as she flipped her name badge toward him. Situated right above her left breast, the fake badge was the best she had been able to come up with on short notice. However, she knew her target audience. Right beside the nametag was, unarguably, one of the most impressive cleavages this man would ever set eyes upon. She was counting on any deficiencies in the name badge to be offset by the spectacular view. When his gaze barely glanced at the badge before moving over and then down, she knew she was home free.

It amused her that a police guard was even here. The woman had a bullet fragment hovering right next to her heart. So close the doctors feared removing it would kill her. All manner of specialists had been called in and were in the process of consulting on how to proceed. Just how dangerous could the woman be? Besides, even in a perfectly healthy state, Alice Callahan was, in her opinion, the stupidest kind of female. She had let a man use her and had gotten nothing for herself. What a waste.

"May I go in?"

The guard jerked his eyes away from the impressive view, and a flush of bright red painted his face. "Uh, yeah. Sure."

Her smile now cool and professional, she pushed opened the door. Flirting with him would be superfluous.

She walked into the room, closed the door behind her. Knowing she had a limited amount of time didn't concern her in the least. She had accomplished tougher jobs with much greater time constraints.

She stood over Alice and watched her sleep for a second. Such a pretty thing. Too bad she had been too stupid to use what she had to her advantage. Not that she cared, but in a way she was doing the young woman a favor. In her book, stupidity was the most incurable disease of all.

Withdrawing the syringe from her pocket, she injected the poison into the IV drip. It wasn't fast acting, nor would it be painful. Making the girl suffer wasn't part of the contract. Termination without suspicion was the goal. The doctors would assume their patient died from the fragment dislodging and hitting the heart. And it *would* dislodge, because they would try to save her. Any autopsy performed would show that the fragment had indeed penetrated the heart. The only way anyone would know that Alice had died from something else was if a specific blood test was performed. And since there was no need for that test, she was confident all medical professionals involved would determine the bullet fragment, and nothing else, killed Alice.

So intent on inserting all of the liquid into the IV, she was startled to look up and see Alice's eyes open. Blue eyes, glazed and kind of sweet looking, blinked up at her.

"So…tired."

"Are you, dearie?" She smiled with gentle compassion. "I'm here to make you all better."

"Thank you," she whispered. Her eyes searched the room. "Where's…Kathleen?"

"Your sister is talking to your doctors."

"Miss…her."

She leaned over the girl and gently brushed a strand of hair off her forehead. "Don't worry, my dearest. Kathleen will join you very soon. I promise. Now go back to sleep. All will be better soon."

"'Umm…'kay." Alice sighed slightly as her eyes drifted shut.

Pocketing the empty syringe, she gently patted Alice's baby-soft cheek and then walked out the door.

On the floor above, five doctors, along with Alice's sister, were deep in discussion on how to save the girl's life. Wasn't it nice that she had taken the problem out of their hands?

Kathleen's mind was so full of information she thought it might explode any second. Five doctors sat at a conference table and argued back and forth over the best options for Alice. While much of the medical jargon was over her head, she understood the gist of the discussion, as well as the consequences. Two doctors believed Alice should be operated on immediately. Two wanted to wait until her vital signs stabilized. The fifth didn't believe she would last through the night.

She wasn't sure how it happened that five doctors, three from another hospital, had examined Alice and offered their recommendations. She was just grateful for their interest. There was no easy answer, though, and she prayed for their wisdom in making the right decision.

The shooter had been identified as Maureen Downey, a lingerie model, and apparently a former lover of Frank Braden's. No one knew how she had gotten inside the courtroom with a gun. No one knew for sure why she had wanted to kill Alice. Had she really been avenging her former lover? A man who was a known abuser of women? Unfortunately, no one would be able to ask her, as she had died instantly from her gunshot wounds.

Everything inside Kathleen felt as brittle as thin ice. With every breath she took, she just knew her fragile veneer of control would crack and she would come apart, disintegrate.

Alice had woken twice since she had arrived at the hospital. Both times Kathleen had been there to reassure her, tell her that she loved her, tell her that everything was going to be okay. But she'd lied. She was lying the whole time. It wasn't going to be okay. Her little sister was going to die, and there wasn't a damn thing she could do to stop it.

At that thought, she pulled in every reserve she had left. No. Dammit. No. She would not give in. She would not allow this to happen. These men were here to fix her sister. There was no other choice. Alice would live. Dammit, she would live.

The medical jargon was still a mile high over her head, but it appeared the vote, four to one, was to wait twenty-four hours to see if Alice's vital signs improved. Whether they did or didn't, they would then operate and remove the bullet fragment hovering so close to her sister's heart.

Now that it was settled, she would go back to Alice's room. When her sister woke, she would tell her the good news. That she would have the surgery and that it would be a success. Kathleen had to make Alice understand that she had to fight, had to hold on. Alice wasn't the most resilient person, but in this she had no choice. She would have to fight for all she was worth.

On decidedly shaky legs, Kathleen stood and gave a sweeping glance to the doctors still sitting at the table. "Thank you for allowing me to listen in. I know you all want what's best for Alice. I'll just—"

The loud speaker buzzed, and then a voice announced, "Code blue. Code blue. All available medical staff. Report to Room 3242."

Alice!

CHAPTER SIX

Kathleen willed her legs to move, one step and then another. Up the stairs to her apartment. She'd shut off her emotions over the last few days. Had barely slept or eaten. Holding on by a thread, just waiting until she could finally let go. The second she entered her apartment, she was planning a meltdown of epic proportions.

The key slid into the door of her apartment, she twisted the knob, and felt the emotions swell.

"Miss Callahan?"

She jerked around. Exhaustion and emotional devastation had slowed her instincts. A man stood in the shadows. He was dressed in black, and she could see nothing of his features other than he was tall, with a muscular physique. If he was here to attack her, he would win. She was way too tired to give a damn. And if he was here to rob her, he was in for a major letdown. She had nothing worth stealing...nothing left, not anymore.

Her fuzzy brain registered that he'd called her Miss Callahan. People weren't generally that polite right before they attacked.

"Yes?"

"I'd like to talk to you about your sister."

Another damn reporter. The burn of hatred was strong and true, singeing and cauterizing the bleed of grief. "Haven't you bottom-feeding reporters had enough fun? Haven't you tortured me enough? What more do you want?"

"I'm not a reporter, Miss Callahan. I'm here to help you."

"Help me how?" Her voice went thick as she added, "I just buried my sister. If you'd wanted to help, you've got piss-poor timing."

"I know. I'm very sorry. I—" He broke off when voices came from the stairwell. Her neighbors were coming home. "Look. May I come in?"

"No, you may not. I have no idea who you are or what you want."

He moved closer, stood in the light. Her breath hitched as she immediately recognized his famous face. This man was on the news more times in one week than Kathleen had been in a lifetime. But what was he doing here?

"My name is Grey Justice, and I'd like to help you find the person who framed your sister."

Grey followed Kathleen Callahan into her home. Though how anyone could call this place *home* would be laughable if it weren't so damn sad. The apartment was one small room with a couch, a small dresser, and a rollaway bed standing upright in the corner. Grey imagined she had to move the furniture into the corner when she was ready to go to sleep, as there wasn't enough room for the bed otherwise.

A small alcove showed an ancient microwave, hot plate, and minifridge. The other side of the room had a toilet, along with a drain in the floor and a hose hanging from the wall above it. Apparently some idiot's idea of a shower.

A beaten-up table with one lone chair sat in the middle of the room. Somehow, that seemed the saddest and most telling piece in the whole place. Kathleen Callahan was alone. Had been for a long time.

"Before we go any further, you need to know that I won't hesitate to defend myself."

Grey wasn't surprised she was holding a gun on him. And he knew her words were true. He knew quite a lot about Kathleen Callahan. What he knew, he liked.

The Callahan sisters' upbringing had been both unorthodox and somewhat difficult. Both women had no doubt been affected by their childhood, but they'd gone about dealing with it in very different ways.

Kathleen had used the skills she'd learned as a child, acquired others as an adult, and had made herself into a force to be reckoned with. Unfortunately, due to circumstances beyond her control, she'd had a reversal of fortune.

"I'm not here to hurt you, Kathleen. I'm here to help."

She studied him for several more seconds, lowered the gun to her side, and then nodded toward the faded brown faux leather couch against the wall. Duct tape and prayer were the only things that seemed to be holding it together.

Grey eased onto the couch, hoping his weight wouldn't tear a new hole in the upholstery. Regret wasn't a normal part of his personality, but as he took in Kathleen's grief-exhausted face, he felt the sting of it. He should have seen to her sooner. After Eli had given him the information on both Kathleen and Alice, Grey had put some of his best researchers on the case. But not in time to prove Alice's innocence. Or save her life. He sure as hell never anticipated that anyone would try to kill the young woman, especially in the middle of a damn courtroom.

"Tell me why you're here. You said you believe my sister was innocent?"

Innocent? He wasn't sure of that. However, he did believe she'd been framed for murder. Grey explained as best he could. "Your sister's case hit my radar a week or so ago. I apologize that it didn't catch my attention until it was too late to give you the assistance you needed."

"I don't understand. Why would you even care?"

Grey had no intention of telling her that she had attracted the attention of the wealthy Eli Slater. It wasn't his place, nor his business. That was for Eli to deal with when the time was right.

"I have a victims' advocacy foundation."

"Yes, I've heard of it. I'm just surprised you seek victims out. For some reason, I thought they came to you."

"They usually do, but sometimes a case catches my attention. Your sister's trial caught mine."

"So do you have some kind of information or proof? Do you know who killed Braden? Do you know anything about the woman who murdered my sister? How can you help?"

The questions were understandable, but as always, Grey walked a fine line when it came to offering a certain kind of assistance. His victims' advocacy group assisted hundreds of people each year, all above board, with no secrets, no fine skirting of the law. Few people were aware that there was another side to Grey's path to justice, one not so straight or narrow. One that often involved secrets, lies, half-truths, as well as a delicate balance between legal and illegal. He never revealed those secrets without absolute trust.

But Eli had asked for his help. Not having heard that much fire in his friend's voice in a long time, Grey had been intrigued. For that alone, he had planned to reach out and offer assistance.

Then, the more he learned, the more he realized how vital it was that he become involved. It was just too damn bad he hadn't been able to prevent Alice's death.

"I don't have a great deal of information. Mostly speculation and theories at this point."

The case hadn't been cut-and-dried before and was even less so now. He had several working theories but none he could share.

The murkiness of the case was now ten times cloudier with Alice's death. The woman who'd shot her was purported to be a former girlfriend of Braden's. The speculation was that she'd wanted revenge for his death. Photographs had been found in her apartment, showing the two together. That lame excuse of revenge had become even shadier when Grey's investigators couldn't find any credible evidence that Maureen Downey had even known Braden. The authorities had accepted the photographs as proof of their relationship. Grey wasn't so trusting.

Other, different clues were emerging, and he didn't like where they were leading. So he would dig deeper until he found the truth, one way or the other.

Until then, he would do what he could to help this woman who'd lost too much already.

From everything he knew of Kathleen Callahan, after his own research and Eli's observations, Grey believed he could trust her. Still, he would tell her only what she needed to know. Revealing more was not only foolhardy, but it was completely unnecessary. Kathleen's focus was on exonerating her sister. Additional information would be superfluous.

This was always the tricky part—revealing facts without showing his hand. "I believe Braden was killed by a hired killer, who set your sister up."

"You know who this man is? Who hired him?"

"Not yet."

"Why do you think it was a hired hit?"

"Contract killers often have signatures. They can complete their assignment in various ways but usually have favored methods, which they often rely on unless their client has a specific preference."

"If Braden's murder had a signature, why haven't the police connected any other murders? It was an unusually gruesome crime."

"The poison was the signature. The rest was...over the top." Grey hadn't quite come to terms with that yet.

"So that means exactly what?"

"The cause of death, the poison, is similar to three other murders committed over the last few months. Similar enough that I believe it's worth pursuing."

Her face was even paler than it had been before. "I don't understand any of this."

"I know you don't. I realize it's hard to trust, but I promise, I am here to help."

"So you know how to find the person who killed Braden? What can you do that the police couldn't?"

Grey had no trouble playing hardball. He could tell her that if she wanted his help, she should just accept certain things without question. It might come to that at some point, but for now he didn't mind sharing more information. Especially since he had an ulterior motive in telling her.

"Sometimes a case is complicated and requires, shall we say, a delicate approach. There are some people who believe there's only one way to pursue justice. I'm not one of those people. The path to get there isn't always a straight, narrow, or smooth journey."

He left it at that. Kathleen Callahan was an intelligent woman, a security specialist. And had recently been hit between the eyes with the knowledge that one could do all the right things and justice still not be served. Justice was rarely black or white. Shades of gray permeated the entire system.

She took another few seconds to study him. She was weighing his words, looking for a trap. Trust didn't come easy for her, and even less so now. He already knew which path she would take. He wouldn't be here if he didn't already know the outcome.

"Where do we go from here?"

"I'd like you to come work with me in Dallas. Unlimited resources will be available to you. Some of the top investigators in the world will be at your disposal. We'll find the truth."

"Why would you want me to work for you? You don't even know me."

"I never offer a job without knowing a prospective employee's abilities. I've researched you. Your training is exemplary, your reputation impeccable."

"What kind of work would you want me to do?"

He saw the doubt, the worry behind the question. Her confidence had taken several blows. However, he knew enough to know she would be an asset.

"With a few variations, much the same as what you were doing in Colorado."

"Variations?" She cocked her head questioningly. No, Kathleen Callahan was not stupid or naïve. "All above board and legal?"

Grey gave her a small enigmatic smile. "Now what would be the fun in that?"

Kathleen stood in the middle of the apartment. Grey Justice had left a while ago but for the life of her, she couldn't seem to gather the energy to move one more step. Getting a job offer on one of the worst days of her life was incomprehensible. At some point, her frozen brain would unthaw, and she would think about what he had offered her, what she had agreed to do. Facing a new job and a new city were inconsequential at this point. Everything was nothing.

It was over. Her baby sister, her only family, the girl she had raised from an infant was gone. Her very own special angel.

Like a tidal wave, everything came crashing down on her at once. The exhaustion, the guilt, the overwhelming need to scream out in agony. Her knees buckled and she fell to the floor with a loud, jagged cry. Covering her face with her hands, she rocked back and forth and sobbed. The soul wrenching sounds echoing around her, mocking her aloneness. A taunt that she had failed her sister once again.

Alice had looked at peace today. So sweet, so incredibly innocent as she lay in that hideous box. Even though it had been a surprisingly nice one, it was still a box. The funeral director had explained about an overstock or something that had enabled him to sell her the coffin at a greatly discounted price. Odd how finding a bargain had always cheered her up before. But not this one. Not this.

Nevertheless she was grateful she had been able to give Alice this one last thing. A nice send-off for a girl who'd never had a lot and had died too young. A precious angel who had made mistakes but hadn't been a bad person—just human.

Raising her head, Kathleen looked around the sparse room, ignoring the hideousness of it for once. Her eyes zeroed in on her hiding place, the one spot she believed was safe from thieves, where she had secreted away the last thing that meant anything to her. Her memories.

Though she wasn't sure her legs would hold her, she refused to allow herself the luxury of crawling. She pushed herself to stand and though her feet shuffled on the threadbare carpet as if she were a century old, she counted it a win that she was even moving.

She removed one of the cushions from the couch and pulled back the material from the bottom. This decrepit sofa had been here when she'd moved into the apartment. It had given her landlord the ability to charge an extra ten bucks a month for a 'furnished' apartment. Ridiculous yes, but it had served its purpose. As large as it was and the condition it was in, no way in hell would anyone ever try to steal the thing. She had figured the massive couch was safe from even the most desperate of thieves.

In between rusted springs and rotting material was where she'd stored her last treasure. She pulled the small box out and held it to her chest. This was all she had left.

Replacing the cushion, she dropped onto the couch, ignoring the additional splits she'd just added to the fake leather upholstery. With shaking hands, she lifted the lid and peered down into the faces of those she'd loved. Forever in her heart, no longer in her life.

As silent tears streamed down her face, Kathleen carefully examined each photograph, remembering the moment each one was taken. The laughter, the tears, the moments that didn't seem all that special at the time but were now priceless and beautiful. She wanted to reach out and grab each one of them back, hold it in her hand and cherish it.

She lovingly fingered the two doll dresses that she hadn't been able to part with. She had often used her doll clothes to dress her sister. These two frilly, nonsensical dresses had been her favorites.

Had she ever told Alice how thankful she was for her? Kathleen had been a devastated little girl who had just lost her mother.

Daniel Callahan had been too grief stricken himself to offer much comfort. So she had poured out all of her love and devotion to her baby sister. She had devoured books on infants and baby care, determined to be the best sister she could be. Alice had been her lifesaver. Had she ever told her how important she was? Had Alice known how much she loved her? How grateful she was for her? The questions would haunt her forever.

Half an hour later, she whispered a soft goodbye to her family, then closed the box and returned it to its hiding place.

Standing straight, resolve settled into her mind and her heart. She would go to Dallas, do the job she was hired to do, and take advantage of Grey Justice's offer. She would find justice for Alice.

But never again would she allow herself the vulnerability or the luxury of loving anyone. Loving meant losing, at least for the Callahans. Never again.

Chapter Seven

Three months later
Hiram Clemens State Correctional Facility
Enid, Texas

The heavy, steel door closed with a loud, reverberating clang. Eli barely refrained from wincing as the sound invoked a memory he could've lived without. Barely a year ago, he'd been visiting his brother Jonah in prison. And today, he was visiting another brother. The last person he wanted to see was Adam, but he had to get some answers. For his children, he'd face Satan himself.

The small room was dingy and smelled of a strong disinfectant that couldn't completely cover the years of piss and vomit the room had endured. He sat in a chair that looked about fifty years old and creaked in protest when he eased his big body into it. The chipped, wood table before him was covered in crude drawings and carved profanities. The fact that many of them were misspelled struck him as amusing. He didn't know why.

The door opened, and his oldest brother shuffled into the room. The changes in Adam weren't as notable as they'd been on Jonah. Maybe because Jonah was innocent—framed by his own father and imprisoned for a crime he didn't commit. Adam was most definitely guilty—responsible for more than what he'd been convicted for. Maybe that was the difference. That and the fact that Adam Slater had little to no conscience.

"Well, if it isn't St. Eli coming to visit his big brother in the slammer. Miss me, little brother?"

"Adam." Eli gave him a stiff nod of acknowledgment.

"To what do I owe this dubious pleasure?"

Eli withdrew a copy of the email he'd received last night. It'd been burning a hole in his pocket and a deeper one in his gut.

"I received this yesterday. Care to explain?"

Adam glanced down at the vague but awful threats, then back at Eli. "What's this got to do with me? I don't know anything about it."

"And I don't believe you, Adam. If you didn't send it, it's a person you know. Someone you or Mathias did business with." Eli leaned forward, glared hard. "Dammit, someone is threatening our family...my daughters...your nieces."

"And I should care...why?"

It was all Eli could do not to take the bastard's head off. "They're your family, too, Adam. My children are just babies. You remember them, don't you? The children of the woman you killed?"

What could only be called a smirk appeared on Adam's face. "Now I thought we'd already gotten past that. No one has proof of any such thing."

"I know what Mathias told me."

"Oh yeah? And when was that, Eli? When did Daddy spill all? And why would he tell you in the first place?"

Eli ground his teeth till they ached. Hell, he was getting in deep when he started spouting things he had no business saying. Just because he knew without a shadow of a doubt that Adam had killed Shelley, he could do nothing about it. Mathias had told him only moments before he was shot and killed. The fact that Eli or any of his other family members had been around when that happened was something he would take to his grave. Not even Adam knew the truth of what happened that night. God only knew what his brother would do with that kind of information.

Eli had already come to terms that Shelley would never get the justice she deserved. All he could do was console himself that Adam, her murderer, would be in prison for the rest of his life. That had to be enough.

He redirected the conversation back to the reason he was here. "Do you know who sent this email, Adam? Who would make these threats?"

Sprawled out in his chair, Adam looked as though he was relaxing in his luxurious home as opposed to wearing an orange jumpsuit and sitting in a vile-smelling prison visitors' room. "What's it worth to you?"

Eli lunged across the table, going for his brother's throat. He squeezed hard, watching Adam's ugly brown eyes bulge. Seconds later, three guards rushed in, pulling Eli back. One brutish-looking guard with a billystick in his giant hand growled, "We got a problem here?"

As much as he'd like to grab the stick and beat Adam within an inch of his life, Eli knew he could do no such thing.

"No…officer," Eli said. "Sorry. Won't happen again."

The man nodded at the two guards holding Eli's arms. "Let him go."

They released him, and Eli seated himself again. The instant the men walked out of the room, Adam smiled. "I see you've managed to influence someone here. Anyone else would've been thrown out the door."

Yeah, he'd greased some palms for the guards to look the other way if he happened to get a little physical. They wouldn't, however, let him get away with beating the hell out of an inmate. Too bad, because he'd never felt as much hatred as he did for the man in front of him. It sickened him to his bones that they shared the same blood...the same last name.

"Since you've seen that I do have some influence here, you might want to reevaluate your answer. Do you know who would threaten the family?"

The amusement dropped from Adam's face. "You've pissed off a lot of people. Any one of them could be seeking revenge. And before you ask for names, keep in mind that Mathias was screwing people long before I came into this world. The things I did weren't a drop in the bucket compared to what he got away with.

"From what I've heard, you're the only Slater available for anyone to seek retribution against. Jonah's on some kind of self-healing sabbatical. Mama and Lacey have disappeared, and no one can find them."

The words sparked Eli's interest. "And how do you know this, Adam? Have you been trying to find them?"

"Hell if I care where they are. Neither one of them has had the decency to even write me, see how I'm doing."

"Answer the question. Why your sudden interest in a family you've had as little to do with as possible? We both know Mathias was the only one you wanted to be around."

Adam shrugged. "We have televisions here, too, Eli. You ever watch the local news? Rarely a week goes by when someone doesn't do some kind of story about one of us." He smirked and added, "Apparently, you've lost a lot of the family's money."

"You mean I've lost a lot of dirty money. It's taken me a year to clean up the shit you and Mathias created."

"Don't matter to me if you end up living in a double-wide outside Dallas."

"If it was a choice between living on blood money or in a double-wide, I damn well know what choice I would make."

"Whatever."

"Who's making these threats?"

"Like I said, I don't have a clue. With nobody around but you and your brats, you're the easiest target."

"I've accepted that I will always be a target. But I'll be damned if I'll allow my children or the rest of the family to suffer any more than they already have for what you and Mathias did. Now tell me who hates you enough to want to come after us."

With a harsh rush of air, Adam expelled a weary sigh. His eyes went even duller than their usual murky brown, and for the first time Eli saw sadness and maybe even a hint of regret. "I'm telling the truth. I don't know. Whether you believe me or not, Daddy set me up to be the patsy for everything, but I knew almost nothing about that side of his business."

"Your hands are far from clean, Adam."

"Maybe so. But the things I did barely got me noticed in those circles. Daddy was the ringleader."

Eli knew that was true. For whatever reason, known only to Mathias himself, their father had set up his oldest son to take the fall for a boatload of illegal activities. Not only did Adam not have the brains to do all those things, there was no way in hell Mathias would have allowed him that kind of power. Since Mathias hadn't known he was going to die, no one knew for certain if he would have allowed the charges to stick.

Still, Eli had absolutely no sympathy for his brother. Plenty of crimes had been attributed to him, including conspiracy to commit murder. And the one crime Adam was responsible for that could never be proven was one Eli wanted to kill his brother over. If it wouldn't leave his children without a parent, Eli knew full well he might have done just that.

Correctly identifying the hatred in Eli's eyes, Adam shook his head. "Hate me all you want, brother, but you're better off without her. Shelley loved only two things. Booze and pills."

"And you made damn sure she had plenty of both that last day, didn't you?"

His mouth twitched as though he was fighting a grin. "She went out with a smile on her face."

Rolling his chair back, Eli shot to his feet. He had to get the hell out of here before he committed murder. "You might never pay for Shelley's death, but your worthless ass will rot in this prison for the rest of your useless life."

A small enigmatic look crossed Adam's face but was gone in an instant. Shrugging, he said, "If you say so."

Eli walked out without a backward glance. Coming here had been futile. How stupid to think that his brother would willingly give him any helpful information. Adam would only ever have one love and that was himself.

He maintained an expressionless demeanor until he reached his car. Once inside, he slammed his fist against the steering wheel and cursed virulently in every language he knew. He'd known going in that it was pointless, but he'd had to at least try.

His phone vibrated in his pocket. He glanced at the readout and then hit answer. "Justice, you got anything?"

"The email came from a computer inside the prison, just like the others. My tech who traced it said this one was almost insulting, it was so easy to track."

"The first one a few months back wasn't so easy to trace. Why'd he change? He knew I'd have it traced."

"We both know your brother isn't the brightest criminal in the world."

Too true. Which was probably one of the reasons it had been so damn easy for Mathias to frame his son. Adam had been their father's confidant and co-conspirator for years. And in the end, he'd been his scapegoat.

Eli shoved his fingers through his hair. No use going back and confronting his brother with the truth. He blew out a sigh, releasing the tension that had built over the last hour. "So we're set for tomorrow night?"

"Yes."

"And you're sure she doesn't know who I am?"

"Yes, but are you sure you know what you're doing?"

Eli knew he was taking a risk. Seeing him again would bring to mind one of the most painful and traumatic times in her life. Not that it would ever be far from her mind, he was sure. But it was time, in more ways than one.

"I've waited as long as I can. And with the most recent events, it's imperative that it happen now."

"Agreed, but…" Amusement entered Justice's voice. "You do know that she'll have a gun, don't you? I've seen her use it. Damn impressive."

"That's what I'm counting on."

His smile grim but determined, Eli ended the call.

CHAPTER EIGHT

Kathleen stood several yards away from the most impressive mansion she'd ever seen. Even while her expert eyes assessed the job, the surroundings, she couldn't quite quell the shiver of excitement that she'd get to see inside. She'd always been a sucker for castles, and this one, in Dallas, Texas, for heaven's sake, was incredible.

Standing at least four stories high, it was a humongous structure of rock and brick, with a classic fairy-tale design complete with turrets and towers. The only things missing were the handsome prince and princess. What kind of family lived in such an extravagant home?

She'd been getting ready for bed when Grey had called and given her this assignment. Said it had to be done tonight, immediately. Even though she'd done numerous jobs for Justice over the past three months, having a half hour's notice was unusual, even for him. There hadn't been time to do more than plug the address into a search engine to discover the homeowner's name. Not that it mattered for her to be able to do the job, but a little more information would have been nice to have.

She sighed. "Expect the unexpected" should be Grey Justice's company slogan.

When she had agreed to work for Grey, she had been an emotional wreck. No matter that he'd promised her access to unparalleled resources to help her exonerate Alice, making a decision of that magnitude without careful study and contemplation had been unheard of for Kathleen. How odd that it had turned out to be one of the best decisions she'd ever made.

Her official title was freelance security operative. Grey had given her carte blanche to reject any assignment she wasn't comfortable taking. She appreciated the autonomy but so far hadn't turned down any jobs. The assignments had been as eclectic as they were unusual. One day she was shadowing a known drug dealer to discover his supplier, the next day she might be leaving incriminating evidence on a prosecutor's desk to help convict a pedophile. Yesterday, she had spent hours flirting with a Swedish businessman thought to be in cahoots with a Spanish crime boss. For three hours she'd giggled and batted her eyelashes just to discover whether or not he'd been in Memphis at the same time a union leader had been assassinated.

She didn't always know the reason the information was needed. Her first day on the job, Grey had explained that a single thread could unravel the most tightly knitted of alibis. Her job would often require that she find that one single thread.

Grey's need for secrecy was of utmost importance. The cases his people were involved in were news stories all over the country. In just the few months she had worked with him, she'd seen legal battles won, cases thrown out, innocent people released from jail, and vile, evil criminals arrested, most of them never knowing that a small group of dedicated people had had a hand in securing justice.

When she'd realized what his secret organization did, she'd been both fascinated and doubtful. Could a small group of justice seekers really make that much of a difference? The answer was an unqualified yes. Okay, some laws were skirted, and a few times she had crossed the line past legal, but when the guilty were locked up and the innocent set free, it was damn hard to quibble with the difference between what was legal and what was right.

At first, her disciplined, too-structured soul had rebelled at the unpredictability of the job. Accustomed to knowing what she would be doing from sunup to sundown had been her way of life for so long, Kathleen hadn't realized how rigid she had become.

Now, if anything, she relished the challenge and variety. Staying busy kept her sane. She still grieved for Alice—would grieve till the day she died. But with each day, with its challenges and variety, she could feel herself healing.

Just because she was healing, didn't mean she had stopped looking for Frank Braden's killer. Exonerating Alice would be one last gift she could give to her sister.

True to his word, Grey had opened doors that had previously been closed. She had uncovered information about Braden she doubted few people knew. So far nothing she had uncovered led her to the person responsible for his death, but like Grey said, sometimes a single thread was all you needed. So she would keep digging until one of those threads led her to a killer.

In the meantime, she had an estate to break into. And what an estate it was. An iron gate, at least ten feet high, surrounded what had to be at least twenty acres. Lights glowed everywhere, illuminating every damn corner. If a spider crawled by, she had a feeling several different sensors would go off. Why did this guy think he had security problems?

With a mental shrug, she pushed the why aside and concentrated on the how. Staying in the shadows, Kathleen stealthily walked the perimeter, looking for the most vulnerable point. It was a tedious, time-consuming task, especially when there didn't appear to be a weak spot anywhere.

Eyes narrowed, concentration keen, she trudged through the wooded area that surrounded what could only be described as an impenetrable fortress. How the hell was she going to—

She stopped so abruptly she almost slammed face first into a tree. A tree whose strong, sturdy branches reached past one of the large brick columns attached to the iron railing. If she climbed the tree and shimmied across the limb, she could step onto the brick column and then drop over to the other side.

Having lost weight that she really couldn't afford to lose, Kathleen knew the limb would hold her. And climbing the tree would be child's play. Her biggest problem would come when she dropped onto the other side and lights as bright as a lighthouse's beacon shone down on her.

Now that she had a plan, she was feeling quite confident as she quickly headed back to the gatehouse. Having already checked out the security guard's activities, she knew what she would find. Still, she peered into a window and confirmed. The man sat at a desk and, in apparent comfort and enjoyment, consumed a large pepperoni pizza as he watched a Cowboys football game. One more security area she'd point out that needed to change.

Opening the small pouch hanging from her belt loop, she withdrew the necessary tools and then eased open the security panel on the side of the gatehouse. Using a small flashlight, she highlighted what looked to be a maze of switches. It was a good system and happily one she was familiar with. Within seconds, she located the security switches that lighted the sector she planned to breach. She flipped two of the switches and froze. No movement from the gatehouse, which told her the guard wasn't looking at the control panel behind him. If he were, he would most definitely notice the warning signal. The guard's lack of attention gave her the opportunity she needed.

She carefully closed the security panel door and took off. In between the noshing of pizza, he might just look behind him and notice the blip. She had no extra time to spare. Reaching the tree again, she jumped for the lowest branch and swung herself up. Within seconds, she was scooting across the branch that hung over the railing. A moment later, she was at the brick column. Bracing herself for impact, she dropped to the ground. Pleased her weak ankle gave no indication it had even felt jarred, she took off into the night.

Evening shadows lengthened into midnight dark, quiet blanketed the house, and night settled in. Eli sat alone in his bedroom and stared at nothing. He thought about and rejected the idea of turning on lights. The darkness fit his mood. Besides, night shadows offered more comfort these days. In daylight, flaws were revealed, armor pierced, blood spilled. In darkness, he could escape the cold light of reality.

His daughters, Violet and Sophia, were tucked in for the night. He hoped they dreamed of magical wizards and beautiful, kindhearted fairies. He hoped they always believed in goodness and light. That they could escape the darkness that permeated their surroundings.

Someone wanted to hurt him by hurting his daughters. He would die before he let that happen. And he would do whatever it took to make sure they stayed safe.

The first threat had been subtle, almost negligible. So much so that if it had been made against him, he would have dismissed it as an amusing incident. But it hadn't been made against him...

it had been made against his children. No way in hell would he stand for that.

The next ones had been much less subtle but still vague. Today's had been different. It had come with attachments—photos of his children taken at various times of the day. The bastard wanted him to know they were being watched...stalked.

Adam had denied sending any of the emails. Having the IP address come from the prison, the location of the threat so easily obtained, screamed setup, not guilt. But he trusted his brother's word as far as he could throw this damn house. So until Eli knew different, Adam would remain his prime suspect.

But if not Adam, then who?

Who the hell was left that hated him enough to do something vile like this? He was an adult, a businessman who dealt with ruthless and conscienceless people. He could handle the heat and any threat made toward him. But to threaten two innocent children? Hell, that was so damn far over the line.

Sure, there were people who didn't like him. More than a few were probably not happy with the way he'd ended his father and brother's business agreements. But he honestly could not name one person he'd pissed off enough to warrant threats against his children.

He wouldn't wait for something to happen. He was being proactive, setting things in place, getting ready. When and if the devil came calling, Eli intended to be well prepared to send him back to hell.

Out of the darkness, a small click sounded, telling him one more thing he'd needed to know. There was no safe place. His home, the one place he believed his children were the safest, wasn't. And yet, when he stood and turned, he couldn't prevent the lift to his heart at the sight before him.

"You're late," Eli said.

Her posture went military straight as her eyes flared with temper. For an intruder, she looked highly insulted. "Well, excuse me, but I just got the assignment an hour ago. Besides, burglars have a tendency to arrive at unexpected times. They don't normally call in advance for an appointment."

He'd never forgotten that husky, almost musical voice. Had been anticipating hearing it again.

"Sorry for the short notice." He didn't add that it was deliberate. If she'd had time to do research, she might not have shown up.

He took in her appearance and fought a smile. Black jeans, long-sleeve black pullover, and black skullcap to cover that glorious hair. She might dress the part of a thief, but she looked delightfully feminine to him. She also looked less stressed than the last time he'd seen her. Though, to his mind, she still had the translucent appearance of someone who'd endured a trauma.

"So...what now? You want me to get down on the floor? Put my hands behind my head?"

"Hmm." She seemed to consider it for a few seconds, and then she smiled. "Since I've never broken into anyone's home before, I don't quite know what the proper etiquette should be."

How odd that for as much as he knew about this woman, he had never seen her smile. He hadn't known about the deep dimple in her left cheek or that those amazing sea-blue eyes could sparkle like diamonds in the ocean.

"You're the one with the gun. Guess you call the shots...so to speak."

She glanced down at the weapon in her hand and grimaced. "Sorry." She slid the gun into the holster at her waist. "Grey didn't give me much information, so I didn't know what to expect."

"Wise woman."

"So…really. I didn't surprise you in the least?"

Her disappointment was obvious. She had expected a stronger reaction. "No. But to be fair, I *was* expecting you." He paused for a second and then added, "If it makes you feel better, your gun is bigger than I thought it would be."

She laughed softly. "Well, that's something."

Eli stayed in the shadows, not revealing his face yet, wanting to enjoy anonymity for just a few more moments. Once she knew his identity, complications would arise and questions would have to be answered.

Not a day had gone by since he'd last seen her that he hadn't thought of her, or regretted that he hadn't stayed longer. He'd already been driving out of the parking lot when the shooting had taken place. Even though they'd yet to share more than a few words with each other, he felt he should have been there for her. She'd had no one.

Staying away from her these past three months had been difficult, but he hadn't wanted to intrude. She had needed time to heal, time to become acclimated to her new job, her new life.

Figuring out a way to introduce himself had proven harder than he'd feared. Hiring her to break into his home wasn't the subtlest of introductions, but it would get the job done, as well as point out the weaknesses in his security.

Her voice broke the quiet, the tone revealing a slight nervousness at his continued silence. "So, umm, now that I'm here, I assume you want to know how I did it…how I broke in?"

"Not particularly."

Her brow furrowed with a frown. "Then why am I here?"

"Because I wanted to know *if* you could break in."

"And now that you know?"

"We're going to make sure no one else can."

The dimple made another intriguing appearance. "Uh oh, you're one of those kinds."

"What kinds?"

"The 'don't tell me about the labor pains, just give me the baby' kind."

"Labor pains I can handle. The intricacies of lock picking and security system failures only interest me when it comes to ways to prevent them."

"You can handle labor pains?"

"I have two children."

That got a raised brow. "Birthed them yourself, did ya?"

Eli grinned, delighted at the unexpectedness of her sense of humor.

"Grey warned me about you. Said you might be stubborn." Frustration flickered in her face. "I can't believe you don't want to know how I got in. It's really interesting. Your system is good, one of the best on the market, but it needs an upgrade. See, once I cut the light in the northeast sector, I used a tree to climb onto a brick column. Took less than a minute. The guard in the gatehouse was chowing down on pizza and didn't see me. You definitely need to have a chat with him. And you need to have the trees surrounding the estate trimmed." She took a step closer, her enthusiasm growing. "Once I got to the house, I overrode the mainframe and bypassed the—"

Eli flipped the light switch behind him.

She jerked to a surprised halt. Suspicion and distrust replaced her earlier enthusiasm. "It's you."

"Hello, Kathleen. At last, we officially meet."

"I don't understand. How? Why?"

Explaining himself without revealing too much, too soon, would be tricky. "I was in Chicago for business. Caught the tail end of an interview you did with some reporters."

"You mean you caught the tail end of one of the many times a reporter blindsided me."

"It's been my experience that they're rarely kind."

"That's been my experience, too." She frowned. "So based on what you saw on television, you what…followed me around?"

"Yes and no. I went to the trial." He didn't tell her that within an hour of being there, he'd called his assistant and rescheduled his entire week.

Eli still had no explanation for his strange compulsion to learn more about her…to help her. He wasn't without compassion, but neither was he known for impulsive actions. Yet the moment he'd seen the interview, he'd felt a connection. An inexplicable pull. The more he'd learned, the stronger the pull had gotten.

"I'm sorry I didn't stay that last day. That I wasn't there to help you."

If she thought the words were odd coming from a virtual stranger, she didn't comment.

"And I'm very sorry for the loss of your sister."

For an instant, grief flared in her eyes. Then, just like those days he'd observed her at the trial, the calm poise returned. "Thank you."

He wouldn't tell her about the medical specialists he'd called in for consultation or the discounted funeral expenses. There was no point. Besides, she would want to know why, and again, he had no reasonable explanation. Or at least one that wouldn't freak her out.

"Grey said Alice's case was brought to his attention. You're the one who told him, aren't you?"

"Yes."

"But I still don't understand. Why would the wealthy Eli Slater of Dallas, Texas, go to the trial of a woman in Chicago? A woman he didn't know?"

"Let's just say the case intrigued me."

"But why?"

He shrugged, finding it even harder to explain than he'd thought it'd be. "Perhaps because of my past experience." When he saw the puzzled look, he explained further. "My younger brother was imprisoned for a crime he didn't commit."

Her mouth went grim. "Apparently, that happens more than most people think. Is your brother still in prison?"

"No. We were able to get him released."

"Grey helped?"

"Yes."

"I'm glad." She cocked her head. "So that's why I received so little notice for this job?"

"I asked Grey not to tell you. I thought you might not come if you knew it was the man you'd met in Chicago."

"I don't like secrets."

If that was the case, she'd definitely hooked up with the wrong people. Grey Justice was all about secrets.

"It was no conspiracy. I promise. I went to several days of the trial, watched the proceedings and heard the testimonies. I told Grey, and he decided to contact you."

"But you helped me with those two thugs. Why?"

"Would you prefer that I hadn't?"

"I prefer not being stalked or lied to."

Eli sighed. He'd known meeting her like this wasn't without risk. "I'm sorry you feel that way. However, I wasn't stalking you, and as far as I know, neither Grey nor I have lied to you."

"Then why the secrecy?"

"Being associated with a Slater in this city isn't exactly good for your reputation."

"I'm not associated with a Slater. I'm here to do a job."

That was something they'd have to talk about later. She was clearly in no frame of mind to discuss a closer association.

Steering the conversation toward a somewhat safer topic, he said, "Any new leads on who killed Braden?"

"You believed in Alice's innocence? That's why you contacted Grey?"

It wouldn't help his case to tell her he wasn't one hundred percent sure of her sister's innocence, that his interest was in her, not her sister. But neither would he lie. "I believed you needed help."

Something like alarm flickered on her face. Her instincts were good. She saw more than he was ready for her to see. "Look, let's cut to the chase. I'm here to show you the vulnerabilities in your security. Nothing more."

Kathleen Callahan was a contradiction on so many levels. She might be just a bit of a thing, but she was as tough as nails. She had deftly handled those idiots in the parking lot. If not for her ankle, he wouldn't have needed to intervene.

The way she'd conducted herself in the courtroom had been both awe-inspiring and heartbreaking. So obviously afraid for her sister, she'd still been poised, professional, and determined.

But now that poise was disintegrating as the nerves appeared. And while he wanted to reassure her that he meant her no harm, he couldn't help but be intrigued by the way she exhibited her nervousness.

A curious kind of tenderness lightened his heart as she began to roam around the bedroom. She lifted the comforter, rearranged it, and then looked beneath the bed. Her steps full of graceful energy, she moved across the room, opened a closet, and stuck her head inside. She then walked back across the room and looked out a window.

"Um. If you'll tell me what you're looking for, I'll be glad to help you find it."

"No, thanks."

"Well, then, make yourself at home."

She picked up a book on the nightstand, flipped through the pages, and set it back down. "Okay. Thanks."

Thoroughly enjoying himself, Eli crossed his arms and leaned against the back of his chair as this intriguing sprite of a girl fluttered around his bedroom. Would she be insulted when she learned that she bore a strong resemblance to Eudora, a fairy sprite in *Starburst*, his daughters' favorite bedtime story?

Her mass of red-gold hair was captured in a ponytail, but several strands had sprung from their confinement and curled around her cheeks. At the trial, she'd either worn her hair in a neat braid or in an elegant chignon. Her mouth was slightly too big for her face and should have made her features uneven, but that wasn't the case. Everything fit together to make her one of the most arresting and attractive women he'd ever met.

Her eyes were probably her most striking feature. They were an unusual shade. To say they were blue would be a mistake. They were beyond blue, reflecting the light from the chandelier and making them glow with a mesmerizing, almost magical, brightness.

Everything this woman did, everything this woman was, both fascinated and enchanted him.

He, on the other hand, apparently made her as nervous as hell.

Kathleen knew full well she was behaving in a bizarre fashion but hadn't yet figured out how to recover. She hadn't expected this. Could never have anticipated that Eli Slater was the man who'd helped her in Chicago. How could she?

And the way he was looking at her was making her damn nervous. As if he already knew her, already liked her. The fact that he looked like Prince Charming and happened to live in a fairy-tale castle didn't help.

Telling herself she was a serious-minded professional wasn't helping either. Instead of behaving like said professional, she was flitting around the room like a hyperactive bumblebee looking for a place to land.

So much had happened since the trial. So much pain, so many recriminations. But this tall, golden-haired, gorgeous man had been a shadow in her mind. She had never forgotten him. Had wondered about him. Now, here he was.

"Seriously, Kathleen, if there's something you're looking for, I'd be glad to help you find it."

The amusement in Eli's voice brought her back to the present. She froze as she realized that she'd just opened his underwear drawer. Closing the drawer with a bang, she whirled around and gave him the haughtiest expression she could conjure. "There could be listening devices anywhere."

Brown eyes glinting with humor, he raised a curious brow. "In my boxers?"

Change the subject, Kathleen!

"So…" She cleared her throat. "What exactly do you want me to do for you?"

She inwardly winced as she realized her words sounded more like a sexual proposition than an offer for security assistance.

Thankfully, even though the smile on his face told her he was thinking the same thing, he was gentleman enough to ignore the implication. "I've researched your background. Your expertise in security is impressive. My number one priority is my family. A security company is coming in tomorrow to upgrade the system. Once they're finished, I'd like you to inspect it for weaknesses. I want to ensure that no one can penetrate the grounds, much less get inside the house."

Glad to be back on solid ground, she said, "I can do that."

"Thank you." Another smile spread across his face, this time even sexier than before. Kathleen felt a little dizzy. How could a man be so masculine and almost pretty at the same time? It wasn't natural.

She really shouldn't be having these thoughts. He'd mentioned his family several times. He was married, had children.

"So...umm. Shouldn't Mrs. Slater be here for this discussion?"

"I'm a widower."

No wonder he had such a tragic air about him, like Heathcliff from *Wuthering Heights*, only not uncouth or cruel. She pushed away her whimsical thoughts.

"I'm sorry, I didn't know." She shrugged. "You mentioned your family."

"I have two daughters. Sophia is six and Violet is four."

Two more reasons an attraction was a bad idea.

"Very well. Once the new security system is in place, I'll return and inspect it for you."

The smile he gave her was filled with promise and had her fanciful mind steering away from Heathcliff and bordering on Prince Charming again. Either way, Kathleen knew that once this job was over, she intended to stay as far away from this man as possible.

CHAPTER NINE

"Why do we gotta have so many babysitters, Daddy?"

"They're not babysitters, Sophia. They're people who are watching out for you."

"But why?"

"Because I want to make sure you stay safe."

"But why?"

"Because I love you."

"But why?"

"Because you ask so many questions."

She giggled, and Eli knew that for just a few minutes the questions had stopped. Very soon they'd start back. His six-year-old daughter spent most of her waking moments wanting to know the *why* of everything.

Violet, who was now four, hadn't started the questioning phase yet. He hadn't even known about these phases until just recently.

Taking them to school each morning had become the most enjoyable moments of his day. His daughters made him forget the kind of world that surrounded him. They saw things in bright, vivid colors. Everything was exciting, new, or different. In their world, bunnies talked, fairies granted wishes, and little girls danced to music inside their heads. There were a thousand different new and exciting experiences to have each and every day.

In his most vulnerable moments, he envied their innocence. In his darkest moments, he swore on his life that their innocence would remain intact. Nothing and no one would hurt his children. This he promised.

"Can we have spa-sketti for dinner tonight?"

"I'll ask Teresa, but she may already have something else planned."

Teresa had been with his family for years. She'd moved with them from England, and not a day went by that he didn't send up a prayer of thanks for the incredibly loving and talented woman.

As if it was a foregone conclusion that Teresa had already planned to serve Sophia her beloved spa-sketti, she added, "And then I'll have ba-nilla ice cream for dessert."

"Got your day all planned, huh?"

She nodded emphatically and then commenced to chatter about one of her friends at school. Eli answered when necessary. It usually took only a one-or two-word answer before she was off on another tangent.

He glanced in the rearview mirror, where Violet snoozed peacefully on the other side of Sophia. Poor baby hadn't gotten her sleep out. Long lashes flickered like butterfly wings on her delicate cheeks, and he knew she was dreaming. He wanted only good dreams for both his girls.

"Daddy, who's that man?"

"What man?"

"On the sidewalk over there."

Eli jerked his head around. A skinny, rat-faced man stood on the sidewalk not five feet from where they were stopped. In his hand was a camera, and he was clicking away.

Eli grabbed his cellphone. "Sanders, there's a photographer standing beside my car. Please take care of the matter."

"You got it, boss."

Thirty seconds later, Tim Sanders, big, brawny, and as bald as a cue ball, towered over the photographer. The man backed away and threw a mean glare toward Eli's car. Then he did the creepiest thing of all. His gaze slid to the backseat, where his daughters sat, and he gave a slimy grin.

"Daddy, green means go."

Eli tore his eyes away from the man. A car behind him honked impatiently. Sparing the photographer one last glare, Eli pressed the gas pedal to move forward. A man jumped in front of the car. Sophia screamed, and Eli jerked to a stop. Though he held a camera, instead of taking photographs, this man just stood and stared at them.

"What the hell!" Eli shouted. "Get out of my way, damn you!"

The guy smiled, tipped the baseball cap he was wearing, and sauntered away as if he was in no hurry at all.

Eli was glad he'd had the foresight to employ a three-man security team to watch over his daughters. While one man dealt with the photographer, another headed toward the creep who'd stood in front of the car. The remaining guard pulled alongside Eli's car and nodded.

"You said two bad words, Daddy. Are you gonna wash your mouth out with soap? Twice?"

Eli couldn't prevent the laugh that erupted in his chest. In a matter of minutes, two different sleazebags had accosted their car, and the only takeaway his daughter had was that her daddy had cursed. Twice.

"You bet I will, sweetheart. Sorry about that."

"That's okay. I won't tell nobody."

"Thank you, Sophia."

"Welcome, Daddy."

Eli pulled in front of the school and parked. The private school was the most exclusive in Dallas with the finest security. That still didn't stop him from walking his daughters inside each day. An added bonus was the kindergarten attached to the school. Other than the time he was with his children in their home, Eli was as sure as he could be that the girls were safe.

He had considered a private tutor but had rejected the idea for now. He wanted his children to experience life, not be so sheltered that they were afraid of everything. They were safe here.

He knew a large part of him was projecting from his own childhood. He'd never been given the chance to just be a kid. His daughters deserved better. Even if he had to watch over them twenty-four/seven, he'd make sure they were given the chance to be "normal." Whatever the hell that was anymore. Lately, he wasn't even sure if such a concept existed.

Eli unbuckled Violet first. She blinked sleepily at him and gave him a smile that melted his heart.

"Daddy, hurry!" Sophia screamed. "That man is coming for me."

Eli twisted his head around. Macon Yates, part of Eli's security team, strode toward them. The man's "I eat nails for breakfast" expression was a normal one for him, but Eli could see where it might frighten a six-year-old.

"He's one of the good guys, Sophia. He won't hurt you."

"He looks like the giant from that story you read us last night."

Even though Yates was an inch or two shorter than Eli, his bulk did make him appear bigger and as mean as the evil giant.

"He's here to protect you."

Sophia nodded, but the fear in her eyes lingered. Giving "normal" to his kids was going to involve more than just taking them to school. He had in mind the one person he believed could make that happen. Now if he could just get her to agree.

Holding his daughters, one in each arm, he acknowledged Yates with a nod. The man's duties when his daughters were inside the building were simple. Keep them safe.

And outside? When they were out in the real world? He had that covered, too. Problem was, just how long would he have to make them live like this? He was prepared to protect them for the rest of their lives. But just how long before it started to take a toll on them?

He had to find out who the hell had made the threats. And when he did? Perhaps the world had not seen the end of the murderous Slaters.

CHAPTER TEN

Kathleen drove down the beautiful tree-lined drive and then pulled to a stop in front of Eli Slater's home. She had agreed to inspect the modifications his security company had installed. Once that was done, once she had fulfilled her agreement, she would leave. There was no reason for her to ever see him again.

In between her Justice assignments, she had been getting ready for this meeting. Armed with knowledge of Eli Slater, she was much better prepared to deal with him. She hadn't handled herself well at their first meeting. She told herself it had been the surprise factor. Finding him to be the man she'd seen in Chicago had caught her off guard. It was nothing more than that.

When she'd left that night, she'd been mildly discombobulated. By the time she'd traveled across town to her apartment, anger had replaced the nerves. It was obvious that she had been set up by both Grey and Eli. She didn't like being kept in the dark or manipulated.

All night long, she'd tossed, turned, and stewed. The next morning, armed with several cups of coffee and a ton of self-righteous indignation, she'd presented herself at Grey's office. Needless to say, the confrontation hadn't gone as planned. She winced at the memory.

"Did Eli Slater ask you to hire me?"

As usual, Grey's expression was unreadable, implacable, the arch of one dark brow the only indication that she might have surprised him. "And good morning to you, too, Kathleen. Did you sleep well?"

"No, I didn't sleep well."

"Bad dreams?"

"Yes...no... That's not the point. Why didn't you tell me that Eli Slater was the man I met in Chicago?"

"Would it have made a difference to the job? Would you have assessed the mansion's security differently? Broken in another way?"

"Of course not, but going in blind was—"

"Discomfiting, I'm sure. Eli's a friend. I'm protective of my friends, including you. If I thought giving you a heads-up about Eli's identity would have been beneficial to the job, I would have included that information in your assignment."

"I'm not buying that, Grey. But I'm past that. What I'd like to know is, did Eli ask you to hire me?"

"I've said Eli is a friend. He's not my adviser, personnel manager, or boss. If I thought you weren't the best person for the job, I wouldn't have offered you a position." He eyed her speculatively. "What happened last night that upset you? Was he rude to you? Did he make advances or say something off-color?"

Since explaining that her discomfort was caused by her extreme attraction to Eli Slater was out of the question, she'd simply shaken her head and mumbled something about having all available information on a client was an important part of assessment.

She was sure Grey could have argued that point and won. Thankfully, he hadn't and had moved on to other things.

Just because she had overreacted didn't mean she was wrong. Eli had wanted to meet her this way. Grey had obliged.

But now that she knew, now that she was prepared, she anticipated this meeting going much differently. She would give him her opinion on the upgrades, make recommendations if necessary, and then she would be on her way. This was just another job… Eli Slater was just another client.

With that self-lecture boosting her confidence, Kathleen got out of the car. The instant she did, the man himself walked down the steps to meet her. His tall, lithe body and commanding appearance were even more devastating in the daylight. Dressed in a pair of black jeans and a black T-shirt that fit tight over broad shoulders, the short sleeves revealing impressive biceps, he was both stylish and masculine.

Her legs suddenly weak, she was glad to have the car behind her to lean on. Who knew a multimillionaire could look that good in jeans?

His movements were surprisingly graceful for a man his size and build. The insane thought that he must be an amazing dancer flashed through her head. She hadn't been dancing since her high school prom, and that had been a disaster. But for some reason, this man made her think of whimsical things her practical brain told her were unimportant. Such as dancing in the moonlight beneath a canopy of a million stars.

"It's good to see you again, Kathleen. Are you well?"

"Um, yes. Fine, thanks."

"Come, take a look at the upgrades and new equipment. Then we'll have lunch and get to know each other better."

He held out his hand and smiled.

At that moment, Kathleen knew all the self-lectures and warnings in the world weren't going to save her this time, because Eli Slater was quite possibly the most dangerous man she'd ever met.

She was nervous again, but this time doing her very best to hide it. Determined to put her at ease, Eli led her into his home. When she stopped abruptly at the entrance to the foyer, he shot her a quizzical look and said, "Everything okay?"

"Yes. Sorry. Your home is beautiful…breathtaking." Her sidelong glance was surprisingly teasing. "Seeing it with a flashlight didn't do it justice."

Glad to see her at ease enough to joke, he gave her a quick grin and then gazed around, trying to see things from her perspective. Having lived here for so long, he took much of the grandeur for granted. It was home to him. The place where his children played, slept, and were growing much too fast.

"My late wife, Shelley, had the home designed to resemble an English castle."

"She was British, wasn't she?"

"Yes. I went to university in England. Met her there, and we married. Sophia was born there."

Shaking away memories he'd prefer to not dwell on, he said, "We'll start on the first floor. I'll show you the cameras they installed, as well as the new motion detectors. If you see anything you feel needs to be changed or added, just let me know."

As they made their way from room to room, he was pleased to see the lessening of tension in her shoulders. Her comments and questions were pointed and intelligent, telling him she was focused on the job and had forgotten for the moment that he made her nervous. He was glad for it. Since he had every intention of spending more time with her, the last thing he wanted was for her to feel uncomfortable with him.

He led her up the stairs to the second floor and heard her sigh.

"What?" he asked.

She shrugged, then sent him a small smile. "I'll bet your daughters love these dual staircases."

He laughed. "Oh yes, we've had quite a few conversations about racing each other on the stairs."

They stood on the landing for a moment and looked down onto the large marble foyer. "I can only imagine the parties you and your wife must have had here. It seems like the perfect home for entertaining."

Eli felt a pang to his heart. "I believe that was Shelley's dream when she had the house designed. Unfortunately, her health never allowed her to live out that dream."

She placed a hand on his arm. "I'm sorry. I didn't mean to bring up sad memories."

"Thank you, but I try to remember the good times." He headed down the hallway toward the east wing and his daughters' rooms. "The girls have separate bedrooms, share a playroom, a media room, and a small music room. However, most nights they want to sleep together and alternate between bedrooms."

Tenderness then sadness flickered on her face. "My sister and I were the same way. Not that we always had a room to ourselves, but even when we did, we slept together."

He had wanted to diminish her sadness and had only made it worse. Hoping to dispel it completely, he led her quickly through the rest of the second-floor bedrooms, parlors, and sitting rooms, the third floor with more bedrooms, along with game room, gym, and media room. Then he took her up to the fourth floor.

"Oh my stars."

Pleased at her reaction, he followed her into the tower room. Though she had made approving comments throughout their tour on both the additional security and the décor, this was the first time she had exclaimed her excitement for a room.

She walked into the middle of the room and turned around slowly, her lovely face glowing with pleasure. "It's like being in the middle of the sky."

The walls were a sky blue with puffy white clouds scattered throughout. The furniture was minimal, with only a few large chaise lounges and oversized chairs. It was a good place for quiet reflection.

"I'm glad you like it. It's one of the few rooms I wanted any say in." He pressed a switch, and the ceiling disappeared, revealing a giant dome-shaped skylight. "One of my favorite places when I was a kid was the planetarium. I could spend hours stargazing, dreaming. And there's just something special about a Texas sky at night. It's especially amazing during a meteor shower."

"It's wonderful."

He looked at her then and had to steel his legs to keep from moving closer. Her lovely face glowed, those miraculous eyes glinted, that beautiful mobile mouth lifted up in a delighted smile. Never had he wanted to kiss a woman more. But it was too damn soon. She didn't know him, wasn't sure if she could trust him. The last thing he wanted to do was scare her off.

"The security upgrade is exceptional. I think you'll be happy with the additions."

He was glad he hadn't made that move. The wary look was back on her face, and she had returned to business mode.

"I really appreciate your help," Eli said. "I know you were upset with both Grey and me about the other night, but I promise you, your input was helpful. I can assure you that my children's safety is priority one for me. Nothing is more important."

"You've said that several times now. Has something specific happened that has you concerned?"

"Come have lunch with me, and we'll talk about it."

She glanced down at her watch. "Oh, I don't know. I should really—"

"Nonsense. Teresa has it all ready for us." He held out his hand. "Come meet her. She said she was dying to meet the woman who broke into the house without her knowing it."

Even as her mind told her she shouldn't, her hand reached out to his. She didn't know what she had expected when they touched. Electrical sparks? Sexual arousal? Nothing? Surprisingly, what she felt when his hand closed over hers was a feeling she'd never had in her life. Safety, security...belonging.

That thought terrified her. Belonging? No way in hell.

Forcing a cool, bland expression on her face, she walked back down to the first floor and into the ginormous kitchen. Teresa Longview stood in the middle of it, grinning from ear to ear. The older woman was in her early sixties, sturdy and dependable looking. She had the appearance of someone who was both compassionate but no-nonsense.

Kathleen liked her immediately.

"What a delight it is to meet you, Miss Callahan."

Kathleen shook the older woman's hand. "It's a pleasure. But please call me Kathleen."

"When Mr. Eli told me what you'd done, I was so impressed. Where did you learn to do such a thing?"

Truth wasn't always the way to go. Not when it involved telling the older woman that her father had been the renowned thief Daniel Callahan, who had taught both his daughters many skills of the trade.

"It comes in handy when assessing structures for security issues."

If Teresa noticed the non-answer, she gave no indication. "I'm sure it does." She beamed up at Eli. "Lunch is already set for you in the small dining room. You let me know if there's anything else you need."

"Thank you, Teresa." Eli glanced at Kathleen. "Shall we?"

She gave Teresa another smile and then followed Eli into the small, cozy dining room. It had a homey and relaxed décor, very different from the formal dining room, which held a table large enough to feed twenty-four and enough ornamentation to suit a royal family. Kathleen much preferred this room, not only for its simplicity, but also because it was obviously the place where Eli and his daughters had many of their meals. A booster chair sat in the corner. Coloring books and crayon boxes were on the sideboard. The knowledge that Eli ate here with his children made her feel less nervous. If she could look at him as a father, instead of a sexy, gorgeous, desirable man, she would be much better off.

He pulled out a chair for her and then sat to her left. With determination, she forced herself to relax. This was a business luncheon with a client. She would ask him about the concern for his children's safety, they would enjoy this delicious-looking Cobb salad that Teresa had prepared, and then she would go home.

She took a sip of tea, delighted that it had just the right amount of sweetness.

"Kathleen?"

She lifted her head. "Yes?"

"I'd like you to come work for me."

CHAPTER ELEVEN

She looked at him as though he'd spoken a foreign language. He could have prepared her beforehand, mentioned earlier what was on his mind, but he'd known she would turn him down flat, without giving it a moment of thought. This way, while she ate lunch, he'd have a chance to convince her to say yes.

"Work for you? I don't understand. I already have a job."

"This wouldn't be full time. Just a few hours each day."

"Doing what?"

"Personal security."

"You mean bodyguard services?"

"That's something you're trained in, right?"

"Yes. The security company I worked for in Denver provided that service."

"I need another bodyguard."

"I'm sure Grey could get you the names of some excellent security companies."

"That's not what I'm looking for. I already have those kinds of bodyguards. I don't need another one."

"Then what are you looking for?"

"I want you to guard my children."

If he'd told her he was an alien and wanted to take her away to his faraway planet, Eli doubted she would have looked more surprised…or appalled.

The words "not just no, but hell no" were the first that came to Kathleen's mind. Every instinct she owned was telling her to leave the table and get the hell away from this man. He disturbed her on way too many different levels already. No way, no how, would she ever want to be charged with protecting his children.

Correctly interpreting that she was about to say no, he held up his hand. "Hear me out. My daughters are in school from eight until three thirty. You wouldn't need to be there with them all day. I already have a man who guards the school. Once they're home, I can protect them."

Moving the plate in front of him out of the way, Eli folded his arms on the table. "Truth is, I have three bodyguards for them already."

"Well, then…?" She looked at him questioningly.

"I want to give my children the most normal life possible. I can't do that when they're surrounded by giant, ferocious-looking men. I need someone who's not going to scare them…someone they can trust."

"I'm sure there are plenty of female bodyguards who wouldn't scare them." Even though she wasn't even remotely considering taking the job, she had to ask, "Are your children in danger?"

"Yes."

"Explain."

"Do you know about my family? About my father and brother?"

She'd spent hours learning about the Slaters over the last few days. Refusing to go too deeply into just how much research she'd done, she just said, "I know before your father was killed and your brother was imprisoned, they were guilty of a lot of things, including conspiracy to commit murder, extortion, money laundering, and pandering."

"I've spent the better part of a year cleaning up their messes. I thought it was over. I had hoped it was behind us, and then I started getting these."

He pulled some folded papers from his jeans' pocket and handed them to her.

She read through them, becoming more chilled with each email. She certainly understood his concern.

"Any idea who's sending them?"

"I have some theories, but nothing's panned out. Until I know who and why, until I can destroy or neutralize the threat, I want my children under protection."

"The protection is wise. But why me?"

"I've done my research, Kathleen. I know one of your primary jobs in Denver was protecting children."

"Then you also must know what happened on my last job protecting a child. She almost died."

"You saved her life. I not only talked to the security company you worked for, I talked to Emily's parents. They all agreed you saved that little girl's life."

Yes, that's what she'd been told, but if she'd done a better job, her life wouldn't have had to be saved in the first place. When Alice had admitted that she believed Frank was responsible, Kathleen had reached out to her former employer, as well as Emily's parents. Though it had sickened her, and she felt even guiltier than she had before, she'd felt the need to let them know.

"I happen to disagree with them, but that's not the point. I can't guard your children." She scooted her chair back, preparing to leave. "Thank you for lunch."

He grabbed her hand, preventing her from moving. "Why not? You have the credentials. The training."

"I just don't want to do that kind of work anymore. And I already have a job."

"I know you work on a freelance basis with Grey, so you have plenty of flexibility. I would need you at the most four hours a day. An hour or so in the morning when the girls go to school. An hour or so in the afternoon when they get out. Once they're home, the house with the new security, along with my full-time bodyguards, will protect them."

"And the weekends? What about then? Don't they go to parks, or the zoo? Movies? Ice cream shop?"

"They'll be with me." He said that with quiet assurance. He could protect his own.

She nodded. "You handled yourself with those thugs in Chicago. Where did you get your training?"

"Mathias, my father, insisted that all his boys know how to defend themselves. The thought of one of us being beaten up by a bully went against everything he believed in. Hell...maybe because he was such a bully himself. I don't know. I took it a step further when I went to university in England. I got into boxing and then mixed martial arts."

"Are you weapons trained?"

"Another skill Mathias insisted all his children learn."

"Your daughters are obviously well protected. Any threats other than the emails? Have you seen anyone loitering at the school? Playgrounds? Anything like that?"

"Not what I would call a specific threat. But at least once a week, sometimes more if it's a slow news week, a photographer or reporter will pop up. Two of them came after us the other day. Scared Sophia. My personal security can take care of these slimeballs, but I need someone up close and personal. I want someone who can not only protect my daughters, but can do so without scaring them. I want that person to be you."

She tried to give him another out. "You barely know me. Just because you saw me in the courtroom…you can't know me."

"Very well. Tell me about yourself."

She went to rise, uncomfortable with the turn of the conversation. His hand was still holding her wrist, and he squeezed gently. She glanced down. The contrast between his large, masculine hand and her small, pale one was a surprise. So was the gentleness, as well as the control.

"Don't like to talk about yourself? Very well, let me tell you what I know. What I saw in that courtroom was courage, poise, tenacity, and a wealth of love I hadn't seen in a long while. Your and your sister's lives were torn apart for public consumption. No stone unturned, no heartache too painful to be bared. Yet you stood there and took it because to do otherwise is not in you."

"She was my sister," Kathleen said faintly. "How could I do anything else but?"

"Exactly."

"What does that have to do with me guarding your children?"

"Nothing other than you've got stamina and grit. Qualities I greatly admire."

"But still—"

"I read some of your college essays. You're very big on patriotism. The need to protect is instinctive."

"My essays? How on earth… You had no right to—"

"My children mean the world to me. Whomever I ask to protect them has to be researched thoroughly. Based on those essays, I was surprised you didn't join the military. And then I thought, no, you wouldn't. You had to take care of your sister. So you put aside your needs once again."

"Alice had to come first."

"Why such a strong affinity for the military? Your father never served, did he?"

"One of my foster fathers did." She shot him a resentful glare. "Apparently, that's something you couldn't dig into."

"He must have made quite an impression on you."

"He did. I didn't have the best experience with foster care. But my last family, Rocky and Georgia Lester, were the best. Rocky was a former marine. He's the one who taught me how to defend myself. Instilled in me the confidence to succeed."

"It must have been hard for you to leave them, when your father was released from prison."

She still remembered the desolation. She'd been torn between returning to her father and her sister—being a real family again—and leaving the two people who'd come to mean so much to her.

"It was hard, but we kept in touch. They moved to Colorado when Georgia retired from teaching. Rocky opened a security company."

"That's why you moved to Denver. To work for him."

"I thought of them as family."

"Are they still there?"

"No. Georgia died a couple of years ago. Rocky about a year ago. When he retired, he sold his company to Bankhead Security."

"I'm sure you miss them."

The gentleness in his tone pulled her from her memories. She'd never talked about Rocky and Georgia, not even to her father or Alice. Those were her memories to treasure.

She waved her hand as if to wipe away the past. "That has nothing to do with this. There are plenty of female bodyguards who are more than qualified to do this job. You don't need it to be me."

"Perhaps. Except it's you I want. You are the perfect person to do this job."

"I'm sorry, but I can't do it."

"Can't or won't?"

When she didn't answer, he gave her one of those charming, winning smiles that both warmed and scared her at the same time.

"Look, come with me to pick them up today. If you decide after you meet them that you can't do it, I won't argue with you again."

Once he saw that just because she had the training didn't mean his kids would take to her, they could move on. He would accept that it wouldn't work out, and then she would never have to see Eli Slater again.

Refusing to dwell on why that thought disturbed her, she said, "Fine, I'll meet your daughters."

The light in his eyes told her he believed he'd already won the argument.

CHAPTER TWELVE

Dark golden liquid swirled in the glass, its murky depths a reflection of the life he lived, the life he'd chosen. Grey took a long swallow of his drink. He rarely drank alcohol, especially at this time of day. Dulling his senses had always seemed like a waste of time to him. If you didn't like your life—had to drink to cope—then you damn well needed to change your life. Drinking did nothing but add to your problems. But now? Hell, this situation just called for a strong one. Maybe two.

His eyes flickered to the map he'd dropped on the table. He'd told himself a million times that he was wrong. She would never be so bold, so careless…so damn cold. He'd seen her humanity, her heart. He'd seen the guilt she'd suffered. These cold acts of violence went against everything he believed about her. But the evidence was here, staring up at him with accusing knowledge. He couldn't deny, prevaricate, make excuses. Refusing to face reality would be pointless. He'd heard from all his sources, in both Ireland and England, and they had confirmed his worst fears. She had been seen, identified.

He slammed the glass onto the table, ignoring the slosh of liquid that fell onto the map. Surging to his feet, he strode to the one place he could still feel her presence, the one place where he could still convince himself she wasn't a cold-blooded murderer. Pushing open the door, he stepped into her bedroom and closed it behind him. This time of day, he was alone, but he would take no chances. No one belonged in this room but he and Irelyn.

He had been stupid enough to believe that she might come back to him. That once she dealt with the blow—with the awful thing he'd forced her to do—she would realize there had been no other choice and she would return to him. That had been over a year ago.

Other than his housekeeper, no one had been in this room since she'd left. At one time, he had planned to discard everything, but he hadn't been able to go through with it. The finality hadn't been something he could abide. So he'd kept the room just as she liked it. This room embodied Irelyn Raine's personality more so than anything else he had of her. He hadn't been able to let go.

Some might think he was being sentimental. Maybe he was. First time for everything, he guessed. Whatever the reason, this room would always be open to her, whether she wanted to be here or not.

He picked up a small porcelain clown, its face both comical and sad. Everywhere they'd traveled, Irelyn had insisted on buying a clown for her collection. He'd known her since they were both in their teens, and in spite of all they'd gone through together, Grey had found her sentimentality charming. There was an enormous amount of depth to Irelyn, and every time he thought he had figured her out, he'd find another layer.

Returning the figurine to the shelf, he surveyed the room. She'd spent a lot of time in here. The cool cream color of the walls and furniture should have clashed with the bold slashes of color in the accent pieces, pillows, and drapery, but they didn't. Every piece spoke of the many facets of Irelyn Raine.

This room had been her retreat…from the world, yes, but mostly from him. Outside this room, she'd had a role to play. She had been his partner, confidant, co-conspirator, employee, and lover. And she had often called herself his prisoner. But if she retreated to her suite of rooms, he hadn't bothered her unless there was an emergency. That had been their agreement… their arrangement.

Grey wasn't one to second-guess his decisions. He wouldn't do so now. What he had made her do that night had been for her benefit—even more so than his. Of course, she hadn't seen it that way. Might never see it that way. Yes, he had wanted the bloody prick dead. Hill Reed had been a dark shadow in his and Irelyn's past. One that had been long overdue for elimination. Assassin, contract killer, defiler of innocents, the bastard had gotten what he deserved. But as much as Grey had wanted the man dead, Irelyn had been the only one who had deserved the privilege of killing him.

She had seen the act in a completely different light.

If Grey had one wish about that night—one do-over—he wouldn't have made her watch. He would've come in before the man died and taken her away. Watching him struggle for air and then breathe his last breath had almost destroyed her. It had most certainly destroyed them.

The chime at his front door pulled him from his regret and from the room. Reviewing past sins didn't do a damn bit of good. What was done was done.

He opened the door, pleased to see the glowing couple in front of him. Marriage looked good on them. "How was the honeymoon?"

Kennedy Gallagher flashed a bright smile as she walked in beside her new husband. "I can attest that the last part was lovely.

You'll have to ask Nick about the first part, though, as I was in the bathroom most of the time."

Sending his wife an amused, loving look, Nick shook his head. "Let's just say I got caught up on all the television shows I've missed over the last couple of years."

Grey chuckled as he led the newlyweds into his office. Though the wedding had taken place last year, they had postponed their honeymoon until after Adam Slater's trial. When they were certain that Adam would rot in prison for the murder of Thomas O'Connell, Kennedy's first husband, they'd planned to enjoy an extended honeymoon. Two days before they were scheduled to leave, they'd learned that Kennedy was pregnant. Postponing again wasn't something either one of them had wanted to do.

"Feeling better now?" Grey asked.

"Feeling wonderful," Kennedy answered. "Nick was worried..." She shook her head. "We were both worried because of what happened before, so I saw a doctor in Madrid. He agreed with my doctor here. The pregnancy is normal, as is the nausea."

"I'm glad." Grey led them to a sofa and then seated himself across from them.

"Your phone call sounded serious. Has something happened? Are Eli and Jonah okay?"

It was a testament to the character of Kennedy and Nick that they cared. Many people lumped all the Slaters together, and either hated them or revered them as one entity. But this couple, who'd been through so much because of two of the Slaters, held no grudge or resentment for the rest of the family. They knew where the evil had existed.

"They're both fine. Sorry to worry you. Not much has changed."

Grey didn't mention the threats Eli was dealing with. They were being handled.

"And Eleanor and Lacey? They're still in France?"

"Yes. I doubt that will change anytime soon. Mathias's death, along with learning what he did to Jonah, isn't something Eleanor will recover from, but hopefully she'll learn to deal."

"What about Irelyn?" Kennedy asked. "Any word from her?"

Would Irelyn be surprised by the concern in Kennedy's eyes? Probably. With their lifestyle and need for secrecy, neither Grey nor Irelyn had ever developed the kind of close personal relationships that most people enjoyed. Forming relationships... friendships was just too damn normal for them.

"No. I've not heard from her."

The disappointment in his wife's face was apparent, and Nick took her hand and squeezed it gently. Looking over at Grey, he said, "So this is another matter? You have a job for one or both of us?"

Nick had become an operative for the Grey Justice Group a while ago, but Kennedy, who had been working for the Slaters in an undercover capacity, had only recently agreed to work for Grey as well. Gallagher was a former homicide detective, Kennedy a highly skilled researcher.

"A job for you both." The murder file lay on the coffee table between them. He slid it forward. "I want you both to investigate a murder."

While Kennedy reviewed the file, Nick stared at him with the keen eyes of a cop. He would know there was more to the case than mere words on the page.

Grey had already decided what he could share. "The victim, if one could call him that, is Bobby O'Leary. Born in Dublin, Ireland. Raised by his granny until he was about ten. Once his grandmother died, he found a way to avoid detection, became a street punk. By the time he was sixteen, he'd raped and killed several women. He then met up with a man who showed him that what Bobby liked to do for fun could be a profitable business."

"Hit man?" Nick asked.

"Yes."

"He took to the job like he was born for it. He had several kill methods, but his favorite was two at a time."

"Two?" Kennedy asked. "How do you mean?"

"He took contracts that often involved killing a couple—a man and a woman was his preference. He'd study them, learn their weaknesses, then lure them with whatever story he had to. He'd rape and torture the woman—usually for hours—in front of the tied-up and helpless man. He would make promises that he'd let them go if she cooperated.

"When he'd gotten his fill, had his fun, he would shoot the woman first, then the man."

Nick gave a low growl of disgust. "And do you want us to find the person who killed this sadistic son of a bitch and give him a medal? Because that's my first inclination."

"I just want a name."

"Grey?" The hesitancy in Kennedy's soft voice told him what was coming. "Do you think Irelyn killed this man?"

Kennedy's instincts, as always, were excellent. However, that wasn't something he could share. "Why would you say that?"

"She's from Ireland, too." Her brow wrinkled. "Isn't she?"

He didn't blame her for her confusion. One of Irelyn's many talents was the ability to perfectly mimic every accent she'd ever heard.

"She's spent a lot of time in Ireland, yes."

Nick's eyes narrowed. "You know, it'd be a helluva lot easier if you'd tell us as much as you know."

"I've told you what I can."

"Once we find out who it is. What then?"

"Get me a name. I'll take it from there."

And he hoped to hell the name was different from the one he feared.

Chapter Thirteen

"Maybe we should have waited until they got home from school."

Eli glanced over at the woman in the passenger seat beside him. Something about him put her on edge. He didn't get the idea that she disliked him. It was more as if he disturbed her composure, unsettled her. And that didn't bother him in the least.

"It'll be better this way. It'll be fine. I promise."

Even though he was no longer looking at her, he knew her eyes were throwing daggers at him. It wasn't as if he'd forced her to come with him. She'd left after lunch, assuring him she'd be back by three o'clock to go with him to the school. He'd been a little surprised that she'd actually come back, but shouldn't have been. One of the many things he had learned about Kathleen was her need to keep her commitments. When she made a promise, she kept it. Since he didn't have a lot of faith in mankind these days, that character trait was damn refreshing.

The dress she was wearing couldn't be more perfect for this meeting. He had chosen well, though she didn't yet know that the dress had come from him.

And her hair. Nothing had prepared him for how lovely she would look with her hair unbound and flowing over her shoulders like a river of red gold. She was both spellbinding and enchanting. A fairy sprite come to life. His daughters were going to love her.

She didn't believe they would take to her, but Eli knew better. Plus, he had a secret weapon. One that he didn't feel the least bit guilty in using.

The first part would be the hardest, for both of them.

Steeling himself, he glanced over at her and said casually, "I like the dress. Very fetching."

Her eyes dropped to take in the multicolored confection. Every hue of the rainbow mingled together to create a mesmerizing, eye-catching mélange of fabric and design. With every move she made, the material shimmered in rhythm with her body.

"I'm attending a cocktail party at the art center this evening. I won't have time to go home and change, so…" She shrugged as if self-conscious and shifted her attention out the window. The soft rosy flush on her face added additional enchantment to her beauty.

"And your hair is lovely, too. You don't wear it down often."

"No. Kind of gets in the way." Her smile was tight. "Breaking into houses and all."

"Ah, makes sense. So, tell me a little more about your childhood. I know that you raised your sister. You were what…nine when your mother died in childbirth? Raising a child is tough enough. Being responsible for one at the age of nine is remarkable."

She didn't respond, clearly uncomfortable with discussing herself. Too bad. She needed to realize that not only did he know almost everything about her, he admired and trusted her.

"I didn't raise Alice by myself. My father was there, too."

Eli didn't comment about that, knowing she wouldn't appreciate Eli's opinion of a man who was not only irresponsible enough to depend upon his nine-year-old daughter to raise her sister, but to make his living as a thief.

"When your father went to prison, you and your sister went to separate foster homes. I can only imagine how hard that was for you."

No response again, but her lovely mouth had become a mutinous line. Being a stubborn, tenacious man, he didn't let that stop him.

"That was what…for three years? Then you were reunited?"

"My father agreed to work for the government. He paid his debt to society. He got the family back together as soon as he could. It worked out fine."

"And you lost him two years later."

"Mr. Slater, you've proven you've done your homework. I don't need my life history verbalized. I've lived it."

He had become *Mr. Slater* again. While he regretted her need to put distance between them, he intended to have his say. He had the odd feeling that Kathleen wasn't as big a fan of herself as he was.

"At eighteen, you were in charge of a nine-year-old. How'd you do that? Go to college and work, too?"

"Very poorly, I assure you. You are apparently aiming to prove that I'm some sort of marvel or saint. I can assure you I'm not. If I were, Alice wouldn't have found herself on trial for murder. And she wouldn't be dead."

"So you blame yourself for all the things that happened to your sister?"

"Who else can I blame?"

"Umm. The scumbag Frank Braden, for one. And how about your sister? She holds no responsibility for what happened?"

Her eyes flashed with both anger and grief. "My sister is dead."

"Yes, and I'm very sorry for that. But you did everything you could for her. The choices she made led her to Braden. Not you."

Fire gleamed in her eyes as a defiant expression came over her face. "So tell me, Mr. Slater. Do you feel any regret or remorse for the fact that your wife died of a drug overdose?"

He was glad she had gone on the offensive, greatly preferring that to her sadness and guilt. And she had made an excellent jab, because he did indeed feel a great responsibility for what had happened to Shelley. How could he not?

"As a matter of fact, I do. More than most people realize or could understand."

Ashamed, Kathleen looked away from him, awash in regret. Yes, his questions and comments had been out of line, but using his own tragedy against him had been deplorable on her part. She rarely lost her cool, but when she did, she had a tendency to lash out in the most hurtful way possible.

"I'm sorry, Eli. I was out of line. If you were at Alice's trial, you had no choice but to hear about my past. And it only makes sense that you've had me investigated." A brief smile cracked her face. "I'm sure you don't allow just anyone to break into your home. However, knowing about my past and talking about it are two different things. I had quite enough of that during the trial.

"Dwelling on bad memories gets you nowhere. I prefer to focus on the here and now."

As if she hadn't spoken, he went on, "The hit-and-run accident in Denver. They never caught the guy who did it?"

Her head jerked around, and she couldn't help herself...she gawked at him. Why would he continue to bring up some of the most painful moments in her life?

"I recovered." Her voice was curt, bordering on rude.

"Your fiancé broke off your engagement not long after your accident. You dodged a bullet there. Guy must've been a giant prick."

Before she could tell him to stop again, or agree with him because Stan had indeed been a giant prick, he continued, speaking at a rapid clip now, as if to dump out all the garbage of her life in one fell swoop.

"And then you had to sell your house to pay for Alice's defense. That had to be painful."

Losing her house had been more painful than losing her fiancé. For the first time in her life, she'd had security, a home of her own. She had no regrets in doing that—Alice had been more important than a stack of brick and mortar. But still, when she thought about her quaint little house with its wrap-around porch and sunny kitchen, the little vegetable garden she'd started in her backyard, her heart bled a little. It had been tiny, not in the best neighborhood, but it had been hers. All hers.

"And still it wasn't enough. You had to take loans out, go into debt. Live in a seedy part of Chicago."

She shot him a silent, resentful glare. He wasn't going to stop. She could see that he was trying to make a point, but damned if she could figure out what it was. He would go on and on, metaphorically shredding her life, bleeding her dry. If they hadn't been moving down the road at a good clip, she'd have opened the door and gotten out. A few bruises and scrapes would be preferable.

"Then you lost Alice."

"Stop it, damn you. Just stop."

He pulled to a halt at a red light and shot her a strange, knowing look. "Close your eyes, Kathleen."

"What the hell are you talking about? I'm not going to—"

"You agreed to cooperate, so I'm asking you to close your eyes."

Though more furious than she'd been in a long while, she closed her eyes and snapped, "Now what?"

"Give me a perimeter check."

Setting the fury aside, she described the scene around them. "Three vehicles directly behind us. In the third one back, the black SUV, are your bodyguards."

"And you know this how?"

"I saw a photograph online."

"Continue."

"In the vehicle directly behind us, the white F-150, is your chauffeur, Gunter. The cream-colored Taurus in the middle is a freelance reporter."

"How do you know he's a reporter?"

"Because he's got the look of a predator without the toughness or attitude to go with it."

"And why do you peg him as freelance?"

"He's got a cheap video camera attached to his rearview mirror and one of the worst comb-overs I've ever seen."

She heard the amusement in his voice when he said, "Okay. Continue."

"Two cars to our right, green Subaru and white Volvo. Both appear to be occupied by innocent civilians."

"Where are we?"

"Forty-second and Seventh."

"If those innocent civilians are not so innocent, or the creep in the Taurus comes for us, what's our exit strategy?"

"One block to the right, two blocks left is a residential area. Lead them there. It's like a maze. We could easily lose them."

"And?"

"A police station is on the other side of the community. Head there."

The car started forward, and she opened her eyes to see triumph on his face. "And that, Kathleen, is the reason I want you to guard my children."

CHAPTER FOURTEEN

Eli knew he was an ass for trapping her like that. Throwing the most painful moments in her life at her, as if they were amusing trivia, had been tasteless to the point of cruelty. But it had proven his point. This woman with her mesmerizing eyes and fairy-tale looks was a highly trained professional. Even while he'd hammered at her about all the trauma in her life, she was still focused enough to know exactly what was happening around them and have an exit strategy if needed. He had no doubts that she could take care of his daughters.

He knew the training she'd had. He'd talked to her former employer as well as several of her former clients. All of them had given her their highest recommendations, praising her as both professional and kind. She didn't just protect the people she guarded, she cared about them.

Under her protection, Violet and Sophia would be safe. And they would trust her. He had ensured that as well.

Eli pulled up in front of the school, but before they got out, he had something else he needed to say. "I'm sorry that I upset and hurt you. You asked me why I wanted you to guard my children. You didn't take me at my word, so I felt the need to show you.

I have a tendency to be ruthless when it comes to those I care about. Bringing up your most painful memories was in poor taste."

She stared at him for several seconds. He could only imagine what was going through her mind. She had her guard up again. His fault this time. He'd put her in a position of vulnerability and felt vaguely sick to his stomach.

She finally nodded. "Fine. Let's go meet your children."

Her tone said she didn't expect the meeting to go well. He chose not to explain why he disagreed. She would learn soon enough.

As they got out of the car, he asked, "You're armed?"

"Of course."

He'd already gone too far with her today but couldn't resist asking, "And your weapon is where?"

The withering look should have singed him but made him want to smile. "I have a bra holster holding my SIG P238, and a knife in a sheath attached to my right thigh."

Now he wished he hadn't asked, because the image that came to his mind wasn't something that would leave him any time soon. Forcing himself to focus on the here and now, Eli explained, "I'll go get Violet and Sophia. You can wait at one of the tables in the side yard."

With a nod of agreement, she headed to the large iron gate to the side. He waved at the camera attached to it and waited until the gate opened then closed behind her before he went into the school. His children were in for quite a surprise. As was Kathleen.

Taking in her surroundings in a flash, Kathleen was surprised and pleased to find that though this was obviously an exclusive private school for the most elite of Dallas, with its gated entrance and security cameras, the playground still had the regular playground equipment of monkey bars, slides, and merry-go-rounds. She was also pleased that it was well maintained and cleaner than the inside of most houses. Not a speck of dirt was on the stone bench she seated herself on to wait for Eli and his children.

She was still furious with him. He had used some of the most horrendous moments in her life to prove a point. In spite of her anger, she also secretly admired the man's ingenuity. The fact that she had fallen for it was a bit of a shocker, but she consoled herself that at least she had passed the damned test. Despite the fact that he knew more about her than she was comfortable for anyone to know, she was also pleased that he had done his homework. He didn't want just anyone protecting his children. He wanted the best.

She knew her strengths and weaknesses. She was confident in her training, abilities, and talents. She had focused her energies on becoming the best.

Navigating the dangerous and choppy waters of personal or intimate relationships was another matter. Kathleen believed in playing to her strengths.

She glanced down at her dress and grimaced. One of the many perks of working for Grey Justice was having her very own stylist and hairdresser for certain events. The phenomenon was still quite new to her, and she loved it. Who wouldn't?

She had planned to wear the simple but elegant Donna Karan dress the stylist had sent her last week. It fit perfectly and was appropriate for the elegant and exclusive gathering she was attending tonight. Her wardrobe plans had abruptly changed a few hours ago.

She'd been getting out of the shower when the stylist had shown up at her apartment with a different dress and a request from Grey to wear it instead. Yes, it was beautiful, but nothing like what she would normally wear. First, it was quite frivolous looking, almost playful.

Secondly, though the dress was multicolored, the main color was almost the exact shade of her eyes. She rarely wore that shade of blue because she'd always felt it was just too much. She'd inherited her mother's eyes, their color a cross between ocean blue and smoky silver. They were pretty, but when she wore anything the same color, the results could be astonishing, almost overwhelming.

The material of the dress was another thing she would never have picked out. It was a delicate, almost flimsy fabric, with several layers that seemed to swish and swirl with her movements.

Grey's request for her hairstyle had been the biggest surprise. When she was on the job, she almost never wore it loose. She either wore it in a long braid or ponytail, or if she was dressing up, she wore it in a loose chignon. The stylist had insisted that the dress called for her hair to be loose and flowing around her. And since the woman had more knowledge of fashion than Kathleen would ever have in a lifetime, she had agreed.

So here she sat in the play area of one of the most exclusive schools in Dallas, wearing one of the most frivolous outfits she'd ever worn in her life. Odd how she felt both silly and ultrafeminine.

At the sound of a door opening and closing, Kathleen stood, waiting for the two little girls to notice her. She had no idea why she was suddenly nervous. She most certainly didn't care if Violet and Sophia Slater liked her or not. It wasn't as if she'd see them again after today.

The salary Eli had offered was off-the-charts generous, the time commitment of four hours a day insignificant. And with the additional security Eli had surrounding his children, the job should be minimal risk. But protecting children again? After what had happened to Emily? She seriously didn't think she had it in her.

They were beautiful children, both bearing a strong resemblance to the tall, devastatingly handsome man following them. The youngest one, Violet, had medium-length, curly, white-blond hair, a button nose, and the softest, sweetest brown eyes Kathleen had ever seen. Sophia's hair was a darker gold, very similar to Eli's hair, and it was long, almost to the middle of her back. She had creamy skin that reminded Kathleen of a gardenia, and her eyes were brown with golden flecks.

Kathleen gave them a cautious, serious smile, waiting for the awkward introductions. Instead, the instant they spotted her, both girls gave delighted shouts of happiness, surprising the hell out of her, and ran to her as if they'd known her all their lives.

"Eudora!" Violet squealed.

They danced around her as if she was the best surprise ever. She glanced over at Eli Slater, who was wearing the smile of a satisfied lion on his too-handsome face. She didn't know quite how yet, but she knew, without a doubt, she'd been set up once again.

CHAPTER FIFTEEN

McGruder Art Center

Laughter and too many conversations going at one time drowned out the soft music of the discreet orchestra in the corner. Grey stood in the middle of a group of people who hung on to his words as if they were made of gold. At events such as this, he didn't mind the attention. Most of them were well-meaning people who actually wanted to do something worthwhile with their money. The Grey Justice Foundation, his victims' advocacy group, gave them the opportunity without having to become involved in the minutiae of the actual work. Resenting their attention would be counterproductive. Actually enjoying the attention was another matter altogether.

Irelyn had excelled at these kinds of events. No matter what was going on in her mind, she could separate herself from her worries and be the charming, delightful companion. It wasn't until after she'd disappeared that he had realized just how much he had depended on her to get him through these things.

Almost a year had passed, and still no word from her. How did she do that? After being in each other's pockets for so many years, he felt as though he'd lost an appendage. Did she feel the loss, too, or did her hatred make their separation easier to accept?

A pause in conversation caused him to look around. The instant he spotted the woman at the door, he wanted to smile. She looked lovely, and though the fire in her eyes said she was thoroughly pissed, she walked through the room with a confidence he couldn't help but admire. Hiring her had been a wise decision.

When Eli had called with the unusual request about her wardrobe, he'd been puzzled. Hearing his reasons behind the strange request had made him laugh out loud. Seeing the results was even more entertaining. While everyone else was dressed in expensive but conservative clothing, Kathleen stood out like a wild rose among a bunch of boring carnations. With each step she took, the dress flowed around her, its colors luminescent, seeming to change shades and nuances with each movement of her body.

The look she gave him, though brief, told him he'd be hearing her opinion on her attire a bit later. Kathleen was a self-possessed woman who didn't like to lose control of any situation. He was quite sure that when the evening was over, he'd be getting an earful, but her irritation wouldn't stop her from doing the job.

Since no one could know of their association, he couldn't acknowledge her presence and wouldn't speak to her until the time was right.

Tonight was all about business. When he'd hired Kathleen and told her what one of her duties would be, she'd been resistant, as only an ethical person would be. When he'd explained further, she had reluctantly agreed. Then, when she'd been given her first assignment and learned the facts of the case, she'd been totally onboard. Sometimes, doing the right thing for the right reasons could at first look wrong.

In his peripheral vision, he watched as she began to work the room, and her target. This would be interesting.

Kathleen settled into her role. Playing the young ingénue was a bit of a stretch for her. She hadn't been naïve in years. Maybe the dress she had been "forced" to wear wasn't such a bad choice after all. The other women were wearing something similar to what she'd had planned—sleek designer dresses that screamed expensive and classy. Her flowing, retro dress definitely drew people's eyes to her. Hopefully, it also made her look more approachable, friendlier, and slightly younger. Or, according to Sophia and Violet Slater, it made her look like a fairy sprite. Eli knew his daughters well. The instant they'd seen her, both girls had assumed she'd popped out of their favorite storybook.

She pushed that aside for now. She was here to do a job—a very important one. She couldn't mess this up.

Taking a glass of wine from a passing waiter, she slowly weaved her way through the crowd. As she sipped her drink, she surreptitiously looked around and spotted her target.

To make sure no one suspected her ultimate destination, she took the scenic route. She smiled at no one in particular and couldn't help but marvel at all the different aspects of this strange and wonderful job. In just a short period of time, she'd broken into a mansion, met a fascinating, albeit arrogant and totally infuriating, man, and had been offered the job of guarding his two young children. Now she was tasked with prying a well-guarded secret from a Mafia princess.

Though she was close to her target, she took a planned detour toward the buffet table. She filled her plate and gave an occasional, somewhat shy smile to the other people standing at the table, wanting to appear pleasant if a little awkward in social situations.

Satisfied that she had just the right items and amount on her plate, she turned and gazed around, as if looking for a place to settle. Since her target was sitting alone at a table in the corner, it should seem only natural for her to head toward it.

Not everyone agreed.

She spotted the brutish-looking bodyguard out of the corner of her eye and was pleased he was the one who'd been sent to deter her. After witnessing him shove an elderly man out of the way a few moments ago, she was more than a little eager to have her own confrontation with the big bully.

"Where are you going?" the deep voice snapped beside her.

As though startled out of her wits, Kathleen whirled around. The glass in her hand, filled with a lovely dark red wine, tipped only slightly, dousing the guy's pristine white shirt with just a few red dots.

"Oh my gosh, you startled me!"

His glare made Godzilla look like a pussycat. "You need to sit somewhere else."

Gazing guilelessly up at him when she'd much rather be slamming his head into the nearest wall wasn't the easiest challenge she'd had.

"But I was just going to sit over there, out of the way. That's the only table that's almost empty."

"I said, find someplace else."

"B-but...but...why?"

Not bothering to explain, he grabbed her arm to steer her elsewhere. Her full plate, already held precariously in her hand, was easy enough to tip over so that the entire contents landed with a satisfying splat against the giant wall of his chest. She was especially happy that she'd thought to include a generous helping of meatballs swimming in tomato sauce.

"Why, you little—"

"Is there a problem here?"

She jerked around, managing to spill a little more of her wine onto the guy's no longer white shirt. "Oh, hi. I was just going to sit down and have a bite. But this man…" She sent a helpless look up at the furious bodyguard. "He wouldn't let me sit where I wanted."

"And why is that?" Grey shot a dark look at the bodyguard.

Apparently realizing that not only had they attracted quite a bit of unwanted attention, but one of the wealthiest and most influential men in the country was challenging him, the man backed slightly away.

"Sorry, Mr. Justice. Just doing my job."

Grey gave him a darkly incredulous look. "Your job is to terrify innocent young women?"

"No, sir. Of course not. I just—"

Grey put a gentle hand on her shoulder. "Where is it you'd like to sit, my dear?"

"I was just headed over there." She pointed to a table. The lone young woman sitting at the table was staring at them with a mixture of astonishment and undisguised amusement.

"You certainly don't look like you'd be a threat to anyone. You did remember to leave all your weapons at home?"

The words were said to be amusing as Grey's eyes danced with a teasing delight.

She laughed as if the idea of her carrying weapons was preposterous. "Yes, I did."

"Then I don't see a problem with her sitting down at that table. Do you?"

The bodyguard backed away. "No, sir," he muttered.

"Excellent. Would you like me to get you another plate, my dear?"

"That would be great. Thank you."

With a look an uncle might give a favored niece, Grey took her now empty plate and headed to the buffet table. Knowing they'd overcome a major hurdle, Kathleen headed to the table where Gabriella Mendoza was sitting.

Grey had given her this assignment a little over a week ago, and Kathleen had spent hours researching the Mendozas. She'd found a tremendous amount to read about the family, much of it speculation and myth, but almost nothing about the youngest member, Gabriella.

Luis Mendoza, head of one of the most powerful Mafia organizations in the world, ruled his family with an iron fist that was apparently as brutal as it sounded. Because of his ruthlessness, as well as his wealth, he was able to be as visible as possible. He flouted so many legalities and laws in every country he conducted business, it would be laughable if not so infuriating. With a team of lawyers whose only job was to keep him out of prison, apparently Luis could do what he damn well pleased.

While the man's lawlessness infuriated Kathleen's sense of justice, Luis was not her primary concern. His grandson, Carlos, was the job. And that was why Gabriella, Carlos's only sister, was Kathleen's target.

"Is it okay if I sit here?"

Speculation and cynicism gleamed in Gabriella's dark-chocolate eyes, and Kathleen's first thought was how incredibly sad that a twenty-five-year-old woman should be so cynical. And wasn't that beyond hypocritical since Kathleen most definitely had a hidden agenda?

"Sure. If you like."

Pulling out a chair, Kathleen took a few seconds to settle herself at the table, all the while studying Gabriella out of the corner of her eye. Since there was so little information on the young woman, she would have to rely on her observational skills as much as anything.

Gabriella's lovely face showed an exotic beauty. With a light olive complexion, thick brownish-black hair that flowed down to the middle of her back, elegant cheekbones, and full lips, along with a tall, slender body, she could easily be a runway model. But for most of her life, the young woman had been kept under lock and key. This particular event was the only one in the US she was allowed to attend each year. And therefore, Kathleen's only chance to discover what she might know about her brother's whereabouts.

"I'm Kathleen. What's your name?"

"Aw, come on. You already know who I am."

"I beg your pardon?"

She gave a small snort. "That innocent act worked for Tito but not for me. His muscles outweigh his brain three to one."

The girl was no dummy, but Kathleen wasn't about to give up her cover. "You think I planned that incident so I could come sit with you?"

"Didn't you?"

"Why would you think that? Are you famous or something?"

Rolling her eyes, Gabriella made a move as if she was about to stand up and leave.

"Okay. Wait. Yes, I set it up to be able to talk with you alone."

Settling back down in her seat, the young woman eyed Kathleen speculatively. "I have no money of my own, which, considering how much that Susan Winslow dress you're wearing cost, you definitely don't need. And I have zero influence anywhere for anything. If you want either of those things, you should pay more attention to your rescuer than me."

"Who's that?"

"Mr. Dark, Dangerous, and Dreamy Justice, that's who."

Both women glanced over at Grey, who was standing at the buffet table filling Kathleen's plate with more food than she probably ate in a week.

"You think Mr. Justice is dark, dangerous, and dreamy?"

"Are you kidding? One look from those deep-blue eyes and every part of me melts."

Kathleen took a moment to study her employer. Tall, well built, with dark brown hair, square, stubborn jaw, and a surprisingly sensuous mouth. Odd that she had never felt the zing of attraction to a man who by anyone's standards was incredibly handsome. Could it be because when she envisioned a gorgeous, hunky man, a tall, blond man with beautiful brown eyes appeared?

"So, anyway. What's your deal? Why did you want to talk to me?"

Kathleen took another second to assess the woman across from her. Yes, she was young, but her eyes held a wisdom that had nothing to do with age and everything to do with life experience. Taking a chance she wasn't making a huge mistake, she said, "It's about your brother."

"Ah yes, the serial rapist."

"You know what he's done?"

"I may be sheltered, but I'm not uninformed." She shivered. "He's a brutal, disgusting piece of dung."

"He's hurt you?"

"Fortunately, incest is not one of Carlos's turn-ons."

"But he's done other things?"

Something like despair darkened Gabriella's eyes. "Carlos only has two uses for women. I can provide neither of them. If I stay out of his way, he doesn't bother me."

"You know where he is?"

Awareness clicked but was immediately followed by wariness. Thinking the woman was going to shut her down, Kathleen opened her mouth, ready to state her case. But shutting her down wasn't Gabriella's intent.

"My main guard dog just arrived," Gabriella said. "You have about forty-five seconds before he gets to the table. What's your cellphone number?"

Kathleen quickly rattled off the number.

"Be warned. The information will not be free."

Before she could contemplate exactly what that meant, the bodyguard approached the table. Though shorter and less muscular than the other guard, this one had the merciless look of a cold-blooded killer. "Gabriella, it's time to leave."

"Of course." She stood and looked down at Kathleen. "It was pleasant chatting with you, Kathleen. I wish you much success in your endeavors."

While her words said one thing, her eyes said something else. A look was shared between them, and Kathleen felt she understood this woman better than she'd ever understood her own sister. It was a shared acknowledgment of pain, sorrow, and the will to survive.

"Good-bye, Gabriella. It was nice to meet you, too."

The bodyguard barely gave Gabriella time to smile a good-bye before he hustled her toward the exit.

Maintaining her pleasant expression, Kathleen tapped her foot to the music. Grey appeared in front of her, a plate of food in his hand that had to weigh five pounds.

"Hope you're hungry."

"Wow. Thanks. That was awfully nice of you."

"My pleasure." He gave her a friendly nod and walked away.

Since it would look suspicious if she got up and left so soon after Gabriella's exit, Kathleen settled into enjoying her meal. She'd accomplished what she'd set out to do tonight, which was to make contact. Now it was up to Gabriella. Would she really be willing to help bring her brother to justice? What had she meant by the information not being free? What would Gabriella want in exchange?

CHAPTER SIXTEEN

Pleased with the evening's outcome, Grey walked away from Kathleen's table. The look he'd exchanged with her made him optimistic that Gabriella Mendoza had revealed something significant.

He moved through the crowd, stopping occasionally to chat with acquaintances and business associates. Able to compartmentalize and multitask, he carried on various conversations, even while his thoughts were on the main reason he'd attended this event: Gabriella Mendoza. The young woman was as well guarded as any member of royalty, but one month a year, she was allowed to attend certain cultural events in various countries. The McGruder art show and auction was an annual Dallas event that drew people from all over the world. This would be Gabriella's fourth season to attend and Grey's one chance to make contact with her, his one opportunity to gain information on Gabriella's brother and get justice for Stephanie Pierce and her family.

A little over a year ago, Stephanie met Carlos Mendoza at a party. Though she admitted to willingly leaving with Mendoza, she'd never anticipated what would happen. Over a three-day period, the bastard brutally beat and raped the young woman.

Once he was finished with her, he'd had one of his men dump her in front of her apartment.

Stephanie's family had done all the right things. Within hours of her going missing, they had contacted the police. Law enforcement had done everything within their power to find her. When she had reappeared, alive but brutally abused, they'd immediately gone after the man she named as her rapist. Carlos had been arrested. It should have been the most clichéd of open-and-shut cases.

Then things had gone sour.

Ignoring the prosecutor's assertion that Carlos was a flight risk, a judge had inexplicably set bail at five million dollars. The Mendozas had more money than some small countries. It was of no consequence for them to post bail. Anyone with a lick of sense or not on the take could have seen what would happen next. Only a couple of hours after his release, Carlos had been on his family's plane headed back to Venezuela. And since the Venezuelan government was sticky about extradition of their citizens, there wasn't a damn thing the law could do about it.

To make matters more confounding and worse, Stephanie wasn't Carlos's first victim. Grey had no idea how many victims there really were. One was too many. Carlos Mendoza was long overdue for justice.

When Landon Pierce, Stephanie's father, had come to the Grey Justice Advocacy Center for assistance, the case had looked to be simple enough. Counseling had been provided for Stephanie and her family. But when Carlos had gotten out on bail and then disappeared, things had spiraled out of control, culminating in Stephanie's suicide.

A family destroyed by the sadistic act of another. Even though it wouldn't bring Stephanie back, Grey was determined that Carlos

Mendoza would pay for his crimes. If Gabriella came through and revealed her brother's whereabouts, then Grey planned to move mountains to make sure the son of a bitch was returned to the States so justice could be done.

Satisfied that progress had been made, Grey turned to head to the exit. In his peripheral vision, he caught a glimpse of a slender, dark-haired beauty. He turned, his heart almost stopping. Irelyn Raine stood at a door only a few yards away. Her eyes, a mysterious blend of various shades of gray and silver, were zeroed in on him. Then, with a strange, almost anxious look, she backed out the door.

Grey took off, and like he was a linebacker moving against an opposing team, people either got out of his way or were in jeopardy of being mowed down. Equal part elation, fury, and old-fashioned lust drummed through his veins. She had come back. Why? Where had she been? He was finally going to get the answers that had been driving him crazy.

He went through the doorway and then stopped. Standing in a narrow, dimly lit hallway, he narrowed his eyes to peer through the darkness. "Irelyn?"

"Down here, Grey," she called out.

His strides as rapid as his heartbeat, he ran down the hallway toward the sound of her soft, lyrical voice. An abrupt tingling on the back of his neck was his only warning, one he knew never to ignore. He dropped into a crouch and then whirled around just as a bullet whizzed by, piercing the wall behind him. If he hadn't moved, he'd be dead.

Pulling his gun from his ankle holster, Grey stood. Even though every molecule in his body was denying it, he couldn't refute the evidence. Irelyn had just tried to kill him.

Grey stalked down the hallway, his anger increasing with every step. He understood her reasons for wanting him dead, but he had just as many reasons for wanting to kill Irelyn. Perhaps it was time for their final confrontation.

He stopped a few feet from the doorway, plastered himself against the wall, and then eased closer to peer inside. The only light came from a single light bulb in the ceiling. He could make out several stacks of chairs, boxes, a few shelves. Leaning against one of those shelves was Irelyn.

"Hello, Grey. You're looking well."

Weapon in hand, ready for whatever more surprises she had for him, he stepped inside. "You're losing your edge, Irelyn."

"And you're as succinctly rude as ever."

"Years ago, you never would have missed."

The sound she released was half gasp, half-husky chuckle. "You think I took the shot."

"Who else?"

"Ah, my darling Grey. You wound me to the core."

There was amusement in her voice, but also a hint of hurt. Grey inwardly cursed his stupidity. If he'd been thinking straight, with his head instead of another body part, he would have realized his mistake. If Irelyn had shot at him, she wouldn't have missed.

"You look good," she said softly.

"It's the clean living. You ought to try it."

"Ach, but my way is so much more entertaining."

Even though he knew she hadn't been the one to shoot at him, he approached her with caution. He was no fool. Irelyn Raine was one of the most dangerous women he'd ever known.

"Where have you been?"

"Miss me?"

Telling her the truth, that he'd spent almost every waking moment missing her, would be damn stupid. Not only wouldn't she believe him, he was long past the days of opening himself up like that. Both he and Irelyn lived too much within themselves to reveal those things, especially to each other.

As he drew closer, concern rippled through him. Something wasn't right. She was leaning against the side of a steel shelf, almost as if... His gaze dropped down. Her hand was holding her side, but he had no trouble seeing the blood seeping between her fingers.

His gut twisted. "What happened?"

"Tangled with the wrong end of a knife."

Every muscle in his body was urging him to grab her and get her to the hospital. With anyone else, that's exactly what he would have done. Not with Irelyn.

"How bad?"

"A tiny scratch, barely worth mentioning. Bastard is as inefficient with a knife as he is a gun. I thought he'd already gone or I would have warned you."

"And who would this bastard be?"

"Hard to say." A wry smile tilted her full lips. "So many people want you dead, Grey."

"Including you."

"You know better than that. With you dead, who would I hate?"

"Good point."

"Besides, how would I—" She swayed slightly, and Grey finally had his chance. Wrapping his arms around her, he caught her before she fell.

"Lean against me."

Her forehead pressed against his shoulder. "Hate for you to see me like this," she murmured.

"What? Beautiful?"

"Weak."

"We both know that's one thing you'll never be."

He leaned a hip against a shelf and kept one arm around her, partly for support, partly because at any minute he expected her to try to escape. Using his free hand, he pulled his cellphone from beneath his jacket.

"Terrance, I need you at the back entrance. And call Dr. Sanderson. Ask him to go to my apartment immediately."

"Yes, sir."

"I see Terrance is still dancing to your every drumbeat."

"And you're still mixing your metaphors."

"Some things never change."

"And thank God for that."

A buzzer on his phone was his signal. Terrance had arrived. Gently, he scooped her into his arms. The fact that she didn't protest told him she was in worse shape than he'd feared.

Knowing he could do nothing until he could check her wound, he carried her out the door. Once she'd been treated and he was sure she was fine, they were going to have a long, overdue talk. He needed answers. He needed information. He needed her.

It was way past time that he and Irelyn came to an understanding.

CHAPTER SEVENTEEN

His children's new bodyguard arrived half an hour before they were to leave for school. Violet's and Sophia's reactions to yesterday's meeting had been everything he could have hoped for and expected. Kathleen hadn't been happy about it, but being the true professional, she'd said nothing in front of the children. He fully expected that once they were alone together, she'd be giving her opinion of his manipulation of events. He was okay with that. She deserved to air her grievances, but nothing would make him regret the outcome. His daughters would be protected, and they wouldn't be afraid. And despite her words, he'd seen the gleam in her eyes when he'd told her the salary he would pay.

She needed the money, he needed her. It was as simple as that.

Eli couldn't deny another reason he was pleased. He wanted her. Had wanted her the moment he had seen her on television defending her sister to that damn reporter. She had stirred something inside him that he had never felt. A protectiveness mixed with an unbelievable desire. She was attracted to him, too, although she did her best to hide it.

None of this was without complications. But if there was one thing he'd learned in the morass that had become his life, it was the knowledge that nothing worthwhile was without risk or complications.

"I'd like to talk to you before the children and I leave for school."

As Eli walked down the stairs toward her, he noted the temper in her amazing eyes. He was about to get a dressing down, but instead of dread or irritation, a strong surge of desire heated his blood. Yeah, this was damn complicated.

"Come into my study. The girls will be down soon."

Kathleen followed Eli, determined to have her say. This morning, while dressing, she had practiced what she would say, how she would say it. Just because she had agreed to do this job—she'd protect Violet and Sophia with her life—didn't mean she wasn't royally pissed at how he'd gone about getting her to agree.

The instant he closed the door, she growled, "You set me up."

"Yes, I did."

"Why?"

"Because I knew you wouldn't do it otherwise. And I knew it would work."

"Using your children isn't a very fatherly thing to do."

His eyes went flat and cold, and for a brief moment, she wondered if he would fire her on the spot. Instead, he spoke as coolly as if he were talking about the weather. "My children mean more to me than anything or anyone in the world. If I have to lie, cheat, steal, or kill to protect them, I will. Yes, I manipulated the situation to get the desired results. You, however, are still free to say no."

He had turned it back on her, and he was right. She could say no and walk away. And if something happened to those little girls because she wasn't there to protect them? Could she live with that? Of course she couldn't. This man knew that as well.

"I won't say no. I will guard them with my life. Just don't manipulate me again. You won't like the consequences next time."

"Fair enough. Shall we go?"

"You're coming with us?"

"Yes, I take them to school every morning."

"I thought the whole point of this was to have me as their bodyguard. If you're going to be with them, why do you need me?"

"You'll pick them up each afternoon. Also, though I hope it's rare, there will be times I can't take them in the mornings. Having them comfortable with you will make it easier when that happens.

"As I said yesterday, I'm trying to give them as normal a life as possible. It was a promise I made to myself after they lost their mother. Having the Slater last name doesn't make that easy. After what happened last year, normal has become even harder. Taking them to school is small, but it means a lot to them. As it does to me."

"Very well. Do you want me in another vehicle?"

"No. I'll drive, you sit in the passenger seat. The children in the back."

Like a family. The image came and went in her mind. She couldn't go there...wouldn't.

How had she not known about the questions? How could anyone ask so many, and in such a short period of time? They had barely been buckled into their car seats before Sophia began.

Where do you live?

What's your favorite flower?

Favorite food?

Favorite book?

Do you have a kitten, dog, hamster, rabbit, bird, gerbil?

Concentrating on their surroundings and answering the multitude of questions was definitely more than a full-time job. And the entire time, Eli had a smile tugging at his mouth.

Glad for her ability to multitask, she answered Sophia's questions and kept her eyes open for any threats.

"Eli. White van, three cars behind. Coming up fast."

His eyes already on the rearview mirror, he nodded. "Yes, I see them."

"Maintain your speed." She looked back at the girls. "Let's play a game. See which one of you can get deepest into your car seats without unbuckling your seat belts."

Giggling, the girls wiggled and maneuvered down into the seats, thankfully unaware of a possible threat.

Her hand on the weapon at her side, she kept a visual of the van, as well as the two SUVs behind them—Eli's bodyguards. If the people in the van were a threat, they would have to go through two layers of security before reaching them. However, she had to be prepared.

The SUVs slowed considerably, blocking the van from getting closer. Alarm went through Kathleen when the van veered off the roadway, rode up on the shoulder and then the sidewalk to try to get around the SUV.

"Step on it. Let's get out of here."

Eli sped the car up. The bodyguard's SUV that the van had tried to pass veered sharply, cutting off the van. Blue lights flashed, coming from the opposite direction, passing their car. Between the police and Eli's guards, the threat, if it had been one, was neutralized.

She glanced over at the tense man driving. "That happen often?"

"Occasionally. Less now than it did during the trial."

"I know your brother Adam is in prison. Has anyone threatened his immediate family?"

"He has no immediate family, at least not anymore. DeAnne divorced him and moved to Switzerland to be with her family there. I've not seen or heard from her since Adam's sentencing hearing. As far as I know, she's not had any problems."

"Could she be making the threats?"

"I thought about that. Even had an investigator tail her for a few weeks. From what we could tell, she's trying to get her life back on track and forget she ever knew the Slaters."

"So she's left town. As did your mother, sister, and brother Jonah. You didn't want to just walk away, too? Take your kids and go start again somewhere else?"

"About a million times over the past year. But I'm no quitter. Mathias and Adam almost destroyed the Slater family. That's not the legacy I want to leave my children."

A cellphone rang, and Eli pressed a button on the steering wheel. "What's the situation, Yates?"

"No threat, sir. Teens running late for school. Police are handling it. I'll meet you at the school. I'm just a few blocks away."

"Thanks for the update." Eli looked in the rearview mirror again, this time at his children, who were snuggled deep into their seats. "Good job, girls. Both of you did so well, I'm calling it a draw."

"What did we win, Daddy?" Violet asked.

He glanced over at Kathleen, and a slow, teasing smile crossed his face. "How about if Kathleen reads you *Starburst* when you get home this evening?"

Shooting him daggers that should have bled him dry, she gritted her teeth and said, "Sure. I'll be glad to." Then, speaking softly so only Eli could hear, she added, "After that, we're going to talk about specific responsibilities, which definitely do not include story time."

Grey stared intently at the empty bed as if he could conjure Irelyn back if he concentrated hard enough. Dammit, he'd been gone less than five minutes. A phone call had come in that he'd had to take. And in that amount of time, she'd woken, dressed, and disappeared.

After the doctor had stitched her up last night, Grey had planned to talk with her, get the answers he needed. Instead, within minutes of Dr. Sanderson leaving, she'd been out like a light. He would have assumed she was faking it if it hadn't been for the shadows of exhaustion beneath her eyes. She had slept like the dead—almost as if she hadn't slept well in months. Stupid and unusually sentimental, he'd had the thought that she knew she was safe at last. Knew she was home. What a fucking fool.

He drew closer to the bed and for the first time saw the note she'd slipped beneath the pillow. Her penmanship was as elegant and feminine as the woman herself. And the terse words so very Irelyn: *Watch your back, Justice. I might not be around to save your ass next time.*

Having someone want him dead was nothing new. He had enemies on both sides of the law. Any one of them would gladly do the deed, or pay millions to see the deed done. It was, however, a new thing for Irelyn to be concerned.

Their relationship, complicated and tumultuous, had lasted longer than many marriages. He had alternated between hatred and adoration for most of that time. No one but the two of them knew the truth of how they began. And no one would understand nor, he figured, comprehend their strange relationship. It had worked for them, though. Or at least, it once had.

He wanted to be angry with her, but relief washed away the wrath. She might have left him again, most certainly she hadn't forgiven him, but he knew to his soul that she wasn't the one behind these bizarre killings. Maybe seeing her again, even for that short while, had knocked some sense into him. No way in hell did Irelyn have it within her to take a life in such a cold-blooded, violent way. At least now he could fully concentrate on finding the real killer, as opposed to figuring out a way to protect Irelyn.

More important, if he were in danger from an unknown person, then Irelyn was also at risk. And that was something he would not tolerate.

CHAPTER EIGHTEEN

West Orange, New Jersey

She leaned against an ancient oak, its long, broad branches obscuring her from view. If anyone looked her way, she wouldn't be seen. Though she knew herself to be one of the most beautiful women in the world, when on the job, she was good at blending in, being invisible.

Not that any of them would look around. When they scurried from the house, as they soon would, their focus would be on getting to their destination. Too self-absorbed, caught up in their own little drama, their own silly little selves, to have an interest in anyone else. Nor would they ever suspect that any harm would come to them. Their minds would be on the future, what they planned to do with their portion of a huge windfall that was about to come their way.

It amused her to know that there would be no future for them.

She had taken many lives in her career. It was a lucrative occupation, and she'd discovered early in life that she excelled at it. How many people were fortunate enough to love their work and make a ton of money doing it? Only a handful, she was sure.

She rarely had a conscience about such things. How awkward would that be? And she didn't discriminate. Old, young, rich, poor. Sex, race, religion, or sexual preference made no difference. She could be the poster child for non-discrimination. An equal opportunity killer.

Usually, she gave little thought to whom she killed. She had a specific target, she did the deed and left. No muss, no fuss. She didn't bother to figure out the whys or nuances of the contract. It was a job and nothing more. But the sheer magnitude of this job was both unique and exciting. Her kill tally was now at two. In about ten minutes, it would be at six. She had two more lined up, but she wanted more. She wanted them all. It would be a contract of a lifetime and, once complete, would make her one of the most-sought-after assassins in the world. But that wasn't the biggest reason she wanted the job. Finishing what her friend and mentor had started would be a tribute to the man she'd loved and lost.

So she had done some research…she was a bit of a history buff anyway. She knew the why and the who. Knowing didn't make her look at the job any differently. Didn't change her plans or her thinking. But it was an interesting oddity she'd enjoyed learning.

She heard sounds like the gobbling of angry turkeys. And yes, there were two of her marks, spilling out of the house, on their fake mission of mercy. She clicked on her earbud so she could listen to their manic frenzy.

"I don't care that you had to cancel plans, Miles," Graham Clancy snarled. "Don't you think I have things I'd rather do this weekend, too?"

"Well, I don't see why I have to be there," Miles whined. "She's your crazy mother, not mine."

"Because she's your grandmother and if you expect to inherit any of her money, you'll be there so she'll damn well remember you. If you think you're getting any of mine, you're wrong. I'm tired of pulling your ass out of the fire. Next time you get arrested for a DUI or shoplifting, you can just stay in jail or pay your own bail."

"Those charges were bogus, and you know it. I got targeted by the cops because of who I am. Any time they see my car, they stop and harass me. I oughta file some kind of lawsuit."

"Yeah, you do that. In the meantime, get your ass in the car." The man turned and glared at the door of the house. "Where the hell are your mother and sister?"

"They're arguing again, as usual. I don't know why we have to have the bitches along anyway."

The man raised a stubby finger and shook it. "Don't you talk about your family like that, especially this weekend. The old lady needs to think we're one big damn happy family. When she croaks, we can go back to normal. Till then, you keep your trash-talking mouth shut."

The boy looked down at the phone in his hand. "Whatever."

She couldn't quite see his face, but she imagined an eye roll had accompanied his answer.

Another gobbling noise sounded, this time higher pitched and even more irritating than the grousing of the males.

"That's not my problem, Kimberly," an older woman snapped as she marched out the door. "You knew we were going away for the weekend when you made your plans. You've only yourself to blame."

Kimberly stomped her foot in frustration. "I don't see why Ritz can't come with us."

"Because, you idiot, your grandmother is about to die. She's the widow of Oscar Clancy. Do you get that?"

"I know who my grandparents are, Mother," Kimberly replied with a sulk in her voice as only a fifteen-year-old could. "That doesn't explain why Ritz can't come with us."

"I will not have you parade that skinny, long-haired, over-tattooed loser in front of your grandmother. We are the old lady's only heirs. This is our last chance to make nice. To make a good impression. Putz is an embarrassment."

"Ritz. His name is Ritz, not Putz."

"Same difference. And get that self-righteous look off your face, young lady." She pointed a finger at her daughter. Any objective onlooker would judge her finger-pointing abilities superior to those of her husband. "If you don't behave in a proper manner this weekend, and your grandmother ends up leaving her money to some freaking charity instead of her rightful heirs, I will send you away to school and make sure you never see that long-haired putz again. Do you hear me?"

Instead of replying, Kimberly stomped to the car, got in the back, and slammed the door.

Giving one another what she imagined were "I hate you" glares, the rest of the family got into the car, the man behind the wheel. The car started up, and they took off. One big happy family.

She glanced at her watch. If Graham Clancy drove at ten miles over the speed limit, as he normally did, the timing would work perfectly. Wet roads, a sharp curve, a steep, rocky hollow, and no brakes. A recipe for disaster.

Or in her case, a job well done.

Feeling quite pleased with herself, she adjusted her backpack and disappeared into the woods. Much to do. People to see; people to kill.

Chapter Nineteen

It had been ten days since she'd talked with Gabriella Mendoza and so far, nothing. Kathleen had almost decided the short conversation would produce no results. Grey wasn't discouraged, saying these things took time.

While she waited and hoped Gabriella wouldn't let them down, Kathleen had plenty to keep her busy. Her workdays started at Eli's home, where, despite her protests, Eli insisted she join him and the girls for breakfast. Although this gave her an opportunity to get to know her charges better, it also felt a little too homey for her liking. She'd been hired to do a job, not become a part of their family.

Storybook time had been just that once, and she would never admit it to Eli, but reading to both girls about Starburst and her merry band of fairies had actually been quite fun. Seeing Eudora, their favorite fairy sprite, and the resemblance to herself had been amusing. She could definitely see why Eli had arranged for her to wear that particular dress for her first meeting with his children. It had been almost an exact replica of Eudora's dress. Even though the deception still riled her, she couldn't help but secretly applaud his ingenuity. Eli Slater knew how to get what he wanted.

Keeping a professional distance while answering Sophia's multitude of questions on the way to school wasn't easy. Eli had assured her it was a phase, but Kathleen wasn't so sure. Even though she had basically raised Alice, she didn't remember her sister having so many questions. Which was probably a good thing, because she'd definitely not had any answers back then.

After breakfast, the girls would get buckled into the backseat, and she and Eli would get into the front. Then the caravan would begin.

Other than a couple of suspicious cars that Eli's guard had not allowed to get close, there had been no problems. Once they arrived at school, Eli would walk the girls inside, while Kathleen followed behind, stopping at the door, her eyes open for any threats.

The most uncomfortable times came when she and Eli were alone in the car. Kathleen felt she needed to maintain her distance, but she also couldn't deny she wanted to know more about Eli Slater, the man behind the public persona.

Ridiculous not to feel comfortable asking him questions when he definitely had no such reservations. The man knew entirely too much about her.

So while she silently struggled to come up with subtle questions to get to know him better, Eli once again showed her that when it came to her privacy, he had no boundary issues. "You ever hear from your ex?"

Though her expression remained blank, her nerves jumped at the intrusive question. Deciding that just because he asked didn't mean she had to answer, she kept her eyes on the outside mirror. They had already dropped the children off for the day and were headed back to Eli's home. Just a few more miles and she could relax her guard.

As if he hadn't noticed she'd ignored his question, he shot her a laughing look. "The guy was way too prissy for you anyway."

"I beg your pardon?"

"Come on, Kat. You have to admit it. Bet that perfect hair of his never moved even during windstorms. I'll also hazard a guess that his socks, underwear, and ties always matched. Didn't they?"

Ignoring the sexy way he was grinning at her, and the jolt of pleasure she felt at the way he'd shortened her name, she gave him a disdainful look. "That's your definition of a prissy man? Good hair and color-coordinated clothing?"

"It's a start."

Since his own thick, golden hair sometimes looked a little mussed, as if he ran his fingers through it a lot, she glanced down at his feet. He wore navy socks. She then looked at his dress shirt, which was casually open at the throat. No tie. Her gazed traveled up to his face. Though she wasn't surprised by the glint of amusement in his eyes, she was startled by the surprising heat behind the laughter. Even more startling was the answering surge of warmth in her body. Oh, this was so not a good thing.

"If you're wondering about my underwear," he continued with that too-charming grin, "you'll be pleased to know I'm wearing white and blue checkered boxers. Quite sedate, if that matters."

Blushing to the roots of her hair, she jerked her eyes back to the mirror outside the car window. "I wasn't wondering. And it doesn't matter."

He laughed again and said softly, "Liar."

"Very well. You want to get personal, let's. Tell me about Shelley. What was she like? How long were you married? Was she a good mother? When did you find out she had drug and alcohol addictions?"

If she had wanted to remove the smile from his face and the laughter from his eyes, she had succeeded spectacularly. A wave of shame seeped through her. He had been teasing her, flirting. She had turned a lighthearted moment into an ugly one.

"Listen, Eli. I'm sorry. Please don't—"

"No. It's a reasonable question. One I'll do my best to answer."

The mood in the car now as somber as a funeral, Kathleen stared miserably out the window, wishing she could cut off her own tongue. When she was uncomfortable or felt unsure of herself, she lashed out.

In a tone holding no animosity or resentment, he said, "I think I told you I met her at university. On graduation day, actually. She had already graduated...was a year older than me. She was at a party I attended. And she was lovely. Tall, statuesque. She looked like a golden goddess. When we started dating, I had no idea of her addiction problems. I found out later she was in the middle of one of her recoveries.

"Her family is quite well-off and had spent thousands getting her the help she needed. She was charming and, looking back on it later, almost too lighthearted. We had some good times. I thought we were the perfect match...so we married.

"For the first few months, it was wonderful. Then I became more immersed in the running of Slater House Hotels. I'd worked there while pursuing my degrees, and when I graduated, Mathias heaped more responsibility onto me. I didn't argue. Why would I? My father and I were often at odds with each other, so when he finally tasked me with the duty of running one of his companies, I hoped we might finally have something in common."

He flashed her a grim smile. "Thank God we never did."

His expression going bleak, he continued, "Shelley was very creative. Loved designing clothes. I didn't realize how frustrated she would get when things weren't working well.

"She got pregnant. We hadn't talked about it. It wasn't the best timing, but we were both thrilled. She occupied herself with planning for the baby. Had a nursery designed. Bought tons of clothing, bedding, furniture. I let her have anything she wanted. She was almost manic in her need to get things for the baby.

"After Sophia was born, Shelley had the blues a bit. I suggested she get back into designing, so we hired Teresa as Sophia's nanny. And things seemed to be back on track.

"It was the drinking I first noticed. You know, three glasses of wine with dinner every night. Then the Bloody Marys or mimosas for breakfast every morning. I did the typical denial thing. Told myself it was just a phase. Creative people have their ups and downs, and Shelley was just on one of her downs.

"I found the pills in one of her lingerie drawers. I had opened it by mistake. I didn't know what they were, so I confronted her. At first she was angry, accused me of snooping. When she realized I wasn't going to let her use anger to avoid answering, she explained that she had headaches and the doctor had prescribed them for her.

"Stupid...so very stupid. I accepted her explanation. Even though there was a small niggle at the back of my mind. Questions like, Why had she hidden them? How long had she been taking them? How often did she need them? But I ignored those niggles and went about my life.

"A few months later, I came home to find her unconscious. I called an ambulance. And that's when the truth came out. She had so much pills and alcohol in her system, the doctors said she would have died within half an hour if I hadn't found her.

"Her parents finally admitted the truth. That they had been hiding her addiction problems. Said they'd hoped with marriage to me, she would be happy and wouldn't need the crutches of drugs or alcohol. Of course, I became the reason for her reverting back to her bad ways."

"They blamed you?"

"It was no less than I deserved. I had ignored all the signs, so immersed in my life, my work, I forgot to be a husband."

Kathleen had her own opinions about that but kept them to herself.

"She went into rehab. Came out and things were great for a few months. By that time, I was monitoring everything. No alcohol in the house. No drugs, over-the-counter or otherwise." His mouth twisted in a grim smile. "Except birth control pills. We had agreed that we wouldn't get pregnant again. She used the pill, and as an added precaution, I used protection, too. But I learned too late that nothing can stop a determined woman."

"She got pregnant with Violet."

"Yes. She said she'd been feeling off for a few days and forgot to take her birth control. She never said, and I never asked, but I suspected she threw the pills away. I also suspected that she sabotaged the condoms. But there was no point in asking. What was done, was done."

"And Violet was born."

"Yes. As much as I resented what Shelley did, I could not, would never, regret Violet's birth. She and Sophia are my greatest blessings."

"So you were living in England then? What brought you back to Dallas?"

"Shelley started being even more unpredictable...erratic. Teresa took care of both girls, but I worried Shelley would go back to her old ways. Her parents had moved to New York a few months after Violet's birth. And being the man who liked to try to fix things, I moved back to the States.

"Shelley was ecstatic. Not only did she get to see her family as often as she wanted, she designed our house. That kept her busy...and seemingly happy for over a year."

"And then it didn't."

"Yes. She—"

He cut off when her cellphone chimed. Cursing the interruption, she glanced down at the readout and noted the number was from an unknown caller.

"Excuse me. I need to take this." She tapped the screen to answer, "Hello?"

"Kathleen?"

"Gabriella?"

"Yes. Can you talk?"

"Go ahead."

"I don't have much time, so I'll get right to it. I can give you my brother's location. All the information you need to go in and get him."

"Wonderful. I'll—"

"Wait. I want something in return."

"What's that?"

"I want someone to kidnap me."

CHAPTER TWENTY

Grey Justice Headquarters

"Kidnap her?" Grey leaned back in his chair, not looking the least bit surprised by Gabriella Mendoza's request.

"I'm sure she sees this as her opportunity to escape…get away from her family who has basically held her hostage her entire life."

"What did you tell her?"

"That I'd get back to her as soon as I could. I realize this isn't exactly your territory, but she sounded desperate."

His mouth tilted slightly. "You might be surprised at all the different territories the Grey Justice Group gets involved in."

"So you'll help her?"

"You're sure this isn't a setup?"

Kathleen thought back to the look she and Gabriella shared during those last seconds of their brief meeting. There had been desperation and an odd kind of pain in the depths of her dark eyes.

"No, I don't think it's a setup. I think she's trying to escape something. I don't know if it's only the confinement. Something tells me there's more to it. Either way, I think she's desperate to get away."

"Good enough for me. When's the next contact?"

"I'm to text her with either a yes or no answer tomorrow at noon. Once I do, she'll send me the locations for both she and her brother."

"You think they're in the same place?"

"No, I didn't get the idea that they are."

"Good. That'll make things easier. Get the info. I'll take it from there." He slid an innocuous tan envelope across the desk toward her. "Leave this on Detective Kowalski's desk. Usual disguise. He got an anonymous tip this morning to be on the lookout for additional information on a case that's gotten stalled."

Envelope in her hand, she took a quick glimpse at her watch. "I've got to pick Eli's daughters up in an hour."

"You've got time. Tonight's soon enough to get it to his desk. Wouldn't want you to miss any of Sophia's questions."

Kathleen laughed. "You know about them?"

He grinned, and Kathleen noted he looked about ten years younger. "I get bombarded every time she sees me."

"I told Eli she would make a good reporter. He looked terrified."

"Can't blame him. How's it going, working for him?"

Inexplicably self-conscious at the question, she felt a flush of color wash over her cheeks. "It's…um…fine. Kids are cute. Pay is good."

She saw a small flicker of humor in his eyes, as if he understood her unease, but all he said was, "I have no doubt that Violet and Sophia are in good hands."

"Eli seems to believe the threats to his daughters are because of his father and brother."

His eyes narrowed with speculation. "You disagree?"

"No, not really. I just think sometimes the obvious answer isn't always the right one." She shook her head. "No matter who the threats are coming from, the girls are well guarded."

"Eli said that they've really taken to you. I imagine that's a load off his mind."

Kathleen was glad that the girls felt safe with her. Other than the inappropriateness of being wildly attracted to their father, things were working out better than she had thought they would.

Wanting to move on, she said, "I have a couple of new theories about Braden I'd like to run by you."

"Excellent." He picked up his cellphone. "One of my investigators indicated he may have something for us today. Let's hear what he has to say, then we'll discuss your findings."

She told herself not to anticipate helpful news. She'd gotten her hopes up too often only to have them dashed. Still, the hope that some vital information that might exonerate her sister had been found was too tempting not too entertain. Alice might be gone, but that didn't negate Kathleen's need to prove her innocence.

Grey pressed a few keys on his phone, and when a growling, masculine voice answered with, "Hold on a minute, Justice," Kathleen's entire body tensed with anticipation.

Seconds later, the voice said, "We got the files. We're going through them now. Nothing's turned up so far. Will keep you updated."

The line went dead.

Kathleen stared at her boss, whose expression was a curious mix of irritation and amusement.

"Ryder isn't one for small talk."

"What files does he have?"

"Braden's financials. He kept a record of his...transactions."

"You mean the amount he was paid for each trick? I saw his records. There's nothing there. He only recorded first names and—"

"We found his real records."

"He had two different sets?"

"The ones you saw were what the authorities found in his desk. A second set was found on his computer, buried beneath a mountain of crap and password protected and encrypted to the hilt."

"He wanted to make sure no one could access them."

"Yeah. The scumbag was quite meticulous in his accounting. I'd say part of that was to keep certain people in line. He had personal information that could make his customers uncomfortable if it was found out."

"So he could blackmail them? That just adds another layer of people who could have wanted him dead."

"That'd be my take. One of my sources in the Chicago PD informed me they had mountains of files going back ten years, detailing Braden's income from both johns and buyers."

Her heart leaped at the news. "So they're pursuing it further? Chicago PD is reopening the murder case?"

Compassion flickered in his eyes. "No. That case is closed."

She acknowledged that with a weary sigh. "Of course. They still believe Alice did the killing. Why pursue it?"

"Exactly, but that doesn't mean we stop. Hopefully, Ryder will have something soon. Now tell me what you've come up with."

"I've dug as deep as I can into Frank Braden. Even went back to his father, Francis, and found that the apple didn't fall far from the tree. He was a sleaze and passed those genes down to his son."

"His choice."

Thinking about her own father, who would much rather have stolen something than buy it, she agreed. And she thought of Eli, who'd arguably had the worst father ever and, instead of following in his footsteps, was doing his best to clean up his father's mess.

"You're right. We all have choices. Braden's were bad ones. He's got a brother in Idaho, Joseph, who hadn't seen him in years. And from our brief, unpleasant conversation, he isn't all that sorry that his brother is dead. I don't see him for the murder, though. He's got a family and is barely hanging on financially.

"So now I'm concentrating my investigation on Maureen Downey."

"The woman who shot Alice. What about her?"

"I've been thinking there's more to her story."

"How so?"

"I don't know. On the surface, it makes sense. She supposedly loved Braden—photos of them together were found at her apartment. She shoots Alice for revenge, then she's killed before anyone can question her."

"And?"

"It's too pat. Too convenient. Those photographs are the only piece of evidence we have that they even knew each other." She grimaced. "Or am I grasping at invisible straws?"

"I've thought from the beginning that your instincts were sound. I agree. It does seem too convenient."

"You've already thought of that, haven't you?"

"Yes." He seemed to hesitate briefly, then said, "So far I've gotten nowhere."

"Then at least I know I'm not crazy for thinking it. I'll delve into her life as deeply as I have Braden's. If something's there, I'll find it."

"If you need more help from me, just give me the word."

Gratitude filled her. Without Grey, she'd be scratching for every little piece of information she could eke out.

The sound of a phone buzzer halted their conversation. It wasn't coming from the phone on Grey's desk, and from the grim look on his face, someone contacting him on it meant bad news.

Pulling open a drawer, Grey grabbed a phone and read a text message. The look that came over his face caused dread to fill her.

"What's wrong?" she asked.

Dropping the phone back into the drawer, Grey stood. "Eli's been taken to Dallas Memorial Hospital."

He didn't need to say more than that. Fear rushing through her, Kathleen was out the door in a second.

CHAPTER
TWENTY-ONE

Panic clawed at her insides as Kathleen ran through the doors of the hospital, Grey right behind her. The thought of something happening to the intelligent, good-humored, honorable Eli Slater wasn't something she could bear to fathom.

A sensible part of her mind, not awash with terror, told her it might well be something minor. Nothing serious. Grey had no details other than Eli had been brought to the hospital in an ambulance. She battled against the horrific images that kept popping into her head.

Halfway down the hallway, she came to an abrupt, skidding halt, barely noting that Grey had to grab her shoulders to keep from plowing into her. Eli was striding toward them, an eye patch dangling from his hand. Though he had a purplish bruise on his left cheekbone and his eye was slightly swollen, he didn't appear to have any other injuries. He was gloriously, beautifully alive.

She fought every instinct to throw her arms around him and never let him go. At that thought, she stiffened her spine. No…just no.

"What the hell happened?" Grey asked.

Eli gave them both a puzzled, confused look. "How'd you know I was even here?"

"I have a contact at the hospital. She alerts me if certain people are brought in."

"What happened?" Kathleen asked.

"I was walking out of our corporate office. Stopped to hold the door open for one of my employees. The instant she stepped out onto the sidewalk, she dropped her purse and the contents scattered. I stooped down to help her pick things up. About that time, a window washer's platform fell from the building."

"And it hit you?"

"Thankfully, no. When it fell, the noise startled the woman I was helping. She jerked her arm, and her pointy and extremely hard elbow slugged me in the eye. I'm going to have quite the shiner come tomorrow."

"You've had plenty of black eyes from boxing bouts," Grey said. "Why come to the hospital for this one?"

"It wasn't for me. Eloise, the woman who jammed her elbow into my eye. She's seven months pregnant, and I thought it best she get checked out. The ambulance showed up, so I offered to ride along with her."

"She's okay?" Kathleen asked.

"Yes. Her husband's with her. Doctor told her to take it easy for a couple of days but said she and the baby are fine."

"Anyone else hurt?"

"No. Thank God. Scared the hell out of a lot of people, but that's about it. Thankfully no window washers were on the platform at the time."

"The eye patch for your black eye?" Kathleen said.

"Yes. Figured Violet and Sophia would get a kick out of it. They have a fondness for pirates."

"You're sure it was an accident?" Kathleen said.

"Just one of those weird things." He looked down at his watch. "It's a little early, but would you mind collecting Sophia and Violet now? Just in case it's a slow news day and this incident made the news, I don't want the girls to hear about it from someone else."

Now that she knew he was all right, Kathleen welcomed the chance to get away. The worry she'd had for Eli had turned into a distinct unease at her extreme reaction. She needed to be alone and regroup. "I'll head there now."

Without waiting for a response, she did an about-face and strode quickly down the hallway.

Eli called out, "Kathleen, wait."

She jerked to a stop but didn't turn around. A hand touched her arm, and she looked up into Eli's concerned face. "You okay?"

Doing what she knew how to do, what she had practiced her entire life, she gave him the calm, poised response he should expect from her, along with a smile that had just the right amount of impersonal professionalism. "I'm fine. Just not a big fan of hospitals. We'll see you soon."

She took off again, this time slower, less frantic. No way in hell did he need to know how very scared she'd been, or the turmoil churning inside her. When she saw him again, she'd have her head on straight and her veneer back in place.

Torn between following her or doing the smart thing and letting her have some space, Eli made himself turn away, returning to where Justice stood.

"Is she all right?"

Eli was a little surprised to see a hint of anger in his friend's eyes. "She's fine. This just brought back bad memories for her."

Justice raised a questioning brow. "You're sure that's all it is?"

"What do you mean?"

"You wanted her to come to Dallas. You wanted her to work for you. Is there something else you want from her?"

"What the hell are you talking about?"

"You tell me."

"You know damn well why I wanted her in Dallas. She needed help. And yes, I wanted her to work for me. My daughters need the protection. She's the best at what she does, and she needs the money."

"And that's it?"

"You got something to say," Eli growled, "say it."

"She's turned out to be an asset to the Justice group. And I like her. I don't want to see her get hurt. She's been hurt enough."

"Why the hell would she get hurt?"

"She was with me when I got the notice you were here. I saw how she reacted. She cares for you more than most people care about someone they work for. If you don't feel the same way, you need to back away before she—"

Justice broke off abruptly, obviously seeing something in Eli's expression. "I'll be damned. How'd I miss it?"

"You've had a lot on your mind. You're entitled to one miss. And before you ask, Kathleen and I are a long way from anything happening. She's still vulnerable, and I doubt she's even admitted to herself she's attracted to me."

He looked back down the hallway where Kathleen had disappeared. "I think for the most part I just piss her off."

"A common feeling among those who know you," was Justice's wry reply.

"Yeah, so I've been told." All humor disappearing, Eli said, "You got a couple of investigators who can do some digging for me?"

"What do you need?"

"Find out who rented that window-washing equipment."

"It's your building. Wouldn't you be able to get that information fairly easily?"

"One would think. I've already checked. It was rented by a dummy corporation. Doesn't exist."

"You think it was meant to hit you?"

"Seems a damn inefficient way to kill someone, but stranger things have happened. Truth is, if Eloise hadn't dropped her purse and I stopped to help her, it would've come right down on me and anyone close-by."

"Do you think Adam could have been behind it?"

"Well, it might give him an opportunity he wouldn't otherwise have."

"Such as?"

"Like get special release to attend his brother's funeral."

"And then find a way to escape."

"Exactly. Last time we talked, he had a Texas-sized smirk on his face when I told him he'd rot in jail for the rest of his life. Maybe it's time for another brotherly chat."

Chapter Twenty-two

Glad to have something to occupy her thoughts, Kathleen picked the girls up from school. Even though Eli had acted as if today's incident had been inconsequential, she wasn't so sure. Because of that, she was hypervigilant on the way home. Nothing would happen to these children under her watch.

Since it was only a half hour or so earlier than their usual pickup time, the girls were as exuberant and chatty as always, never suspecting anything unusual had happened. But, just in case Eli's black eye looked even worse when they got home, she wanted to prepare them.

"Your daddy got a new boo-boo today."

"Like a splinter in his finger?" Sophia asked.

"Kind of. Except it's on his eye. He's going to have a little bruise there. But the fun thing is, he's going to wear an eye patch to cover it."

Sophia's eyes went wide, shining with wonder. "Like a pirate?"

"Yes, just like a pirate."

That was all she needed to say to get their imaginations soaring. They whispered to each other the rest of the way home, and the instant they walked into the house, the girls rushed upstairs.

Even though she told herself to leave before Eli came home, Kathleen followed them. They'd seemed so excited, and she couldn't resist seeing what they were up to.

She walked into the playroom, which was situated between the two girls' bedrooms. Filled with every conceivable doll, toy, and children's book imaginable, the room was a children's treasure trove.

The girls immediately sat down at a table in the corner and began to work furiously on something. She stood in the doorway and watched them for a few minutes, loving the way they whispered to each other. Because of their age difference, she and Alice had never had that kind of closeness. Assuming the role of caretaker instead of sister prevented that kind of camaraderie.

Pushing aside the sadness and regret, she came to stand behind the girls. "So, what are you two up to?"

Sophia looked up briefly and gave her a gap-toothed grin. "We're writing a book."

"About what?"

"About Daddy Pirate."

Swallowing laughter, Kathleen gazed down at their progress. The drawing had started first. The first surprise was that she was going to be in the book, too. It wasn't hard to identify herself, what with the long, red hair and blue-green eyes. Both girls had drawn her, and it was quite the surprise to see that Violet could well be an artist. The picture she'd drawn of Kathleen had a surprising resemblance to her face. She was slim, willowy, and, even to her own mind, quite lovely. And Eli, with an eye patch and golden-blond hair, was holding a sword, apparently armed to defend her honor.

Sophia, however, wasn't the artist her sister was. She had drawn Kathleen as a stick figure with wild, kinky, red hair and long, skinny arms and legs. Oddly enough, the picture reminded her of how she'd looked growing up. Wild red hair and stick thin.

Eli hadn't gotten much better treatment from Sophia. He too was a stick figure, with spiky, yellow hair, an eye patch, an unfortunate bulbous nose, and oversized teeth.

Spotting a large, comfortable-looking chair in the other corner, Kathleen sat down to watch them for a few minutes. It was peaceful here, and the girls added to the calm with their little stage whispers as they shared what they should write or draw.

The quiet also forced her to acknowledge what she'd been avoiding. Her reaction to the possibility of Eli being injured had been off the charts. When had she started to care? And not just care...but have such strong feelings for him? Yes, she had admitted an attraction and had been fighting like crazy to keep it at that—a mere attraction. The anguish she'd felt was totally unexpected. Completely unwelcome. Falling in love with Eli Slater was a disaster in the making. One she could not allow to happen.

She closed her eyes, fighting the need to have a good cry. Wouldn't that top off her over-emotional day? Forcing her mind away from her worries, she allowed her thoughts to drift. The quiet, other than the soft, conspiratorial whispers of the girls, lulled her into a restless doze. And as often happened, the nightmares weren't far behind. Like dark wisps of clouds, they swirled around her. Knowing what was happening, she tried to push herself awake, told herself not to let them take her. Instead, she found herself falling, falling.

As usual, the dreams were a jumble of some of her most horrific moments.

She stood in a cold, sterile room, felt small, insignificant, helpless to stop what was happening. A man, a stranger, lifted Alice in his arms. Kathleen screamed—*"Alice! Alice!"*—and ran after her. A pair of strong hands caught her, held her back. "You can't go with her," a firm, female voice said. "She'll go to a good home, and you will, too. We can't find a family who wants both of you. Sorry."

"No, no, no! We're not puppies, damn you! You can't do this!" She screamed, cried, begged. Told them she could take care of Alice, but they wouldn't let her. She fell to her knees, sobbing as they took away her baby sister.

The nightmare shifted. "Skinny Kat, Skinny Kat, can't even swing a bat!"

They taunted, laughed, made fun of her. Pinched her so hard she had bruises for days. The house was full of kids. She was just another one. No one cared until it was time to blame someone.

"Kath-a-leen." Her foster mother stood over her, her face lined with wrinkles, her breath stinking of cigarettes. "Did you break that vase?"

"No, ma'am."

"Don't you lie to me. Joey saw you do it."

"But I didn't."

Smack! "Don't you talk back to me. Don't I give you a roof over your head and food to eat?"

Mouth pressed together, Kathleen knew not to answer with the truth. She shared a room with three other girls. Barely had room to move. And the food was minimal and tasteless.

"I'll teach you not to lie if it's the last thing I do!" Slap! Slap! A thick belt replaced the slapping hand.

Kathleen fought back the tears, refused to show the pain and remorse the woman wanted.

Another shift, another shadowy figure.

"I'm sorry, Miss Callahan. We found your father on the bank of the river. Coroner has ruled it an accidental drowning. He must've fallen from the bridge."

Daddy was gone...but she still had Alice.

"I don't care what you say, Kathleen. I don't have to stay with you, and I don't want to stay in school. It's boring. I'm twenty years old. I have my own money that you can't touch. I can do what I damn well please."

Kathleen reached out for her, her mind screaming for her to say something, say anything, to keep Alice with her. And then she was gone, a puff of smoke in the wind.

The horror came faster now. A screech of tires. People shouting. Emily screaming. And the pain...oh, sweet heavens, the pain was agonizing.

The blast of a gun made her jerk. Alice! She was screaming over and over. Kathleen fell on top of her, protecting her, already knowing it was too late. No. No. No. Not Alice. No!

Doctors, their eyes sad but resigned. "We're sorry, Miss Callahan. The fragment dislodged. We couldn't save her."

Alice lay on the bed. So pale, so pretty. So dead.

The scene shifted again. She stood over another dead body. Murky at first, then her vision cleared. Eli lay facedown, blood pooled around him. Just like Alice.

Not Eli! No, no, no!

"Kathleen! Wake up. It's a dream. You're having a dream. You're safe. Kat. Wake up now. It's just a dream."

Opening her eyes, she blinked up at Eli, who was on his knees in front of her. His hands gripped hers, his eyes filled with worry.

"Sorry." She shook her head quickly to dispel the horror. "Must've fallen asleep." Then, gasping, she looked over her shoulder, fearful that Sophia and Violet had heard her scream.

"They've had dinner and have already been settled into bed. Teresa said she hated to wake you, you looked so peaceful."

She blinked again, trying to get a grasp on reality. It had been too real. That last part. It had just been too damn real.

"Didn't mean to drop off like that." She tried for a smile, then winced as she saw the bruising around his eye. "Looks sore. How does it feel?"

"Not bad. I've had worse."

"Did you wear the eye patch for the girls?"

Brown eyes twinkled with amusement. "Yes. I'm now Pirate Daddy."

"They've drawn pictures and were already planning a series of books when I dozed off."

He stood and, since he already had hold of her hand, pulled her up with him. "Come see what they've done."

He didn't move away when she stood, and she bumped into him, the heat of his body against hers causing a visceral reaction she hadn't anticipated. Heat flooded through her as an unexpected need rose within her.

Refusing to acknowledge her reaction, Kathleen took a step back, tugging at her hand. Instead of letting her go, Eli said softly, "Kat? Look at me."

She lifted her eyes to his, saw tenderness, a simmering desire. Her heart pounded, part want, part panic. If he kissed her, what would she do?

A little smile twitched at his mouth, and he looked like he was about to say something but then stopped himself. Instead, his hand squeezed hers gently. "Come see what they've done." He said again as he pulled her forward, toward the table.

Both disappointed and relieved, she followed him to the small table where several pages were neatly stacked and a small trash can beside the table held multiple wadded pages. Apparently, several story attempts had been started and scrapped. Though Violet was most definitely the more talented in drawing, Sophia was well on her way to being a storyteller. She already had five paragraphs about her Pirate Daddy.

"You might possibly have a writer and an illustrator in your midst."

"Looks like. Although we might have to talk to Sophia about plagiarism. Read the first line of the story."

Daddy was a pirate. One of the good ones.

Kathleen laughed, recognizing the first sentence as the beginning of *Starburst*, which started with *Starburst was a fairy. One of the good ones.*

"Hopefully, it's just a first draft."

He squeezed her hand again. It had felt so natural, she'd almost forgotten he was still holding it.

"So...um. I guess I'd better get home."

"Stay for dinner."

"I can't. I have a job to do for Grey tonight."

"A job, this late?" A glimmer of amusement glinted in his eyes. "Not breaking into another house, are you?"

She laughed. "No, you were my first and last."

For some reason, the words invoked an image that had nothing to do with breaking into a house. Pushing aside the emotion, the rising heat, she said, "It's a drop-off at the police station."

Truthfully, she was going to wait until midnight to place the envelope on the detective's desk. But to stay and have dinner with Eli? Just the two of them, without the children there as a distraction? She couldn't risk it.

"Please, Kathleen. I'd like to have dinner with you. Just us."

"Why?"

"Why not?"

"I..." There were a thousand reasons, yet she had no answer.

"You've got to eat. I've got to eat. Why not share a meal?"

"Is it as simple as that?"

"It's a meal. Nothing complicated about it."

Oh, if he only knew.

She took a breath, let it out slowly. "Then yes, I'll stay."

Chapter Twenty-three

Eli felt as if he'd won a major battle just getting her to stay for dinner. She was attracted to him and fighting it with every breath she took. It had been years since he'd wooed a woman. He was so out of practice he found himself wishing that caveman-style wooing was still an acceptable practice, because his body was urging him to forgo the social niceties. Throwing her over his shoulder, carrying her to his bedroom, and kissing her into submission sounded like a damn fine idea. The knowledge that she was trained in self-defense and could take him on full force did nothing to diminish his desire. If anything, the very idea made him harder.

Pushing those heated thoughts aside, he walked side by side with Kathleen down the stairs and into the dining room. She halted uncertainly at the door, and Eli inwardly winced as he noted the table setting. He'd told Teresa he was going to persuade Kathleen to stay for dinner. She had taken him at his word and then some. The table was set with fine china, silverware, and sparkling crystal. Candles were lit and flickered romantically in the dimmed lighting. It looked nothing like an impromptu sharing of a meal, but a scene set for seduction.

Since Teresa had a tendency to remind Eli almost daily that the girls needed a mother, he should have anticipated that she'd see this as a special occasion. Although it was, the last thing he wanted was to scare Kathleen away. She was skittish enough as it was.

"Looks like Teresa went to a lot of trouble." The hesitancy in her voice was apparent.

Eli shrugged. "I don't have dinner guests very often. Teresa doesn't get to use the fine china most of the time because of the girls. I imagine she had fun setting the table."

The wariness in her eyes receded, and she moved into the room, her body relaxed. "That was sweet of her."

"Yes, it was." He pulled out a chair. "Shall we?"

The instant Eli sat across from Kathleen, Teresa rolled their meal in on a dining cart. Since inviting Kathleen for dinner had been unplanned, Eli figured the roast chicken, potatoes, and green beans that the girls had eaten earlier would be their meal as well. Instead, Teresa had worked magic.

She set a plate overflowing with T-bone steak, baked potato, and asparagus in front of Kathleen and then one in front of Eli.

"Oh my, Teresa. This looks amazing," Kathleen said.

She beamed like she'd won a million dollars. "Just a little something I whipped up when Mr. Eli told me you were staying for dinner. It's so nice to see him having dinner with such a lovely young woman. He doesn't—" She broke off when she saw the subtle shake of Eli's head and then finished, "He doesn't eat near enough red meat."

Kathleen had been admiring the food, but her head popped up at Teresa's odd statement.

Swallowing laughter, Eli said, "Thank you, Teresa. You're a jewel."

Looking relieved, Teresa backed out of the room with a quick, "Enjoy your meal. And don't worry about the dishes. Just stack them in the sink, and I'll get to them tomorrow." Then with one last bright, encouraging smile, she said, "Good night."

"Good night, Teresa. And thank you," Kathleen said, then shot Eli a mischievous smile. "So you eat red meat only when you have lovely dinner companions?"

"Something like that." He held up a bottle of his favorite Cabernet. "Wine?"

"Yes. Thank you."

She took a sip and then cut into her steak. "So, about what happened today. You don't really think it was an accident, do you?"

He wasn't surprised at the question. Kathleen was as astute as she was lovely. "I wasn't sure at first. Just seemed an odd, inefficient way to kill someone. But, I've changed my mind."

"Why?"

"Got video feed showing two men in hoodies setting up the equipment in empty office space on the fifteenth floor."

"Did you know them?"

"Couldn't see their faces. Looks like they knew where the cameras were. As soon as the platform fell, they were gone. Another security camera caught them running out the back on the first floor, into the alley. They disappeared out of sight. The equipment was rented by a fake company."

She nodded slowly, and he could see her mind working out the logistics, the scenarios. "But if someone really wanted to hurt you, why choose such an unreliable way? The timing would have needed to be just right to make it work."

"I agree. A sloppy way to off somebody. If you're going to take someone out, even if you want it to look like an accident, there are a lot better ways to get it done."

"I'm not sure which is scarier, that someone wants you dead or that they're willing to take out others without caring who or how many."

That grim fact chilled him a helluva lot more than someone wanting him dead. "There's a disturbing level of recklessness, carelessness."

"You think this is related to the emails?"

His mouth twisted in a wry smile. "I sure as hell hope so. Unsettling enough to know somebody wants me dead. Having more than one out there is doubly disturbing."

"And doubles the chance of one of them succeeding."

"There's that, too."

"And you have no leads?"

"No. But I'm going to go see Adam again tomorrow."

"If it is Adam, why threaten your children, too? What's the point?"

"To torture me." Eli shrugged. "Could be more for distraction than anything else. I hope that's all it is."

"I can't imagine all the things you had to do after your father died and your brother went to prison."

"It all kept me focused. I had goals, knew what I had to do. Plus, I had my children."

"They seem well adjusted, happy."

"I've worked hard to make sure none of this touches them. Hopefully, by the time it matters to them, the Slater name won't have the stigma it does now."

"You're a good dad."

"Most important job I'll ever do. Tell me about yours."

She gave a half-hearted wave of her hand. "You know most of it. He was a thief, got caught, went to prison. Gained an early release by agreeing to work for the government."

"Those are facts. Tell me about the man."

She took another sip of her wine, another bite of her food. He got the idea that her hesitation wasn't so much a reluctance to share but that she was trying to come up with the right words.

"In many ways, he was a wonderful father. He made us laugh. We knew we were loved. Before my mother died, I never understood what he did for a living. I just knew he worked nights. When he brought Alice home...after we lost our mom, he changed. He was so sad...morose."

"But he continued with his chosen profession?"

"You mean stealing? Yes, he did. He took Alice and me on a couple of jobs. That's when I found out what he did."

Eli ground his teeth to keep from saying exactly what he thought about Daniel Callahan exposing his children to a potentially dangerous situation. The affection in her voice as she spoke of her father told him any kind of criticism would shut her down.

"What kind of jobs?"

"Hmm." She took another bite, stared in the distance as she remembered. "A jewelry store break-in. At least, I think that's what it was. We waited in the car. Alice was only a baby. I wasn't sure what was going on until he and a few other guys came running out of the building. They got into another car. My dad threw a bag in the passenger seat and took off, following them to an old warehouse. He made us sit on the other side of the room, but I definitely saw some sparkles as they went through the take.

"Then we came home, and he tucked us into bed."

"Did you ask him about it?"

"Yes. Not that night, but later on I did. He explained that it was his job. Said all daddies had jobs and that was his. I accepted it, and that was that."

Eli could see that happening. Even as much as Sophia had a ton of questions, whatever Eli told her, she took to heart and accepted as fact. If Daddy said it was true, then it was.

"When did you realize he was breaking the law?"

"I'm not exactly sure. I guess a part of me knew all along, but I didn't dwell too much on it. When he was arrested, it was a brutal awakening."

"And you and Alice went into foster care. Separate families."

Her mouth twisted into a painful smile. "You've already proven you know quite a bit about that."

Yes, he did. However, he didn't know her thoughts and feelings. He could only imagine what it must have felt like for her to have her only family ripped away like that. She'd been caretaker to Alice from her sister's birth.

He was surprised she continued to talk, had feared she would shut down.

"Even though it hurt to be separated from Alice, I was glad she went to a stable, loving home. They were good to her. She was only six when it happened." She paused, then said softly, "They treated her like one of their own."

The words "unlike me" went unspoken.

"Yours wasn't as happy?"

She shrugged, and he left it at that. Bringing back more bad memories was the last thing he wanted. "It must have felt like your birthday and every holiday combined when your father was released and you were reunited with him and Alice."

"In a way, yes. It was wonderful. I missed Rocky and Georgia, of course, but it was great to be a family again." She cocked her head a little, a wistful smile on her mouth. "Still not the same, though. It could never be the same. You think it can be, but…"

Sensing she was about to end the conversation and call it a night, he asked, "Was Rocky the only reason you went into private security?"

"Not totally. When my dad got out of prison, he was more serious, focused, as if he was on a mission, determined that Alice and I learn something. He made sure we spent at least two solid hours together each night learning from him. From how to pick a lock to how to defend ourselves. When he realized I'd learned a lot of self-defense skills from Rocky, he let me train Alice."

Eli could see why she said things hadn't been the same. Their father had gone from being a foolish, irresponsible man who took his children to a burglary, to teaching them the business. Perhaps he'd had a premonition that he wouldn't be around much longer.

"Sounds like he changed a lot."

"We never had any deep, philosophical discussions. Prison definitely changed him but not all for the better. He was harder to reach, less talkative." She grimaced. "Sadder."

"Yet he wanted you to learn from him, prepare you for the world."

"Yes." She cocked her head again and speared him with a "now it's your turn" look. "Tell me about your father. What was he like? What did you learn from him?"

Turnabout was fair play, but that didn't make talking about Mathias any easier. "I learned what not to do as a father, as a man, as a husband. Doesn't mean I haven't screwed up, especially with Shelley, but I was determined not to make the same mistakes."

"He was cruel to you?"

"Mathias alternated between cruelty and his own brand of affection. As I got older, I realized there wasn't that much difference between the two. He was a sadistic bastard who got what he deserved."

It wasn't the time to go into all the secrets and lies the Slaters still lived with. At some point, she might need to know, but for now, he didn't see the need to put her off the family any more than she probably already was.

"It's getting late. I'd better go."

The mood had turned somber, not what he had intended. Still, he knew not to push. She'd shared more than he'd ever anticipated. He felt humbled, as he knew she didn't like to talk about her past.

He wasn't surprised to see her pick up her plate and head to the kitchen. She was a self-sufficient woman, and he admired that. Both his mother and Shelley had always had servants to cater to their every need. Kathleen took care of herself and would want to pull her weight no matter what situation she was thrust into.

They worked together in silence for several moments, clearing the table, putting dishes in the dishwasher. Eli often took care of kitchen duties but usually by himself. Even though they said little to each other, he enjoyed the small intimacy.

Kathleen wasn't feeling quite so pleased. For the last half hour, the urge to run out the door had been strong. She didn't consider herself a coward, but in this instance, she accepted she might be. Eli was becoming too much of a temptation for her to handle. He listened to her, actually listened to her. As much as she didn't like to talk about herself, having an astonishingly handsome man so interested in what she had to say was a seduction of its own.

Spending more time with him like this couldn't happen. She had agreed to do a job. She would guard his children with her life, and no harm would come to them under her watch. Anything beyond that, anything more, was impossible.

They walked out of the kitchen together, and she headed to the foyer closet where she had stored her purse and jacket. Before she could open the closet door, he was there before her. Instead of handing her the jacket, he held it out to help her into it.

She slid her arms into the sleeves and reached for her purse. "Thanks for dinner."

"Kathleen, look at me."

She lifted her gaze and, without a thought to how it would look, gently touched her fingers to the bruise on his cheekbone. "Does it hurt?"

"Only when I laugh. Can I ask you a question?"

He'd asked so many questions at dinner, what could one more hurt? "Yes."

"Are you attracted to me?"

Her heartbeat went to a rapid thud; her mind went into a mild panic. "Eli…I…um…"

While she was so ineloquently trying to explain that nothing could happen between them, he bent his head and touched his mouth to hers. All thoughts, including why this wasn't a good idea, disappeared like wisps of smoke.

The kiss was soft…warm, tender, his taste heavenly.

Wanting more, she moved into him, pressed her body against his, and began to drown in a whirlpool of exciting, new sensations. Heat, need, want swirled together, creating a vortex of desire, the likes of which she'd never felt.

Her mouth opened on a moan, and Eli took quick advantage, sliding his tongue inside. Only it wasn't rough or forceful. He still kept the kiss light, tender, as his mouth moved over hers. She could feel the simmering passion, the controlled strength. He could easily overpower her, but she knew instinctively that she could trust him. Knew that he wouldn't push her further than she wanted. Problem was, what she wanted and what was smart were in complete contradiction.

Her body heated, and arousal, like a warm, soft-flowing river, slid through her. She wanted to urge him to go deeper, imagined his hands caressing her, his body moving over hers, his hard length thrusting deep.

It was the most delicious, beautifully intense moment of her life. She wanted more, ached to have it all. She wanted everything. Skin to skin, every part of him connected to every part of her.

The insane image of Eli sweeping her up into his arms and carrying her Rhett Butler-style up the stairway to his bedroom flashed through her mind.

She had to end it. Now.

She pulled away from him, breathless. "This can't happen, Eli. We can't happen."

He said nothing for a moment. Instead, he just looked down at her, his eyes brimming with both need and tenderness. Then he said very gently, very quietly, "Why?"

Oh-so-many answers to that, none of which he would accept. Since telling him she wasn't attracted to him was out—he had disproved that, and the heat in his eyes said he would be glad to disprove it again—she gave him the truth. "I'm not interested in any kind of romantic relationship."

"Never? Or just not right now?"

The truth was never, but she was much too tired tonight to explain her reasons, so she gave the easy answer. "There's too much going on right now. Everything's too complicated. You've got someone out there trying to hurt you…maybe even hurt your children. You're my employer. I'm still trying to find out who killed Frank Braden. Getting involved with each other is simply not a good idea."

"That's a lot of words for a non-answer."

"It's all I've got."

"Fine. Okay. We won't get romantically involved."

His easy acquiescence was like a sharp kick to her heart. Disappointment swamped her. Before she could deal with the hurt, try to deny its existence, his mouth was on hers again, kissing her voraciously, as if he couldn't get enough. His tongue thrust deep as he ate at her mouth. Every single thought in her head disintegrated. This time, there was more passion, more heat. More everything. This time he held nothing back.

Kathleen whimpered her need beneath his mouth. Oh yes, how she wanted…how she needed. She rose up on her toes, wrapped her arms around his neck, and offered him everything he asked.

Long, heated moments later, he raised his head, his eyes glittering. "Okay," he growled. "No romance. I promise."

Her mind still blurred from pleasure, she had no opportunity to compose a coherent thought, much less a verbal response. He abruptly opened the door and led her down the steps to her car. She was sitting behind the wheel of her car before she realized it.

He closed the car door with a click. Before she could lose her nerve, she switched the engine on, rolled down the window. "What was that kiss about?"

"Passion. You say romance is out. That's a shame, because I'd really like to romance you, but I'll settle for passion."

She stared up at him in openmouthed amazement. He gave her a small smile, leaned down, and dropped a quick, hard kiss on her surprised mouth. "Drive safely, Kat. Text me when you get home. See you tomorrow."

Figuring if she didn't leave she'd either say something she would regret or she'd figure out a way to kiss him again, she put the car in drive and headed down the driveway. Before she rounded a corner, she looked in her rearview mirror. He was still standing there, watching her.

Why did this one man, with his strength, tenacity, and elegance, threaten her equilibrium? She didn't know but one thing she was sure of: She had to shut it down and quick.

No one—man, woman, or child—would penetrate her armor ever again.

CHAPTER
TWENTY-FOUR

The instant Kathleen stepped into his house the next morning, Eli could tell all her defenses were back in place. Last night, for a very brief period of time, he'd been able to break through.

He hadn't planned on kissing her, but no way in hell would he regret something so damn fine. She had tasted better than he had imagined, had felt perfect in his arms. He was going to do everything within his power to get her back there again. And from the look in her eyes, he was going to have to work extra hard at it.

Eli liked a challenge, and Kathleen was definitely worth it. He tapped down his impatience and gave her what he hoped was a somewhat reassuringly bland smile of welcome as he waved her inside the house.

"Everything go okay last night?"

"What do you mean?"

"The job for Grey."

"Oh. Yes. It was just a drop-off. No problems." The smile she gave him barely moved her lips. "Thanks."

"That's good, then." He glanced up at the stairway. "The girls are almost ready, and Teresa is just finishing up their lunch boxes."

She backed away from him, put her hand on the door as if to leave. "I'll just wait on the porch for them."

"That's fine. I'll have Teresa bring you out the cup of coffee she's already poured for you. I think she used the fine china again."

"Yeah, right."

"Very well." He turned and called out, "Teresa!"

"Oh, for heaven's sake." With a huff of exasperation, she dropped her hand from the door and went to walk around him. She jerked to a halt when she spotted Teresa standing in the foyer, holding a cup of steaming coffee in a sturdy mug.

Okay, so he'd got that part wrong.

"Good morning, Miss Kathleen. Here's a nice hot cup for the road."

"Thank you, Teresa. That's awfully kind." She shot a look at Eli out of the corner of her eye, and he could only grin at her.

"Teresa, would you tell the girls to be down in five minutes? I need to talk to Kathleen."

"Of course, Mr. Eli."

The instant she was out of hearing range, Eli said, "I want you to go in the limo today. It's bulletproof and a helluva lot safer than my car."

"You're not riding with us to school?"

"No. I've got some things to take care of at the office. Then I'm going to go see a rat in prison."

"Your brother?"

"Yes. Time for the gloves to come off."

"And what about you? Don't you need some kind of protection?"

"My daughters' safety is my priority."

Hearing the childish giggles as his girls raced down the stairs, he turned but was startled to find a hand on his arm, stopping him. Eli looked down at her hand. Slender and graceful, like its owner. Though her nails were short and well cared for, he wasn't surprised at the lack of polish or rings. This woman, who continued to fascinate him, wasn't into adornment. With her serious, no-nonsense persona, dressing up probably seemed frivolous to her. And for that reason, along with a few others, Eli suddenly wanted to buy her something sparkly and shiny.

Since that would likely send her running in the other direction, he ignored that urge. At least for now.

"Be careful, Eli. I know you have good security and you're trained, but a bullet is hard to dodge."

He squeezed the hand still resting on his arm. "Don't worry about me. I've got way too much to live for."

Kathleen eased her hand away from him and stepped back. The warm, intimate look in Eli's eyes was a temptation she refused to indulge in. The stern lecture she'd given herself last night, along with another one this morning, was now as shaky and substantial as melted pudding. She could not, would not, allow this.

"About last night. I don't want—"

"Oh yes, you do, Kathleen," he growled softly.

Her heart stuttered. "What? No I—"

His fingers gently trailed down her cheek. "Yeah. In fact, you want it almost as much as I do."

Heat swept through her at his arrogant and much-too-truthful words.

"Don't be—"

He drew closer and his fingers pressed against her mouth. "Shh."

Her body softened, accepting, as a groan of longing welled within her. He was right. She did want, she did need. She did—

"We're ready, Daddy!" Sophia squealed as she entered the room.

Violet, only a step or two behind, yelled out, "Me, too!"

A cold dash of reality slapped at Kathleen. What the hell was she doing?

Tearing her eyes away from their father, she turned to see Sophia and Violet running toward them. Though the girls were two years apart in age, they often dressed alike. Kathleen spotted a streak of competiveness in both of them and had a feeling Eli's hands would be full as they grew older. She ignored the tug to her heart that she wouldn't be around to watch them grow up.

As they said their good mornings, Teresa rushed out with their lunch boxes, and then Eli was hustling them out the door and into the limo. While he secured Violet into her car seat, Kathleen buckled Sophia into hers.

Once both girls were secured and Eli had kissed each one good-bye, he stood outside the car with Kathleen and Gunter.

"I really don't expect any trouble." Eli kept his voice low. "But if you see the slightest cause for concern, come back home. If need be, I'll bring in a teacher for them until this has passed."

"Will do, sir." Gunter nodded and then slid behind the wheel.

There were a lot of things she wanted to say to Eli. Most of them weren't appropriate, and she could never say them out loud. How he'd gotten under her defenses wasn't something she wanted to contemplate, because she couldn't let him stay there. Being vulnerable and open with this man would only lead to another heartache. She couldn't risk it.

"Be safe, Eli," was the best she could do.

Eli wasn't of the same mind. Grabbing her hand, he pressed a kiss to the back of it. "You, too, Kat. Take care of all of my girls."

Not giving her a chance to respond, he opened the door and gently nudged her inside. "Be good girls today. I'll see you all tonight." And then closed the door.

Still reeling from his words and actions, Kathleen forced her mind back to her priority. The limo rolled down the drive, and then she found herself distracted again when Sophia said, "Do you gotta boo-boo on your hand?"

Pulling her thoughts together, she faced the two little girls eyeing her so curiously. "No, I don't have a boo-boo."

"Then why did Daddy kiss your hand?"

Another reason, just as important, that she and Eli couldn't get involved. Sophia and Violet had already had too much upheaval in their life. The loss of their mother, no matter how young they were, would have a tremendous impact. And with the Slater family in disarray, they needed stability. Having Kathleen come into their life for a short while was one thing. Having them think that their father had an affection for her was something else. When they no longer needed her protection and she left, they could be hurt. She had to make Eli understand that getting involved with her, in any capacity other than as his children's bodyguard, was out of the question.

Aware that Sophia would not let go of the question until it was answered to her satisfaction, Kathleen explained, "He was being a gentleman."

"You mean like when the prince kisses the princess's hand?"

"Umm. Yes, like that."

Thankfully, that sent Sophia off on another questioning tangent. Kathleen answered when necessary, her mind whirling. She and Eli needed to talk, to come to an agreement. This little flirtation had to end. It wasn't good for his children, it wasn't good for her. Kathleen Callahan and Eli Slater did not belong.

Chapter
Twenty-five

Slater House Hotel
Corporate Offices

Standing at his office window, Eli looked out over the Dallas skyline. He'd grown up in this city. Knew it as well as he knew his own home and most of the time loved it like it was family. Dallas had been good to the Slaters, and even though some of them had screwed her royally, she was a forgiving city.

They'd been damn lucky the entire family hadn't been run out of town. Instead, things were flowing once again, flourishing. Slater House Hotels were running at peak occupancy throughout the world. The family's other businesses, though scaled down due to all the shuffling Eli had employed, were also thriving and growing.

Yet there was the lingering darkness. The emails had stopped. He hadn't received any in a couple of weeks. Was that because of the protection he'd added for his children, or was there another reason? Was someone about to step up their game, or stop altogether?

Yesterday's incident had been bizarre. What kind of idiot tried to kill someone in such an inept and half-assed way? Someone who wasn't totally onboard with killing him? Or had someone hired an inexperienced killer?

Going to the police with these vague, obscure threats would be useless. And every investigator he'd hired had come up with nothing substantial. He felt like he was in an odd kind of waiting game but had no idea what he was waiting for. Death or some sort of revelation?

Despite those worries, he did have light in his life. His daughters were healthy, happy, and thriving. And he was falling for a beautiful woman who, though as prickly as a cactus, was at last showing some interest in him. Yes, she'd tried to hide it. He didn't expect her to just fall into his arms, but he'd felt the warm softness of her lips, the receptiveness of her body. She might not be as ready as he was for something more, but at least he now had hope.

The buzzer on his desk sounded, and his secretary's voice came over the intercom. "Eli, you have a visitor. Kathleen Callahan."

A rush of pleasure swept through him that she felt comfortable enough to come to his office. "Thank you, Rose. Tell her to come in, please."

Seconds later, Kathleen walked into Eli's gigantic office. Seemingly miles of sky-blue carpet and rich, dark hardwood covered the floor. On one side was a sitting area with a black leather sofa and chairs. The other side had a small conference table and a small bar. In the middle was a large desk. Behind the desk were three giant windows showing an astonishing view of the Dallas skyline. And in front of that window stood a man who fascinated her, scared her, excited her.

"Welcome to Slater House. This is an unexpected pleasure."

The resolve she'd built up over the last hour dissipated slightly. He seemed genuinely pleased to see her. His eyes gleamed with pleasure, and his beautiful, sensual mouth was curved up in a delighted grin.

She had come here to tell him to stop flirting, teasing, and treating her like she was his girlfriend. He was her employer and nothing more. But seeing him like this melted her resistance. Why did she have to want him so much?

At her continued silence, the smile disappeared. "Is everything okay? My daughters?"

She shook herself back to reality. "Yes. Sorry. They're fine. We dropped them off at school, and they were as excited as always."

"Good." His hand swept toward the bar. "Would you like some coffee or a soda?"

"No." She straightened her posture, steeled her resolve, determined to do what she came here to do. "I wanted to talk with you about the way you're behaving."

"And how am I behaving?"

"Like you're interested in me."

"I am interested in you."

"I mean romantically."

He cocked his head slightly, warm amusement on his face. "So do I."

That wasn't exactly what she had expected. Okay, yes. She knew he was attracted to her, but still. "I don't want your daughters to be confused. If they see you do something again like what you did this morning, they may think there's something more to it."

"What did I do this morning?"

"You kissed my hand."

He came toward her, and she had to dig her heels into the carpet to keep from backing away. When he stopped within a foot of her, she told herself she was glad he'd stopped.

"It's a lovely hand." Surprising her, he picked it up and kissed it again, this time slower, softer.

Rattled, she tugged at her hand, but he refused to give it back. "You can't do stuff like that."

"Why not?"

"Because it's…I'm not…" She huffed out a breath. "Like I told you last night. I do not want to get involved with you."

There, she'd told him, succinctly, somewhat brutally, but it had to be done.

"Liar."

"I beg your pardon?"

"You heard me. I don't believe you. I think you do want to get involved with me, but you're afraid to get hurt. I get that. I don't blame you. Caring about someone else is a risk. But it's a risk I'm willing to take."

She blinked in confusion. Where had this gone wrong? "No, I do not want to get involved with you. I just want to do my job. That's it. And if you can't honor that, I'll have to quit."

"Prove it."

"Prove what?"

"That you don't want to get involved with me."

"And how do you propose I do that?"

"Kiss me."

Her heart began a rapid gallop. "How would that prove anything?"

"It won't, but I think it'll prove something to you."

Despite her best intentions, she backed away. She didn't get far, though, since he still held her hand.

"Listen, Eli. You're an attractive man. You could have any woman in the world you want, at any time."

"I don't want anyone else in the world. I happen to want you."

"But why?"

"Kathleen, are you really so unaware of your own appeal?"

"You don't even know me."

"I think we established that I know quite a lot about you."

"The things you know…that's surface stuff. You don't know the real me."

"I know you better than you think. And what I don't know, I want to learn. I want to know everything about you, Kathleen. Is that so hard to believe, to understand?"

Before she could answer, he said, "I walked to you, Kat. I've told you what I want. I was open and upfront. Now I'm asking you. Take one step forward, toward me. Show me that I'm not the only one feeling this way. Show me it's not one-sided."

Step back, step back, step back. The words were a rhythmic warning in her head. But the seduction of his words infused her entire body with heat, and her heart was whispering in counter rhythm. *Take a chance!*

Without even knowing she was going to do it, she took a step forward. The warm approval in his eyes sent heat shuddering through her before he even touched her. Lowering his head, he put his mouth on hers, and she remembered his taste from yesterday, warm rich flavors, like a good wine. She had expected passion, prepared herself to be drawn deep into the same vortex of heat and need she had experienced last night. She hadn't expected tenderness. His mouth, soft as a whisper, made love to hers slowly, gently. This was a slow, sweet seduction. She told herself she could have fought the explosion of desire. But this… Oh, this just made her want to sink into him and let him take control.

Kathleen moaned as she stretched up on her toes, wrapped her arms around his shoulders, and gave in to the need.

Even as tenderness swamped Eli for her bravery, desire consumed him. His hands cupping her bottom, he pressed her hard against his arousal, molded his body to hers, and let passion take them both. Every fantasy he'd ever had, every dream he'd ever wanted, was here in his arms. As their lips melded together and their bodies heated with desire, Eli knew this was a pivotal moment for them. He could take it further, make her burn even brighter, quench the need. But a quick fix wasn't what he wanted from this woman. This was no short-term romance for him. He had forever in his mind. And she wasn't ready to know that, accept that.

With the fiercest willpower he'd ever known, Eli did what his body told him was impossible. He pulled away from her delicious lips and stepped back.

She was breathing heavily, in panting little gasps that he'd probably hear in his dreams tonight. The fire in her eyes was more than he could have expected, and it took every bit of that willpower to keep himself from diving in again.

Holding his arms loosely around her, he touched his forehead to hers. "Have dinner with me again tonight. Just you and me. We'll go out...someplace crazy romantic and seduce each other. I'll take you dancing, or we'll take a drive and make out under the moonlight."

He had expected confusion, maybe a bit of shyness. He hadn't expected anger.

"Just what do you think you're doing?"

"What?" He took a step back, shook his head. "What are you talking about?"

"You cannot and will not seduce me. You're my employer and nothing more."

"I'd say we were doing a fine job of seducing each other. Or did you forget you took that step forward?" Maybe it was wrong to throw that in her face, but dammit, he knew what she had felt, knew she wanted him. "Why are you denying this, Kat? What are you so afraid of?"

"Get someone else to guard your children, Eli. I'll stay until you find a replacement. Until you do, stay away from me." She whirled and headed to the door.

"Like hell." Doing what he'd never done in his entire life, he refused to comply with a woman's request. Instead, he strode quickly to his desk and flipped a switch, clicking the locks on the doors, keeping her from leaving.

Either she hadn't heard them lock or she refused to believe he'd do something so arrogant. She tugged on the door handle, and when it didn't open, she growled, "Open the damn door."

"Not until we talk. Until you tell me what the hell's the matter. I know you want me, dammit."

She whirled again, and though her body was trembling, he was glad there were no tears. Tears from this woman would do him in. He'd do anything to prevent them.

Leaning back against the door, she whispered harshly, "Yes, you can turn me on. Yes, I'm attracted to you. But that's it. Nothing more. I can't get involved with you. I won't. It's not fair to your children to see you involved with a woman and have it go nowhere."

"What makes you think it would go nowhere?"

"Because it can't. We both know that."

"No, we don't." He was tipping his hand a lot sooner than he'd planned, but what the hell? "You say I don't know you...the real you. Well, dammit, you're wrong. I do. And what I know,

I'm crazy about. I don't want short term. I don't want an affair. I want long term. Maybe forever."

Her flushed face went pale. Tears glimmered in her eyes. "No. Just no. Now open the damned door before I scream and your secretary calls the police."

That would never happen, but neither did he want Kathleen to feel trapped as she so obviously did. But before he clicked the locks, there was one thing she needed to hear.

"I don't know what's got you so scared, but I won't give up, Kat. You're not a coward. You've proved that. With every adversity you've faced, you've overcome and triumphed." Eli flipped the switch, and the door lock clicked open. "I sure as hell never thought you'd look at my feelings for you as an adversity."

He saw a flicker of regret in her face, and then it went blank, much the way she'd looked at her sister's trial. "Any woman, anywhere, would be flattered and thrilled to have someone like you interested in them, Eli. You're every woman's dream. You just can't be mine."

She turned, opened the door, and walked out.

CHAPTER TWENTY-SIX

Hiram Clemens State Correctional Facility
Enid, Texas

"This is getting to be a habit, Eli. Are you back for more advice from your big brother? What's the matter? You finally figuring out you don't have the smarts to handle the Slater holdings?"

It had been a few weeks since he'd seen Adam. Why had he thought the incarceration would make a difference to the asshole? If anything, Adam looked healthier and even more smug than before.

"Prison life seems to suit you."

His brother swaggered to the table and sprawled back in his chair. "Three squares, plenty of time to exercise and read. It's a great life. I really hope you get to experience it someday." He grinned and pointed to Eli's black eye. "Whereas you, little brother, look like warmed-over dog shit. Somebody finally beat the hell out of you like you deserve?"

Unfazed by the showy rhetoric, Eli said, "I know it's you, Adam."

"It's me, what? Eli?"

"You're the one who sent the emails threatening my family. Did you think I wouldn't find out?"

"Oh, little brother. How sad you are. Here I am, locked in a cell, twenty-four/seven, eating shit I wouldn't give a stray dog, listening to men fart, belch, and get off with their hands or with each other only a few yards away from me, and you come complaining about some stupid email? Daddy was right all along. You're too soft. Don't have it in you to be the head of the Slater family."

"I'm through playing your games, Adam. You think listening to your fellow prisoners entertain themselves is unpleasant? You don't know what the word means. I just met with the warden, and we had what you might call an enlightening conversation."

Something like fear flashed on Adam's face, but he quickly covered it up with a smirk. "You've got me shaking in my prison-issue loafers. What has my badass brother got cooked up for me? You going to take away my pillow and blanket?"

Eli realized he'd been wrong. There was worry behind the bravado. Adam was feeling the stress, the pressure. This was the perfect time to lay down the law.

"Here's how it's going to be. You're going to tell me if you sent the emails threatening my children." When Adam opened his mouth to speak, Eli held up his hand. "I'm not finished. You're going to tell me the truth. If you do, I'll believe you and will do nothing other than make sure you have no access to the Internet."

"And how are you going make me do that? Truth serum? Lie detector?"

"Daddy once said you couldn't lie your way out of a paper bag because you were too stupid. And since you are indeed one of the stupidest men I've ever known, I figure he was probably right. So tell me, Adam, did you send the emails?"

"Screw you, Eli. I'm not saying another damn word."

"Fine. Not only will you be barred from any electronics, a camera will be installed in your cell. You'll be monitored twenty-four/seven."

"You think that scares me? Hell, a man can't take a piss in this place without somebody getting splattered."

"Then get ready, brother, because it's about to get a helluva lot wetter for you. The warden will be adding someone to your cell."

"He can't do that. I have to have a cell to myself. I've got a doctor's order. I've got a condition. Warden can't change a doctor's orders. I've got rights."

"Funny, he couldn't seem to find anything like that in your file. Guess that quack doctor didn't come through for you, after all."

Adam surged to his feet. Eli prepared for an attack. Instead of going after his brother, though, Adam began to pace.

"You don't understand, Eli. I'm not like those other men. I have to have a place to myself. You put somebody in there with me, I'm going to die."

"All you have to do is tell me the truth."

"And you'll believe me?"

"Yes."

"Then, all right, yes. I sent a stupid note. It wasn't anything more than a little smartass one-liner. Meant nothing."

"Just one?"

Eli pulled out the small stack. He now had six. He thought he knew which one Adam had sent.

"Now wait just a damn minute. I'll cop to one, but I didn't send any others."

"Show me which one you sent."

Adam sat down and read each one, then pointed. "This is mine."

"And what did you expect to gain from sending it?"

"It was a joke. You're so friggin' serious all the time."

"Joking about my children's safety is not amusing."

"Yeah. I get that." He looked down at the other emails, the attached photographs. "Who do you think sent the others? Could I be in danger here?"

Adam's question didn't even surprise him. The man had always had only one concern—himself.

Having endured his brother's company as much as he could stand, Eli stood. "Good-bye, Adam."

"You believe me, right?" Adam grabbed his arm. "You're not really going to make me share a cell with anyone, are you?"

A strong wave of disgust hit Eli, but it was tempered by a dose of pity. His brother, the most spoiled of Mathias's children, was also the weakest and least stable. Eli had figured the threat of sharing a cell would do Adam in. Had banked on that. When they were kids, Adam had pitched a fit if he had to share anything with his other siblings, most especially a room.

"You'll keep the cell to yourself. And whatever other privileges you're provided. I'm done with you."

Eli walked out the door, hoping like hell he never had to come back here again. He gave a nod to everyone he passed but barely saw their faces. The air felt thick, and even though he figured much of it was in his head, the stench of the place roiled his stomach. His strides ate up ground until he got outside, and then he took in great, deep breaths, cleansing his lungs.

Wearier than he'd been in months, he got into his car and headed out of the parking lot. He'd gotten the answer he'd come for. Despite the evil that resided in Adam's heart, Eli believed him about the emails. But they'd all come from the prison. Justice's tech person had verified all of them had the same IP address. So if

Adam sent only one, who had sent the others? And why from the prison? Was it to set Adam up? To make it look like his low-life brother was making the threats, and all the while someone else was out there waiting to hurt his family?

He hadn't mentioned the incident from yesterday. Adam might be a sleazebag, but Eli didn't believe his brother was behind the attempt on his life.

So where did he go from here? The answer was obvious, but he had hesitated taking the next step. Hadn't wanted to make it. But now he had no choice. He needed to get his daughters to his mother and sister in France, away from immediate danger. As long as they were close to him, Eli knew he wouldn't be able to concentrate, do what needed to be done.

And Kathleen? The image of how she'd looked when she'd walked out of his office haunted him. He had told Justice yesterday—just yesterday, dammit—that he wouldn't push her. That he knew she was too vulnerable, wasn't ready. And then what had he done? He'd damn well pushed her to the point of quitting.

But now what could he do? Get her out of his life until everything settled down? With Sophia and Violet going away, the job no longer existed. If he let her go, what would happen? He knew the answer. He wouldn't see her again. She would take the opportunity to get out and stay out.

If he asked her to stay, to work with him, using her expertise to help hunt down who was behind the threats, would she? Or would her fear, her stubborn pride make her turn him down?

And if anything happened to her?

His mind whirled, argued, and turned itself inside out with what he should do versus what he wanted.

Who was behind the threats? Were they really that serious? A few emails and a lame excuse for an assassination attempt? Was he making too much out of it all?

His foot lifted from the accelerator, easing his speed to take a hairpin turn. A glint in his peripheral vision caught his attention. He glanced over at the heavily wooded forest. What had he—

The instant his mind registered what he was seeing, he instinctively ducked. A loud pop sounded, the windshield shattered. Eli jerked on the steering wheel. Another *pop*, *pop*. Bastard had shot out at least one tire.

He slammed on his brakes and the car went into a wild, uncontrollable spin. Seconds later, he knew he was a dead man as the car went airborne, flying off the road and down toward a small valley.

Saying a quick prayer that his children would not lose another parent, Eli prepared for the bone-jarring impact.

Chapter Twenty-seven

For the second time in twenty-four hours, Kathleen's feet flew down the hallway of the hospital. This time, there was no Eli heading toward her with a bruised eye and an eye patch to entertain his children. Instead, Grey was standing in front of the reception desk, his mouth set to grim, dark blue eyes sparkling with fury.

She skidded to a stop. "Is he okay? Where is he?"

"I don't know. The doctors are still in with him. He's alive. That's all I know."

Kathleen closed her eyes, relieved he was alive, but she knew from experience that there were different levels of being alive.

"Let's sit down." Grey took Kathleen's elbow and led her to a chair. He sat beside her, his expression troubled.

"It wasn't an accident, was it?"

"No. The police were here when I arrived. They couldn't give me a lot of details on his condition other than he was able to tell them that he'd been shot at."

Her heart stopped. "He was shot?"

"I don't think so. At least, they said they couldn't find any entrance wounds. The paramedics indicated the blood was from a head wound, not a bullet wound."

Apparently seeing the blood drain from her face, he reached over and squeezed her hand. "Eli's a tough SOB."

That was true. Despite his elegance and sophistication, he did have a dangerous edge and could handle himself in most any situation. But he wasn't immortal. Bullets could penetrate his flesh. And his head, though as hard as a rock, could still be crushed.

At that image, a wave of nausea swelled within her. Dammit, she had told herself she wasn't going to care for him and now...? Now she felt as though her heart was breaking.

Unable to sit still, she sprang to her feet and began to pace. "Who could be doing this? Who would want Eli dead? We have to find out. Is it his brother? Is Adam that evil?"

"Evil? Yes. But he's got no money to speak of any longer. Paying for a hit would be hard for him to do."

"Then who? Eli said he's gone through every one of his father's enemies, all the people who had been wronged, and couldn't pinpoint anyone. Who's left?"

"Eli said this feels personal, and I agree."

"I can't see anyone hating him enough to do this. Or hurt his children."

"That's the pisser. I can't either." He threw Kathleen a grim smile. "The man's not perfect and can tick off a saint when he's brought to the line. But killing him? That's buggering stupid."

"You're helping him investigate?"

"I've got a couple of people assigned, but we've found nothing substantial. I'm going to add to that. I've contacted two of my main investigators, Kennedy and Nick Gallagher. They'll be on it full time until this thing is over."

"I want in on the investigation."

A knowing glimmer appeared in his eyes. "I thought you might."

She ignored Grey's inference, refusing to contemplate that he was seeing something that she could not allow herself to entertain. Finding who was doing this was her only focus. It angered her that she hadn't asked to be involved before. She'd been too concerned with protecting herself. And had it helped? Of course not. She already cared too damn much.

"Mr. Justice?" A tall, slender man dressed in scrubs stood before them.

"Yes." Grey went to his feet.

"Mr. Slater is asking for you. Follow me."

Not bothering to ask if she could come, too, Kathleen walked beside Grey to a curtained-off area. Hearing Eli's deep, slightly hoarse voice, Kathleen felt her knees turn to melted rubber. She stiffened her spine and watched as the nurse pushed aside the curtain. The instant she saw Eli, she wanted to cry, in both relief and worry.

The crooked smile he gave was probably supposed to reassure her. It didn't.

"It's not really as bad as it looks."

A white bandage was wrapped around his forehead, his left arm was in a sling, and hideous bruises were already mottling his bare chest.

"What's the damage?" Grey asked

Before Eli could answer, a doctor walked in and said, "Lucky to be alive. A mild concussion, sprained wrist, a dozen or so lacerations, and bruised ribs."

"You weren't shot?" Kathleen asked.

Again, the doctor answered. "No bullet wounds. Like I said, damn lucky to be alive. Still, he's going to be hurting for a few days. I'm trying to convince him he needs to stay the night for observation, but he insists he has someone at home who will monitor him." He glanced down at a chart. "Someone named Kathleen. Is that you?"

Her eyes shot to Eli, who was looking like a little boy hoping not to get called out on a lie.

"Yes, that's me. And he's right. He'll be well taken care of at home."

The doctor nodded. "I'll give you a copy of instructions for his care." He looked at Eli. "No overdoing it for a couple of days. Resume normal activities then, but if you start feeling dizzy or unusually tired, rest."

"Thanks, doc. Appreciate it."

The doctor nodded again and walked out. The instant he did, Kathleen whirled around. "What happened?"

"The doctor's right. I got lucky. Just before the first shot, I caught a glimpse of the sun glinting off something. Rifle, I'm guessing. I ducked. Good thing I did, since the bullet would've gone through my head. Then the bastard shot out my tires. I lost control, went down a ravine."

"How can you act so calm? Dammit, someone tried to kill you, Eli."

At her statement, his eyes flared with acknowledgment, and she realized his casual attitude had all been an act. Beneath the cool façade was a burning fury.

"Yes, they did."

"What'd the police say? I only got the bare facts from them when I came in."

"They're investigating, but nothing, not even a shell, was found. I was out for a few minutes. Not sure how long. By the time I woke, the ambulance and police were there, and the shooter, along with any evidence, was long gone."

"I didn't see any reporters. How'd you manage that?"

He shrugged and then winced. "Called in a few favors."

"You did all that while you were being treated?" Kathleen asked.

"I had to act fast." His eyes went back to Grey's. "Justice, can you give us a minute?"

"Yes. I'll bring the car round."

The instant they were alone, Eli said, "I need you to bring my daughters home. The gloves are off now, and this thing is only going to escalate."

Fighting the need to smooth the lines of both worry and pain that furrowed his brow, she nodded. "Of course, I'll go now."

She went to back away, sure that if she stayed another moment she'd be touching him merely to reassure herself he was all right.

"Wait."

She halted. "Yes?"

"I also want to apologize."

Surprised, she asked, "For?"

Eli struggled for words and vaguely wondered if his throbbing head had anything to do with his inability to form the right words, say the right things. Telling her he was sorry for kissing her would be a flat-out lie. But he was sorry for how things had gone at his office. He needed to apologize for pushing her then, scaring the hell out of her now. And maybe for what he was going to do once his daughters were safely away.

"At my office. I shouldn't have pushed you like that."

"That's not something we need to talk about now."

"Maybe not, but it needed to be said. I'm also sorry for scaring you now. I know this brings back a lot of bad memories for you."

She shook her head, denial stamped firmly on her face. "I wasn't scared. I was concerned for my employer."

"Your employer?"

"You're my employer until you find my replacement."

Maybe any other time he might've let her get away with that, but not now. "You've never been a coward in your life, Kat. Don't you damn well start now."

"What's that supposed to mean?"

Ignoring the pain, Eli bent forward, grabbed her wrist, and pulled her to him. Trapping her between his spread legs, he used his good hand to cup her face and pressed a hard kiss to her soft mouth. Beneath the surprise, he felt the give, the surrender.

When he raised his head, he locked his gaze with her startled one. "This is what I mean. Don't deny it. Don't brush it off as something less. I'm not just your employer. You're not just an employee. You damn well know it."

Her slender body shuddered, and Eli told himself once again not to push. But things were changing, escalating, and the need to grab on to everyone he cared for and hang on for dear life was strong.

But that would have to wait. Dammit, all of it would have to wait. He released her arm, watched her back away again, out of his reach.

The curtain rustled as the nurse came back in. "Looks like you're set to go, Mr. Slater. Your clothes are ruined, so I brought you some snazzy scrubs to wear home."

His teeth grinding against the pain, Eli slid off the exam table. Apparently realizing that all that had covered him was a sheet over his lower half, and it was now on the floor, Kathleen backed away even more. "I'll follow you and Grey home, then I'll collect Sophia and Violet…bring them home, too."

Eli wouldn't stop her from leaving the room but refused to let her believe the conversation had ended. "This isn't over, Kat."

"You're right, it's not over. Because it never even started." She walked out of the room.

Eli cursed softly, then gave a grimacing smile of apology to the nurse as she helped him dress. He wanted the kind nurse to go elsewhere for a half hour so he could show Kathleen that her words might say one thing but her body had said something else. The heat in her eyes when he'd dropped the sheet told him she wanted him. That was something he could build upon.

But that, too, would have to wait. His entire body felt like he'd just gone twelve rounds with a heavyweight champ. Engaging in anything remotely physical was well beyond his capabilities for the time being. But that wasn't the biggest deterrent. He had a family to protect and then a killer to uncover.

The instant he was dressed, Eli grabbed his cellphone again. It was a call he hadn't wanted to make, but this time, he had no choice.

CHAPTER
TWENTY-EIGHT

Kathleen ushered Eli's daughters inside the house. She had explained that their father's car had crashed and he had a few minor boo-boos. Hopefully, the girls wouldn't be too frightened once they saw him.

Grey had driven Eli home. Kathleen had followed in her car, looking for a threat in every car they passed, every person she saw. The moment they arrived, she'd jumped into the limo and headed to the school. She had called ahead to let the principal know she was coming. She didn't give any more information than that, but had a feeling Eli would be contacting the school this afternoon. He hadn't said so, but she knew the girls wouldn't be going back to school. Not until this was over.

She and Eli might disagree on personal issues, but this was one they could both agree on. When your loved ones were threatened, you gathered them close and rode out the storm. That was something she'd learned way too late.

Teresa was standing in the foyer waiting for them. Though she gave the girls her usual cheerful greeting, there was worry in her eyes.

"Your daddy is upstairs in his bedroom. As soon as you put your school supplies away and change into your play clothes, he wants you to come see him. I'll bring you some milk and cookies."

With the optimism of the young and the bright promise of cookies, both girls ran up the stairs, giggling and cheerfully unaware their father had almost been killed.

The instant they were out of hearing range, Kathleen said, "Are you all right, Teresa?"

Her arms wrapped around herself, she rubbed them for comfort. "I'll be fine. I'm just so worried about Mr. Eli. I can't imagine anyone wanting to hurt him or those precious babies."

"There're a lot of people working to find who's doing this. And in the meantime, Eli will make sure he and the girls stay safe."

"Including you, Miss Kathleen? Will you be staying to help?"

That was something she would have to talk with Eli about. If he planned to keep his daughters out of school and confined to the estate until the threat was gone, there was no reason for her to be here. She'd been hired for one reason only. That particular reason no longer existed. But another reason for her to stay did exist. She just needed to figure out how she would tell him. Explaining her reasons without him reading anything into it would be tricky. Especially since she didn't believe them herself.

Since Eli deserved that answer first, Kathleen just said, "I'm not sure yet. How's he feeling?"

"He said he was fine, but I saw the pain in his eyes. He's lying down. I'm supposed to wake him every other hour." She glanced down at her watch. "That's about an hour from now."

"Why don't I take that responsibility off you? You get the snack ready for the girls. Once they see their father, I'm sure the comfort of milk and cookies will be even more welcome."

"Yes…all right. That sounds good." She turned to head toward the kitchen, then stopped and looked over her shoulder. "I do hope you'll stay, Miss Kathleen. You're good for him. Good for the girls, too."

"Why do you say that?"

"There's a light in his eyes when you're around. A spring in his step. I think you make him happy. The girls see that, and it makes them happy to see their father that way."

Kathleen had no answer for that. She couldn't take on that kind of responsibility. Couldn't take that kind of risk.

Eli settled himself carefully into his chair. As long as he didn't breathe too deeply, he figured he could control the pain, at least long enough not to scare his kids. He'd persuaded the nurse to take the gauze bandage off his head and replace it with a small cartoon Band-Aid. With his black eye from yesterday and his new injuries today, he figured he looked damn rough. Downplaying was his best bet.

He'd dozed off for a little while but woke when he heard the rapid steps of little feet rushing up the stairway. He couldn't have Sophia or Violet see him lying in bed this time of day. He wanted to be alert and sitting up when they came in to see him. Today was going to be difficult enough for them. They sure as hell didn't need to see their daddy looking like a zombie movie extra.

How he delivered the news would make all the difference. They could either be excited, looking upon this as a new adventure, or fearful at all the changes taking place. They'd already had too much upheaval in their young lives.

Once they were acclimated to their new location, books, movies, games, and a large outside play area should keep them occupied. The instant the bastard responsible for terrorizing his family was dealt with, he'd bring them back home. Until then, they needed to be as far from danger as possible.

Kathleen was another matter. Was he being selfish by wanting her to stay? The thought of anything happening to her churned his guts. If her association with him caused her any harm, he couldn't handle it. On the other hand, if she stayed here, not only could he keep an eye on her, they could work together. She was a professional, trained to defend herself and others, trained to dig deep and uncover secrets.

The original job he'd hired her for was no longer relevant, but would she consider working for him in another capacity?

And again, was he being selfish simply because he couldn't bear to let her go?

A soft knock on the door told him time was up and he damn well needed to make a decision.

"Come in," he called out.

She came into the room, calm, competent, and so damn beautiful his entire body, though aching and sore, went hard with desire. She was dressed in black slacks that molded to her slender legs and a sky-blue cashmere sweater that enhanced the beauty of her eyes. She rarely wore that color, and he thought he knew why. Her eyes practically glowed.

Her clothing, while casual, was both feminine and flattering. However, he also knew that beneath the slight bulk of the sweater was the gun she favored, a Ruger LC9. And beneath one pant leg and wrapped around a slender ankle was a holster holding her secondary weapon. Kathleen Callahan, delightfully feminine and dangerous as hell.

"Why aren't you in bed?"

"I was. I'll go back in a few minutes. Thought it best that Sophia and Violet see me sitting up. It'll alarm them less. What did you tell them?"

"Just that you had a little smash-up with your car and got a couple of bumps and bruises." Her mouth moved from grim to a slight grin for a second. "They'll like your bandage."

"Before they get here, I want to tell you the plan."

"I figure you'll pull them out of school until this is over."

"Yes. But I'm also going to send them away."

"Away? Where?"

"To a little town off the coast of France, where my mother and sister are staying. Only a handful of people, and only ones I trust, know about the small estate I purchased there. It's right on the water, but secluded and well guarded. They'll be safe there until this is over."

"I see."

"My brother Jonah is coming to get them. I called him from the hospital and got lucky. He's in the States and will be here soon. They'll be in good hands."

Wanting to get a reaction one way or the other, he added, "I appreciate your protection of them. You've done a great job."

"That's it? I'm dismissed?"

He tried for a smile, figured it looked pretty lame since he didn't feel the least amused. "You quit your job. Remember? Besides, your charges won't be here. The job no longer exists."

"I'm staying here with you. Remember?"

"Why?"

"You told the doctor I would see to your care."

"Teresa can do that."

"She's not going to France?"

"No."

"She's got a lot on her plate, taking care of this house, seeing to your meals. It'll be easier for her if I stay and help."

"One could argue that now that she doesn't have two rambunctious little girls to care for, she'll have a lot more time on her hands."

She put her hands on her hips and started toward him. "Why are you trying to get rid of me when an hour ago you…you…"

"I what, Kat? Acted like I couldn't keep my hands off you? Maybe I'm tired of doing all the pushing. Maybe I'm waiting for you to make a move toward me for a change."

"That has nothing to do with this. I want to stay and help you find out who's trying to hurt you."

"And that's the only reason?"

"The only one there can be, Eli."

He saw the fear, the worry. Was it the threats that worried her, or the fear that she was beginning to care for him? He had a feeling it was both. For right now, he'd have to worry about the first and hope the second worked itself out. But he saw no reason to keep his concerns from her.

"I would appreciate the help, and I want you here. But I'm concerned for your safety."

"How so?"

"Your association with me. I don't want you to get hurt."

"I can take care of myself."

"Very well." He was aware he'd accepted her offer too quickly for her to think he'd considered any other option.

She surprised him by not calling him on it and instead said, "I'm actually astonished that you didn't insist on it."

"Why, Miss Callahan, are you accusing me of being a bully?"

The glimmer of humor on his face was such a relief, Kathleen couldn't help but tease him a little. "Not a bully... More like a dictator."

"Dictator Eli. I like it."

She had to smile at that. Despite the cartoon bandage on his head, he did look quite arrogant and dictatorial. "I'm sure you do. So, the girls feel comfortable with your brother?"

"They adore Jonah. And since they haven't seen him in months, it'll be even more exciting for them. I'm hoping they'll be so happy to see him, to know that they'll be seeing their grandmother and their Aunt Lacey, that they'll not be upset about leaving."

"Have they ever been away from you like that?"

The pain in his eyes had nothing to do with his injuries. "No. I've been away from them on business, but they've never even stayed overnight with anyone."

"They're happy, well-adjusted children, Eli. They'll be fine."

"I'm counting on it."

Hearing the patter of running feet, she backed away, knowing he'd want to spend this time with his daughters, preparing them for their adventure. "I'll head home and get my things."

"Kathleen?"

She stopped at the door and turned. "Yes?"

"No matter your reasons for staying, I want to thank you. You've come to mean a lot to me, to my daughters."

If there was one thing he could have said that would make her regret staying, that was it.

Putting aside her worries for her own emotional well-being, Kathleen set her mind to concentrating on her new job—keeping Eli out of harm's way. Not that she had included that in her reasons for wanting to stay with him. She knew him well enough to know that the thought of her putting herself in danger to protect him went against every bone in his body. That would remain her secret. She would help him find who was threatening him, plus keep him safe. He didn't need to know.

That thought foremost in her mind, it was a bit of a shock that when she walked out of the house to get into her car, Eli's main bodyguard stopped her.

"Where are you going?"

Although they exchanged greetings every morning when she arrived to take the girls to school, Macon Yates rarely said much more than that.

"My apartment to pick up some clothes."

"Let's go, then."

"Excuse me?"

"Eli's orders. Neither you nor Teresa go anywhere without protection."

She didn't know if she should be insulted or touched. Eli believed her association with him might put her in danger. Being the one protected instead of the protector felt odd, but arguing was pointless.

"Very well."

"We'll take one of Eli's cars since yours has been towed to a garage."

"What? Why?"

"Eli wanted to make sure it hadn't been tampered with."

He was taking no chances, and while his autocratic ways were once again irritating, the knowledge that he was thinking of her safety even when he felt like hell lessened the sting.

"The limo, I'm assuming?"

His eyebrows shot up. He had apparently expected an argument. "Yes. That's his preference."

Saying nothing more, Kathleen went to open the front passenger's side door, but Macon was there before her, opening the back door. She shrugged and got into the back. She had a feeling she and Eli would be having arguments on many issues in the coming days.

CHAPTER
TWENTY-NINE

Kings Crossing, Vermont

Striving to appear powerful and in charge, William Johnson sat behind his desk. Since this was a videoconference call, no one could tell that he had placed a couple of pillows on the chair so he'd look taller, or that he'd added a bit of padding to his suit coat to make his shoulders broader and his body bigger.

As a slender man of somewhat small stature, William always took great pains to make himself appear larger. People were intimidated by strength and size.

He strived to ignore the voice in the back of his mind whispering to him that the reason this man had failed was because of his own shortcomings.

Setting his face in a practiced scowl, William snapped, "You've disappointed me once again."

"Making murder look like an accident isn't easy."

"If you want easy, you're in the wrong line of work. You took the job, knowing my rules…my parameters."

"He's a difficult man to get to."

Despite all the prep work beforehand, William was glad he'd insisted on a videophone meeting. Instead of relying on a voice inflection, he could see the man's face. The killer he had hired had proved to be an abysmal disappointment. Not only did he lack creativity, the arrogance was still there. No apology for screwing up. He would pay dearly for his lack of humility.

"Your predecessor had no such problems."

A flinch in the man's right eye showed that a point had been scored. Even as William fought a smile, he thought that perhaps it was unfair to compare this idiot to Hill Reed, a man who, by anyone's standards, had been the perfect killing machine. But when it came to eliminating enemies, fairness was a weakness William would not allow.

Although the outcome had already been decided, William deserved an explanation for what had happened, or hadn't happened, to Eli Slater. "You changed your tactics today. Shooting him was not to my specification."

"Your request to make it look like an accident wasn't working."

"That wasn't a request."

Another slight flicker of discomfort, this one a bit more obvious, flared in the man's eyes. "That kind of killing takes time. You were becoming impatient. It was a judgment call."

"You have poor judgment."

"James Johnson understood that—"

"You dare speak of my father?"

"I meant no disrespect. I was just going to say that I accomplished several jobs for James. He was pleased with my work. We had a good partnership."

That was an extreme exaggeration. The man had eliminated only two people for James. Both hits had been outright assassinations, unrelated to this current contract. Which was probably a good thing for this man. William knew for certain that James would not have tolerated this man's ineptitude and lack of creativity.

"That was then, this is now. Your incompetence offends me on many levels. It's time for new blood. Your services are no longer required."

"You can't just fire me. We have a contract."

"A contract you've not honored." William added slight amusement to his tone. "And who are you going to complain to? I don't believe the EEOC will be interested in hearing how unfairly a contract killer feels he's been treated."

The glare the man gave him might concern someone else. William paid it no mind. He had a backup plan, as always.

"You'll regret this."

No, he wouldn't, but much the way a cat would play with a dead mouse, William couldn't resist taunting the man.

His voice low and lethal, just like he had practiced earlier, William said, "I won't take that as a threat because I refuse to believe you are really that stupid. However, you need to know that if anything happens to me, I've already made arrangements for you to be taken out. Do you really want to spend your twilight years running for your life?"

At last, fear leaped into the man's eyes, and a surge of power swept through William.

The killer said at a rapid clip, "I misspoke. I won't let you down again."

"Excellent. Then we're on the same page."

A knock sounded at the man's door, and another bolt of power swept through William, practically lighting up his surroundings. Fighting to keep smugness off his face, he murmured, "You'll want to get that."

Before he ended the call, William heard two distinct, soft pops, telling him a silencer had been used. Though he longed to see the results, he told himself that was a crass desire. One does not stare at the remains of a meal once one has finished eating. Still, he entertained himself by imagining the brain matter that was now decorating the man's low-budget motel room.

Though still infuriated at the imbecile's screw-up, William was relieved to be rid of the man. It had been a mistake to hire him.

Once again, he lamented not only his father's death, but the death of his father's favorite employee.

Hill Reed had been the best when it came to killing. Not a year had gone by that James hadn't employed the renowned contract killer to take out a competitor or enemy. There had been so much more to do. Reed had died last year, much too soon and under suspicious circumstances.

His death had been a blow to James. Only days after learning of Reed's death, James had ordered William to his bedside. What he'd asked him to do was no surprise. William had known for years about certain enemies who were being put down in a variety of ways because of past sins. James Johnson had been a man of enormous vision and immense patience.

William had both feared and revered his father who had been larger than life. Whatever James wanted, so did William. Which was why the son had promised the father he'd continue the vendetta. Nothing would stop him from carrying out his father's wishes. All his life he had strived to please James and had often failed. He wouldn't fail at this. It had been too important to his father, which made it of utmost importance to William.

Perhaps if Reed had still been alive to handle the remaining contracts, all would have been well. After his father's death, William had felt overwhelmed. Not only had he been grieving, he had taken over the family's businesses and he'd had to see to this matter. Interviewing contract killers was a time-consuming, tedious, and enormously scary thing to do. Since there were so many people to eliminate, William had thought that spreading out the work to several assassins was the smart thing to do. For the most part, things had worked out well, but the man he'd hired to handle the Slaters had been as inept as he'd been unimaginative.

William had learned his lesson. Diversification was not the way to go. Only one killer would be charged with eliminating the remaining targets. Even though he'd made a few mistakes along the way, William comforted himself that at least the hired killer who'd just put down this dud had worked out phenomenally well. He had found her himself. And not only had she proven her competence and skill by completing several assignments, she had come to him and asked for more. He liked her initiative and drive. Having been trained by Hill Reed himself, she came from good stock.

Besides, who was he to turn down a lovely lady's request?

Chapter Thirty

Dallas

"I've seen people in the morgue look healthier than you do right now."

Eli's eyes popped open to see his younger brother standing over him. He'd thought to rest his eyes a little before getting to work. Apparently, he'd fallen asleep instead.

Pulling himself from his chair, ignoring the throb of his head and vicious aches throughout his body, he grabbed Jonah in a hard hug.

"It's damn good to see you."

"You, too, but seriously, bro, you look like dried-up ape shit."

Eli eased back into his chair, grinning. "And that's one of the things I've missed about you. Your poetic way with words."

"What the hell is going on?"

"I've had a few issues lately."

Dark green eyes glimmered with temper. "And why am I just now hearing about it?"

"Because you had your own issues to deal with. Watching over Mother, on top of the other stuff you're doing. You didn't need me piling anything extra on you."

Jonah dropped into a chair across from Eli and slouched. The relaxed pose didn't fool Eli. Before his stint in prison, Jonah hadn't exactly been soft, but he had been less wary, more trusting. After all that had happened—prison, losing his fiancée in such a horrific way—any softness that had remotely existed was gone. In its place was a hard-eyed, edgy man who rarely smiled and trusted only a handful of people. Eli felt honored to be among that handful. Especially since he felt a great guilt for not preventing what had happened.

"Since arguing with you is like trying to reason with a rock, I'll let that go for now. Tell me what's going on."

In a few succinct sentences, Eli explained about the emails, the odd incident with the window-washer platform, and today's near miss.

"And you actually believe Adam's claim that he only sent the one email? That he isn't the asshole behind the whole thing?"

"Yeah, I do. Not because he's not evil enough. We both know he's that and then some. But doing this without direction from someone else? That's not Adam. Without Mathias calling the shots, the man's as helpless as a turtle on its back."

"I'll reserve judgment about that, but nevertheless I trust your instincts. So, if Adam only sent one of the emails, there's someone on the inside doing the others."

"Yeah." Knowing how Jonah would take it, Eli sighed as he added, "I've asked Justice to use his influence to get Adam moved to another prison."

Jonah shook his head slowly in disbelief. "You're protecting the man responsible for your wife's death."

"Don't you think I know that, Jonah? There's a huge part of me that says just let him die in prison. But if I do that, I'm not any better than he is. This family's had too much heartache as it is…too many deaths."

"You're a better man than I am, Eli."

Eli wasn't going to argue with him. Beneath Jonah's hard shell of bitterness and indifference was the good, kindhearted brother he'd grown up with. He hoped like hell he'd see that man again someday.

"So what's the game plan?"

"Find out who's doing this and shut them down. Justice has assigned Kennedy and Nick to help out. Between the four of us, we'll find him."

"Four? Who else is working with you?"

"Kathleen Callahan. She's a bodyguard I hired for the girls a few weeks ago. She's a trained security specialist, freelances for Justice. She's agreed to stay here and help out."

"Is that right?"

The gleam in his brother's eyes told him he hadn't hidden his feelings. Jonah had a way of reading him when no one else could.

"I'll look forward to meeting Miss Callahan. But for now, tell me what I can do to help."

"Take care of my daughters. There's nothing more important than their safety."

"With the bodyguards already there for Mother and Lacey, they'll be safe. There's gotta be something else I can do."

"There isn't. I promise. The estate is well hidden, the chalet invisible until you're practically at the doorstep. Only the family, with the exception of Adam, knows I own the property. They'll be safe there."

No need to discuss the reason he'd originally purchased the small estate. His plan to get Jonah out of prison, one way or the other, and hide him there had never materialized. Jonah had managed to escape from prison through the most surprising source imaginable.

"Knowing Sophia and Violet are safe will free me up to find out who's behind this."

"If that's the way you want it, no problem. You know I won't let anything happen to them."

"Thank you. Now, what about you? Any news on your end?"

Any lightness Jonah had in his eyes died. And though it wasn't easy to see, Eli was encouraged that the rage had been tempered by determination. Jonah was on a quest to find the man who had murdered, at Mathias's orders, Teri Burke, Jonah's fiancée. After her body had been discovered, Eli didn't think he'd ever see anything in his brother other than a pure, unadulterated hatred. It was still there, but focusing on finding the bastard had steadied him, channeling the anger toward that goal.

"I have leads but no name yet."

"You still doing side work for Justice?"

"Yeah. Here and there. I'll turn down anything he offers until this is over."

"I'm sending two of the bodyguards I hired to watch the girls along with you—Macon Yates and Trevor Yost. They can protect them if you need to take a job."

"They'll be in good hands, but I'll stay there as much as I can."

"Appreciate it."

"Before I go see my nieces, why don't you tell me a little more about Kathleen Callahan?"

"Like what?"

His brother gave him a knowing look. "I grew up with you, remember? You might look like hell, but that gleam in your eyes is unmistakable. Tell me how, in just a few short weeks and with everything that's going on, you managed to fall in love with your children's bodyguard."

Kathleen finished unpacking and then gazed around the bedroom Teresa had assigned her. It was lovely, feminine without going overboard. The color scheme of sea foam blue and off-white was both restful and elegant.

When she'd asked the housekeeper if Eli's late wife had decorated it, sadness had come over her face. "Mr. Eli had the entire house redecorated. I just think there were too many bad memories for him."

After what Eli had told her about his marriage, that was understandable. How sad that drugs and alcohol had stolen Shelley Slater's life. Sadder still for the ones she'd left behind.

But Eli hadn't given up on Shelley. That, more than anything, showed what kind of man he was. Tenacious and stubborn to a fault, Eli Slater did not give up.

So many things to think about right now, so many things to accomplish. None more important than finding out who was behind the attempts on Eli's life. What she felt for him, what she couldn't allow herself to consider feeling, would have to be shoved aside.

Smoothing down her hair, straightening her spine, she opened the door and walked out. Eli's bedroom was right across the hall from hers. She told herself that was a good thing—expedient. She'd need to check on him through the night, and being so close was convenient. And when he was well again? She ignored the shiver that zipped through her at that thought.

She was startled when Eli's bedroom door opened. A large, dark-haired man with glittering, emerald green eyes and a stone hard face walked out. He closed the door behind him and then, turning to face her, gave her a quick up-and-down perusal. "Kathleen, I assume?"

She gave him a smile, held out her hand. "You must be Jonah."

He took her hand, shook it in a brisk, business-like manner. "That would be me. Mind if we talk a few minutes?"

Puzzled by his cold, almost adversarial attitude, Kathleen said, "Sure. Here?"

"Let's go to the sitting room at the end of the hallway. Less chance of being interrupted."

More than a little curious, Kathleen followed him to the room, unsurprised when he closed the door.

"Is something wrong? Is Eli okay? I—"

"He's fine—or as fine as he can be since he feels like hell and someone's trying to kill him. Eli told me who you are, how you came to be here."

"For some reason, that sounds more like an accusation than a statement. Do you have a problem with me being here?"

"No. My only concern is making sure neither Eli nor my nieces are hurt."

"How would I hurt them?"

"I don't know. Maybe by having them care for you and then leaving, breaking their hearts."

She had said something similar to Eli earlier today. Hearing her point thrown back at her by a virtual stranger wasn't comfortable.

"Eli, Violet, and Sophia mean a lot to me. I would never hurt them."

"Perhaps not intentionally. But they've been through too much hurt already. They already care for you. Maybe more than care. If you're not serious about them, stay out of their lives."

"I don't believe my relationship with Eli or his daughters is any of your business." She started toward the door. "And you, Mr. Slater, are an ass."

Something seemed to soften in his hard expression. "Can't argue with the truth. I just don't want to see them hurt."

"A brother protecting a brother is an admirable thing to do. Your execution needs a bit more finesse, though."

A knowing smile spread across his face. "Eli knows what he's talking about."

"About what?"

"He said I would like you. And damned, if he isn't right."

.

CHAPTER THIRTY-ONE

Eli stood at the end Sophia's bed, his heart literally breaking as he watched his six-year-old daughter snuggle close to her sister. Even as young as they were, they were independently minded but still often slept in the same bed. Tonight was no different, but he'd sensed an even deeper need in them to be close to each other. As much as he had tried to make this trip seem like an adventure, they were sensitive enough to know there was more to it than they'd been told.

Sending them away was the right thing to do, but Eli didn't know if doing the right thing had ever been so hard. His daughters had been his light in all the darkness that surrounded him. Protecting them was his number one job. But, damn, this was hurting.

"Eli?"

He turned, surprised to see Kathleen at the door. She'd said good night earlier, and he had assumed she'd already turned in. Dressed in light blue flannel pajamas, her long hair falling down her back in a single braid, she looked about twelve years old. But he'd held her in his arms, knew that beneath the sweetly prim attire were womanly curves and a delightful feminine softness.

In a move that felt completely natural to him, he held out his hand for her to join him. He saw the indecision on her face, but he also saw something she probably didn't want him to see and might not even acknowledge. There was the light of hope in her eyes.

Even as she told herself not to, Kathleen found herself joining Eli and taking his hand. He pulled her to stand beside him, and then they both smiled as a protective, even in sleep, Sophia wrapped her arms tighter around her little sister.

When she and Alice were growing up, they rarely had rooms or a bed to themselves. However, even when they did, Alice would inevitably steal into Kathleen's bed every night. She'd woken almost every morning to find her sister snuggled up to her exactly like this.

"Do you think it's possible to love too much?" Eli asked.

"Doesn't seem like there could be too much of something so good and pure."

"Were you and your sister like this?"

"Yes. Mostly when we were much younger. When she got older, she had an independent streak." She grimaced, remembering some of the shouting matches they'd had. "It was hard to accept."

His hand squeezed hers in comfort. She glanced up at him, feeling in this moment closer to him than any man she'd ever known. She took in his pale features, the lines of strain around his mouth, the hint of pain in his eyes, and was reminded of why she'd sought him out.

"Let's get you to bed."

Rough laughter rumbled up from his chest. "I've fantasized about you saying those words, and now that you have, I can't do a damn thing about it."

She tried not to smile, but it was hard. He was really so outrageous about his attraction to her. "Come on, Romeo, and I'll ignore the obvious sexual harassment of an employee."

Still holding his hand, she led him from the room. Eli stopped at the door, gave one last glance toward his sleeping daughters, and then switched off the light.

The master suite was five doors down the hallway. Kathleen led him inside and went to the bedside table, where she'd already placed a bottle of water and a pain pill. She turned and handed them to him. "I'll wait until you take this before I leave."

"Don't trust me?"

"Not in this, I don't. I know you've been in pain all day but haven't taken any of the pills the doctor prescribed."

"I don't like to take pain pills. They make me feel stupid."

"Well, you'll be asleep and won't realize how stupid you are."

Another rumble of laughter, and then he winced, grabbed his ribs. "Stop making me laugh. It hurts."

"Take your medicine, or I'll tell you all the jokes I know."

He swallowed the pill. "Happy?"

"Ecstatic. Now get into bed."

He glanced down at his jeans and shirt. "You're going to stick around while I strip?"

"I know you're hurting. Do you need me to help you undress?"

A sexy smile curving his mouth, his hand went to the zipper of his jeans and moved it slowly down. "Yeah. Thanks."

Kathleen backed away. Okay, so maybe she'd taken this nursing thing a little too far.

"Call me if you need me. I'm right across the hall."

He waited until she got to the door and said, "Thank you, Kat. It's been a long time since I've had anyone take care of me."

Refusing to let her heart melt the least little bit, she gave him a perfunctory nod and walked out the door. Even injured, sad over his daughters leaving, and angry about someone trying to kill him, Eli Slater was the sexiest, most dangerous man she'd ever met.

Just what had she gotten herself into?

Saying good-bye to Sophia and Violet had been harder than she'd believed possible. Kathleen had hugged each of them tight, finding it incredibly difficult to let them go. She could only imagine how Eli felt.

The girls had been heartbreakingly brave. Though their little lips had quivered and soft brown eyes had glistened with emotion, there had been no tears. She was glad of that, because she had the feeling if even one had started, everyone would have broken down, including her.

The instant the limo disappeared, headed to the private airport where the Slater family jet would whisk them away to France, the stoic smile disappeared from Eli's face, and his shoulders slumped as if he were exhausted. She'd checked on him on and off during the night and knew he hadn't slept well. His face was pale, and the pain in his eyes wasn't just because he'd said good-bye to his children.

"Have you taken anything for your headache?"

"No. I need clear thinking today."

"If you're in pain, how clearly can you think?"

"When I find out who's behind this, I'll worry about myself." His eyes went to the drive where the car carrying his children had disappeared. "If anything happens to them…"

She put a hand on his arm. "It won't, Eli. You did the right thing, sending them away."

"I know. Doesn't hurt any less." He gave her a puzzled look. "You and Jonah have words?"

"Why would you say that?"

"I know my brother well. And even though you're often harder to read than a book written in ancient Greek, I definitely sensed the tension between you two."

"Let's just say you have a very protective brother."

His eyes went hard. "Did he say something to upset you?"

Since putting a wedge between the brothers wasn't something she wanted, she said quickly, "Absolutely not. He just has a gruff demeanor."

"He didn't used to. Out of all of Mathias's children, he was the most softhearted, the kindest. I haven't shared a lot of our family history with you, but it might help you to understand Jonah better if you knew what he's been through."

"I know your father punished him by framing him for a crime he didn't commit and that he served time in prison."

"Yes. There is that. But my father also had Teri Burke, Jonah's fiancée, murdered."

Kathleen gasped, shook her head in disbelief. "How could a father—"

"Mathias Slater had more evil in him than anyone I've ever known. If he wanted something bad enough, he'd kill one of his own kids without compunction. In fact, he'd planned to have Jonah killed in prison, but thankfully, he trusted the wrong person to take care of it."

"I'm glad I never knew him. And thank you for telling me about Jonah. It explains a lot."

His expression was even grimmer than before. She imagined that talking about what his father had done hadn't helped his headache. Since they would soon start digging into Mathias

Slater's past, she had a feeling it would get much worse before it got better.

He turned and headed toward the house. "I've got some things I need to take care of this morning. Kennedy and Nick Gallagher will be here at ten. We'll meet in my office and start tearing into things. Have you met either of them?"

Following him, she said, "Grey's mentioned them, but I haven't had the pleasure of meeting them yet."

"You'll like them, especially Kennedy. You two have a lot in common."

"Really? How so?"

His eyes went warm with appreciation as he gave her a charming, mischievous grin. Kathleen felt the impact to her toes and had to swallow back a sigh of longing. She was so mesmerized by the look, and so happy to see his sadness disappear, that she didn't protest when he took her hand and led her up the porch steps into the house.

"For one, you've worked for two of the same employers. The irascible one and the charming one."

"She's worked for both you and Grey?"

"Yes."

"Good. I'll see if she can give me tips on dealing with my irascible boss." She glanced at her watch. "Now I'd better go make a call to the charming one."

He grinned again and then kissed her hand before letting her go. "I'll see you in a couple of hours."

Kathleen stood at the entrance to Eli's office. She could hear his voice, but since his office was empty, she wasn't sure where it was coming from. Seconds later, a portion of the wall opened, and Eli stood there, holding a cellphone against his ear. When he saw her, he motioned her forward.

Curious, she walked toward him, and Eli backed away, allowing her to enter. A few feet inside the room, she jerked to a stop and swallowed a gasp. Not only was this a hidden room, it was filled with stacks of files and reams of paper. More than a half-dozen whiteboards stood against the wall, covered with the names of people and companies.

"She's here now, Justice," Eli said. "I appreciate the help. No, that's okay. I'll call you if we come up with something."

The instant the call ended, Kathleen asked, "What's all this?"

He gave a broad wave of his hand. "Welcome to Eli's World of Insanity."

"I don't understand."

"After my father died and my brother was arrested, I tore apart every business deal, legitimate, illegitimate, and in between. This is the result."

She was speechless and more than a little ashamed of herself. Even though he'd made reference to the work he'd had to do to repair all the damage left by his father and brother, she had never fully comprehended what that had entailed. But looking at the evidence, she could only imagine the endless months this had taken him. To do this in addition to handling the day-to-day details of running the Slater House Hotels enterprise, plus his family's other businesses and being a father, was nothing short of remarkable.

Seeing all of this only reinforced what she already knew. Eli Slater was a man of tenacity, grit, and enormous strength of will.

Though she already knew the answer, she had to ask, "You did all of this by yourself?"

"I'm fortunate to have many good people working for me. It's in everyone's best interest that the Slater empire survives. While they handled the legitimate businesses, I concentrated much of my efforts on this." He shrugged. "It was either that or lose every damn thing. I couldn't let that happen."

"So this is Eli's famous war room."

At the sound of the deep masculine voice, they turned. A tall, dark-haired man stood at the door. Beside him was a lovely woman with chestnut-colored hair and an obvious baby bump.

"Hey, guys, come join the fun. Kathleen, this is Kennedy and Nick."

As she'd told Eli, she hadn't met either of the Gallaghers, but Grey had mentioned them several times. He seemed to think a lot of both of them, and it was a testament to his friendship with Eli that three of Grey's employees were going to devote all of their attention to finding out who was threatening Eli and his family.

"Teresa told us to come on in," Kennedy said. "She said to tell you she's headed to the market with Gunter."

"Thanks." He nodded toward a narrow table against a wall. "There's coffee and pastries. Help yourselves. Then we'll get started."

The instant Kathleen, Kennedy, and Nick were seated, Eli began. He'd conducted hundreds of business meetings in his life, but none like this one. Determining who was behind the threats was forcing him to have to go back through shit he had hoped to never have to deal with again.

He could almost hear Mathias's evil laughter. One more way to torture the son he'd despised.

Standing at one of the whiteboards, he said, "This is the list of all the shell companies Mathias and Adam created. Fortunately, most of them were dormant. Mathias would use one for a short time, close it up and move on. He had five employees totally devoted to overseeing these companies. He played them like Whac-A-Mole. As soon as one shut down, another was ready to pop up. The employees saw to the emptying, refueling, and making sure that nothing blew back on Mathias."

"What happened to the five employees?" Kathleen asked.

"Good question. I don't know. The shit fell all at the same time. Mathias's death, Adam's monumental screw-up." He shot Kennedy a pained look. "I can't believe you're here helping me, after all that the Slaters did."

"Eli, stop it," Kennedy said. "We all know who was responsible. Blaming yourself is ridiculous. If it wasn't for you, I never would have found justice for Thomas and our baby."

Eli acknowledged her words with a grateful look. What his family had done to Kennedy and to Nick was unforgivable. Thank God they didn't see it that way.

"Anyway, it was days before I started digging. By that time, the five were in the wind. I know they existed, but their names were as fake as the shell companies they oversaw."

"So that's five people, possibly more, who could have a grudge," Nick said.

"Yes." He threw out a grim smile. "I thought I'd start with the bad news first. These are five unknowns who could show up on my doorstep and I'd have no idea who they are."

Walking to the next board, he said, "These are the companies my father swindled and betrayed. Beneath each one, I've listed the major shareholders. I've done my damnedest to mitigate the damage done, going so far as to reimburse them for all their losses."

Nick whistled. "That must've cost millions."

Eli nodded. "And then some." He looked back at the board. "I'm sure there are many who are still angry. Not because of money, but maybe embarrassment."

"That's going to be the biggest problem, isn't it?" Kennedy said.

"What do you mean?"

"The human factor. You can detail the money...there's a trail to follow. But all those hidden feelings. People holding grudges rarely out themselves."

"You're right," Kathleen said. "Getting revenge isn't always about money."

Eli's gaze swept around the room, taking in all the names of the people Mathias had screwed. Kennedy and Kathleen were right about the human factor. Hatred or the need for revenge wouldn't show up on a ledger. But within this morass of names had to be the man or woman they were looking for. And if not?

Refusing to even consider such a thing, he trudged on.

By the time Eli finished and called a break, his throat was hoarse and his head felt as though a mariachi band and a rock band were competing with each other inside it. A year of repairing the damage that had taken his father decades to create had been a monumental undertaking. But explaining this mess was harder, at least emotionally. Kathleen saw what he'd come from. Hell, was it any wonder she was so hesitant to have a relationship with him?

Slumping into a chair, he rubbed his forehead and wished he had the energy to get up and take one of those damn pills the doctor had prescribed. He'd left them in his bedroom, determined to get through the day without needing them. Being such a stubborn ass could be a real pain.

As soon as he'd called a break, Kathleen had slipped out of the room. He couldn't blame her for wanting to get away. Having lived with this shit for so long, he thought he'd become inured to the impact. Apparently, he'd been wrong.

Both Kennedy and Nick had gone out, too, but he somehow felt less embarrassed for revealing all of this to them. They had lived and survived Mathias's and Adam's evil schemes. Neither of them could be surprised. But Kathleen was a different deal altogether. She had to be sickened by it all.

The door opened and closed, and Eli lifted his head. Kathleen stood in front of him, holding a glass of water and one of the pain pills.

"Take this before your head explodes."

Without looking at her face, he accepted the water and pill, swallowed both, and said, "Thanks."

Expecting her to leave again, he was surprised when she sat beside him. "Eli, look at me."

When he did, he wasn't surprised by the anger in her eyes. No decent person could help but be disgusted by what his family had gotten away with for all these years.

"I'm so very sorry."

Jerking at the apology, he asked, "For what?"

"For what you had to do, what you had to endure."

"Hell, Kathleen. Most people would figure I haven't done enough."

"No, they wouldn't. Not if they saw what I've seen. And not if they know you. Even Kennedy and Nick, who by rights should hate the Slater name, like and respect you. I'm proud to call you my friend."

The tension in his entire body loosened. There was nothing she could have said that meant more. "Thank you for that."

"Kennedy and Nick are taking a walk outside before lunch." She glanced over at the sofa in the corner. "I'm going to lower the lights so you can lie down for a few minutes. Give that pill a chance to take the edge off your headache."

Whether she wanted to admit it or not, Kathleen was a nurturer. She tried to act tough and unaffected, but the longer he knew her, the more her true nature was coming out. Wondering just how far he could push that nature, he said, "Come with me?"

Surprise flickered on her face, but she stood and held out her hand. On the way to the sofa, she stopped and dimmed the lights, then sat down. "Use my lap for a pillow."

Eli stretched out on the sofa and settled his head into her lap. The light was too low for him to see her expression clearly, but he saw the outline of her face and what looked like the curve of a soft smile on her lips. And just before he fell into sleep, he felt her fingertips brush gently, tenderly over his face.

Chapter
Thirty-two

Boise, Idaho

The bar with its dim lighting and nineties decor was just seedy enough for her purposes. Most people who came to places like this were here for two things: getting drunk or finding a one-night stand. It was the perfect place for her and the lowlife sitting across from her.

Joseph Braden gave a loud belch, grinned an apology, and said, "Did I mention you're the most beautiful woman in the world?"

Willing herself not to throw up at the rank smell of her target's breath, she gave him a sultry "let's do bad things together" smile. Only a few more minutes and she'd have him exactly where she wanted.

A cocktail waitress appeared at their table. "Can I get you another drink?"

Before he could refuse—she wanted him good and drunk—she smiled her thanks. "Yes, two more, please."

"You're trying to get me drunk."

The statement startled her, until she saw the wicked pleasure in his glazed eyes. Apparently, he didn't care if she had to pour him into his hotel room or that he wouldn't remember a thing tomorrow. Not that the remembering part mattered, since he wouldn't be alive.

"Not drunk." With a smooth, sexy move, she flipped her long black hair over a slender shoulder. "I just love to party, don't you?"

His eyes followed the movements of her hair, just as she'd planned, and then he gave her a goofy grin. "I live to party, darlin'."

No, he didn't, but not from lack of trying. She knew her mark well. A traveling salesman for a small computer company, Joseph Braden was only slightly less disgusting than his sleazy brother, Frank, had been. When he was out of town on business, he tried—and failed—to be a ladies' man. More often than not, he spent lonely nights in his hotel room watching porn and being harmless. Which was not what he was when he was home.

Depriving a wife of her husband or children of their father wasn't a concern for her. She had a job to do. However, she had to admit that this kill was a little more satisfying than most. Braden's wife had visited the emergency room four times in the past year. Clumsy woman apparently kept falling down and breaking bones. Their two kids, a twelve-year-old boy and an eight-year-old girl, had had two ER visits apiece in the past twelve months. Clumsiness and broken bones seemed to run in the family.

Killing an abusive bastard wasn't any more difficult than killing a saint. However, it did add an additional element of satisfaction.

Fresh drinks appeared before them, and she drank hers in three swallows. A high tolerance for alcohol was an asset in many ways, not least when challenging a low-life misogynist. Joseph Braden would not allow anyone, most especially a woman, to out-drink him.

As she watched him throw his whiskey back like a wannabe cowboy in a bad Western movie, she wished his death could be more brutal. That was unusual for her. Killing was a job she did well, but rarely did she want to prolong the actual event. But this man with his big fists and cruel twist to his mouth just made her want to give him some of what he'd been giving his family.

At that thought, she pulled herself out of her head. There were three basic rules an assassin learns early. Do the job. Get the money. Move on to the next target.

Forget those rules and get dead.

Knowing he was near his limit, she moved in for the figurative kill. Making sure her assets were on display, she leaned forward. "What do you say we make this party a private one?"

His glazed eyes took on an even sleazier glitter. "I got a motel room bout a block from here."

Oh she knew all about the motel room. In fact, she had already made a visit there in preparation.

"I've got a bottle of bourbon in my bag, along with a box of condoms." Just in case he didn't get the message, she leaned over even farther, so her breasts were directly in his face, and whispered, "I want it rough and wild. You up for it, cowboy?"

"Oh yeah, baby," he groaned. "I'm ready for a hard ride."

Glad to hear it, she stood and held out her hand. "Let's go."

He got to his feet, teetering slightly, and then straightened up the way people do when they're stupidly drunk but want to pretend otherwise. As she wanted him stupidly drunk, she smiled widely.

Since he was too far gone to remember to pay the check, she threw down enough for their drinks, plus an appropriate tip. Having anyone remember them wasn't in her plan. They were just two drunk, horny people. No different than ninety percent of the patrons in this dump.

With her arm wrapped around him, they weaved toward the door. She was glad she was in such good shape since the creep was practically making her carry him. Maybe that last drink had been one too many.

Refusing to contemplate that she'd have to do this all over again if he passed out on the street, she moved as rapidly out the door and down the block as she could.

Five minutes later, she took the key from his hand, unlocked the door to the motel room, and pushed him inside. He turned around, belched loudly, and gave her a drunken leer. "Get naked."

"Let's get something to drink first."

She took the bottle from her purse, set it on the dresser, and poured two generous glasses. Turning back around, she handed him one and chugged down her own glass. Watching carefully to make sure he downed his as well, she turned back and poured another.

He belched again, then shook his head. "Don't want no more. I drink anymore, gonna puke. Get naked." He reached out for her. "Now."

She laughed and skirted his grasp. "Come take a bubble bath with me."

He wasn't so drunk that he misinterpreted her delay tactic. Beady eyes going mean, he snarled, "Get naked, or I'll rip your clothes off."

As threats went, it was as lame as any she'd ever heard. Still, one did what the job demanded.

With one swift movement, she pulled her dress over her head and knew exactly what he would see—perfection. Dressed in a cherry-red demi bra that barely covered her nipples, a dental-floss thong, and four-inch stilettos, she was every man's fantasy. Her body, created by nature, perfected by man, was second to none.

"Take your clothes off, too, and then come find me, baby," she whispered softly and walked into the bathroom.

Having prepared the bath earlier, she only had to get him into it. She touched the water, grimacing at the coldness. Wouldn't do for him to jump out the minute he hit the water. She let out a little of the water, then ran more hot.

Not hearing any noises telling her he was coming inside, she opened the door and then growled softly. Slumped into a chair, his chin resting against his chest, her mark was snoring like a giant hog.

Her gaze dropped to the chair legs, and she smiled when she noted the rollers. Actually, this would work better. She hadn't been looking forward to fighting him. Bruises on him would invite questions she didn't want.

Going to the chair, she stood behind it and wheeled the unconscious man into the bathroom.

Her hands quick and efficient, she quietly undressed him. His pants were a challenge with him sitting, but he was so out of it, he never woke as she tilted his hips and pulled his pants off.

Now completely nude and sawing logs like a lumberjack, the man didn't appear to feel a thing when she pushed the chair all the way to the tub and upended him into the water. He hit his head on the edge on the way in, and she laughed softly. Really, this one had been one of her most cooperative marks in years.

Righting his body, she pressed his head beneath the water and held it down. Whether he was so drunk he couldn't wake up or the hit on his head had knocked him out, she didn't know. Whatever the reason, he didn't fight. When he'd been under a good five minutes, she pulled him up slightly. Checked for a pulse. Nothing.

She stood, watched as his head submerged again. Returning to the bedroom, she took the bottle of whiskey and brought it back to the dead man in the tub. She set the bottle beside the tub and then stepped back to take in the scene. Yes, exactly as she'd wanted it to look.

Taking five minutes or so to wash the glass she'd used and wipe down the rooms for her fingerprints was an irritant but had to be done. Her prints weren't on file anywhere, and she wanted to keep it that way.

Satisfied that she'd erased all evidence that Joseph Braden had been entertaining company when he'd drowned in his bathtub with a belly full of booze, she slipped her dress over her head.

The song *Another One Bites the Dust* playing cheerfully in her head, she walked out the door.

Now on to Dallas.

CHAPTER
THIRTY-THREE

Dallas

Eli channeled his fury and slammed his fist into the heavy leather bag so hard that it swung wildly. He grabbed it, held it still, and then began a series of rapid, focused hits. Every one of them designed for maximum force.

Two weeks. Two frigging weeks, and they weren't any closer to finding the fucker than they'd been before. Tons of information had been dissected and decimated, dozens of people had been investigated, with many more to go, and all they had to show for all their efforts were more questions and a crapload of possible suspects.

This wasn't going to work. Eli had felt all along that the attacks were personal. And though he didn't have a rational reason for that belief, his opinion hadn't changed. Kathleen and Kennedy had also both mentioned that the attacks might have nothing to do with the business at all. If that was the case, they were wasting time while the bastard was just sitting and waiting, looking for another opportunity to strike.

Damned if he would allow that to happen. He was ready. The injuries he'd sustained in the wreck were healed. It was time to be proactive. Being reactive was pointless.

Another series of punches slammed into the bag as he thought about today's revelations. It had started with a statement from Kathleen that had been well justified and one he should have been prepared for. Instead, it had taken him by surprise when she'd said, "Perhaps it would be helpful if we're all on the same page here. You, Kennedy, and Nick have information I've not been privy to. You need to tell me everything about your family."

Eli had frozen, knowing where it was leading yet unable to verbalize a reasonable objection. She was right. All of them needed all the facts and not just what the general public knew.

So, he had sat down and told her all he knew about what Mathias and Adam had been guilty of, including the murder of Kennedy's first husband, Thomas O'Connell. Both Kennedy and Nick had lived and suffered through that. They already knew about Mathias's responsibility in Jonah's incarceration and Teri Burke's death, but Eli had felt the need to take it one step further. For the first time, he'd also revealed that Adam, at Mathias's urging, had practically forced Shelley to overdose and kill herself. He hadn't gone into detail of when he'd learned this. That was a revelation he wasn't quite ready to make.

After that, Eli had called a break. The shock and pity in his friends' eyes had been hard enough to see. He hadn't been able to even look at Kathleen. He'd walked out the door and come down here to beat the shit out of a boxing bag because the people responsible were out of his reach. Mathias was dead, Adam was in prison, and Eli couldn't reach up and kick his own ass.

Bottom line, he had failed Shelley. He might not have known how ruthless Mathias was at that time, but he'd known enough. Enough to know that his family might be in jeopardy. Shelley had been vulnerable, an easy target. Eli had failed to do his job of protecting her.

Another wave of fury swept through him, and his fists slammed, slammed, slammed again.

Her heart breaking for him, Kathleen watched as Eli punished himself. She had come to the gym to work out, not knowing he was here. When he'd abruptly walked out of their meeting, she hadn't known where he'd gone, only that she was sure he wanted to be alone. She should have figured he'd come here to work out his demons.

She had been standing in the doorway for at least half an hour watching him deal with those demons. These last two weeks had taught her more than she'd ever believed possible about this man. Honorable, fierce when challenged about something he believed in, yet open-minded enough to listen to other points of view. She'd already known that he was protective about those he cared about, but she hadn't fully grasped how very deeply he took his responsibilities.

How had Eli grown up with a hideous father and disgusting older brother and survived? Not just survived. How had he developed into a man of honor, integrity, and depth? The answer, though not simple, was obvious. Eli Slater had purposely become the exact opposite of those two men.

Was he perfect? Absolutely not. He had proven time and again that he could be ruthless in pursuing what he wanted. But never with intent to harm.

When at last he stopped pummeling the boxing bag, he pressed his forehead against it. Sweat poured down his shoulders and back. The muscles in his arms and legs bulged from the strain. She had known he was in excellent shape. Having been in his arms, felt the power of his body, the solid strength of his muscles, she had known. Beneath the elegant, expensive clothing, the sophisticated veneer, was a body that spoke of discipline and good health. A man in perfect physical condition.

Her mouth watered, with appreciation, with delight, with desire.

And she knew, with one hundred percent certainty, that she was falling in love with him. Question was, what was she going to do about it?

The last couple of weeks had been so focused on uncovering the person behind the threats, they'd had little time to have any more intimate moments. She had a feeling Eli was deliberately giving her some time and space. He had already apologized for pushing her. And silly her, who'd insisted that she wanted him to stop his advances...she found herself missing them. His touches, those delicious slow kisses, the sexy looks. Even the handholding. She missed it all.

He abruptly whirled around, startling her. "I'll leave if you want to work out alone."

Instead of backing away, she walked toward him. "I don't want to work out alone." She jerked her head toward the mat on the other side of the room. "If you've still got some juice left, come take me on."

A sexy smile replaced the grim line of his mouth. His eyes smoldered with the wicked gleam she had missed. "Oh, I believe I have plenty of juice left in me."

Kathleen headed toward the mat, trying with all her might to ignore the sane, cautious voice inside her asking just what the hell she thought she was doing.

She stopped in the middle of the mat and turned to face him. It had been months since she had sparred with anyone. She kept in shape by running, lifting weights, and yoga. Not only was she out of practice, she was about to take on a man who, with one touch, could turn her body to liquid heat. She wasn't quite sure if this was the worst idea she'd ever had or the very best.

Eli stopped about five feet in front of Kathleen, took in the sight of her, and decided that the person who invented spandex should be given some kind of humanitarian award, because… damn, she was beautiful. A black, cropped top covered small breasts that showed delightfully tight nipples, as though she was already aroused, and revealed a generous portion of pale, smooth skin and flat, firm abs. Mid-thigh shorts hugged a taut, firm ass and slender, muscular thighs. Her hair was pulled back into a ponytail, and her lovely face already glistened with a fine sheen of perspiration.

He grinned. "Sweating already, baby?"

Those glorious eyes widened slightly, and he saw knowledge in them. Yeah, she knew this would end only one way. They'd been dancing around each other for weeks now. He'd backed off his advances, giving her time to breathe, to think. Telling himself the next move needed to be hers. The waiting had been harder than he'd anticipated, but he was glad he'd waited. No way in hell had he coerced her. She'd made this move on her own. And now, no matter who won this bout, he intended for both of them to come out supremely satisfied.

They circled each other silently, tension thickening with every second. If she looked below his waist, there would be no question of what was on his mind. He was rock hard. The thought of touching her firm, smooth flesh, of putting his tongue on those tight nipples, of sliding between her thighs into her hot, sweet body put him on the point of explosion.

It shouldn't have surprised him that she attacked first. If he hadn't been so immersed in his fantasy, he would have been better prepared. As it was, when she nimbly jumped and kicked his shoulder, it was all he could do to keep his balance. Righting himself quickly, his grin grew broader. "Score one for you. Now, let's play."

He went after her, ready to tackle her and bring her to the floor. She jumped out of his way, whirled, and managed a stinging punch to his stomach. Eli grunted, laughed again, and threw out a leg, tripping her. She fell onto the mat, and he was on top of her in a flash.

She heaved her body, trying to buck him off. When that didn't work, she wrapped her legs around him and tried to twist, to turn him over. Eli laughed again and did what he'd been dreaming about for what seemed like forever. Pushing her arms above her head, he loomed over her and kissed her.

The instant Eli's mouth touched hers, she stopped struggling. Kathleen had known where this was headed, and while the rational, self-protective part of her screamed dire warnings of impending heartache, she shushed them and went with what her heart, soul, her very being wanted. This man, this beautiful, exasperating, honorable, sexy as hell man, was what she wanted, needed...had been searching forever for. And he was hers. His intent was clear—he would take her. And her intent was just as clear—she would take him, too.

Though her arms were still stretched above her head, she could still use her legs. And since they were already wrapped around him, she made it easy for them both by spreading her legs wider and wrapping them around his hips. When his hard length settled against her sex, she moaned against his mouth. Never had anything felt so good...so damn delicious.

Opening her mouth, she welcomed his tongue, reveled in his taste, in his mastery of how to kiss like no one had ever kissed her. Eli kissed like it mattered. As if he were already making love to her, already inside her. He kissed with purpose.

Arousal swelled within her, and she became a writhing, wanton, needy creature who wanted only one thing. This man... her man, inside her.

Panting slightly, Eli pulled away from her luscious mouth to look down at her. Never had he seen anyone lovelier, more desirable. Eyes glittering with heat and need, she gazed up at him with approval, but beneath that, he also saw vulnerability, fear. He knew the fear had nothing to do with him physically and everything to do with her heart. When this need was sated, Eli swore he would get to the bottom of that worry. But for now... for now, this was what they both needed.

Using one hand, he shoved her top up, revealing small, gorgeous breasts. Groaning, he dropped his mouth onto a raspberry-colored nipple and suckled hard. She screamed softly and jerked upward, causing his cock to press deeper into her sex. Growling his frustration at the clothing impeding their final connection, he rolled away from her. Before she could react, he was pulling her shorts down and flinging them across the room. She surprised him by pushing him onto his back and straddling his knees. Hooking her fingers into his pants, she pulled them down, freeing him.

Eli kicked off his pants, rolled her back onto the mat, and came over her again. They were both breathing heavily, their mouths raking across each other's skin, their hands grabbing, caressing.

Looking down at her, he checked once more to make sure she was still onboard, that this was still what she wanted. When he saw the acceptance in her expression, he knew there was no going back for either of them. This moment, this first time, was more than sex, more than the need to connect or satisfy an urge. This was commitment in its most elemental form. She was his... he was hers. It was as simple, as basic, as that.

Pushing her legs farther apart, Eli thrust deep.

She came on a scream. Bright, blinding lights exploded behind her closed eyes, and her entire body took flight, soaring like a rocket. Her face buried in Eli's hard shoulder, her arms tight around his firm, damp body, Kathleen exulted in the most outrageous pleasure she'd ever experienced.

"Kat?"

"Yes?"

"Okay?"

"Oh yes."

"Ready to go again?"

Before she could explain that there was no way her body could experience an ounce more pleasure, he was proving her wrong. With short, fast thrusts, followed by long, hard plunges that reached deep inside her. Kathleen felt pleasure spiraling up all over again. Her hands tightening on his back, her fingers digging into his skin, an orgasm, stronger than the one before, approached.

"Eli. Eli. Eli," she whispered as she plunged over a cliff and once again flew into glorious, mind-blowing ecstasy.

With an animalistic groan that sounded both tortured and exultant, he shouted her name, and she felt him pulse inside her as he came.

They were still panting, his body only beginning to come down from the incredible high it had just experienced, when he felt her pulling away from him. Not physically. They were still wrapped around each other. Their damp skin almost glued them together. He was still inside her, softening but continuing to nestle within her warmth. But she was retreating from him all the same.

Raising his head, he looked into her eyes and confirmed his thoughts. The regret was there, and behind that, the fear had returned. He was determined to confront them both.

"Talk to me."

"This isn't a good time to talk."

He barked a laugh. "It's the best time. We're connected, as close as two people can be. We can't hide from each other. Tell me what's on your mind."

"Very well. I…" She closed her eyes briefly and when she opened them, they were swimming in tears.

"What, sweetheart? Tell me."

"This shouldn't have happened," she whispered. "I realize I instigated it, but I—"

"You instigated it? I think we can both take credit for that. And I totally disagree that it shouldn't have happened. In fact, I think it should've happened a long time ago."

She shook her head. "No." Pushing at him lightly, she said, "Let me up."

"Not until we've talked this out. Every time I try to get you to talk to me, you walk away. Not today. Tell me what's wrong. What are you afraid of?"

"I just can't have a relationship with you, Eli."

"Too bad, baby, we already have one."

"No, I mean…yes, of course we have a relationship. But we can't have a…a…an intimate relationship."

"That's exactly what we have, Kat." He pressed into her and hardened, stirring to life inside her. "What the hell do you call this?"

She released a small moan of pleasure and then shook her head. "This...this was just..."

"What?" Eli fought it, but the anger was setting in, erasing the incredible pleasure. "Tell me what you think this *just* was."

"Sex."

"You've never been a liar, Kat. Don't start now. No way was this just sex."

"Then what was it?" she challenged.

"This was two people making a commitment to each other in the most elemental way possible."

Her eyes went wide with horror. "No." She shoved at his shoulders. "No, Eli. Let me up."

Eli eased out of her, gritting his teeth at the residual pleasure. He sprang to his feet, now angrier than he'd been before. Grabbing their clothes that he'd flung across the room, he dropped hers beside her. "Deny all you want, Kathleen. Pretend you don't feel anything. Act like you just enjoyed a casual fuck. I know different. And you damn well do, too."

Turning his back on her, he slid into his pants and stalked away. If he stayed, he'd say things he would regret. Having their first time together turn into an argument sure as hell hadn't been in his plans.

CHAPTER THIRTY-FOUR

Kennedy took another sip of her iced herbal tea, hoping it would settle her queasiness. She'd read somewhere that being sick past the first trimester was a good sign of a healthy baby. If that were true, then this darling one would be the healthiest baby born in Texas. Which, despite the discomfort, was just fine with her. She'd gladly put up with nine months of nausea to have a healthy, happy baby.

She took another sip and then squinted at the computer screen. Her eyes were a little bleary, but something about this particular news piece had caught her attention. A niggling thought at the back of her mind made her keep coming back to it.

She twisted her neck to relieve the tension and then smiled as Nick came up behind her and began to knead her shoulders. She let her approving moan tell him he had hit the right spot.

He pressed a kiss to the top of her head and then sat down beside her. "How about we call it an early day? Start fresh tomorrow."

She glanced at the open door. "It's only a little after three. Kathleen and Eli will be—"

She stopped when he shook his head, a little smile playing around his beautiful mouth.

"What?"

"I went looking for Eli. Figured after his revelations today, he might need someone to talk to. Knowing him, I thought he might head to the gym to work out some of that anger."

"And?"

"Let's just say I stood outside the door and listened for about ten seconds and left."

"Why?"

"Because he and Kathleen were working out together."

"So? Why would that—" She broke off and found herself blushing a little. "Oh."

Nick laughed and leaned forward for a quick kiss on her mouth. "Yes. I've got a feeling we won't be seeing them again today."

"I'm glad. It's so obvious they're crazy about each other. About time they admitted it."

"So what do you say? Want to head home? Take a little siesta of our own?"

"Sounds lovely. Besides, if I have to look at one more hideous thing about Mathias Slater today, I'll probably have nightmares."

"Hey." He took her hand and squeezed it. "Is this too much? Digging back into the guy who destroyed your life can't be easy. It was selfish to even ask for your help."

"Thank you, but no, it's not too much. Mathias can't hurt me anymore. What evil that man perpetrated is in the past."

"And he's in hell, where he belongs."

"Yes." She kissed the hand holding hers and then twisted back to her laptop. "I'm at a dead end on this anyway. The thread kind of petered out on me."

"What were you pulling on?"

"Something Kathleen said a few days ago got me to thinking."

"What did she say?"

"About how Mathias couldn't have started being evil so late in life. That there must be decades of things he did that we know nothing about."

"That's probably true, but that's way too much crap to wade through without knowing what we're looking for."

"I know, but all the research we've done hasn't turned up anything substantial, so it makes sense that if the threats are related to something Mathias did, maybe it's not anything recent. Right?"

At his nod, Kennedy went on, "Mathias covered his ass probably more than anyone will ever know. So I started digging for crimes that didn't have his name attached to them, but looked like something he could've been involved with."

"Holy hell, Kennedy, that would take years to sift through."

"Yes, but I looked specifically for something that smelled like a cover-up but wasn't recent. Crimes that might fit Mathias's MO."

"That's an interesting thought, but again…a lot of shit. Did you find anything?"

"Yes and no. I found a lot of crap"—she grinned—"as you so succinctly put it. But nothing that screams a Mathias Slater cover-up."

"But?"

Her grin got bigger. "You know me so well." She slid her laptop around so he could see the screen. "Most small-town newspapers don't have online archives. This one did."

His eyes quickly scanned the information, not that there was that much to read. "This is some little town in Nebraska. Several robberies occurred on the same night. No names are listed but the suspects are referred to as 'youths'.

"Crazy. Right? But I keep going back to it."

"Why?"

"Because of this." She pulled up another article from the same little town. It had a newsy hometown feel, mentioning various goings-on in and around the town. His eyes zeroed in on one line that mentioned that the Slaters from Dallas, Texas, were visiting relatives outside Omaha.

"See? These robberies happened during the time frame Mathias and his family were there."

Nick gave a slow nod. "He would've been young back then… might've even been before he and Eleanor married."

She sighed and then slumped in her chair. "It was decades ago, though. So crazy. Right?"

Instead of agreeing with her, Nick began to click on more sites. The gleam in his eyes told her he was on to something.

"What? You see something?"

He held up one hand. "Just a sec."

As he worked on the laptop, Kennedy took another sip of her tea. Then, propping her arms on the table, she rested her head on them and gazed dreamily up at her husband. A year and a half of marriage and she was more in love with him than she'd ever thought possible. Not a day went by that she didn't marvel at how blessed she was. When she'd lost Thomas and their baby, she had thought her life was over, that finding information on Mathias Slater to put him away would be her only purpose in life. She'd never believed she could find happiness again. Now, with Nick, she was unbelievably, ecstatically happy. And in a few months, she would be a mom.

Showing that after more than two years off the job, her husband still had a cop's observant eyes, he kept his gaze on the computer screen as he said, "You keep looking at me like that, we'll be going to find the nearest guest bedroom and have that siesta you promised me."

Her heart skipped a beat. "Why don't we—"

"Hot damn."

She sat up straight. "What? You found something?"

"Yes. Maybe." His eyes blazed when he looked at her. "Mathias was supposed to spend the summer with relatives in Dorman, Nebraska. Six weeks into what was supposed to be a three-month stay, his father came for him."

"How old was he?"

"Twenty."

"Over eighteen. He would've been charged as an adult. How could he—" She cut off at Nick's cynical look. "Of course, his father paid to get him out of trouble. No wonder no names were mentioned. I wonder if all the boys had parents who paid."

"Either that, or the others were minors."

"So do you think this is something, or are we just whistling Dixie?"

"You do have a sweetly seductive whistle." His phone chimed with a text message. Glancing down, he read it and then reached over to close her laptop. His eyes twinkling with amusement, Nick held out his hand and stood, pulling her to her feet. "That was Eli. He said something's come up. Wants to call it quits for the evening. Start back again tomorrow."

She beamed up at him. "Gee, a whole night off. What will we do?"

"Oh, I think we'll find something."

She leaned into him. "We make a good team, don't we?"

"In every way possible."

Standing on her toes, she pressed a kiss to his mouth. "I love you, Nick Gallagher. You're my heart."

All the love in the world in his eyes, he said quietly, "And you, Kennedy Gallagher, are the very beat of mine."

No matter how often she told herself that hiding in her room for the rest of the evening was a cowardly thing to do, Kathleen couldn't make herself leave. Every dire warning she'd given herself had come true. She had known that staying here with Eli, working side by side with him every day, would be dangerous. This was one time she hated being right.

She paced back and forth across the bedroom floor. A sensible, reasonable person would have showered by now. She still wore the workout clothes she'd put back on after—

Shoving her fingers through her hair, she shook her head. Stupid, silly, sentimental Kat. Eli's scent was all over her. When she showered, it would be gone. And all she would have was the memory of something she could never have again.

The tears started before she even realized it. Everything blurred, and with a hopeless sobbing sigh, Kathleen fell across her bed.

In her weakest moments, she had dreamed of how it would be if they'd made love. She had imagined it would be enjoyable, memorable. What lifeless words for the utter magnificence of what had happened. Eli had said their lovemaking had been making a commitment in the most elemental way possible. Despite her denial to him, she agreed. That's what it had felt like.

She had hurt him with her lies, her refusal to accept what she felt, what he felt. Hurting Eli was the last thing she wanted to do. But if she didn't continue to deny these feelings, if she accepted what her heart wanted to accept, what then? How many times did it take for her to see that when she loved, she lost? Everyone in her life, beginning with her mother, who she had adored, was gone. Everyone. If she lost Eli, too?

No, she couldn't take the chance. Could not risk her heart. Losing him would destroy her.

She would do her job, help him find out who was trying to kill him, and then she would be gone.

But until then... She closed her eyes and allowed herself to relive the most intensely beautiful moments of her life. Moments that could never be repeated.

CHAPTER THIRTY-FIVE

Eli had spent a miserable night alternating between hurt and fury. Knowing that Kathleen was across the hall and all he had to do was walk a few steps and confront her was of no use. More than a couple of walls separated them.

He tried to force the regret away, but it kept getting in the way of his self-righteous anger. He had known damn well she wasn't ready for more, wasn't prepared to face her feelings, much less his. And what had he done? He'd railroaded her into an ultimatum. Was it any wonder she'd shut him down?

He was groggy and out of sorts. However, he wasn't about to change his routine. Breakfast with his daughters was the highlight of his day. Everything always seemed brighter after spending a few minutes with them, even if it was only through a webcam.

After breakfast, he had a morning full of meetings at his office, then it would be back here at home for another afternoon of research, conjecture, and more damn guessing games.

If there was one advantage to sleeplessness, it had given him plenty of time to come up with a plan. He was tired of the non-action. Tired of waiting around. This shit had to stop. And the only way to stop it was to bring the bastard out in the open, trapping him in his own game.

After showering, Eli dressed and then walked out of his bedroom. Kathleen's door was closed. The temptation to knock and have it out with her was great, but he resisted. Until the threat against his family was neutralized, perhaps it was best to back away, pretend yesterday hadn't happened. When things were calm and his life didn't resemble a nightmare, he'd pursue her to the ends of the earth.

Feeling slightly more optimistic with a plan in place, Eli pushed open the kitchen door, looking forward to having breakfast with his daughters. He didn't expect to find that Kathleen had arrived ahead of him and was already seated. Even though she usually joined them for breakfast, somehow he had assumed she would skip today. It showed him, more than anything else she could have done, that she wanted to be with him...with them. Whether she was ready to admit it or not, they were already a family.

Throwing her a small smile, he settled at the table, prepared to have breakfast with his three favorite girls.

They sat across from each other, she and Eli, pretending for his daughters' sake that everything was fine. And even though Eli had smiled at her a time or two during breakfast, Kathleen knew things were far from fine.

"And Gammie bought us new shoes and socks and pillows and a truck."

She'd been listening while Sophia listed all the things their grandmother had purchased for them. From the sound of it, Eli's mother and sister had been making up for lost time by purchasing everything two little girls might want. But the last thing was different.

"A truck?" Kathleen said.

Sophia nodded emphatically. "Gammie said no, but Aunt Lacey said Texas girls should have a truck. Mine's blue. Violet's is green."

"That sounds really pretty."

Thrilled to have an audience, Sophia said, "I'll go get it." Before Kathleen or Eli could protest, she'd jumped from her chair. While Sophia went to get her truck, Violet started with her own litany of gifts her grandmother and aunt had purchased.

"It's not really all that much, Eli." An older woman appeared on the screen behind Violet. In her mid-sixties, Eleanor Slater was still a beautiful woman. Fragile-looking, with skin stretched tightly on her face, she had a delicate, refined air about her. When Kathleen had first met her, via their video calls, she had seemed stressed, uncertain. The longer her grandchildren stayed, it seemed the more relaxed and happy she became.

"I'll have to send a second plane to bring back all the stuff you and Lacey are buying them," Eli joked.

At the mention that they would at some point be leaving, Eleanor's eyes darkened and her smile disappeared. "I've so enjoyed having them here, Eli."

"When this is over, Mom, you can come back home. See them every day."

"Oh, I don't know." She waved a fluttering hand. "After everything…"

"It'll be time, Mom."

Eleanor's gaze flickered nervously over to Kathleen and then back to Eli. "Does Kathleen know about—"

"No." The abruptness of Eli's answer was startling. A tense silence followed, and for the first time, Kathleen felt like an outsider.

"Here's my truck!" Sophia dropped a large toy truck on the table.

Everyone laughed, and the tension disappeared as Violet insisted on showing off her truck, too.

Breakfast ended with "I love you's" to Eli, and for the first time, Sophia, followed immediately by Violet, said, "I love you" to Kathleen.

Her throat clogged with emotion, Kathleen barely managed an "I love you" in response before the screen went blank.

The instant the call ended, Eli went to his feet. "Are you finished?"

She glanced down at her empty plate. Even though she hadn't acknowledged her hunger, missing dinner last night had given her an appetite. She'd eaten her omelet and toast without even realizing it.

"Yes."

"Come into my office. I need to talk to you."

Eli then thanked Teresa for breakfast and walked out the door.

"He's not upset with you, Miss Kathleen," Teresa said. "He's missing his young ones so much."

Knowing that Eli's grimness wasn't just about missing his children, Kathleen smiled, thanked Teresa for breakfast, then headed toward Eli's office. She stopped at the door. She rarely came in here. It was his domain, masculine without the extreme tidiness of the rest of the house. It wasn't junky so much as it gave her an idea that Eli's management style was more hands-on than most CEOs.

"I wanted to talk to you before I left for the day."

Kathleen braced herself to deal with the aftereffects of yesterday's monumental event. "The condemned ate a hearty meal" flitted through her mind. Though she had no real clue what he was going to say, she got grim amusement that at least she'd had a good meal before Eli told her to leave.

Instead, he completely took her off guard by saying, "I'm going to trap the bastard."

"What do you mean by trap?"

"This research is getting us nowhere. Our only option is to take the fight to him."

"And how are you going to do that?"

"Be as visible as possible. A helluva lot more visible than being chauffeured to and from work every morning in a bulletproof limo. When he makes another try for me, we'll take him on. If he's a hired gun, which would surprise me, as inept as his attempts have been, we'll have him lead us to the person behind this."

The very thought of Eli putting himself out there as a target chilled her blood. "I think it's a bad idea."

"You have a better one?"

No, she didn't. And the reason she didn't like the idea of using Eli to set a trap for the killer had nothing to do with the plan itself. As these kinds of plans went, it was fairly straightforward. No, it wasn't the plan, it was the target she had a problem with. Explaining why she didn't want him to take this risk would require her to acknowledge something she refused to give a name to. So, she went with a lame comeback.

"It's too dangerous."

"What's the alternative, Kat? Bury myself here at home until the guy gives up and goes home? He's not going to give up, and I refuse to let him control my life any longer."

"Putting yourself out as bait is too big of a risk."

"But one I'm willing to take. I'm not going to hide under the covers."

She wrapped her arms around herself and walked to the conference room door, seeing the boards they'd been working with. All of this information and not one solid lead. He was right. Staying inside, hiding from this unknown threat, was counterproductive. Her rational self said this was the best way to catch a killer. Her emotional self was shouting that it was too risky. She hadn't wanted to care for this man. And now that she did, she was thinking with her heart and not her head. To hell with that.

She whirled around. "Fine. I want to be in on it."

"In on it how?"

"No one but those closest to you know I was guarding your children. Anyone who saw us taking them to school might assume we were doing so as a couple. So we can keep up with that pretense. If you're out and about, putting yourself in the crosshairs of this person, I'll be with you. It'll be assumed we're dating, and I'll be there to watch out for you. No one has to know it's fake."

In a half-dozen strides, he was in front of her. Grabbing her arms, he shook her slightly. "Fake? You think what's between us is fake?"

"This isn't the time, Eli."

Pulling her closer, he smashed his mouth against hers in an angry kiss. "When would be a good time, Kat? When this is over and you can leave? You do your job, kept my kids safe, help me find the asshole trying to kill me, and then when it's over, you can leave with a clean conscience?"

Eyes glittering with anger, he shook his head. "No, I think now is a damn fine time to talk about us."

"There is no us."

"Then what was yesterday about? You weren't faking that, baby."

"That was—" She stopped, swallowed, and tried again. "It was just—"

"Don't say it, Kat. Don't say it was just sex. Don't you dare try to pretend you don't feel anything for me."

She wondered what was more painful. Seeing something you desperately wanted and being too afraid to go for it? Or having it within your grasp, opening your heart to all the possibilities, and then losing it?

Showing that he was more attuned to her than anyone she'd ever known, Eli asked quietly, "It's time to tell me. The truth this time. What are you afraid of?"

No longer able to hold back, Kathleen gave him the answer he deserved. "I've lost everyone I've ever loved, Eli. My entire family is gone. One at a time. How the hell can I take the risk of loving someone else? I can't go through that again. I just can't."

"I understand that fear. But if you don't take that risk, what have you lost?"

Beautiful dark eyes filled with so many emotions—compassion, frustration, affection, and desire—stared down at her. The shadows beneath his eyes told her that he had slept as poorly as she had last night. The scar on his forehead reminded her of the close call he'd had a couple of weeks ago.

And now he was wanting to go out and put himself in danger again?

No, she couldn't do it.

She backed away, pulling out of his arms. "We'll pretend to be a couple. You can still set the trap, but you'll have additional protection."

"That's it, then? Pretend and nothing else?"

"That's all I have to give you, Eli." She turned her back on him, walked to the door. "Let me know when you're ready to begin, and we'll plan accordingly."

She left the room before he could say anything to stop her. If she turned back to look at him, she feared what she would see. Not just hurt, not just sadness. She feared she would see disappointment, perhaps even disgust at her lack of courage. She might feel those things herself, but she could not bear to see them in Eli's eyes.

Eli watched her go. He wanted like hell to call her back, reassure her that he wouldn't ask her again for something she wasn't ready to give. Problem was, he didn't know if she'd ever be ready. Yes, she had lost a lot. And while he understood her fear, he couldn't deny his frustration.

Pushing anyone into anything wasn't his way. And pushing Kathleen into a relationship with him was definitely not what he wanted. But, dammit, she cared for him. He knew she did. He saw the tenderness in her eyes, felt the passion in her body. Saying yesterday had just been sex was ridiculous. He'd seen the lie in her face even as she uttered the words.

How many women had pursued him? He was smart enough to know part of his attraction was his wealth, but more than a few women, just as wealthy or wealthier, had made their interest known. Hell, he'd even had a couple of them, disgusting as it was, come up to him during Shelley's memorial and offer to comfort him. No one, until Kathleen, had interested him. And no one in his life had enthralled him as much as this woman did. So how ironic was it that the only woman he wanted was too frightened to love him?

He picked up a framed photograph of Shelley from his desk. After her death, he hadn't wanted to hurt the children by taking away any of the pictures that had been around the house. He never wanted them to forget her, and never would he taint their memory of her with his own bad ones. Shelley had been a beautiful woman. A tall, slender blonde with an infectious laugh and good sense of humor. Before she'd started using again, they'd had some great times together. And after the first couple of stints of rehab, when he'd tried to convince himself she would stay sober, there had been some good times. After that, not so much.

If Adam had been right about one thing, it was that Shelley's first loves were alcohol and drugs. But she hadn't deserved what happened to her. Hadn't deserved Adam's and Mathias's cruel interference. Without them, perhaps she would have stayed on the road to recovery. But just like everything else his father and brother had touched, she had been destroyed.

Eli opened a bottom drawer and dropped the photograph inside. He had stopped loving Shelley long before she finally left him. It was time to let her go for good.

Hell, even if Kathleen wasn't afraid to get involved, was it any wonder that she had reservations? His family wasn't exactly a 1950s sitcom. And she still didn't know everything. His mother's reference this morning had been a grim reminder of that. When this was over and his family was no longer being threatened, he would tell her everything. Deciding she didn't want to be with him because of his screwed-up family was one thing. Making the decision because she was too afraid she'd lose him was ludicrous. Nothing worthwhile was without risk.

Turning toward the door, he made a decision. He was in love with the prickly, unpredictable, frustrating, amazingly strong, vibrantly beautiful Kathleen Callahan. She was the woman he wanted. And if there was one thing he *had* inherited from his father, it was sheer dogged stubbornness. He would not give up.

CHAPTER
THIRTY-SIX

Kathleen rushed into the conference room. She was late. She and Eli usually had lunch with Kennedy and Nick in the small dining room before coming into the conference room for the afternoon. Not only had she missed lunch, but she was fifteen minutes later than she had intended. She did, however, have a good reason.

She gave a quick nod and smile to both Kennedy and Nick who sat at a table, laptops in front of them. Eli was standing at one of the whiteboards, apparently staring at it and hoping for answers. Kathleen didn't have any yet—just more questions. But she had discovered something that might lead to another avenue.

"Why didn't you tell me Lacey almost died when she was a child?"

Eli jerked around, the expression on his face more puzzled than startled. "It was a long time ago."

Showing that both she and Nick were in the dark, too, Kennedy asked, "What happened?"

Eli gave a one-shoulder shrug. "It was Lacey's fifth birthday. My parents threw her a lavish party at one of our hotels downtown. I remember that Lacey wanted to go to one of those pizza joints that cater to kids, but Mathias insisted on the party since he wanted to invite some of his business associates.

"Lacey is highly allergic to peanuts. Can't even be in the same room with them. My mother swore she'd talked with the kitchen staff and warned them. Lacey took one bite of her birthday cake and went into anaphylactic shock."

"Did your parents not have epinephrine close by?" Kennedy asked.

"Yes. My mother always carried an injection with her. When she opened her purse to get it, it wasn't there. Fortunately, someone else at the party had a similar allergy and had one with her. It saved Lacey's life."

He frowned at Kathleen, confused. "What does any of this have to do with Mathias?"

Instead of answering his question, she continued on the same path. "What did the kitchen staff say about the cake?"

"They denied using anything related to peanuts in any of the cooking. Adam has a similar allergy, though not as strong. He ate the cake and was fine. It was decided that someone must've given Lacey something to eat that had peanuts in it, and she didn't remember." He shook his head slowly. "I never would have related that incident to any of this. It'd make no sense."

"It might not be that big of a coincidence," Nick said. "We wanted to wait until Kathleen arrived to tell you about a thread Kennedy uncovered yesterday."

"What's that?" Eli asked.

"Kathleen actually helped me with it," Kennedy said.

"How so?" Kathleen asked.

"A few days ago you asked what if this had nothing to do with Mathias's or Adam's businesses. What if it was a personal vendetta? So I started going farther back to when Mathias was a young man."

Kennedy told them what she'd uncovered last night about some robberies in Dorman, Nebraska. And Nick added in the information he'd found about the Slaters of Dallas, Texas, visiting relatives during that time.

Before they finished, Eli was shaking his head. "I appreciate you guys for digging that deep, but relating everything that's happened to my family over the last fifty years to what's happening now is crazy. Every family has odd, scary things happen to them. Lacey's incident is no different.

"And the robberies in Nebraska? We don't even know if that had anything to do with my father's family. There was more than one group of Slaters in Dallas. Though, to be fair, I'm sure we're the craziest of them. But there's no way to be sure that it's the same—"

"But there is," Kennedy said softly.

"How?"

"I found an article from the social section of the *Dallas Times* in the summer of 1966. It said that Silas and Hazel Slater, along with their son, Mathias, would be visiting family in Nebraska during the summer."

For the first time since the conversation had started, Kathleen saw a sparkle of hope in Eli's expression.

"It's something, Eli. A thread we didn't have before." Not giving any thought to how it would appear to Kennedy and Nick, or what she was conveying to Eli, Kathleen reached for his hand and squeezed it. "Let's explore this for a few days before you set yourself up as a target."

She saw the doubt in his eyes and pressed forward, not feeling the least bit guilty for using his feelings for her. She'd do anything to keep him safe. "Please. For me?"

A cynical light entered his eyes, and he pulled his hand from hers. Kathleen felt the loss of his touch like a slap. He had seen her plea as the manipulation it had been. Still, she was happy to hear him say, "Fine. Let's dig up what we can about some crimes that happened half a century ago. See if there's anything to it. Then we'll go from there."

Without looking at her again, he walked out of the room.

Kathleen stood at the doorway leading out onto the balcony of the second-floor parlor. Eli sat in a chair at the corner, staring into the dark. She could literally feel his exhaustion and frustration, his sadness. Three additional days of digging were yielding results, and they all believed they were finally on the right track. There had been plenty of people to look at. Mathias had betrayed, screwed, and manipulated people long before he became a business tycoon. Narrowing it down to one event had felt impossible, but there was light, though only a dim pinprick, at the end of the tunnel.

Earlier today they'd been optimistic, if not exactly jubilant. There was still so much to unearth, but heading in the right direction after so many wrong turns was such a refreshing change, they'd all been more upbeat. That had changed an hour ago. Eli had received a phone call that had practically sent him over the top. Violet had tripped over her new toy truck and had broken her arm. It was a clean break, and Eli had talked to the doctor himself, who had assured him it would heal fine. But that hadn't stopped Eli from being worried or desolate that he wasn't there to hold her and comfort her. Even Violet, with her new purple cast, had reassured him she was fine, but Kathleen had seen not only the worry but also the resolve in his eyes. He wouldn't be able to hold out much longer. If something didn't break within the next twenty-four hours, she was certain he would be putting plans in place to trap a killer.

If he did that, and something went wrong? If the killer finally finished his job? No. She could not accept that.

She watched him shift his shoulders in a weary shrug. And, suddenly, she knew the answer. Reassuring him with platitudes and smiles wasn't what he needed. He needed her.

Even though her knees were knocking as she approached him, she had never been surer that she was doing the right thing.

She touched his arm, felt the hard muscle and, beneath that, the tension. Since she had no words to make him feel better, she did what he had done for her so many times in the past. She simply took his hand and held it in hers.

He squeezed it gently, and then, as if it was the most natural thing in the world, he pulled her down into his arms. She put her head on his chest and closed her eyes to prevent the tears from escaping. He hadn't touched her like this since their argument. Even as she told herself the distance was best, she had been afraid he would never touch her again.

They stayed like that for several long moments, taking comfort from each other until it wasn't enough. She raised her head and gave him the words they both needed her to say. "I want you, Eli."

His eyes searched hers, and what he saw in them must have been what he needed.

With a sexy, low growl, his mouth covered hers in a devouring kiss and melted any remaining doubts away. This gentle, kind, infuriating, gorgeous man needed her. And despite all her fears for the future, she knew without a doubt she needed him.

Eli didn't know what had changed, didn't care right now. All he knew was she had finally come to him. This woman he felt like he'd waited a lifetime for was once again in his arms. She tasted better than he remembered, felt delicate and beautiful. He wanted to cherish her and at the same time take her hard, fast.

"Come to bed with me."

At her soft sigh of acceptance, Eli stood with her in his arms and headed for his room.

She laughed softly. "In a hurry?"

"You have no idea." Need surging like a tidal wave, he was surprised he could even speak, much less walk.

"Oh, I don't know about that. I'm feeling decidedly needy."

He glanced down at her, surprised at the sultriness in her voice. Amazing eyes glittering with desire, full lips glistening from their kiss, Kathleen Callahan was the most beautiful creature he'd ever seen. And tonight, she was all his.

He pushed opened the door to his bedroom and strode to the middle of the room. Lowering her to her feet, Eli forced himself to slow down. The last time had been all about heat and the need to quench a massive thirst. And though that thirst was still there, he wanted to cherish her...love her the way she should be loved. He undressed her slowly, carefully, savoring the moment. She was wearing a light blue blouse, and with each button he undid, he glimpsed an inch more of creamy skin. When at last the blouse was undone, he slipped it off her shoulders and went dry-mouthed at the loveliness he'd uncovered.

"You're beautiful."

"No one has ever made me feel this way, Eli. No one."

Lifting his gaze to her face, he saw the truth in her words. All the tumultuous emotions and raging desire he felt for this woman was reflected in her eyes.

He had vowed to go slow, to relish every second, but when her fingers began to unbutton his shirt, he forgot that promise. Swooping down, he took her mouth in a ravaging kiss. Drowning in desire, in heat and need, he raised his head moments later to realize his hands had a mind of their own and they had been busy.

She stood before him, nude, beautiful, and delicate, almost fragile. Her skin gleamed beneath the dim glow of the chandelier, glowing as if she had an inner light. His eyes roamed over creamy shoulders, slender arms, then traveled to her small, firm breasts with rose-pink nipples. He remembered that the other day, after his mouth had ravaged them, they had turned a ripe raspberry color. He wanted to see that color again. He lowered his head and licked at one, delighted that it tightened against his lips. Opening his mouth, he captured her nipple and suckled, gently and then harder. Beneath the roaring in his ears, he heard a gasp and then a whispered, "Yes."

It was all the encouragement he needed.

Pushing her gently onto the bed, he followed her down and devoured every sweet spot. First with his hands, then he kissed, nibbled, licked, and lapped. Ravished. Cherished.

Kathleen was drowning in a pool of whirling desire, her body heating from the inside out, throbbing with need, aching. Eli's hands and mouth were everywhere at once, but she wanted more of him. Needed to taste him, take him as he was taking her.

"Clothes," she gasped out.

"Hmm? What?"

She laughed, glorying in the happiness, rightness of this delicious moment. "You were incredibly efficient in getting my clothes off, but you need to work on yours."

He lifted his head. "Damn. I'm still dressed?"

"Much to my disappointment, yes."

"Let me just take care of that. One." A kiss on her mouth. "More." A suckle at her breast. "Moment." A long, gentle lick in the crease of her thigh.

She lay gasping as he rose to his feet, sure she'd never breathe right again. And then her breath stopped altogether when he stripped. The hard, sleek muscle of him was a delight. How could she have forgotten in just a few short days how very beautiful this man was?

Her eyes drifted below his hard, flat stomach and settled on the evidence of how much he wanted her. Unable to resist, she sat up and wrapped her hand around the steel-hard shaft with its silky covering. At his groan, she looked up into his eyes and saw the glittering heat, the monumental need. Keeping her gaze on his, she leaned forward and licked the opening at the head, savoring the salty, musky, masculine taste of his desire. Before she could go further, take him in her mouth and give them both the pleasure they craved, Eli pushed her until she fell back onto the bed.

He was over her in an instant, his mouth everywhere, kissing, licking, sucking. Taking everything she had to give, asking for more than she ever believed she had to offer. Their gasps and moans mingled into the music of rapturous sounds. When at last he settled between her legs and slid inside her, Kathleen almost cried at the incredible, indescribable moment. After that one sleek glide, he allowed her a second of acceptance of the hard length inside her, and then he began to hammer into her. Laughing with joy at the glorious taking, she joined in the rhythm, meeting every hard thrust with as much force as she could, delighting in the elemental power of their bodies. This was heat, need, absolute surrender. This was love.

They reached their climaxes together. Need had wrapped her up as tight as a rubber band, and in letting go, she was flung up to the stars, where she was suspended in complete ecstasy before she peacefully floated back to earth.

Gasping as though he'd just run a marathon in record-breaking time, Eli caught himself before collapsing on top of the beautiful woman beneath him. He'd just battered her body like a jackhammer. Damned if he was about to crush her, too. Rolling onto his side, he gathered her close, relishing the aftermath of the incredible experience. Her body, glowing with perspiration, snuggled into him, and Eli closed his eyes, at peace at last.

An hour ago, he had been as close to detonation as he'd ever been. Violet, his precious little girl, had broken her arm, and he couldn't be with her. Couldn't hold her, reassure her...hell, reassure himself. When he'd seen Violet's eyes gleaming from recently shed tears, saw her little chin wobble before she bravely set it to firm, he had wanted to reach through the screen and grab her.

This maniac...this freak was keeping him from his daughters. If he hadn't already been infuriated at the situation, today's incident had topped it off. He could wait no longer.

"I can hear you thinking."

He squeezed the woman in his arms, marveling at both the delicacy and strength in her body. "That another superpower you have? Hearing people think?"

She shifted in his arms to look up at him. "What other superpower do I have?"

"Making me want you more than I've ever wanted anyone in my life."

"Wow. That's quite a superpower."

"The question is, will you use your superpowers for good or evil?"

"What do you think?"

Trailing his fingers down her body, his hand stopped on her mound, and then his fingers touched the still-swollen nub at the top of her sex. At her gasping groan, he whispered, "I think for the good. Don't you?"

She arched her back as he slid one finger, then two inside her. "Oh yes…good," she whispered. "I'll only use them for good. I promise."

Eli chuckled softly. "That's my girl."

He wanted to see her come again. Before, he had been focused on giving and taking pleasure. Now, he wanted to concentrate on her reaction, witness the spiraling need blossom within her. Watch her take her pleasure, relish that he could give it to her and she would take it from him. As his fingers plunged, retreated, and plunged again, he watched her go from the beginnings of arousal to full-fledged bliss. Eyes wide, lush mouth opened and rounded, gasping for air, graceful body arched in surrender and pleasure, she groaned loudly and then softly, sweetly screamed her release.

"Beautiful," Eli whispered. "Perfect."

Supremely happy and relaxed, Kathleen snuggled back into Eli's embrace. She had never felt so safe, so cared for in her life. In Eli's arms, she was the most desirable woman in the world, all because that was the way he treated her. The pleasure he gave her, the care he took with her.

"I wish it could be like this forever." She hadn't meant to say those words out loud. She didn't want to spoil what had just happened, or the happiness she felt.

"When all of this is behind us, when we uncover the truth, we'll go away together, the four of us, forget about what we've been through."

Could she do this? Could she actually give in and allow herself to love, totally and forever? She had lost so much. What if she lost Eli? What if something happened to Sophia or Violet? How could she bear that?

"Now I can hear you thinking, Kat."

She tried for a laugh, knew it sounded strangled, fake. "So we share the same superpower, Mr. Slater?"

He rolled them over so that she was on her back. "Don't borrow trouble, sweetheart. You can't predict the future, what's going to happen. There's nothing wrong with being happy in the moment."

Even though fear still gnawed like a roaring beast, she determinedly pushed it away. This time with Eli was too special to spoil with her insane fears about the future.

"I am happy, here with you. And I would love for all of us to go away together."

He smiled, pressed a warm kiss to her mouth, and then gathered her in his arms again. And even though she knew he was comforting her, to reassure her, she saw the fear in his eyes as well. What if the threats never stopped? What if the path they'd headed down was the wrong one?

What if they never knew when death would come?

CHAPTER
THIRTY-SEVEN

Teresa Longview considered herself one of the most fortunate people in the world. She was healthy, had a job she loved, and lived in a castle with a family she adored. Sophia and Violet were precious and a delight to care for, and Eli Slater was the most generous and kind employer she'd ever had.

Having lost her husband years ago and never being interested in being married again, caring for Eli's family was her idea of the perfect life.

And now Miss Kathleen was with him. Even though their journey to love hadn't been easy—what with the threats made against Mr. Eli's family—Teresa delighted in seeing their feelings grow for each other. She was a romantic at heart, and watching them fall in love was just about the sweetest thing she could imagine. When their troubles had passed, she was sure they would stay together. The girls would return home, and the family would be complete.

Now if only those troubles would end.

Going to the market every few days used to be a treat. But now, with the knowledge of danger, Teresa found herself preoccupied with looking for threats more often than she did the ripest melons or the freshest asparagus.

She used to drive herself to the market, using one of Eli's cars—another treat for her. But now, Gunter, Eli's chauffeur, drove her wherever she needed to go. The first few times had been fun, but now it felt stifling.

"I only need a few items today. Shouldn't take me more than fifteen minutes or so."

Gunter gave her a polite nod in that patient, serious way of his. Teresa had tried several times to engage him in conversation, and though he was never rude, he either just nodded at her or answered with one or two words. Still, she had a small affection for him. Her late husband had been a man of few words, too.

Knowing he'd gotten out of the car and watched as she walked into the grocery store, Teresa paid little attention to her surroundings. Her eyes skimming the short list she'd made, she went quickly through the store. Having shopped here for years, she knew each aisle as well as she knew her own kitchen. She was reaching up for a jar of olives when a soft voice with a distinctive Texas twang said, "Oh, let me get that for you."

Turning, Teresa took in the young woman smiling sweetly at her. Tall, with long black hair pulled back with a barrette, she wore a Cowboys sweatshirt, jeans, and boots and was quite possibly one of the loveliest women Teresa had ever seen.

"Thank you," Teresa smiled at her. "These shelves seem to get higher every year."

Reaching up, the woman grabbed the jar and handed it to Teresa. "My pleasure. Um… Do you shop here often?"

"I have for years. Is there something I can help you find?"

"I was looking for the local honey. My husband has allergies and was told if he ate local honey it might help." She took a jar of honey from her buggy. "This one comes from Houston. It's not local, but it's still Texas, so maybe that's local enough."

"Oh no, dear, you don't want that one." Teresa took the jar from her. "Let me show you the local section. It's two aisles down."

"I hate to trouble you. I've not shopped here before and feel so lost."

Taking young people under her wing was as natural as breathing to Teresa. "It's no bother at all. You just follow me."

Pushing her cart forward, Teresa headed toward the aisle where the local products were shelved. She pointed to several different brands of honey. "These three are made here in Dallas. I've tried all three, and there's not much difference between them. All of them have nice, smooth taste."

"Oh, thank you so much." The young woman took a jar from the shelf and then held out her hand to Teresa. "My name is Mary Ellen Wilson. We moved here from El Paso a month ago, and it's taking me forever to feel comfortable."

"I know exactly how you feel. You'll get the hang of it, though. The city is large, but the people here are very helpful and friendly." And because she truly was interested in people, she asked, "It's just you and your husband?"

"For right now." Tears glistened in her eyes as she said, "We've been trying to get pregnant, but so far it's not happening."

"Oh dear." Teresa patted her arm. "Don't you worry. When you least expect it, I'm sure it'll happen for you."

"I hope so." She sniffed delicately. "Vinnie's getting really discouraged."

Teresa gave an exasperated sigh. "Men can be that way."

Wiping away the tiny teardrop that was glistening on her flushed, pretty cheek, Mary Ellen said, "You're so sweet. I miss my mama and granny back in El Paso." She paused and then haltingly asked, "Would you…I hate to impose, but would you be interested in having coffee with me in that coffee shop next door?"

Teresa thought about poor Gunter having to wait on her. "It's no imposition at all… It's just, I have someone who brought me here. I'm—"

Teresa broke off when she saw the disappointment in Mary Ellen's face. "Tell you what, I'll go see if he minds waiting. If he doesn't, I'll meet you over there as soon as I finish paying for my groceries."

"Oh, thank you. While you do that, I'll just pay for this honey and then meet you there."

Teresa quickly paid for her purchases, noting Mary Ellen was two registers down from her. The young woman waved and smiled at her as she exited the store.

Teresa rolled the cart loaded with bags toward the exit and wasn't the least bit surprised when Gunter met her at the doors. "I'll take that for you," he said.

Feeling only slightly guilty, she said, "Do you mind if I run into the coffee shop for a few minutes? There's nothing in the bags that needs to be refrigerated, and I—"

"Not at all. I'll be waiting."

Promising herself she wouldn't keep him waiting long, Teresa entered the coffee shop and saw Mary Ellen sitting in a corner, already sipping coffee. "Come on over. I took the liberty of getting a latte for you. Hope that's okay."

Teresa took a seat, thinking what an unexpected delight it was to make a new friend.

She took a sip of her coffee and gave the older woman a sweet, simple smile. Playing the innocent was one of her favorite roles, simply because of the challenge. She'd left innocence back in Ireland decades ago, so when she got the chance to pretend, it was extra fun.

Teresa Longview was a lovely woman with a friendly smile and that motherly instinct that seemed to come natural to some people. Apparently, that particular trait had been left out of her own gene pool. Even though she had little sympathy for stupid people, she did appreciate the kind ones. They were so eager to do good and were, therefore, so much easier to mislead.

Wanting to make sure Teresa felt completely at ease and would therefore be all the more rattled later on, she kept the conversation light and frivolous. They talked weather, the differences between El Paso and Dallas, and the best kind of casserole for a winter meal. Happy to see Teresa completely relaxed, she took another sip of a truly excellent latte and then smiled brightly. "I have a confession to make."

"What's that, dear?"

"I didn't really invite you to coffee because I'm lonely."

Teresa got that look on her face most people did when they were fearful that they'd been hoodwinked into a meeting about selling cosmetics or vacuum cleaners. It always amused her, because once she finished explaining the reason for the meeting, they no doubt would have much preferred the sales pitch.

"I have a small favor to ask of you."

"Favor?"

"Yes. Would you like to save two lives?"

Teresa jerked back in surprise. "What on earth are you talking about?"

Seeing no need to delay further, she explained, "You have a sister and brother-in-law in England. Linda and Douglas Abbot. Just outside Surrey."

"How could you know that?"

"Oh, Teresa, my dear, I know everything." She took her cellphone and flipped to a photo. "You'll be happy to know that your sister's arthritis is much better. She and Douglas were able to take a nice long walk in the park just the other day. See?"

Teresa's chair made a loud screech when she scooted it back. "I don't know what this is about, but I am not amused."

"Now don't be getting too hasty. I'm just getting to the good stuff. Besides, I didn't arrange this meeting to amuse you, dear."

"Your accent." Teresa shook her head. "You're not from Texas at all. You're from Ireland?"

"Dublin. Ever been there?"

But Teresa, the dear lady, was no longer in the mood for chitchat. "Tell me what this is about. How do you know my sister and brother-in-law? What do you want?"

She swiped a finger across the screen of her phone. "Here's another photograph of your sister and brother-in-law. They don't look near as happy, do you think?"

The elderly couple sat back to back in wooden chairs. Their torsos were tied with the same rope. A single long cloth was wrapped around both of their heads.

"Secured this way, they can barely move a muscle. Very difficult to stay that way for long. Very painful, especially for poor Linda. Her arthritis must be hurting her badly."

The horror in Teresa's eyes was exactly the reaction she was looking for.

"What have you done to them? What do you want?"

"I've not had the pleasure of meeting them yet. My associate is seeing to their care. It's up to you to make sure I never do meet them."

"What do you mean?"

"Just that you work for a man who needs to die, along with the young woman who's living with him, Kathleen Callahan. You arrange for their deaths, with my help, of course, and your sister and brother-in-law will be released, unharmed. They'll be allowed to live out the rest of their lives with the last few days as only a bad memory."

Her face now as white as the tabletop holding their coffee, Teresa whispered, "You're the one who's been trying to hurt Mr. Eli and his family."

Instead of answering, she clicked on another photograph. "The saying 'a picture's worth a thousand words' might be cliché, but in this instance, I think it stands the test of time. Take a look at the relatives of the last person who refused me."

She shoved the phone just inches beneath Teresa's nose. "I was actually quite proud of my work here. No muss, no fuss. Bullets to the head, point-blank range."

Teresa let loose a sound between a strangled moan and a gasp. "You...you killed an entire family?"

"Of course I did. 'Twas quite easy, really. But that's neither here nor there." She withdrew the small vial from her purse. "There's enough poison here to fell several horses. Shouldn't be any problem to handle two people. Just pour it into their coffee or tea. It'll be over quickly, and then you can move on. I do advise you to get out of town as soon as the deed is done, though. The pesky authorities have a tendency to look down on murder."

"How dare you ask such a thing of me!"

Teresa went to rise but stopped when her wrist was grabbed. "You will be responsible for killing the only family you have left. What would your mum say to such a thing?"

When Teresa didn't say anything, she went on, "You've got two days to get it done. If I don't hear about the deaths of Eli Slater and Kathleen Callahan within forty-eight hours, I'll be heading to England to put bullets in the heads of your beloved sister and her husband."

Satisfied she'd made her case, she took one last sip of her coffee and rose, leaving the vial on the table in front of Teresa. "No need to reimburse me for the coffee. This was such a treat for me."

When Teresa called out, "Wait," she stopped at the door.

Looking nothing like the cheerful little woman she'd met an hour ago, the obviously devastated Teresa said, "Why do you do things like this?"

A wicked smile lit her eyes and for the first time she allowed Teresa to see her real nature. "Because it's fun."

CHAPTER
THIRTY-EIGHT

Time was running out. Kathleen felt the tension as if a timer attached to a bomb was clicking the seconds down to zero. Eli was getting ready to put his plan into action. He hadn't said so in words yet, but she knew it was just a matter of time before he did. She stood before the whiteboard, seeing the connections but still not seeing everything she needed to see. They still didn't have that one missing piece that would complete the picture. Who the hell was doing this?

"We're getting there, Kathleen."

She turned to Kennedy, who sat at the table, working diligently.

"I know we are, but I'm afraid if we don't have it soon, Eli will do something to bring it to a head."

"If he does, he'll have plenty of backup. You have to trust him."

"There's no one I trust more. I just—" She couldn't say it. Couldn't even think it.

"Despite what's happened, I'm glad you two found each other."

She wanted to be glad, too. Oh, how she wanted to be able to let go and just be in love. Feel the joy, the giddy excitement. Instead, fears and anxieties smothered all the wonderment.

"What are you so afraid of, Kathleen?"

"Why would you even have to ask that? Isn't it obvious? I'm afraid for Eli and his children. For—"

"That's not everything, though, is it?"

Seeing the warm compassion on the other woman's face, Kathleen shrugged helplessly, unable to keep up the pretense. "I've lost everyone I've ever loved. How can I not be afraid? What if something happens to Eli? To his daughters? What if I fall in love with all of them only to lose them?"

"Would not loving them keep them safer?"

That stopped her in her tracks. "No. I—no, I guess not."

"Then why wouldn't you cherish every single moment instead of being so afraid? Is a lifetime of being miserable and alone really better than an undetermined time of happiness with a man who adores you? With precious children who love you?"

Just because she could see what she would be losing out on didn't diminish the fear. In fact, that almost made the fear stronger. If she let her guard down, let go and allowed herself to love, what then?

But just how stupid was it to be afraid to be happy? Was the certainty of being miserable and alone for the rest of her life really better than having all she'd ever dreamed of, even if how long it lasted was uncertain?

"Let me tell you a story." Kennedy's soft voice broke through Kathleen's misery. "About a little girl who had everything—loving parents, a wonderful childhood that anyone might envy. And then one day she had nothing. Her parents were killed, and she went into foster care. She hated it, but she learned to cope. She grew up, not always strong and brave, but resilient. Then one day she meets this amazing, kind-hearted man and falls madly in love. They marry and are ecstatic to learn they're having a baby. It's the perfect life she'd always dreamed of. Then, in one endless nightmare, she loses everything again. The husband she adores, the baby she desperately wants. She's forced to leave behind everyone she cares about."

Kennedy was talking about her own life. About losing her first husband because of Mathias and Adam Slater. Kathleen knew the basic facts, but Kennedy had never talked to her about the specific events.

"How in the world did you cope?"

"I was frozen for a while, and then I got to work. It helped to know who my enemy was, my target for revenge. Focusing on getting justice for Thomas and my baby was my goal. But I was still alone, still brokenhearted. Just a shell of a woman with only one goal: to make the Slaters pay.

"And then Nick came back into my life. He had been Thomas's best friend and was my rock after his death. I didn't plan it...never believed it would happen. But I fell in love with him, completely and forever.

"Everything I've lost, every heartache and tear, led me to him. I never imagined it was possible to have this kind of happiness again. But I'm so incredibly grateful for it, and I plan to cherish every single moment. And if, for whatever reason, I lose them, I will be shattered, heartbroken. But not for one single, solitary moment will I ever regret what we had."

Her voice went to a fierce whisper. "This is living, Kathleen. This is what life is about. The good and the bad. The agony and ecstasy. Being afraid to live life to its fullest is a death all in itself."

Tears filled Kathleen eyes. This woman had lost even more than she had and still had the courage to love. Shame filled Kathleen for her own lack of courage. How awful of her to have denied her love for Eli. He had told her she was a coward, and she acknowledged the truth. But no more. Dammit, no more.

Kathleen jumped up from the sofa and raced toward the door. Then, stopping in the middle of the room, she turned and ran to Kennedy, giving her a hug. "Thank you. Thank you for talking some sense into me. For being my friend."

Kennedy laughed and hugged her back. "You're welcome. Now go get your man."

Kathleen ran down the hallway. She could see Eli and Nick standing on the side patio, talking. Their grim expressions said the conversation was serious and heated. As much as she hated to interrupt them, she didn't want to wait any longer to tell Eli she loved him. A noise coming from the kitchen stopped her in her tracks. Was that someone crying?

Knowing the sounds could only be coming from Teresa, Kathleen shifted direction. She pushed open the door and stopped, startled to see the stoic Teresa Longview with her head on the kitchen table, sobbing her heart out.

"Teresa? What's wrong?"

The older woman jerked in surprise and then jumped up. "Nothing's wrong. I...I..." Teresa looked around the kitchen, her expression panicked.

Recognizing fear and emotional overload, Kathleen pulled up a chair and sat at the table. "You can talk to me, Teresa. What's upset you?"

"I can't talk about it, Miss Kathleen. I just can't..." She looked out the window, her eyes unfocused.

Something was terribly, terribly wrong.

Kathleen stood, went to the cabinet for a glass, and then filled it with water. Placing a hand on Teresa's shoulder, she said, "Take a few sips."

Teresa drank half the glass. Then she looked over at Kathleen, and her face crumpled.

Feeling real fear now, Kathleen grabbed the woman's hand. "Did you lose someone? Is someone in your family ill?"

Tears rolled down the older woman's grief-ravaged face. "I can't...I can't..."

"I'm going to go get Eli. I'll be right back."

"No." She grabbed Kathleen's arm. "No. I—" Then she began to sob again. "Yes. Yes. Go get Mr. Eli. He has to know. I can't go on like this."

Jumping up from her chair, Kathleen went out the door and to the patio where Eli and Nick were just headed inside.

"Eli, something's wrong with Teresa."

He was running by her in an instant, Nick right behind him.

She ran after them but stopped when Kennedy called out, "What's going on?"

"Something's wrong with Teresa," Kathleen said. "Eli and Nick are with her."

She and Kennedy pushed open the kitchen door just in time to hear a violent, vicious curse from Eli, who was sitting in the window seat at the other end of the kitchen, holding Teresa. The woman was sobbing on his shoulder as if her heart was breaking in two.

Nick was in the corner on his cellphone, his voice urgent and hard.

"What is it? Did she tell you?" Kathleen sat beside Eli, patted Teresa's shoulder, and waited to see what the hell was going on.

"I wouldn't do that to you, Mr. Eli." Teresa sobbed against his shoulder. "To Miss Kathleen either. No matter what. I wouldn't. But I'm just so worried."

"I know you wouldn't, Teresa. I'm sorry this is happening. Now, let's go over it again, once more."

Eli listened once again, his fury building as Teresa recounted her experience at the grocery store and coffee shop.

"When she showed me the photograph of Linda and Douglas, I almost fainted. I just couldn't comprehend someone doing something like that."

"No one could." Even as Eli said the words, he cursed himself for not thinking about it. He thought he had protected his loved ones, but dammit, he had forgotten about Teresa's family. He had made it easy for the culprit. So damn easy.

"We've got to do something, Eli," Kathleen said.

"Nick's on the phone with Justice right now. He's got people in London."

"Can you describe her for us?" Kennedy asked.

"Yes. She's a beautiful woman. Long black hair, almost exotic looking. Silvery-gray eyes. She's about five-seven or so. Slender build but curvy, too. She pretended to be from Texas. Introduced herself as Mary Ellen Wilson from El Paso. But when she told me about…" Teresa's mouth trembled. "She changed her accent. She's Irish."

"She had an Irish accent?" Kennedy's tone held shocked alarm.

Eli knew exactly what Kennedy was thinking and refused to even contemplate such a thing. "It's not her, Kennedy. I know her. She would never do something like this."

"Who?" Kathleen said. "You know who it is?"

"I don't think she would either," Kennedy said, "but Teresa just described her to a T."

"Her? Who?" Kathleen said. "Will someone tell me who you're talking about?"

Looking sick, Kennedy answered, "Irelyn Raine. Grey's former partner."

Grey stormed into Eli's house, prepared for war. Nick had told him what he'd needed to know to get people on the ground in London and find Teresa's family. Once that was in place, Grey had called back for more details. When he'd gotten those, he'd become livid.

No way. No fucking way had that woman been Irelyn. She liked Eli. He knew she did. There was no way she would hurt him. And to arbitrarily want Kathleen dead, too? No. There was a helluva lot more to this than met the eye.

They were gathered in the main parlor. Nick and Kennedy sat on one sofa, Kathleen and Eli on another.

"Where's Teresa?" Grey asked.

"I persuaded her to take a mild sedative," Kathleen said. "She's sleeping."

"Where's the bottle?"

Eli nodded at the table, where a small innocuous-looking bottle sat, holding about an ounce of liquid.

"I'll have my lab guys analyze it. Hopefully, we'll have the results in a few hours. I'll have them check for fingerprints, too."

"I've already checked," Nick said. "I had a print kit in my car. Only one set of prints are on them. They're Teresa's."

"Grey," Kennedy said. "I don't believe this woman is Irelyn either, but I'm not sure anyone else is convinced."

Eli shook his head. "I don't want to believe it's her, Justice, but if it's not, then who the hell is pretending to be Irelyn and wanting both Kathleen and me dead?"

Dropping into a chair, Grey blew out a ragged sigh. He had known he might have to share some of his suspicions but had hoped for more time. Time had run out.

"A few months back, I learned about a couple of murders. The victims were not of the highest quality of individuals. They were in different parts of the world, seemed to have nothing in common with each other. Except for the way they died."

He glanced over at Nick and Kennedy. "One was Bobby O'Leary."

"Who's Bobby O'Leary?" Kathleen asked.

"He's a former hired killer that got dead," Nick answered. "Kennedy and I have been trying to determine who killed him. So far we've come up empty."

"What does this have to do with what happened today?" Eli asked.

"The method of murder was poison."

He could see the comprehension hit them at once.

Kathleen stood. "That's how Frank Braden was killed."

"Yes. Just that way."

"So you knew all along it wasn't Alice? You knew and you didn't tell me who else it could be? Why would you—"

"I had no names, still have no names, or suspects. I hoped that by digging into each one of their deaths—Braden's, O'Leary's, and the other men's—we would find a link. And find the killer."

"You're trying to determine if it was Irelyn, aren't you?" Nick asked.

"I was trying to make sure it wasn't. I don't believe it's in her to—" He shook his head. "I just wanted to make sure it wasn't her."

"I don't understand," Kennedy said. "Why would you even think it was Irelyn?"

There were certain things Grey could still not share, and the reason he suspected Irelyn might be behind the murders was one of them. At some point, he might have to reveal certain secrets about his and Irelyn's past, but not yet. Not until it was an absolute necessity. He owed Irelyn that, if nothing else.

"That's something I can't say right now. And again, I don't believe it is her. Besides, Irelyn can emulate any accent. There's no reason for her to be so blatant about her Irish background, unless…"

"You're right. It's too obvious," Kathleen said. "But why would anyone try to frame her?"

"Damned if I know."

A sound had them all turning toward the doorway, where Teresa now stood. Grey had met her only a couple of times, but she now looked totally different from the self-possessed motherly woman he remembered. She appeared to have aged a decade.

Eli's heart turning over in regret for what she was going through, he went to his feet. "What is it, Teresa?"

"I can't believe I didn't remember this before. I was just so…" She waved her hand, obviously overcome with emotion.

Kathleen went to her, put her arm around her. "What didn't you remember?"

"My brother-in-law, Douglas. He's been having memory problems. Not diagnosed with dementia or Alzheimer's quite yet, but there's the worry. Linda, my sister, is a proactive sort. She bought Douglas a watch for his birthday a few months back. It was from one of those places that puts a locator device inside. That way, if he became lost, and his memory grew worse… She never told him. He's been self-conscious about not being able to remember things. But if he was wearing it when he was taken…"

Grey had already pulled his phone out. "I'll call my guys."

Teresa's eyes swam with fresh tears. "So they might be able to find them? Before it's too late?"

"Yes. That's definitely a possibility," Eli assured her.

"Well that's good. That's good," she whispered.

Showing the compassion and warmth that were such an intrinsic part of her, Kathleen squeezed her shoulders in a hug. "Why don't we go get you a cup of tea?"

Teresa nodded, gave a small smile. "That sounds lovely."

The instant Kathleen led Teresa away, Eli glanced at Justice, who had just ended his call. "What do your people know about Linda and Douglas so far?"

"They found signs of a struggle at their apartment. Said it was apparent they'd been gone a day or two. Their two dogs and three cats were frantic and starving."

"They can trace the chip?"

"Yes. They're working on it now."

"Having them found…that's the main issue right now. I can't believe I didn't get them protection. Just so damn shortsighted of me."

"None of us thought it would go this far, Eli. It's on all of us that we didn't think of it." Justice glanced at the door and then turned back to Eli. "There's something else we haven't talked about that concerns me."

"What's that?"

"The woman pretending to be Irelyn. She wanted Teresa to poison Kathleen, too?"

"Yes." Just the thought scraped his insides raw.

"We need to discuss why," Justice said.

"What do you mean?" Kennedy asked.

"Why include her at all? If Eli's the target?"

"You're saying, if she's a professional, she would only focus on her target? Not someone else?"

"Yes. Contract killers don't normally kill without purpose or a reason. I'm not saying there's not collateral damage sometimes, but this is too specific. Poisoning only you should be no problem. Why include Kathleen?"

"What are you thinking?"

"I'm thinking this is more complex than one person with a grudge. We need to dig deeper."

"You're right," Kathleen said from the doorway. "There's got to be a link between Frank Braden and Mathias Slater."

"You've already done a ton of research on Braden," Grey said.

"Yes. I'll get my notes and start digging. We've found so many threads. Maybe this is one more. One that might lead to the final piece in the puzzle."

"Could it be that two different people hired the same killer?" Kennedy asked. "And that's the only connection?"

Nick shook his head. "That's stretching coincidence beyond the breaking point. There's a connection, we just need to find it."

"I'll go get my files and bring them to the conference room." Kathleen shot Eli a look. "Could you help?"

Eli was on his feet in seconds, headed to her. Maybe he read something of what she wanted to talk to him about, because his expression went hot and fierce. Without a word, he took her hand and led her up the stairway.

They waited until they were in her bedroom to speak. He shut the door and turned. Before he could ask what was going on, she blurted out, "I realize this is quite possibly the worst timing in the world for this, but I've put this off for too long. I'm bad about putting everything else in front of what's really important. I can't do that with this...with you. Not anymore." She paused a second, swallowed past a dry throat, and continued, "I never expected this…it's inconvenient as hell. Absolutely terrible timing."

A brilliant smile spread over Eli's face as if he knew exactly what she was trying to say.

Kathleen forgot every word except what mattered most. "I love you, Eli. I'm in love with you."

Letting go a rough laugh, Eli grabbed her up and whirled her around in a circle. "You are incredible, and I love you beyond measure, Kathleen Callahan."

She buried her face in the crook of his neck, embarrassed by her incredibly inept declaration of love and enormously relieved he had ignored all the garbage she'd spouted beforehand.

"I'm so bad at this."

"You're better than you think you are." He pushed her head up so he could see her face, the tender look in his eyes melting her. "And I'll give you plenty of opportunities to say it over and over again. Say, about sixty, seventy years."

Emotions swelled to a fever pitch inside her. "I don't deserve you, Eli. You've put up with so much crap from me. Can you forgive me for—"

His fingers pressed against her mouth. "You deserve everything good, my sweet Kat. I plan to spend the rest of my life making sure you get it."

They shared a kiss of promise and hope. Wonderment.

Heated moments later, Eli raised his head. "We've got a lot to talk about…plans to make."

"Yes. But first…"

"Yes." He dropped a hard kiss on her mouth. "But first we have a killer to hunt down."

With reluctance, she pulled out of his arms and went to her laptop on the desk. "I brought everything with me. It seems crazy, doesn't it? That there's a connection between your father and Braden?"

"Hell if I know. They were both sleazebags. As far as I know, Mathias never got involved in prostitution or human trafficking, but I wouldn't rule it out."

Eli grabbed her laptop while she grabbed several notebooks. As they headed out, Eli stopped at the doorway. "Whatever we find…no matter what it is, we'll get through it together. Right?"

"Yes. If there's one thing this whole ordeal has taught me, it's that I don't want to go through life alone." She flashed him a bright smile. "You're stuck with me, Mr. Slater. Deal with it."

"Oh, I intend to, Miss Callahan."

CHAPTER THIRTY-NINE

"Linda and Douglas were found outside London in an abandoned farmhouse," Justice said. "Both are suffering from exposure and dehydration. Your brother-in-law may have had a small stroke. They're evaluating him. Other than a slight blood pressure problem that's being treated, your sister is fine."

Teresa took in a ragged breath and released it with a sob blended with laughter. "We Longviews are a hearty bunch."

Eli squeezed her shoulder. "You saved their lives, Teresa. Remembering that tracker in Douglas's watch was the key to finding them."

Teresa gave him a teary smile and then turned to Justice. "Thank you for sending your people to save them. I owe you…" Her gaze went around the room. "I owe all of you for saving them."

"I'm just glad we were able to help." Justice stood. "I've got an appointment to get to. Keep me posted on any new developments."

"Will do." Eli gave Nick and Kennedy a telling look. "If you don't mind, Kathleen and I would like to talk to Teresa alone."

Nick nodded. "We'll get set up in the conference room."

Eli waited until they left to turn to Teresa. Regret beat at him, and though he dreaded the answer, he had to give her the words.

"I want to apologize again, Teresa. None of this would have happened if not for my shortsightedness." He raised his hand to keep her from speaking. "No matter what you say, I hold myself responsible."

He took her hand in his and squeezed it gently. "Tell me what you want to do. If you want to be with your family, I'll have a plane ready for you in an hour. Douglas and Linda are under protection. No one can get to them now, but I completely understand if you want to be with them."

Teresa patted his hand. "Don't you fret, Mr. Eli. I'm exactly where I want to be. My sister would be the first person to agree. And you need to stop apologizing. You can't predict what bad people will do."

"Maybe not, but protecting my family is my responsibility."

"A few months before Miss Shelley passed away, she said something to me. I didn't know quite what she meant at the time, but now I think I do."

"What's that?"

"She said that you have a hero complex. That you have a tendency to want to save people, even from themselves. And even when it's not your place."

Eli didn't know how to respond. He sure as hell hadn't been able to save Shelley, especially from herself.

"She also said that's one of the reasons she fell in love with you. Said that chivalry was one of your greatest gifts." She patted his hand again. "Now I'm going to go call the number Mr. Justice gave me so I can talk to my sister. Then I'll get started on dinner. And don't even think about telling me not to bother. Staying busy is a gift."

He watched her go, wishing he could have done more. Wishing he could figure out just what the hell he was supposed to do.

"It bothers you, doesn't it?" Kathleen asked. "What she told you that Shelley said. That you try to save people."

"It's what I did...what I do. When it's something I want or feel strongly about, someone I care about, I do manipulate people to get my way." He looked at her then. "It's what I did with you. Manipulated the situation."

She smiled at him then. This beautiful woman he loved to distraction. "You want me to be angry about that?" she asked. "Too bad, because I'm not. You did it because you wanted to help me. I don't think Shelley meant her words to be an insult. There's a shortage of heroes in the world. I love that you want to help people."

She moved into his arms. "And I'm particularly grateful you wanted to help me."

Eli buried his face in her hair, inhaled her scent, took solace from her strength. "I don't know when this will be over...if it'll ever be over."

"It will, Eli. With all of us working on it, I promise it will."

"And then what, Kat?"

She raised her head and spoke with a quiet confidence. "We'll live happily ever after. Just like we're supposed to."

Slater House Hotel
Downtown Dallas

She shot up from the fragrant bubble bath she'd been thoroughly enjoying. "What do you mean they disappeared?"

"Just that. I left them there overnight, tied so tight one of 'em couldn't scratch an itch without the other saying thank you. Came by this morning to see if they were still kicking. The door was busted open. I didn't go in. Figured the place was being watched."

"This is very disappointing."

"Hey, I followed every direction you gave me. You said there was no need to watch them. You said—"

"I know exactly what I said. But, as one might expect, that doesn't diminish my disappointment."

"It's not my fault they're gone. You still owe me three grand."

"I take care of my obligations. It's such a shame you don't do the same."

She ended the call before she could say anything more. She didn't have time to deal with this right now. Going all the way back to England just to kill one stupid criminal was pointless. He could be found under a rock at some point later.

Stepping out of the delicious bath, she dried off quickly and then began to pace across her hotel room. Staying in the most luxurious accommodations was one of the many perks of her job. That it was the Slater House Hotel was an amusing coincidence. Luxury and decadence often soothed her, but not tonight.

Dammit, she had read Teresa Longview wrong. Her kind usually believed that family was the most important thing. How many times had she used this technique in the past? Dozens? It had always worked like a dream. Where the hell had she gone wrong?

Anger ignited. Looking around the room for an outlet, she picked up a vase, threw it across the room, and watched it shatter. No, that hadn't helped. She whirled around, grabbed a small statue, and lifted her arm. Out of the corner of her eye, she caught a glimpse of herself in the mirror. Turning, she faced herself fully and felt the rage drain from her body.

Being beautiful had been a gift. She hadn't always looked like this. The man she had loved and lost had given her this. What woman wouldn't want to have this face? This body?

Soothed by her beauty, she regrouped. Obviously, she had underestimated the housekeeper. Not only had she not served Slater and Callahan the poison, she had apparently told them. And if she'd told them, it was only a natural step for Slater to have called the one man with the kind of worldwide connections that could find and rescue people in trouble. Grey Justice had been a thorn in her side for as long as she could remember. Even while she hated him, he had fascinated her, enthralled her. And for one very specific reason, she wanted him dead.

But that was for another day. Right now, she had to go to her backup plan. Frustrating, because she hadn't done the recon she normally would beforehand. But it was reasonable, sensible. And it would have to be done soon, before Slater suspected her next move. He now knew no one was safe.

She picked up her cellphone again, this time to make flight arrangements. Maybe once this part of the job was finished, she'd take a few days there and relax. She certainly deserved it, and France was so nice this time of year.

Rubbing his hair dry with a towel, Eli walked out of the bathroom and then stopped at the sight before him. Kathleen Callahan, beautiful, sexy, and without a doubt the love of his life, sat in the middle of the bed. He had dreamed about having her here, all the wickedly delicious things he wanted to do to that sweet, luscious body. But this image had never entered his mind.

The entire bed was covered with stacks of papers, most of which carried his father's name. Kathleen sat in the middle of those stacks, reading, studying, researching. It had been a helluva long day, and he'd looked forward to holding her in his arms for a few hours without the stench of his family invading.

Only a few hours ago, she had told him she loved him. Despite all the troubles still facing them, he wanted to celebrate that miracle. Hold her in his arms and convince himself that for a few stolen moments, all was right with his world.

He gestured at the bed. "This is one place I really don't want my father."

Lifting her head, Kathleen gave him a weary smile and started gathering papers together. "Sorry. Still looking for that connection between Braden and your father."

He had some thoughts on another kind of connection, but he wasn't about to bring that up tonight. He needed to do a little research on his own before destroying her world once again.

"We've dug enough to know there doesn't appear to be a business link, but you're talking personal? There was a big age difference between the two. They lived across the country from each other. Other than they were both sleazebags, their perversions of choice weren't related. What kind of personal connection could there be?"

"I don't know."

"Let's get some rest and tackle it tomorrow." He gave her his most lascivious leer. "My eyes are so blurred it's almost impossible for me to tell if you're wearing clothes or not."

She laughed and shoved a stack of papers off the bed. "Is that right? Well, I guess this sexy, see-through gown I'm wearing is pointless."

He gave an exaggerated blink. "How about that? I think they're clearing up again. But where's that sexy see-through?"

"Come down here and help me find it."

"My pleasure."

He sat on the bed beside her and helped her stack the rest of the papers. "What's this?"

She peered over his shoulder. "What's what?"

"This list."

"Oh, it's a list of companies Braden had an investment or interest in. I thought maybe someone had him killed either for revenge or to possibly get his stock at a good price." She shrugged. "I was scraping the bottom of the barrel, I admit. I—"

Obviously noting the stiffness in his body, she sat beside him so she could see his face. "What?"

His heart pounding, he surged from the bed and grabbed up the papers. "Come with me."

CHAPTER FORTY

Grey arrived just as Kathleen and Kennedy finished setting up. Kathleen and Eli had worked until after three this morning. When she could no longer hold her eyes open, she'd convinced him to come to bed for a few hours. They'd fallen into bed, arms wrapped around each other, believing they had finally found that connection.

A few hours later, she'd woken alone and found a note beside her pillow to meet him in the conference room when she was dressed. She'd walked in to see he'd already consumed half a pot of coffee but looked as triumphant and optimistic as she'd ever seen him. Kathleen felt an almost euphoric glee.

By the time Kennedy and Nick arrived, she and Eli had completed half the boards. When Eli explained what he'd found, they'd gotten to work, too. Once they'd seen the thread…where it was going, it had been easy enough to follow, connect, and then tie them together.

When they'd felt they had gone as far as they could, Eli had made a call to Grey.

Now armed with more information than they'd believed possible, Eli stood at the front of the room and faced the small group.

"Since Justice hasn't heard any of this, and I want to make sure we're all on the same page, I'll begin with how we believe it started. After that, we'll move to what we can prove and are certain of. And then, we'll talk about what we speculate." Eli's gaze went to Grey. "That's where you come in. There are certain things I think you can find faster than we can."

At Grey's nod of acknowledgment, Eli continued, "Forty-nine years ago, a twenty-year-old Mathias went to visit his cousins in Dorman, Nebraska. It's a little town right outside Omaha and at that time had a population of right under ten thousand.

"Since it was such a small town, there was little to do. Except a special event happened to be taking place in Dorman. One of their own, Frisco Durango, was coming for a visit."

Justice's arched a brow. "Frisco Durango?"

Eli grinned. "I kid you not. Anyway, Frisco had made it big on the rodeo circuit and, wanting to give back to the community, arranged a rodeo for the town. People came from all over the state, some from neighboring states."

"That would've been a great boon to a little town," Grey said.

"Yeah. Businesses that weekend were going to reap the reward. And Mathias, most likely bored and restless, saw an opportunity."

Eli glanced over at Kathleen, who continued the story from where she sat. "Three businesses—a mom-and-pop grocery store, a little ice cream shop, and a hole-in-the-wall barbecue joint—were all held up late that Saturday night. Wearing ski masks, several young men—we're still not sure of the number yet—stole an estimated $128,000."

She glanced over at Nick, who picked up the story. "This is where the speculation part comes in. The money was recovered, but no arrests were made. We figure Mathias's father, who was by far the wealthiest among the families involved, paid off each of the businesses so they wouldn't press charges. Maybe encouraged them not to talk about it."

"If no arrests were made, how do you know the robberies even happened?"

"Kennedy found it in an old newspaper article, which got us onto the trail," Nick said. "With the money being recovered and no one ever charged, it was apparently a big mystery that local residents talked about but never solved.

"I called the local law in Dorman. Took some time and more charm than I knew I had, but I managed to persuade the records clerk to look up the emergency calls from that night. She confirmed that three robbery calls came in, from those businesses.

"Then, I talked to a few old-timers in Dorman who remembered what happened. They all agreed the robberies happened, and then it was all hush-hush, and no one spoke of it."

"It might have stayed this way—like it never happened," Kennedy said. "Except the day after the robbery, the wife of the man who owned the barbecue place had a heart attack and died."

Justice didn't speak, but his confusion was clear. How could a woman who died of a heart attack almost fifty years ago have anything to do with the death threats Eli and his family were experiencing? Eli appreciated the man's restraint in not questioning.

"The name of the man who owned the barbecue place was Bruce Johnson. We believe," Kennedy continued, "that Johnson had a son named James, and he was in on the hold-up."

"James robbed his own father's restaurant?" Justice asked.

"Yes. And when the mother found out her son had been involved in the robberies, she had a heart attack," Kathleen explained.

"The old-timers we talked to," Nick said, "claimed it was widely known that the wife had a heart condition and that the father blamed his son for her death."

"What happened next?" Justice asked.

"That's where things get shady," Kathleen said.

"How so?"

"A year later, Bruce Johnson closed down his barbecue place and moved out of town. It was assumed his kid, James, went with him. But when Bruce showed up in Tulsa, Oklahoma, a few months later, he was alone, a childless widower. There's no clue what happened to his son. All we know is the father worked as a cook at a local diner in downtown Tulsa."

"So you think Bruce Johnson killed his son?"

"That was our first inclination," Eli said.

"But not now?"

"We know the kid graduated high school that year," Nick said. "And that father and son left town the next day."

"Okay, you've sold me on the fact that there was a crime and that it was covered up. And I agree that it's likely Mathias was involved. But what are we looking at? Revenge? If so, why the hell wait almost fifty years? Also, what about the other young men involved in the robberies? What happened to them? Why the hell target you, Eli?"

"Give us a minute," Eli said, "and it'll all become clearer, I promise. None of this made sense or seemed connected until I spotted a familiar name in some of the research Kathleen did on Frank Braden."

That sparked a light in Justice's eyes as his gaze targeted Kathleen. "You found a link between Frank Braden and Mathias?"

Kathleen gave a quick smile. "Actually, it's a link between Francis Braden, Frank's father, and Mathias."

Eli went to a board and turned it around. "Like clockwork, on the twelfth day of each month, both Mathias and Francis Braden made payments to the Grinstead Foundation."

"Which is?" Justice said.

"Supposed to be a non-profit foundation for conservation and ecology," Nick answered. "Turns out, it's a fake charity. There's nothing behind it."

"Using that information, we've confirmed that at least three other men made contributions to the same company. George MacDougal, Oscar Clancy, and Monty Owens."

"How did you find that information?"

Kennedy grinned. "With a little hacking, a lot of digging, three doughnuts, and a half gallon of decaf."

"We also confirmed that all three—MacDougal, Clancy, and Owens—lived in Dorman at the time of the robberies," Eli added.

"Okay, so you have at least five men that you know of who contributed a certain amount of money each month. For how long?"

"Thirty-six years," Kathleen said. "And then, nothing. There's no indication that these men donated any more money to this company."

"How much money?" Justice asked.

"Five hundred at the beginning. Then the amounts increased—perhaps as each man's income increased. But each man paid the same amount."

"Up until thirteen years ago," Kathleen added. "After that, the payments stopped."

"What was the amount of the last payments?" Justice asked.

"Five thousand," Eli said.

"All right. I'll buy that it might've been a mutual agreement to stop the payments and that whoever was on the receiving end might've been pissed at the loss of income. But as Kathleen pointed out, that was thirteen years ago. Why wait until now to do anything? And again, why you, Eli? I don't see—" Justice stopped and then said, "Wait. The other men involved in the robberies. What happened to them?"

"All dead," Eli answered. "The first death was nine months after the last payment was made. It was ruled an accident. As were all subsequent deaths."

Going to another board, he turned it around. "Monty Owens was the first to die when scaffolding from a building he was working on fell and crushed him. Eighteen months after that, Francis Braden died in a house explosion. Ruled a gas leak. Three years later, George MacDougal went fishing alone. His body was discovered three days later. It was ruled an accidental drowning. Oscar Clancy fell from the twentieth floor of a hotel balcony. Also ruled an accident."

"What about Mathias? Why wasn't he targeted?"

Anger flashed through Eli as he recalled the phone conversation he'd had with his mother a few hours ago. "I couldn't believe he'd escaped either. That's why I called my mother to jog her memory. She admitted there had been two different incidents, possibly attempts on his life. One was a mugging four years ago, when they were in San Francisco. We all know that Mathias was a tough old bird. He beat the hell out of the mugger. Never reported it to the police. Mathias considered the matter done. The second time was a year after that. They were vacationing in France. My father opened his suitcase to unpack and found a rattlesnake in his underwear.

"Mother said he threw a towel over it, strangled the damn thing, and then pitched it out the window."

"That's it?" Justice said. "He didn't suspect that someone had placed it there?"

"If he did, she said he never let on to her. She said he insisted on going through her luggage. They found nothing else."

"Hell, I know we live in Texas and see more than our share of snakes," Nick said, "but damned if I wouldn't suspect some foul play if I found a snake in my underwear."

"With Mathias, who knows?" Eli said. "By then, he probably had so many people gunning for him, it would have been difficult to pinpoint one person."

"What about your father's death last year?" Kathleen asked. "Could Cyrus Denton, the man who shot him, have been a hired killer?"

If anyone other than Justice noticed that Eli stiffened at the question, no one said anything. Shrugging, Eli said truthfully, "We know for a fact that Cyrus did a lot of my father's dirty work, which included murder. But I'm reasonably sure he was not hired to kill Mathias."

Before anyone could question why Eli was so certain of that, Justice helped him out by saying, "Okay, so we know these five men, whom we speculate were involved in a robbery with this James Johnson, are dead."

"Yes. And though James Johnson disappeared off the radar, we're assuming he's the one behind it."

"Why are you looking at the son, James, and not his father, Bruce? He'd be an old man by now, but that doesn't mean he couldn't hire someone to take out these people. Seems like he'd be the one who would be holding a grudge or wanting revenge."

"Because Bruce Johnson was killed three years after he moved to Tulsa. House burned down, ruled an arson but no one was ever charged."

"You figure the son did him?" Justice said.

"That would be my take," Eli said.

"Okay, let me see if I can sum this up. So far, you have three robberies that happened forty-nine years ago. At least five of the men believed involved in those robberies are dead. And four of those deaths look somewhat suspicious."

"Yes."

"And now, I assume you're going to tell me that those men's relatives have had similar misfortunes."

Eli gave a grimacing smile. "Give the man a prize. That's exactly what we're going to tell you. Each one of us took a family and followed it through.

"George MacDougal never married but had a son with his onetime live-in girlfriend. That child, a boy, age twenty-four, was found in his apartment with a bullet in his head. He'd had some depressive episodes, so his death was ruled a suicide."

He nodded at Kathleen, who walked over to another board and said, "Francis Braden had two children. Frank was killed by poisoning. And only a few weeks ago, his brother, Joseph, was found dead in a bathtub in a motel in Boise, Idaho. He had a high alcohol level in his system, and his death was ruled an accidental drowning."

Kathleen gave a nod to Kennedy, who said, "A few weeks ago, Oscar Clancy's only child Graham, along with Graham's wife, Helena, and their two children, Miles and Kimberly, were killed in a one-car crash. Car burned to a crisp. It was ruled an accident."

Nick looked at the board he was standing beside. "Howard Owens, Monty's son and only child, along with Howard's wife Vonda, were killed in a single-engine plane crash. Howard, who was piloting the plane, called in a Mayday that they were having engine trouble. They were flying over the Atlantic Ocean when they disappeared off radar. The wreckage and their bodies were found by some divers a few months later.

"Seven months after that, Russell Owens, Howard and Vonda's only child, was found at the bottom of a ravine in Delamore, New Mexico. His neck was broken. Since it was a known fact that he liked to hike and climb by himself, it was assumed he was doing so when he fell to his death."

Justice sat quietly for a few seconds, taking it in, then blew a long, soft whistle. "So this bastard is patiently and systematically eliminating every man's direct blood tie."

Eli nodded. "Plus anyone else who happens to get in the way."

"And you're thinking that James Johnson is the one responsible for this massacre?"

"Only makes sense that it's him," Eli said. "Problem is, we can't find him. Johnson is a common name and there are thousands, if not hundreds of thousands of James Johnson's. Finding the right one is proving almost impossible."

"You don't think he changed his name?" Justice said.

"There's the possibility but more than likely there wasn't a need," Nick answered.

Justice sat silently for a few more seconds, his eyes scanning each board. "You guys have done amazing work. What do you need from me?"

"Find the right James Johnson," Eli said.

Standing, Justice said, "Send me everything you've got. I'll take it from here."

CHAPTER
FORTY-ONE

His arm wrapped around Kathleen's shoulders, he guided her up the stairs to their bedroom. The dark shadows beneath her eyes and the translucency of her skin were a testament to her exhaustion. She'd had only a few hours' sleep last night. And though he'd had even less, Eli couldn't really rest. Yes, he was relieved that they had apparently identified the source of the threats, and he had faith that Justice, with his resources and contacts, would be able to locate the bastard behind all of this. But there was a new dark cloud hanging over them. One that Kathleen wasn't even aware of yet. When she learned about it, he knew without a doubt, her heart would be broken once again.

From the moment he'd first suspected a connection, he'd debated what he should do. Had even considered not telling her at all. She'd been hurt enough, and knowing the truth would do nothing more than hurt her once again. Eli wouldn't feel an ounce of guilt by keeping it from her. When it came to those he loved, he could be cold-bloodedly ruthless. Protecting them would always be his number one priority.

So not telling her wouldn't bother him a damn bit. But if he didn't tell her, what did that say about his belief in her? Kathleen was one of the strongest, most courageous people he'd ever known. If he didn't tell her, then he was making a mockery of that strength. Bottom line, he trusted her to handle this new heartache just as she'd handled every adversity before. But there was a difference this time. He would be with her every step of the way. Her champion and biggest supporter. She was no longer alone.

"Everything okay?" Kathleen's soft voice broke into his thoughts. "You've been awfully quiet."

Standing in the middle of the bedroom, Eli held her shoulders and gazed down at her. No way in hell would he tell her now. She looked ready to drop. After a long sleep, and a good meal, she'd be more fortified and able to handle the news.

But first, he wanted to be with her, show her in the most elemental way possible that she would never be alone again.

She frowned up at him, the beginnings of worry in her eyes. "Eli?"

"Do you know how beautiful you are? Or how much I love you?"

A lovely smile curved her lips. "Never in a million years did I ever believe I'd be so blessed."

Lowering his head, Eli took her mouth in a soft, tender caress. He wanted to go slow, savor every sigh, swallow every gasp. Her lips yielded under his as she wrapped her arms around his neck, sinking into him, surrendering. With sensual intent, he made love to her mouth as his hands slid over her body, loosening and removing clothing as he went. In less than a minute, her shirt, jeans, and underwear were scattered on the floor at their feet.

When he lifted his head, her eyes were brimming with warm laughter. "What?"

"Should I be worried that you can strip me without me even being aware of it?"

"Another one of my superpowers."

"I hope you never use your superpowers on anyone else."

"This one is reserved strictly for you."

"I love you, Eli. More than I can ever say, ever communicate."

"I know you do, and that's why you're going to let me have my way."

"Oh yeah? And just exactly what do you want?"

"I want to love you until you're breathless. Until every bone and muscle in your body is limp from pleasure. I want to be so deep inside you that my heartbeat will become yours. Will you let me?"

Her eyes were dreamy, already glazed with passion and heat. "Only if you let me return the favor."

"Deal." Scooping her into his arms, he carried her to the bed. Lowering her gently onto the pillows, Eli followed her down. Then, beginning at her forehead, he trailed kisses down her body, stopping and savoring tender or fragrant spots along the way. How he adored this woman. From the moment he'd seen Kathleen, he'd felt a connection with her unlike any other person he'd ever known. It was inexplicable, yet he had never been more sure of anything in his life. This woman was meant for him.

Supple skin, covered in a light dew of perspiration, pliant under his mouth, tasted like heaven. Breathy moans, groaning sighs of acceptance, were the most erotic sounds he'd ever heard. And were driving him crazy.

Pulling away, he looked down at her and smiled. Eyes closed, skin flushed pink with arousal, she was undulating on the bed, almost as crazed as he was. He wanted her more crazed, hotter, needier than she'd ever been before. So consumed with desire, her only thought would be to let herself go, to lose herself in him.

He moved to the end of the bed.

She raised her head slightly. "What are you doing?"

"Loving you." This time, he started from the bottom. Holding a slender foot in his hand, he peppered kisses down her arch, over her heel, and then up her firm, shapely calf.

"What are you doing to me, Eli?"

"I'm driving you as crazy as you drive me."

"Come up here, and let's drive each other crazy together."

"Be right there." Lifting her leg, he bent it forward, opening her up to his gaze. Strawberry-red curls covered her sex. Eli bent over her, inhaled the delicious scent of arousal and the delicate fragrance that was a natural part of her essence.

"Eli, please."

He blew softly over her curls, and she arched up, her body asking, seeking. He obliged. Burying his face between her legs, he plunged his tongue into her, loving her taste, the contractions of her soft as silk flesh as she came, the scream of his name from her lips.

No longer able to hold back, he went to his knees and slid his length deep into her. He groaned at the hot silk enveloping him. Leaning over her, balancing himself on his arms, he cupped her face in his hands and locked his gaze with hers. He wanted to watch her come again. See those amazing eyes go blank with pleasure.

"I love you, Kat." He thrust hard, then held still. "You're mine. Always."

"Yes, I am. And you are—" Her breath hitched as she clenched around him.

"Say it, Kat. What am I?"

"You are…" She let loose a scream as she came again.

Laughing his triumph, Eli thrust harder and then exploded. Burying his face against her neck, he growled, "I am what? Tell me, Kat. What am I?"

"My everything, Eli," she whispered softly. "You're my everything."

Kathleen gave a luxurious stretch and opened her eyes. Deliciously slow loving, then a few hours' sleep, and she now felt fabulous. She smiled as she remembered how incredible Eli had been. No one had ever treated her so tenderly, with such reverent passion. His hands and mouth had moved softly, slowly, sweetly over her body as if she were the most precious of jewels. She had felt cherished, treasured. They'd held on to each other for several moments afterward, cherishing the rare moment of peace and fulfillment. Seconds later, she had fallen into the sublime sleep of complete contentment. And now, every part of her body sang with supreme satisfaction.

Turning her head, she saw the empty pillow and frowned. She had hoped he would sleep longer. He'd had even less rest than she had last night and had to be exhausted.

She could barely comprehend that the nightmare was almost over. After living with intense fear every day when Eli was out of her sight for even a few seconds, she felt as light as a fluffy cloud, as though a tremendous weight had been removed from her shoulders. Yes, there were still unanswered questions, but within a few days, if not less, they should have all the answers they'd been searching for. And once they did, they would hunt down this man and end his evil.

After it ended…after it was over, Kathleen, Eli, Sophia, and Violet would be a family. She had no doubts about that. Was she terrified? Absolutely. This wasn't what she'd ever thought to have…would ever allow herself to have. But now? She wanted nothing more. The joy of loving him, being loved in return, far outweighed the fear of losing them. One day or a hundred years, whatever amount of time she was given, she wanted to spend with Eli, and with Sophia and Violet.

She couldn't wait to get started on their life together.

Like a cloud that appears from nowhere and shadows the sun, an ominous darkness washed over her bright optimism. She didn't know why, but she had the sudden compulsion to be with Eli. Almost as if he needed her with him this very moment.

Kathleen jumped out of bed and threw on the clothes Eli had taken off her earlier. In less than a minute, she was out the door. By the time she made it to the stairway, she was running. Practically flying down the stairs, she skidded to a stop in the foyer, unsure where he'd be. Soft music came from the small private dining room, and Kathleen headed toward it. If he wasn't there, she'd find Teresa and ask her where he was. She told herself everything was okay. That she was in a panic for nothing.

She stopped at the door, startled at the scene before her. Her instincts must be way off, because this wasn't Eli upset or in danger. This was Eli at his finest. Dressed in a pair of gray slacks and a royal blue cashmere pullover, standing at the head of the table, he was every woman's fantasy. A wave of longing and immense love swept through her. How on earth had she gotten so lucky?

Tearing her eyes away from him, she took in the room. Candles flickered in the soft lighting, creating a romantic ambience. Dreamy, instrumental music played in the background, setting the mood for seduction. A bouquet of roses sat in the middle of the table, which was set with fine china, gleaming silverware, and sparkling crystal stemware.

Eli moved toward her, the expression on his face one of tenderness and love. Kathleen figured she was going to melt on the spot. Never had anyone looked at her like that.

"What's all this?" she asked.

When he reached her, he took her hands in his, kissed her forehead, her nose, and then very softly, but thoroughly, kissed her mouth. Lifting his head, he said quietly, "You need to know how much I love you, adore you. If it were within my power, every day of your life would be filled with flowers, sunshine, music, and laughter."

Emotions clogged her throat. She wanted to say something equally as eloquent and beautiful. She wanted him to know just how incredible he was and how very much she loved him. All she was able to manage was, "You're like a dream come true."

"I want to make all your dreams come true. Will you let me?"

"If you let me return the favor."

"Deal," he answered softly.

She glanced down at her clothes and grimaced. "I'm not dressed for anything fancy."

"You're beautiful in anything. Don't you know that, Kat?"

If he said anything more, she was going to dissolve in a puddle in the middle of the floor. Hearing a slight sound, Kathleen peeked around Eli's shoulder. Teresa stood in the doorway with a tray in her hand and a beaming smile on her face.

"The table looks lovely, Teresa."

"Oh, that wasn't me. Mr. Eli insisted on setting it." She laughed and added, "I supervised, though."

Kathleen looked up at Eli. "It's going to be a perfect night."

Something flashed in his expression. Before she could decipher the look, he said, "You must be starving."

Wanting to return to the earlier, sexy moment, she whispered so only Eli could hear, "In more ways than one."

Heat and gentle amusement glittered in his eyes. "Let's start here, and we'll go somewhere else for dessert."

Eli pulled a chair out for her and then seated himself. The plan was for Teresa to bring the entire meal to the table and leave. He had debated how to do this. There was no simple way to break someone's heart. A part of him wanted to just say the words and get it done so he could start helping her heal. Another part of him wanted to delay for as long as he could. He was compromising. She'd had almost no food today. Half a pastry and coffee this morning and no lunch. The least he could do was provide her with sustenance to deal with what lay ahead.

Determined that she relax and enjoy the meal, Eli concentrated on light topics. Where would she most like to go on holiday, favorite books, movies, music. Even though he had an agenda, he was enjoying himself, too. Watching her eyes dancing with amusement, that beautiful, mobile mouth curve in a sweet smile, seeing her completely relax and be herself was a gift.

All too soon the salad, lasagna, and wine had been consumed. He'd refilled her glass a couple of times. He didn't want her drunk, but he had the hope that the alcohol would numb the pain, at least a little.

She relaxed in her chair with a happy sigh. "Hands down, best meal ever." She glanced at his plate and frowned. "Did you not like it?"

He'd barely eaten a bite. A lump of dread had almost blocked his ability to swallow. "I had a snack when I woke up so I'm not that hungry."

Placing her napkin beside her plate, she pushed her chair back. "I'm going to let Teresa know how fabulous the meal was, then we'll clean this up."

Eli stood. "You can tell Teresa tomorrow. And she said to not worry with the dishes, she'll take care of them."

"Okay, if you're sure. I—" Concern darkened her eyes. "Eli, what's wrong? Do you not feel well?"

Reaching for her hand, he pulled her from the room. "I'm fine. I—" Eli shook his head to clear it. If he weren't careful, he'd screw this up worse than it already was. "While you were sleeping, I did a little more digging. Found something else."

"Really? What?"

As inane as it sounded, he'd fretted over where to tell her this news. The place he told her would most likely taint it with the memory of devastation. He didn't want any room in the house to have a bad memory for her. But there was one place they could go that was already contaminated. "Let's go to the conference room."

She let him lead her, a worried little frown still on her face. Hoping to lighten the mood, he said, "Once this is all over, I'm going to have this room gutted. Maybe even replace it with something else."

They stopped at the door, and she gave him a crooked, awkward smile, so unlike the natural ones during dinner. Despite his efforts, she sensed whatever he had to tell her would upset her.

"Sounds good to me. If I never have to see this room again, it'll be too soon for me."

"Agreed." He opened the door, and they walked in together.

She was nervous and had no idea why. Eli's somber, serious expression told her whatever he'd learned was more than some tidbit of information they hadn't had before. And he believed it would upset her.

"Let's sit down."

"You're scaring me, Eli. Whatever it is, just tell me. Okay?"

"I'm sorry. That's the last thing I want. It always struck me as strange that the woman who approached Teresa at the store wanted her to poison you, too. The more I thought about it, the more it got me to wondering."

He glanced down at a small stack of paper on the table. "There were dozens of names on the list of contributors to the Grinstead Foundation."

Kathleen nodded. "I never went through the whole list, but I figured there were probably others. This guy was too smooth to only have a handful of people he was blackmailing."

"There was another name on that list. I didn't catch it at first, because the amount was much less than for Mathias, Braden, and the three others. But the name caught my eye, so I did some more digging, and I'm now certain an additional man was involved in the robberies."

"Really? Why didn't you say so? Who is he? What do you know about him? Did he—" She stopped abruptly when she saw the truth in his eyes. She shook her head slowly, denying.

"The name was Daniel Callahan. Sweetheart, I believe your father participated in those hold-ups."

Her legs shaky, she dropped abruptly onto the sofa, barely noting that Eli sat down beside her, took her hand in his.

"But how is that… I don't understand how… He never said… In Nebraska…where? I don't…" She knew she was rambling incoherently, but for the life of her, she couldn't seem to piece together a complete sentence.

Eli's voice, deep and reassuringly calm, broke into her stuttering mind. "He would have been a little younger than Mathias. Maybe nineteen. Likely before he even met your mother."

Her heart set up a loud pounding in her chest as reality slapped her in the face. "He was the first one killed, wasn't he? The payments stopped thirteen years ago. My father was found dead thirteen years ago."

She closed her eyes as the awful truth slammed through her. "It wasn't an accident. He didn't fall from that bridge."

"There's no evidence to say otherwise, but after we saw what happened to the others, my best guess would be no, he didn't fall. He was pushed."

Tears sprang to her eyes, and emotion clogged her throat. "All this time... I never told Alice, but all this time, I thought he might have committed suicide. He wasn't the same once he got out of prison. There was no light in his eyes, as there had been before.

"We tried, Alice and I, we tried to make it like it was before. But he..." She trailed off as another, more devastating thought occurred. Shoving Eli's hands away, she jumped to her feet and then whirled around. "Alice."

It was all she said. All she needed to say. She saw the truth in his eyes.

"Tell me. Everything, Eli. Just tell me every damn thing you know."

"The woman who shot Alice."

"Yes, Maureen Downey."

"The photos of her and Braden together. Grey had them analyzed. They were Photoshopped."

"Fake?"

"Yes. Those photographs were the only real proof that she even knew Braden."

"But why would she shoot Alice? She—" Kathleen closed her eyes briefly. "The woman. The hired killer. She forced her?"

"That's our best guess. Maureen had no family, but when she was a teenager, she gave birth to a daughter that she gave up for adoption. The girl disappeared for three days a few months back. She claimed to have been kidnapped but, out of the blue, was let go. The girl's been in some trouble before, so no one believed her. The timing coincided with Alice's shooting."

"So the woman did to Maureen what she tried to do to Teresa. Blackmailed her into killing."

"Yes. Unfortunately, it worked."

Kathleen shook her head. "All this sadness, all this loss, because of one man's need for revenge…or money…or what? What the hell reason is there for all these deaths? All this heartache?"

"I don't know, sweetheart. I don't know."

She wrapped her arms around herself. "It hurts. It hurts so damn much. So senseless and pointless. My father made so many mistakes. And one of them cost Alice her life."

"It almost cost you yours, too."

"You mean the poison? Yeah, I—" She gasped, comprehending his words. "The hit-and-run in Denver. You think she's the one?"

"If not her, one like her, hired to kill you. We know this bastard has patience. He's spread these murders out over decades. It would be no skin off his nose to wait awhile and go at you again. Who knows? The two men who attacked you in Chicago may have been another attempt."

She shook her head in disbelief. How had she not seen the pattern? It didn't help in the least that no one else had seen it either. That had been the bastard's plan all along.

"I want him to pay, Eli. He's taken my father and my sister from me. I want him to pay."

"He will. I promise you that."

"And I want her to pay, too. I don't care if she turns out to be Grey's friend. She's going down."

"I agree." He waited a heartbeat and then added, "That's not everything."

"What do you mean, not everything? They're both dead. I know they were both murdered. What more could there be?"

"Sit down."

"No. Just tell me." She was no longer afraid. Fury had replaced the grief. Her family was dead. There was no more truth that could hurt her.

"Hired killers are paid to do a job. When it doesn't work out, they continue until the job is done, the target eliminated. When Maureen Downey shot Alice, she didn't kill her."

"Yes, she did. She—" A lump of dread settled in her chest. "What are you saying?"

"I had an investigator talk to the deputy in charge of guarding your sister's hospital room. Ten minutes before she died, a woman dressed in a nurse's uniform went into Alice's room. She matched the description of the woman who approached Teresa."

She stood, frozen in place at the horror of his words. "No. No. No." She heard the whispered words as if from very far away. The room whirled around her, and Eli caught her before she fell. He sat down, pulled her into his lap, and wrapped his arms around her.

But she couldn't hear any more tonight. Just couldn't be here. She had to go. Had to get out of here.

She jerked out of Eli's arms and started toward the door with no idea of a destination. Rational thought was gone. To survive, she had to leave. Get out. Now.

"Kathleen. Wait." Eli's heart broke for her as he watched her world crumble. Having no clue what to do, only knowing she needed to know she wasn't alone, he reached out for her, touched her shoulder.

Whirling around, she lashed out at him, slamming her hand toward his face. He managed to sidestep, and perhaps at the last moment, she realized what she was doing and pulled back, because the hit wasn't as hard as it could have been. Still, he felt the sting in his jaw.

Covering her face with her hands, she let out a keening, wild cry of grief and fell to her knees. Eli followed her down, wrapped his arms around her, and let her grieve.

Ugly, retching sobs filled the room. Tears stung Eli's eyes, and he wished with all his might that he could take away her pain. Make all of this go away. Since he couldn't do that, he did the only thing he knew to do. Standing, he pulled her up and then scooped her into his arms. There was one place he loved to go to when his heart was heavy or he needed solace. The tower room.

She didn't ask where they were going. He didn't even know if she was aware they were moving. Her face was buried against his neck, and though the awful sobs had stopped, she was still weeping silently. He thought that might be sadder than the loud sobs. The silent tears spoke of hopelessness, sadness.

Finally reaching the fourth floor, Eli pushed the door open and then kicked it shut behind him. Grateful for the good weather and mild temperatures, Eli used one hand to push the switches up. A humming sounded, the ceiling opened, and the night sky exploded above them.

Settling into an oversized chair, Eli pulled Kathleen closer and then leaned his head back. When it was time, when she stopped crying, the heavens would be above her, showing her beauty. Giving her peace.

Slow moments passed. Eli didn't speak, giving her time to come back to herself in her own time, her own way. When he felt her move slightly, felt the loosening of her tense muscles, he squeezed her lightly, another touch of assurance that she wasn't alone.

Several more moments passed, and then she whispered in a raw voice, "I failed her. It's my fault."

Eli sighed. He had known she would take this on herself. She had assumed the responsibility of her sister at age nine and had never let up.

"I should have looked out for her, should've taught her better. She never would have fallen for Frank Braden's act if I had prepared her for people like him."

"How could you have prepared her for someone like Braden?"

"I don't know. I just..." Horror shuddered through her. "I just think of her lying there. So alone, so vulnerable. And that bitch comes in. I never should have left her alone. The doctors didn't really believe she would live. I saw the truth in their eyes, but dammit, she deserved a chance."

"Yes, she did. So let's make sure we blame the ones responsible. Not the one person who did everything within her power to save her."

"Did you tell yourself the same thing when Shelley died?"

Of course he hadn't. He had blamed himself for not being able to save her. Then, when he'd learned what Adam did to cause her to kill herself, he'd blamed himself even more.

"Maybe it's time for both of us to let go of the guilt."

"I want the sadness to go away. I want to catch the bastard who's behind this and the bitch he hired. Once they're behind bars, I want to be happy. To remember the good times I had with Alice and my dad." She shifted to look up at him and saw the stars above them. "It's beautiful here. Thank you for that."

"Marry me, Kat."

"What?"

This wasn't how he'd planned to ask her, but suddenly, nothing seemed more important than having her agree, right here, right now, to be his forever.

"Let's start a life together that has nothing to do with our past. If you don't want to live here, we'll find another house. Or build one. Or, if you want, we'll go somewhere else…away from Dallas. We'll go where no one knows us and start over again. The girls are young enough so they'll easily adapt to a new environment."

He pressed his forehead against hers. "Don't let them win. Don't let them destroy what we've found together."

"Oh, Eli," she sighed softly.

"I know this is terrible timing. And we've only known each other a short while, but I love you, Kathleen. You're the one I've been waiting for." He winced. "That was kind of corny, wasn't it?"

She gave a half sob, half giggle and shook her head. "I think it was perfect."

"We'll go to Denver, Detroit, Duluth. Anywhere you want. We'll—"

She pressed a finger to his mouth. "It doesn't matter where we live. Dallas, Denver, Detroit, Duluth. Or even a city that doesn't start with a D. As long as we're together, you, me, Sophia, and Violet, I don't care where we live."

"So that's a yes?"

"I love you, Eli. So very much. And I would be honored to be your wife."

Relief flooded through him. This had to be the poorest timing of any marriage proposal, but he didn't care. She had said yes.

That was all that mattered. His kiss was a soft one of promise, of commitment. He wanted this moment to be in her memory, wanted to erase the last hour.

She sighed as she buried her face in his neck, hugging him to her. "It feels so weird to be so happy and sad at the same time."

"Someday soon, we'll both be happy. Together."

"You're right. We will. It's strange, though, don't you think?"

"What's strange?"

"We've been connected for years and never knew it. Through our fathers." She nuzzled her face against his neck, pressed soft kisses to his throat. "How extraordinary is it that you happened to be in Chicago, saw me on the news. How amazing is it that we even met?"

Everything within Eli froze at her words. "Son of a bitch."

She jerked back, looked up at him. "What? What's wrong?"

Instead of answering, he pulled out his cellphone and hit the speed dial for Justice. The minute he answered, Eli said, "I know who it is."

Justice said, "I just got the name myself."

They said the name at the same time. "William Johnson."

"Dammit, I can't believe I didn't piece it together."

"We've got him," Justice said. "That's all that counts."

"Where is he?" Eli asked.

"Kings Crossings, Vermont," Justice answered. "I'll set things up with the local law. You and Kathleen get your gear together and meet me at the airport."

Eli put Kathleen on her feet and then hugged her hard, barely believing that the nightmare was almost over. "Let's go catch a monster."

CHAPTER
FORTY-TWO

Grey Justice's Private Jet

The Boeing 767 sliced through the night, winging its way to Kings Crossing, Vermont. Kathleen glanced over at Eli, who sat across from her, quietly talking to Grey. Dressed in black jeans, black sweater, black boots, he had the appearance of elegance, sophistication, and wealth. As if with one arrogant look, he could get things done without lifting a finger. But she knew the man beneath the clothing. Eli Slater could be just as dangerous and ruthless as any man she'd ever met. His veneer of sophistication hid a well-trained fighter. There was no one she'd rather have at her side—to fight with or to spend the rest of her life with.

Kathleen's blood pumped with exhilaration, masking the exhaustion she wouldn't let herself feel. When this was over and done with, she would let go. Until then, she'd live off coffee, hope, and Eli's love.

"You okay?" The concern in Eli's voice was another reason she adored this man.

She flashed him a reassuring smile. "I'm good. Just looking forward to the takedown."

"From what I remember about Johnson," Eli stated, "he won't put up much of a fight."

The things she'd learned about William Johnson over the last few hours made her agree. Though he had a reputation of being a wealthy, eccentric recluse, she had found a couple of old photographs of him when James Johnson, William's father, was still alive. Eli was right. William was barely five-five, probably weighed only a few pounds more than she did, and had a sallow complexion. He looked as harmless as a child. But knowing what he had done, what he still wanted to do, she could only see him as a monster. Evil lay beneath that dull looking façade.

"We'll be prepared just in case," Justice said. "Anyone that evil will have some tricks."

Hearing their conversation, Nick and Kennedy got up from the sofa they'd been sitting on and seated themselves beside Kathleen.

"He's right about Johnson's appearance," Nick said. "Some of the most evil people I dealt with as a cop looked as unthreatening as a kitten. Those are the ones you have to look out for because people assume they're harmless."

"I still can't fathom why Johnson manipulated things so you would be in Chicago during Alice's trial," Kennedy said. "What was his motivation?"

"Hell if I know," Eli said. "The meeting was legit. Mathias and James, William's father, had been negotiating a deal for several months. The Johnsons have several different businesses, including a chain of discount stores spread throughout the Northeast. Mathias had been considering purchasing them. When James died, William took over."

Kathleen's brow furrowed with confusion, and Eli was glad to see her sorrow over what she'd learned about her father's and Alice's deaths had been replaced with a new light of determination. "Why would Mathias do business with a man who was blackmailing him?"

"The workings of Mathias's mind were always a mystery to me. For any other person, I'd say it was because he felt like he owed the man something, but Mathias was the least sentimental person I've ever known and had absolutely no conscience. My best guess is, he thought he could make some money off the deal. That was always his primary motivation when it came to business. After Mathias's death, William Johnson contacted me, offered his condolences and suggested, after a proper time of mourning, we reconnect. He wanted to continue to negotiate a deal."

"But if he doesn't live in Chicago, what reason did he give to get you to go there?" Kathleen asked.

"A few months after we first spoke, he contacted me again. Said he was going to be in Chicago for several business meetings and if I could see my way to meeting him there, it would be most appreciated. Since I have other business interests there, I agreed."

"But you decided not to go through with the deal?"

"I didn't like the numbers. When James died, the stock went down. From my perspective, William was doing the wrong things to stop the decline. I made some suggestions—he didn't like them. I bowed out, never heard from him again."

Eli shook his head, still cursing himself for not seeing the setup sooner. "Never crossed my mind that he was manipulating me. The bastard, for whatever reason, wanted us to meet."

"But why?" Kathleen asked. "And how could he even be sure we *would* meet?"

Trying to figure out an insane person's motives was like walking through a minefield. "He knew Alice's trial was being held. Knew I'd probably see it on the news. How he knew I'd be interested? I have no idea."

"The chances of you two meeting were slim to none," Justice said. "Probably wanted to see what might happen."

"But he had to know that if we did meet, at some point we'd put two and two together."

"True, but I doubt that he even considered that you would come to Dallas, or that you and Eli would fall in love."

Eli didn't bother to hold back a grin at the lovely blush coating Kathleen's cheeks. Their relationship was still new to her, but he figured that would soon change. Once Johnson was behind bars, Eli planned to move mountains to make her his wife as soon as possible.

"So," Nick said, "between the two of them, James and William Johnson are responsible for how many murders?"

"We're certain of fifteen," Kathleen said. "Including my father and my sister."

"Sixteen," Kennedy sent an apologetic look at Kathleen. "I know it's hard to see Maureen Downey as a victim, but…"

"You're right. I—" Kathleen swallowed. "No. You're right."

"I'd like to see William charged with every murder," Eli said, "including the ones his father ordered. James might have been calling the shots, but William would've had knowledge of them, maybe even helped with the planning."

"Agreed," Justice said. "The DA's office in Montpelier, Vermont, has every piece of information we've come up with. After he's arrested, a search of his home and offices should give us enough evidence to do just that."

"What about the murdering bitch he hired?" Eli asked.

"We'll make sure Johnson tells us where we can find her," Justice said. "We'll get her."

"You're still convinced that this woman isn't Irelyn?" Kathleen asked Justice.

"There's no doubt in my mind. I've known her for years. Irelyn Raine is many things, but a cold-blooded killer, especially of innocents, is not one of them. When we—"

Justice broke off when his cellphone buzzed. The instant he answered it, Eli knew something was wrong. The man's grim expression didn't give anything away other than what he was hearing was not good news. His answers to the caller were a terse and short, "Yes," "No," and "All right."

When the call ended, Justice pressed a speed-dial number. Everyone remained silent, knowing whatever bad news he had just received, the man was already taking steps to correct the situation.

Justice spoke into the phone. "Johnson's in the wind." His expression granite hard, he listened intently for several seconds and then said, "Good enough for me. Set it in motion. Call me if you need help."

"How the hell—" Eli began.

Justice held up his hand to stop him as he pressed a button beside his chair.

"Yes, Mr. Justice?"

Eli recognized the voice of Lily Turner, Grey's pilot.

"Change of plans. We need to head to Tennessee instead. Winston will call you with the coordinates."

"Very well, sir."

Eli wasn't surprised at Lily's serene response. From what he knew of the pilot, few things rattled her. He imagined that was an asset in working for Grey Justice.

Grey ended the call and then turned his attention to four pairs of questioning eyes.

"The police went to arrest Johnson and found him missing. The bed was made, as if he'd never slept in it. Several personal items were missing, too. He left no note, no indication where he'd gone."

"Dammit." Eli blew out a disgusted sigh. "Someone tipped him off."

"That's my take." Satisfaction glittered in Justice's eyes. "Not that it's going to do him any good."

"How do you know he's in Tennessee?" Kathleen asked.

"The man's been planning this a long time. No way in hell he didn't have a contingency plan."

"As did you," Eli answered.

"Of course." Justice shrugged as if it was a foregone conclusion. "We'll get to him before he has a chance to settle in."

"And then?" Kathleen said.

"And then we strike."

CHAPTER FORTY-THREE

Great Smoky Mountains
East Tennessee

Flexibility and preparedness were the keys to a happy and long life. If William had a motto, that would be his. It paid to have contacts, especially in the DA's office. When the call had come, warning him of the arrest warrant, he'd been ready to leave within the hour.

It was an inconvenience to have to leave his home but no real worry. What might be a devastating event to others was a minor nuisance for William. Just like his father, he was a man of great vision.

Truthfully he had been anticipating this since he'd made that silly maneuver in Chicago months before. As a disciplined man, such an indulgence went against everything he believed in. Which was probably one of the biggest reasons he was the least bit put out about it now. It had been avoidable, and he had only himself to blame.

His father would be disappointed in him for indulging in a bit of fun. James Johnson had been a strict disciplinarian who didn't believe in frivolities. In the early years, the lack of light-ness had been cumbersome. But William grew used to it and began to crave the harshness. The Johnsons were serious-minded, no-nonsense men. His mother, whom he barely remembered, had quietly faded away when William was just a boy. Then it had been just he and his father.

So yes, it had been a bit of fun he shouldn't have allowed, and he was paying the price. But as he looked around his new surroundings, he couldn't exactly complain. Nestled in the mountains, his hideaway had every amenity he'd had in Vermont, just on a smaller scale.

It would all work out fine. As a man of vision, there was no contingency he hadn't thought of, no situation he couldn't handle. While other men dreamed of doing great things, William simply and quietly did them.

He was also a man with a noble goal. Some goals were nobler than others. One might become a doctor to save lives. Another might become a world-famous opera singer to create beauty. And one might become a killer to rid the world of scum.

Not that William considered himself a killer. He'd never picked up a weapon in his life. In fact, if he held a gun in his hand, he'd be more likely to shoot himself than anyone else. No, he was most definitely not a killer.

But he was a promise keeper. He had made a vow and intended to keep it. If that wasn't a worthwhile, noble cause, he didn't know what was. A promise to his father. What could be more important than that?

It didn't matter that his father was no longer living. Debts didn't disappear, promises didn't go away simply because of death. Promises had to be kept.

Almost from the time he'd been able to walk, comprehend words, he had heard about the hatred his father had for the men involved in the robberies. His father had been coerced, lied to.

He'd been the youngest of the men, only seventeen. They had forced him to go along with them, and his life had been destroyed. All the other men had gone on to enjoy their lives and never had to pay the consequences.

The measly amount of money they'd paid his father through the years had been nothing. A small, insignificant token, an acknowledgment of guilt. His father had accepted it as such, but then they had stopped paying. It had been an insult to turn their backs on the guilt they should have borne for the rest of their lives. When it became apparent that there was no remorse, probably never had been, his father's path had become clear. They and their blood kin must all be destroyed.

William had learned to hate what his father hated. And even if death claimed him, as it had his beloved father, the vendetta would live on until it was finished. It was almost biblical, really. Well, with maybe a little twist. Sins of the father would be visited upon his children. The fathers were dead, many of the children had paid with their lives. So far, the Slaters, and one Callahan, had eluded justice. But that was about to end.

Of course they didn't know that. They believed they'd won. But he would show them…he would show them all. He was a winner through and through. And they were the losers.

He glanced at the wall clock and deemed it a reasonable time to make the call. Even though he was paying the woman—she was his employee—he knew to be careful with her. One didn't rile a wild dog.

Taking a burner phone from his desk drawer, he punched in a number, and felt a minor embarrassment at the resentment for having to punch in eleven numbers. He really had become quite spoiled.

She answered on the first ring and, as usual, got down to business. "The targets have become unreachable. We'll need to wait until they come out of hiding before pursuing it further."

"There's been a development."

The silence was his cue to continue. This one didn't waste words.

"They know my identity."

"How do you want me to proceed?"

She exhibited no worry or concern for his safety. He let the brief flash of anger pass. He didn't pay her for fake platitudes, he paid for results.

"The plan hasn't changed."

"If you're caught?"

"You'll still be paid," he answered a little irritably. Really, her uncaring attitude was a bit irksome.

"How?" If she heard the irritation in his tone, she didn't let on. She had an agenda.

"I have a man in Geneva, Switzerland. With each fulfilled contract, he'll wire you the appropriate funds."

"Very well."

"The gloves can now come off. Since they know who I am, accidents or subterfuge are no longer required. Feel free to do what you must, any way you prefer. Take out the whole damn family with one fell swoop if you like."

"That will make things easier."

For the first time since their association began, he heard a hint of emotion in her tone. One that sounded distinctly like condescension.

Deciding to ignore the mild insult, William went on, "The contract continues, no matter what happens. Even if I'm dead. Even if years pass, I want the job completed. Do you understand?"

"Perfectly." The line went dead.

William dropped the phone on the desk beside him, unsurprised to see his hands shaking. She might be his employee, but the truth was, she scared the hell out of him.

CHAPTER
FORTY-FOUR

High on a mountain, secluded deep in the dense woods, with only a small access road, the large stone and log home was a formidable well-hidden fortress, blending into the background as if it were part of the forest itself. Anyone looking with the naked eye wouldn't be able to see it, even from the sky.

But William Johnson wasn't nearly as clever as he believed. Locating the hideaway had been no challenge for Grey's researchers. Within an hour of being given the assignment, his people had found it.

As far as hideouts went, it was luxurious to the point of ostentatious. Johnson most likely believed he was roughing it. The man enjoyed his luxuries.

Grey knew his own lifestyle could be considered quite lush, but it hadn't always been so. When he'd first come to the States, he'd had to scratch and scrape for everything.

William Johnson had inherited his wealth, and if allowed to continue unencumbered, he would lose most of that wealth within a couple of years or so. The man was a piss-poor businessman. But they weren't going to give him the chance to go bankrupt. The bastard was going down. Tonight.

"We're set?" Grey said it a low voice.

"Yes." Standing on one side of him, Nick said, "Place is surrounded. Two deputies covering the back. One on each side, if he decides to go through a window. Eli, Kathleen, and I have the front."

"The sheriff and I will go in first," Grey said. "Once he's secure, I'll let you know."

"I still don't like this," Eli said behind him. "The asshole could have any number of traps set."

Grey didn't like it either, but he'd had to compromise to get the cooperation of the local law. "He might not blink at hiring a killer, but Johnson is about as physically dangerous as a mouse. Besides, this guy thinks he's smarter than everyone else. He doesn't believe for a second that his hideout could be found, so there's no reason for him to set traps. Bastard is sure he's safe."

With a grim nod to the sheriff, they started toward the house. He was well aware that two of the people behind him deserved to be going in with him. Grey planned to make sure they got their pound of flesh.

A gung-ho, damn-the-torpedoes method could be a helluva lot more efficient but didn't always produce the needed results. William Johnson had information they needed to find the killer he'd hired. The fake Irelyn. The very concept infuriated him. When she was caught, Grey planned to spend a few moments alone with her. He had his own theories of why she was impersonating Irelyn. He'd damn well get answers.

"I'll knock on the door," the sheriff said. "You stand to the side."

Sheriff Ronald Sanders was nobody's fool. His faded blue eyes held both wisdom and knowledge. With the scruff of a beard covering half his face and a body the size of a grizzly, he didn't need the nine-millimeter in his hand to look intimidating. Despite

Grey's frustration of having to play by the rules, if the authorities had to be involved, he was glad it was a man like Sanders.

When the knock yielded no response, Sanders called out, "Sheriff Ronald Sanders, here to serve a warrant, is entering the premises." He turned the doorknob, and when it opened, he didn't spare Grey a glance when he said, "Be ready."

His favorite handgun, a Glock 17, steady in his hand, Grey followed Sanders. They were in the middle of the living room when a querulous voice called out, "Who's there?"

"Mr. Johnson? It's Sheriff Ronald Sanders. Would you please come out?"

They heard a mechanized humming sound before William Johnson appeared before them. Though his face had the appearance of a healthy, if somewhat slight, man, and his shoulders, though not broad, looked strong, the fact that he was in a wheelchair was a surprise. Grey had no intel that William Johnson was physically handicapped. Eli had said nothing about it either. So either his intel was faulty, which he doubted, or Eli hadn't thought it pertinent, which he knew better, or Johnson was faking it, making the bastard even lower than the slug Grey knew him to be.

"What are you doing here?" Johnson asked. "What do you want?"

"I have a warrant for your arrest," Sheriff Sanders said. "Please place your hands above your head."

Though Sanders hadn't holstered his gun, he had lowered it to his side. Grey couldn't tell if he'd bought Johnson's act or not.

Johnson complied immediately and raised his hands above his head. The sheriff stepped forward, took Johnson's hands, cuffing them to one of the arms of the wheelchair.

"What's this about?"

"You're under arrest for the murders of Alice Cavanaugh and attempted murder of Eli Slater."

"Murders?" Johnson's eyes were wide, but Grey swore they were gleaming with excitement, not fear. "I don't know anything about any murders."

Determined to show the man he wasn't the least bit fooled by the man's innocent act, Grey snapped, "Cut the crap, Johnson. We know everything." He glanced over at Sanders. "Do what you need to do, and then we'll need that ten minutes I asked for."

As Sanders read him his rights, Grey spoke into the mic on his wrist unit. "You guys can come in now."

Fighting back the anger at this indignity, William barely paid attention to the sheriff as he eyed the big man in front of him. He'd recognized Grey Justice immediately. Ego maniac got featured all the time in magazines and on television specials. Just because the man had a charity, the media acted like he was something special. Like he was some kind of big deal.

If he'd wanted to, William knew he could be just as popular and get just as much press. He just didn't want to.

Grey Justice was a friend of Slater's. Probably pulled all kinds of strings and paid a boatload of money to dig out his location.

None of that mattered. He was a Johnson. And a Johnson always had a contingency plan. What happened over the next few minutes was what counted.

Even though his heart was pounding and his palms were wet with sweat, he would play this out. No, it wasn't exactly what he had planned, but it would still work out fine. These people were so damn arrogant, so sure they could outsmart him. He had worked all his life to get respect, and no one had ever truly appreciated his genius. He would soon prove that underestimating a Johnson was a foolhardy thing to do.

"I assume you have some solid evidence, or you wouldn't have been able to persuade the law to come with you. I'm willing to cooperate."

"Fine," Justice said. "Before we leave, though, there are a couple of people who want to meet you."

The door opened, and the two people he'd never thought to see alive were standing before him. Hatred boiled within him. It didn't matter that they wouldn't be alive for long. He shouldn't have to suffer their presence.

Determined to play the game to win, William smiled brightly. "And who are these two lovely people?"

"Cut the crap, Johnson," Eli Slater growled. "We have everything we need on you and your screwed-up father, but before we leave here, you're going to tell us how to get in touch with the woman you hired to kill us."

"Why, I never. I—" William chuckled, unable to keep up that much pretense. Besides, he could have fun another way. One they would never suspect.

"What's the woman's name?" Slater asked. "Where is she?"

"I don't know her name, and I have no idea where she is." He was delighted that they would assume he was lying when he wasn't.

Eli pulled out a cellphone, dropped it on William's lap. "Call her."

"And say what?"

"Tell her the contract is canceled."

"She's already agreed to that."

"What do you mean?"

"Our agreement is, if I'm captured, the contract is void. I can't very well pay her from prison."

Perhaps he had overplayed his hand. Both Slater and the Callahan girl looked at each other, and then the girl moved

382 | CHRISTY REECE

forward. She'd holstered her gun the moment she'd seen him in his chair, which had tickled him, but as she came closer, she pulled a long knife from a sheath at her waist.

"Call her. Now."

William bristled at the woman's bossy, unladylike tone. He had expected rudeness from Slater. Considering who'd sired the man, he was surprised he wasn't crawling on his belly. The girl surprised him, though. He remembered his father talking about Daniel Callahan being quite genteel—a gentleman thief, his father had called him. Too bad the girl hadn't learned her daddy's manners.

When she held up the knife, it glistened in the light, and William swallowed thickly, imagining how easily she could stick him and how much pain it would cause. The very thought of pain caused his bowels to loosen.

"Very well." Inwardly wincing because he knew the woman wouldn't be happy to hear from him again so soon, he punched in the numbers.

"Put it on speaker," Slater said.

William pressed speaker, and there was complete silence other than the ringing of the phone. As they waited for her to answer, William worked to settle himself down. This would take subtle finessing.

As they waited, Kathleen glared silently at Johnson. He looked even more like a pip-squeak than she had imagined. How could someone so innocuous and harmless-looking cause such destruction? He had thinning black hair, a small goatee, and light green eyes. He didn't look like a man who'd destroyed so many lives. The wheelchair had been the biggest surprise. None of their research had indicated a physical disability, which made her doubly wary.

After about the tenth ring, the phone was finally answered. "Yes?" Though it was a one-word answer, the tone indicated suspicion, disdain, and irritability.

"There's been a change of plans," William said.

"In what way?"

"I've been captured."

"I see."

"As per our agreement, the contract is now voided."

Total silence.

"Do you understand?" William asked.

"Perfectly," she said without the slightest hint of emotion. And then she added with surprising amusement, "Have a nice life...sentence." The phone clicked dead.

"Satisfied?" Johnson asked.

Kathleen saw the arrogance, the contempt in his eyes. He believed he was far from beaten.

"No." She took the phone from him and handed it to Grey.

Eli had pulled up two chairs, and sending him a quick smile of thanks, she sat down in one. The minute he'd settled into the other, Kathleen leaned forward, making sure the knife in her hand gleamed with sharp brilliance. "Now, we're going to talk. You're going to tell us everything we want to know."

"And why would I do that?" Johnson asked in a pleasant voice, as if they were discussing the weather.

She held up the knife and said softly, "Because I asked you to. That's why."

Eli relaxed into his chair, preferring to stay quiet for the moment and give Kathleen the floor. She had lost so much and deserved to be the one to begin the questioning.

"Tell us why you hired a hit on our families," she said.

"I thought you said you knew everything. Why then must I repeat it?"

"Because killing two generations of families for something that happened half a century ago seems quite lame."

Johnson sniffed. "You weren't the injured party."

"Yeah, well, neither were you, pal," Eli scoffed.

"My father suffered, so I suffered. It was a sin that carried consequences beyond death."

Kathleen cut her eyes over to Eli, who gave her a slight nod of agreement. Ego and overconfidence would be Johnson's downfall.

Eli took the first shot. "Something that petty?"

As first shots, it was enormously effective. Johnson's face went to an unhealthy, florid color, and his handcuffs rattled as he gripped the armrests of his chair. "Petty? You call the death of my grandmother and the ruination of my father petty?"

Sending a "can you believe this guy?" look over at Eli, Kathleen took her own shot. "Was your father not in on the robbery? Didn't he cause the whole mess in the first place?"

"He was just a young man. They coerced him in to going along with it."

"So he was such a weakling, a coward, that he couldn't say no." Eli nodded. "Yeah, I can see why he'd carry a grudge. He blamed other people for his own spinelessness. Much the way you have."

Johnson's body began to shake. "You know nothing of what he suffered, we suffered. He was disowned by his family, forced out into the world to fend for himself."

"You know," Eli continued, "what I can't for the life of me understand is why those men, who obviously did have some guts, if questionable ethics, would pay your weasel of a father a penny, much less thousands of dollars for decades."

"They had reputations they didn't want ruined."

"But the amounts were so measly," Eli said. "Why not ask for more. The men, other than Daniel Callahan, had millions. Why only a few thousand?"

"It wasn't the amount that mattered. My father didn't need the money. It was the acknowledgment of their guilt, their perfidy. My father asked for so little. Then they refused to pay even that. It was an insult. A slap in the face to a man who had lost so much. They had to be punished. Put down."

"We know Braden's death was a setup and Alice was innocent," Kathleen said. "That the woman who shot Alice was forced into it to protect her daughter. We also know that a woman posing as a nurse killed Alice in the hospital while she was struggling to stay alive."

"Really?"

A surge of pure hatred went through Kathleen, the smug smile on Johnson's face almost more than she could bear. It would be so easy. One swipe of her knife to his throat and he'd never hurt anyone again. He and his father had taken so much from her.

She felt a comforting hand on her arm and looked up into Eli's sympathetic eyes. He knew exactly what she was going through, what she was feeling. Just from that small touch and look, she gained the strength she needed to resist temptation.

Johnson chortled. "You two are in love. How precious is that? And you owe it all to me."

"Why'd you want us to meet?" Eli asked.

"An indulgence on my part, I must admit. I just had to see what would happen." He gave an eerie kind of giggle. "It was a little like playing people chess."

"You enjoying playing people, don't you, Johnson?" Eli said.

He sniffed disdainfully. "You should thank me for bringing you together."

A memory flashed in her mind of one of the last conversations she'd had with her sister. The man in a wheelchair who'd asked Alice so many questions. "You saw Alice in Chicago. When she was still under Braden's thumb."

A thin smile twitched at Johnson's mouth. "Another indulgence, I admit. I had seen photos of her on her website. Such a lovely treat. She was hard to resist."

Nausea roiled her stomach. "You didn't touch her. She said you didn't."

"I don't pay for whores."

She lunged toward him, her knife drawn. Eli wrapped his arms around her, holding her in place. "He's not worth it, Kat. He's nothing."

"You're right." She gave Johnson one last glare of disgust. "He's not."

Eyes glittering with evil excitement, Johnson was clearly enjoying being the center of attention.

"How'd you get my brother to send those emails?"

"What emails?"

"The games are over." Eli's voice held a lethal edge. "What did you promise Adam?"

His disappointment obvious, Johnson's eyes lost a little of their shine. "An opportunity to escape prison."

"You never intended to help him escape, though. Did you?"

The self-satisfied smile returned. "But of course not. He was going to be killed trying to break out. It was amusing to use him, play him." Johnson gave that odd, mad little giggle again as he added, "He's not very bright."

Judging by the bubbling fury she could feel about to explode within him, Kathleen figured Eli was within a second or two of killing the vermin in front of them. "Let's go, Eli. I can't be in the room with this filth any longer."

They were halfway to the door when Eli turned back around. "When we met in Chicago, you weren't in a wheelchair. Why are you now? What's wrong with you?"

Johnson sniffed indignantly. "That question is in poor taste. Though I should expect nothing less from a Slater."

"Answer the man's question," Grey snapped.

"I have a deteriorating condition of the spine. In a couple of years, maybe less, I'll be completely bedridden."

"Breaks my heart," Eli said. "Doesn't it yours, Kat?"

"Yeah. Real tragedy."

"Let's get him out of here." Sheriff Sanders, who'd been kind enough to allow them this time, stepped forward.

Eli took Kathleen's hand and pulled her from the room. Neither of them needed to be around Johnson any longer. They had accomplished what they'd intended. Prolonging it would have done nothing but give the bastard more opportunity to gloat.

Justice walked out with them. "When did you figure out it was Adam who sent all the emails?"

"I wasn't for sure until Johnson confirmed it, but Adam's smugness kept playing in my mind. There had to be a reason for it." He shook his head in disbelief. "Idiot actually believed Johnson would help him escape.

"Funny, I told Jonah I didn't think Adam was involved because he needed somebody to lead him to be able to carry anything off. Naive of me to not realize he was working for the enemy."

"I'll make sure Adam's notified that he's been had," Justice said. "I'm sure he'll be quite disappointed." He jerked his head toward the door they'd just exited. "You heard everything you needed to hear?"

"It was enough," Eli said. "Were you able to trace the woman's location?"

"Yes. She's still in Dallas." He gave Eli a small, pained smile. "At the Slater House Hotel."

"Shit," Eli muttered softly.

"I've got people headed there as we speak," Justice said.

"Think they can take her alive?"

"That's my intent."

"No way in hell is that contract canceled."

Justice nodded. "Agreed."

"She's got nothing to lose now. She'll be gunning for us any way she can."

They all turned at the sound of the mechanized motor of Johnson's wheelchair. He wasn't looking quite so confident now as a small bead of perspiration rolled down his forehead. To keep him from being able to hurt Kathleen any further, Eli put an arm around her shoulders and led her to the other side of the porch. If Johnson even knew they were there, he didn't let on. Eli figured the man had more on his mind now than taunting them.

Once he rolled down the ramp at the other end of the porch, they watched as his hands were uncuffed so he could be lifted into the backseat of the patrol car. The instant the cuffs came off, Johnson went into action. Knocking aside the deputy who was assisting him, Johnson took off running down the hillside and into the woods.

Eli, Kathleen, Justice, and Nick, along with the sheriff and the deputy, ran after him. Something inside had told Eli that the man was faking his handicap. He should have listened to his instincts.

Darkness hadn't yet set, but a thin, damp fog was swirling through the trees, obscuring their vision. They were all armed. Johnson had no weapons, and despite his ability to escape the sheriff's deputy, he wasn't in good physical condition, nor was he trained to evade his pursuers. The mountains were dense with trees, filled with wild animals and hazards of all kinds.

One way or the other, William Johnson would be caught.

His lungs burned from overexertion, and the air wheezing from his mouth sounded like a dysfunctional teakettle. When this was over and he was safe, he'd go to a place where he could get in better shape. He'd always preferred exercising his brain more than his body, but since he would be on the lam for the rest of his life, perhaps it would be best if he were in better shape.

As his feet crunched over wet leaves and rotted branches, a part of him wanted to sit down and cackle at how he'd fooled them all. He'd been using the wheelchair ruse for years. People were always extra careful and considerate toward people with disabilities. They had been so arrogant, so rude with their weapons, their insults. If only he could see their faces as they pursued him. He was a phantom. They would never catch him, because he had a plan. He always had a plan.

Slipping and sliding down the hill, William spotted the headlights of the car waiting for him. The minute he'd heard the caravan of vehicles arrive, he'd set this exit strategy into action. The extra time of questioning had been excruciating but important for his getaway plan.

The minute he was in the car and safely away, he'd call his hired gun and reassure her that his phone call to her canceling the contract had been a ruse. He thought she knew that already, but he'd double check, just in case. Eli Slater and Kathleen Callahan would both get a bullet in the head. Then he'd have the remaining family members picked off, one by one. The entire Slater family would be crazed with fear, not knowing who would be next.

Yes, it was all working out just as he'd—

His feet flew out from under him, and he landed with a painful, bruising impact on his butt. Then kept sliding. William reached out to grab a limb, and it came apart in his hands. His heart thudding with a new kind of fear, he grappled for anything he could grab hold of to catch him. The lip of a drop-off loomed ahead. If he didn't catch on to something soon, he would go off the cliff. As he slid downward, he spotted a tree stump directly ahead. He dug his heels into the wet ground, trying to slow his descent. The tree stump would stop him, but he didn't want to hit it too hard. His plan worked perfectly. He skidded into the stump, stopping abruptly just before he went off the ledge. Giddy with relief, giggling at the adventure he hadn't expected, William stood on tired, shaky legs.

A noise behind him startled him, and he jerked around.

Eli Slater and Kathleen Callahan stood before him.

"It's over, Johnson," Slater growled.

Shaking his head, William jumped back and stumbled. The stump that had saved him from falling, tripped him. Arms swinging like windmills, he tried to find something solid to grab.

Something stopped him from falling. He looked up to see that both Slater and Callahan had hold of his jacket. Their expressions were grim with resolve; they had saved him from certain death.

Laughing at the irony and their stupidity, he took a step forward, toward them. It wasn't over. He'd find another way to escape. He was a Johnson and a Johnson always had a—

The ground crumbled, then disappeared beneath his feet, and William plunged downward. His cry echoed through trees as he fell into cold dark nothingness. The last image in his mind was the bitter disappointment on his father's face.

CHAPTER
FORTY-FIVE

Dallas

It was a somber group that disembarked onto the tarmac at the private airstrip. The night hadn't ended in the way they'd hoped. Not only had William Johnson gotten off easy by getting himself killed, the killer he'd hired was nowhere to be found. Grey's people had arrived at the location of the cellphone ping only to find an empty hotel room. The added insult that it was a Slater House Hotel was of no consequence. She had disappeared, that was all they cared about.

Sitting beside Eli, Kathleen had managed about an hour's sleep. Eli hadn't slept at all. His eyes were bloodshot and filled with worry. That worry grew only stronger when his cellphone rang a few moments after landing.

Taking in his grim expression, Kathleen knew something dire had happened.

"What the hell do you mean the house blew up?"

Only able to hear one side of the conversation, she stared at Eli in horror.

Apparently seeing her worry, he punched a button and put the call on speaker. "It's Jonah."

"The house in Toulouse where Mother and Mathias used to vacation each year. I caught it on the news this morning. Happened a couple of days ago. No one hurt. House was empty."

"Dammit," Eli said. "She took the chance it's where the family is staying. She didn't care who she hurt."

"You want me to get them out of France?" Jonah asked.

Eli's gaze connected with hers as he said, "We're headed there in a few hours. Alert the guards and stay on lockdown."

"Will do."

Ending the call, Eli immediately made another one. "I need the plane ready to leave for France in two hours."

As soon as he ended that call, Kathleen grabbed his hand. "Tell me."

"My parents vacationed in Toulouse every year at the same house. It's where they honeymooned. It exploded yesterday."

"So she wasn't even sure if her targets were in the house. She's getting reckless."

"And more dangerous." Eli closed his eyes. "If they'd been there…" He shook his head. "I've got to get them out of there."

Squeezing his arm, she whispered softly, "We will. We'll take them someplace safe, and then we'll go after this bitch with everything we have."

He pressed his forehead against hers. "I love you, Kathleen Callahan. And as selfish as it seems, there's no one else I'd rather have at my side right now."

"That's because you know I can kick ass with the best of them."

"Yes, I do."

"We'll get through this. And once this is over, we're going to have a wonderful life together. I promise."

"Yes, we will."

This was beyond irritating. The house where Mathias and Eleanor Slater had vacationed each year had seemed like the perfect spot for Eli to hide his family. Okay, yes, it had seemed too easy, but the correct answers were often the most obvious. It had taken days to uncover the location, and now she had nothing to show for it.

She allowed herself an indignant sniff, a little shrug of her shoulders, and then moved on. Other than lost time and the aggravation of needing to do more research, she wasn't really out anything. But still, it was a setback she didn't like. And, if she were being honest, it was a bit embarrassing. Two failed attempts were unheard of in her line of work. Admittedly, now that Johnson had been arrested, she had all the time in the world to get the job done, but she had a reputation to uphold. She had planned for this job to be a career triumph for her. Instead, it was turning into a giant bust.

She had to step up her game.

So she had returned to Dallas to do a little recon work. Not her favorite thing. She much preferred making the kill. But busy work was part of her job. She had put off this particular method simply because it could get so messy. She was a goal-oriented killer. Meaning she didn't like to include other people who weren't on her agenda already. Okay, yes, she'd used the killer by proxy method several times because…honestly, it was fun. Screwing with people's heads like that was an enjoyable byproduct. But this? No, this wasn't a favorite part of her job, but it had to be done.

She stood in front of the modest but obviously expensive home. She knew enough about this family to know only one woman occupied the house most of the year. A widow with no children, Phillippa Morton stayed busy with her church, her charity work. She had a reputation for being somewhat of a loner with only a few friends, but she was apparently quite loyal to those few. A test of that loyalty was about to occur. Would Phillippa pass or fail?

She knocked on the heavy oak door. When no one answered, she rang the doorbell. At last she saw the outline of someone through the thick glass. With a sweet, sincere smile pasted on her face, she waited. The door opened, and Phillippa Morton, Eleanor Slater's best friend in the whole world, stood before her.

"Yes?"

The woman had the look of a pampered, spoiled woman who'd never seen hardship a day in her life. Unfortunately, before the day was over, Phillippa would know a horror most people could barely fathom. She had just answered the door to her very own nightmare.

Holding out her hand, she took Phillippa's and said, "Mrs. Morton? I'm a friend of Eleanor Slater's. May I speak with you?"

Like any friendly Southerner, she opened the door wider and smiled. "Why, of course. Please come in."

His feet slapping against the wet pavement in a hypnotic rhythm, sweat dripping from every pore, Grey pushed himself harder. For convenience sake, he usually used the treadmill in his private gym, but tonight, fresh air was a necessity. It was well past midnight, so the streets were mostly empty. Which was good, because right now he needed solitude.

For as long as he could remember, he'd had a plan. One that had worked with surprising success. Escaping his past had been his number one priority. Once that was achieved, he'd concentrated on building the life he wanted. Creating his wealth hadn't been difficult. He'd had good luck, made sound decisions, worked hard, and reaped the rewards. It had helped that he enjoyed his work. Once he had established himself, had the wealth he desired, he'd developed his victims' advocacy group. The organization did valuable work, and he was proud to be a part of it, but that hadn't been enough. So he had done more.

Perhaps because of his heritage, perhaps in spite of it, he had needed to do more.

His life, though not perfect, and God knew he wasn't perfect, had been a good one. He had been satisfied. Was that because she had been with him for so long? From the beginning?

But now, Irelyn was out there somewhere, and she was in trouble. He felt it to the marrow of his bones—she needed him. How to get to her, to help her? That was the clincher. She no longer trusted him, no longer wanted their partnership. While he understood her reasoning, he couldn't accept it. He had to find her.

His cellphone rang in his pocket. Skidding to a halt, Grey slid his finger over the screen to answer. As if his need had conjured her, he heard Irelyn's voice say, "Ivy Roane."

So relieved to hear from her, to know that she was alive, Grey didn't immediately comprehend her words. "What?"

"The woman trying to kill Eli and his family. That's her name. It's not me."

"I know it's not, baby."

He heard an odd choking noise that sounded almost like a soft sob. "It's been a long time since you called me anything sweet, like baby."

"We haven't had many sweet moments."

"No, I guess we haven't."

"Where are you, Irelyn? I'll come to you. I—"

As if the intimate words had never occurred, her voice went serious, hard. "Those in the business know her as Poison Ivy, as that's her preferred kill method. She's been a contract killer for a half-dozen years." She paused a beat. "She's one of his."

Something he'd already figured out. "He made her look like you. Hell, her name is even similar to yours. Why?"

"That's something I'll ask when we're finally face-to-face. Unfortunately, we can't ask him directly."

She would be forever throwing that back in his face. Yeah, nothing less than he deserved. But damned if he would regret the bastard's death. Hill Reed had deserved death more than any person he'd ever known.

"She'll have it out for you, Grey. She may not wait until her current job is done before she comes after you."

"She'll be after you, too, Irelyn."

"Yes, I know."

"Then lets fight her together. Come back to Dallas."

"I can't. You know that. You know why."

"I can keep you safe."

The soft laugh was one he often heard in his dreams. "You know I can protect myself."

"Then come back and protect me."

"You have an advantage. She doesn't know how deadly you are, what you can do. That doesn't mean she won't get you in a weak moment, though. Watch your back, Grey. I'd be very pissed off if she got to you before I did."

The line went dead. He cursed softly. Even though he knew it was pointless, Grey put an immediate trace on the call. And as expected, got nothing. Irelyn was too smart to be that careless.

Once again he was left with more questions than answers, along with an ache that would never cease until he found her again.

CHAPTER FORTY-SIX

Lorient, France

Eli and Kathleen sat on the small sofa, the children snuggled between them. They'd been huddled like this for at least an hour. If it were up to him, they'd stay like this forever. But he had only a limited amount of time to act. They were leaving in a short while. The Slater yacht he'd had docked at the marina for such an event as this was being prepped. In a few hours, everyone he loved would be on the water, safely away from danger.

But first things first.

"And then Aunt Lacey drew a picture of me and Pia and put it up on the wall. Want me to go get it?"

Violet had yet to stop talking, and though he was happy to be back with his children, it broke his heart a little that his baby girl had grown so much in such a short time. The last time he'd seen her, she'd been the quiet one. Now, as if she were trying to catch up with her sister, she'd been chattering nonstop. Even Sophia was having trouble getting all of her questions in, which, thank you, God, hadn't stopped.

Eli resented that he'd missed a single second of watching them grow.

As if she could read his thoughts, Kathleen squeezed his shoulder gently. "You'll catch up, Eli."

He sent her a smile of appreciation. "I know it."

"Do you want me to go and get it, Daddy?"

"Maybe in a few minutes, Violet. I want to talk to you both about something."

Both his daughters looked up at him, so innocent, so sweet. Dammit, they deserved every good thing. And he was going to start with the very best thing right now.

Shooting Kathleen a look of apology, since they hadn't talked about how they would do this beforehand, Eli said, "I asked Kathleen to marry me."

Two little golden-blond heads turned from him and looked up at Kathleen who was looking both startled and extremely nervous.

"Really?" Sophia said. "You mean, we'll be a real family, with a daddy and a mommy?"

"Mommy? Oh, sweetheart...I..." Kathleen gave Eli a quick help-me look. "Your mommy is—"

"Yes," Eli said. "We'll be a real family, with a daddy and a mommy."

Accepting her father's statement, Sophia continued, "And you'll come live in our house, too?"

"Yes," Kathleen said.

"And you won't leave?"

"No, I won't leave."

"Ever?"

Kathleen shared a tender look with Eli and then said softly, "Ever."

Not to be outdone, Violet had her own demands. "Will you read *Starburst* to us?"

Kathleen gave a relieved laugh. "Yes, I will."

"Every night?"

Kathleen enveloped both girls in a fierce hug. "Every single night."

"Okay." Then, showing that she hadn't forgotten her daddy's promise, Violet looked back up at Eli. "Now can I go get the picture that Lacey drawed of me and Pia?"

"Yes," Eli said. "I'd love to see it."

The girls sprang up together and took off running. Sophia stopped at the door and said, "Do I get to call you Mommy?"

Her eyes glimmering with tears, Kathleen shot another anxious, pleading look his way. He understood her dilemma. She didn't want to take anything away from Shelley. And while he appreciated that, Sophia barely remembered her mother. Having her accept Kathleen as her mother was what he had hoped for.

Nodding his approval, he said, "That sounds good to me."

"Then yes, please, Sophia. I would love for you to call me Mommy."

Her smile bright, she said, "'Kay," and then ran after her sister.

Kathleen turned to Eli, so full of emotion she could barely think straight. "I don't know what to say," she whispered softly.

"Before they come back in, there's something else I need to ask you."

"What?"

"Marry me now."

"Now?" she squeaked.

"Yes, now. Today. As soon as we get on the water."

"But...I..."

"We can have another wedding later on, so Kennedy, Nick, and Justice can be there. And anyone else you want to invite. But let's do it officially today, privately."

"Why?"

"I want you to be mine as soon as possible."

Dread washed over her. "You're doing this, in case…" No, she couldn't finish the sentence.

"I want you to be part of the family, Kat. Immediately. I love you, you love me. There's no reason not to make it official. Is there?"

Peace settled within her. Even though she knew Eli's rush to get married was in case Johnson's hired killer found them, he was right. There was no reason to wait. Whether it was one day of marriage or fifty years, she wanted it to begin immediately, too.

"But what about a minister?"

"He's meeting us on the yacht."

She grinned. "Pretty sure of yourself, aren't you?"

"Sure of myself? Occasionally. Sure of you and of my love for you? One thousand percent."

At the naked emotion in his eyes, the sweetness of his words, love swelled within Kathleen, almost overwhelming her in happiness. "Then yes, I do believe I'd like to get married today."

Eli's arms closed around her, and they shared a tender kiss. In just a few hours, she and this wonderful man would be married. And they, along with two beautiful little girls, were going to have a happy, long life together. She refused to think anything different.

"Can I take this one, too?" Sophia asked.

Kathleen looked at the dolls and books already lined up to be packed. Eli had asked her to help the girls gather a few toys and books to take with them on their trip. From the looks of things, they might need a bigger boat.

"How about just the ones who want to go on vacation with you? Then, when we get back, we'll gather them all together, and those who went can tell those who stayed behind all about their trip." She nodded at the line of dolls. "Which ones are the very best storytellers?"

While Sophia made that choice, Kathleen went to the other side of the room, where Violet was gathering up a year's worth of art supplies. Thankfully, everything was flat and fit perfectly in the small suitcase designated for toys.

"You don't want to take one of your dolls or animals?"

Violet's lip trembled, and her brown eyes glimmered with tears. Panicked, Kathleen crouched down. "What's wrong, sweetheart?"

"That lady took my fluffy puppy and won't give it back."

"What lady?"

"The one standing over there."

Icy fear sliding through her veins, Kathleen's hand surreptitiously went to her ankle holster and pulled her weapon. "Stand behind me," she whispered to Violet. "No matter what. Okay?"

Innocent eyes wide with fear, Violet nodded quickly.

Kathleen gave her a quick, reassuring smile. Then, as if she had all the time in the world, she stood and slowly turned. A tall, slender woman with black hair, silver-gray eyes, and a pouty little smile was standing in the doorway. In one hand she held a dingy white, floppy-eared stuffed dog, in the other hand was a Glock pointed directly at Sophia.

"We meet at last, Kathleen."

A calm resolve washed over Kathleen. Damned if she would allow the slightest harm to come to these children, her children.

Her hand steady, she pointed her weapon directly at the woman they now knew as Ivy Roane. Without taking her eyes off the hired killer, Kathleen said calmly, "Sophia, come over here with me, sweetheart."

Ivy surprised Kathleen by allowing Sophia to move to her. As soon as Sophia was close enough to touch, Kathleen reached for her and put her behind her back, where Violet stood.

"Now, Kathleen," the woman mocked, "do you really think you're going to be able to protect those little chicklings when you're lying dead on the floor?"

"Maybe not, but if you shoot, so will I."

"I've studied your portfolio. You're quite the marksman."

"Which you apparently aren't."

She tilted her head. "Now why would you be saying a thing like that?"

"Getting someone else to do your dirty work for you?"

"Ah, you're speaking of your little sister, Alice."

Kathleen's gut churned. Everything within her wanted to shoot the woman in the head and be done with it. It would be a selfish, irresponsible act, because if something happened and the woman shot Kathleen instead, the children would be at this woman's mercy. And she had none.

"You forced someone to shoot Alice, and then when that didn't work, you killed her yourself."

A little smile lifted Ivy's mouth. "Took you forever to figure that out, didn't it? But I put the poor, dear girl out of her misery. She wasn't going to make it."

"You murdered a helpless, innocent woman who couldn't defend herself."

"Innocent? Oh my dear, your little sister lost her innocence long before she met me. To be honest, I did the girl a favor."

"Killing her was a favor?"

"Well, not that part, but the other."

"Killing Frank Braden was no favor. She was framed for a murder she didn't commit."

Surprise flickered on her face, and then she laughed. Kathleen was struck that though her beauty was almost too perfect, her true nature revealed itself in her laugh. It was one of the most evil sounds Kathleen had ever heard.

"You really don't know, do you? Perhaps I gave you too much credit for being the brainy one."

"What are you taking about?"

"Alice put the poison in his brandy. She really did kill Frank Braden."

It shouldn't have surprised her, but it did. Why Alice had never told her the truth she didn't know. Didn't matter now, but the hurt was there all the same.

"Now before you go and get all mad at little Alice, let me explain. I approached her when she was coming out of a hotel where she'd spent the night servicing one of Braden's clients. We went for coffee. Poor, dear girl looked so alone and desperate, like she really could use a friend."

That comment, more than any other, slashed at Kathleen's conscience.

"I offered her the choice of killing Braden or me killing you. Poor thing already felt guilty for the hit-and-run that almost killed you. She thought Braden had done that because she'd run away from him. You probably know by now that he had nothing to do with it. Anyway, it was easy enough to get her to put the poison in his brandy. She knew he drank a glass every night."

As much as it hurt her to know Alice had been forced into doing that, it didn't surprise her. Alice had felt so alone. And she had been protecting Kathleen.

But there was one thing she was sure of. "You're the one who used the knife on him. Alice didn't do that."

"I did that for Alice. Frank Braden was a despicable human being. Mutilating him was quite satisfying. It was just unfortunate that he was dead before it happened."

Kathleen had heard enough…more than enough. She needed to get the children away from this murdering bitch. The things they'd already heard would give them nightmares for years.

Still holding the gun on Ivy, Kathleen began to walk backward and used her other hand to wave at the girls to back up, too.

"Now, now, now. No cheating."

"You only know how to destroy the defenseless and weak. Why don't you give yourself a real challenge?"

"And what would you be proposing?"

"Take me on, hand to hand. Loser dies, winner lives."

"Not that I think I would lose, but you must understand, you cannot live. I have a contract to fulfill."

"Not anymore. William Johnson is dead."

A brilliant smile brightened her features into an otherworldly beauty. "So the little bastard finally bought it. Good riddance, I say. He was an irritating little prick. I can't, however, shirk my duties. The contract is still valid. Besides, I have a reputation to maintain."

"A reputation for only killing the weak and innocent is pitiful."

She shrugged. "It pays the bills." But Kathleen could see that her interest had been piqued. And perhaps her ego slightly dented.

"What are you afraid of, Ivy?"

When the woman started slightly, Kathleen knew she had surprised her. "You're not as smart as you seem to think."

"But of course I am. You think it matters that you know my name?"

"Yes, I do."

"Put the children in the closet. I'll take care of them when I'm finished with you."

Without taking her eyes off Ivy, Kathleen spoke softly to the children. "Girls, go get in the closet." And lowering her voice even more, praying only they could hear her, she added, "When I shout 'go,' run downstairs and out the door. Don't stop for anything."

Both girls were whimpering in fear, and she wished with all her might she could turn around and reassure them. But Ivy Roane was as unpredictable as she was deadly. No way in hell would Kathleen trust her to keep her promise.

Out of the corner of her eye, she saw the girls run to the closet and then close the door. Her heart sank. Had they not heard her about running? Knowing she had no choice, she turned back to her opponent.

"So I guess it's best that we lay our weapons down at the same time," Ivy said.

"Very well. On three." Wary of a trick, Kathleen kept her eyes on the weapon in Ivy's hand. If the woman reneged, she had to be prepared to shoot.

"One. Two. Three."

At the same time that Ivy placed her gun on the bed, Kathleen put hers on the table beside her.

They walked several steps toward each other and then began to circle, each looking for the opportunity to strike, for that one vulnerable spot.

Noting how Ivy kept her shoulders rounded, her hands loose at her sides, Kathleen knew the woman was expecting an upper-body strike. Ivy was about five inches taller and probably weighed a good thirty pounds more, mostly muscle. Since she'd always been small, Kathleen had learned how to use an opponent's size and weight against them. But first, she had to get the woman off guard. Springing up, Kathleen kicked out, slamming her foot into Ivy's kneecap.

Ivy stumbled back, and Kathleen took advantage and leaped toward her, slamming the woman into the wall. At the same time, she shouted at the girls, "Go!"

Beneath the rush of blood, she heard the girls screaming as they emerged from the closet and ran out of the room. The next second, Ivy retaliated, and Kathleen went headfirst into a nightstand. Her ears ringing from the blow, she glanced up to see a fist coming at her full force. Kathleen rolled away, dodging at the last second. Jumping to her feet, she leaped onto Ivy, the momentum carrying them both to the floor.

Eli loaded the last of the bags into the back of the SUV. He'd told both his mother and Lacey to pack light. Their interpretation of light wasn't the same as his.

"Looks like we're ready to roll," Macon Yates said.

"I don't think there's room for anything else in the back." He checked his watch. "You go ahead with my mother, sister, and Teresa. Kathleen's helping the girls pick out some toys to take. We'll catch up with you."

Yates nodded. "We'll see you in a few minutes."

He waited while the SUV backed out of the drive. Jonah, Trevor Yost, and two other guards were already on the yacht, ensuring its security. As soon as they were all on the boat, they'd head out to the middle of the ocean. No way in hell could Ivy Roane get to his family there.

Pulling his phone from his pocket, he pressed the speed-dial number for Gunter as he walked toward the chalet. Frowning when the man didn't answer, Eli sped up, running toward the steps. His heart almost stopped when he heard Sophia and Violet screaming. Taking the steps three at a time, he met them on the porch.

Grabbing them in his arms, he asked, "What's wrong?"

"A woman with a gun is fighting with Kathleen!" Sophia shouted.

Eli picked both girls up and headed down the steps.

"Mr. Eli!"

Turning, he saw Gunter coming around the house, holding the side of his head. "Sorry, sir. Got caught from behind."

"Take the girls and get out of here."

"But, sir. She's—"

"I don't have time to argue. Kathleen and I will handle her. Take care of my children, Gunter. That's all I ask."

Dropping a quick kiss on each daughter's head, he handed them over. Turning his back on them, knowing Gunter would protect them, Eli dashed back up the steps. Kathleen was somewhere in there, fighting for her life.

CHAPTER FORTY-SEVEN

Bruised, breathless, and aching, Kathleen circled the other woman. With the children safe, she'd been able to concentrate solely on bringing this bitch down. Ivy Roane was a tough, well-trained killer, but Kathleen had an advantage this woman would never understand. She had a lifetime of love to fight for. This woman killed for money, only knew how to destroy.

Ivy wasn't looking quite as lovely as she had when she arrived. Her left eye was swollen closed, blood seeped from her nose, her lip was busted, and she now had a distinct limp. She was also panting, and anger had replaced the earlier smugness.

"You think you're winning, bitch? I'm just getting started. When I'm through with you, I'll gut those two brats in front of their father, and then shoot him in the head. Then I'll do the rest of the family, one by one."

"Your threats are as laughable as that crooked nose you're now sporting."

"So we're resorting to cheap shots about our appearances now?"

Kathleen shrugged. "It was an easy one to make." She cut her eyes right, as if someone had come up behind Ivy. The woman jerked her head a bit. It was exactly the diversion Kathleen needed.

In one smooth move, she bent and slid her knife from the sheath at her ankle and threw it. Ivy jerked back. The knife landed with a thud in the wall where Ivy's head should have been.

Something like respect gleamed in Ivy's eyes. "Well, now, aren't you full of surprises? Yet, it's very tacky to change the rules in the middle of our game."

"I save my classy moves for those who actually know what class is."

"Ouch."

A movement behind Ivy told her Eli had arrived and that meant the girls were safe. He was holding a gun in his hand, pointed directly at Ivy.

"It's over," Eli shouted. "Get on your knees, put your hands in the air."

Ivy stiffened for a moment. Then she grabbed the knife embedded in the wall and twisted around to Eli.

Kathleen yelled, "Eli, watch out!" And sprang forward, tackling Ivy.

Eli fired his gun just as the knife flew from Ivy's hand. Kathleen landed on the woman's back, slamming her down onto the floor. When her body went still, Kathleen rolled over. Ivy's eyes were closed, her face pale and still. She was unconscious, but the hit hadn't been hard. They needed to restrain her.

Thinking to ask Eli to find something to tie her up, she looked up, and then her heart stopped. He was leaning against the doorframe, Kathleen's knife sticking out of his chest.

Scrambling to her feet, she ran to him. "No, no, no."

"Damn, that hurts."

"Sit down, Eli. Sit down. Let me see how bad it is."

"I'm okay. I think I deflected it a little. Hit bone more than flesh."

Her hands shaking, she jerked at the buttons and looked beneath his shirt. The knife had hit him on the upper left side. Though it was embedded at least a couple of inches in his chest, he was right. The bone had likely deflected it, but he was bleeding profusely.

"I turned at the last second. She missed her mark. I don't think—shit! She's getting away."

Kathleen twisted around to see Ivy limping out of the room.

"We'll worry about her later. For right now, we need to get you some help."

"No. This ends today."

"But you're bleeding."

His expression unyielding, Eli gripped the knife handle and pulled it from his chest. Standing, he stalked to the attached bathroom and returned with a hand towel covering his wound. "This'll do for now. Let's go."

The sound of a boat engine starting up told them Ivy had reached the private boat dock, which was apparently how she had arrived.

Eli took a step toward her, held out his hand. "Let's go."

She took his hand and then watched as the blood drained from his face. "Eli?"

"Ah. Damn." He gave an odd, rough sort of laugh and then fell unconscious at her feet.

CHAPTER
FORTY-EIGHT

As twilight softened the day around them, Eli stood on the deck of the Slater yacht. Dressed in a black tuxedo, he waited for his bride. The last day and a half had been a whirlwind of gathering information, preparing, and oh yes, getting a couple of pints of blood.

Keeling over at Kathleen's feet hadn't exactly been his finest moment. It'd scared the hell out of her and had stopped them from being able to pursue Ivy Roane. And while that was hard to accept, it had been for the best. Not only had he been bleeding like a sieve, Kathleen had needed treatment for her sprained ankle, bruised ribs, and wrenched shoulder.

Eli had been stitched and received the blood he'd needed, Kathleen had gotten her injuries bandaged. Then they'd gathered everyone together, discussed options, and made plans. Setting a trap for a ruthless killer was hard enough. Setting the trap while ensuring that everyone came out alive, including the killer, was somewhat more complicated. Justice wanted to have a face-to-face with Ivy Roane, and Eli had promised him that if it was possible, they'd capture her alive.

It wouldn't be simple, and he was doubtful that it would come out as clean as they hoped. But, dammit, it would end here, tonight. He had a lifetime to look forward to, and he wanted to get started on it as soon as possible.

At the sound of the wedding song, Eli turned and faced the most beautiful sight this side of heaven. Kathleen, wearing the multicolored dress he'd purchased for her months before, walked toward him.

This woman, with her courage and her capacity for love, humbled him. If he looked the world over, he would never find anyone as fine, as lovely, or as perfect for him. Or for his daughters. He swore with everything within him that he would spend the rest of his days making sure all three of his girls were safe and knew how very loved they were.

But first they had a killer to capture.

Her heart racing for myriad reasons, Kathleen reached for Eli's hand. The two-carat diamond ring caught the last rays of sunlight, reflecting the hope and promise of the bright future that lay before them. In between making plans to bait and capture a killer, Eli had pulled her aside last night and surprised her with the most beautiful engagement ring she could ever have imagined.

Every fantasy she'd ever had of a handsome, charming, sexy man who would make all her dreams come true had happened. This man, with his good heart, integrity, and determination, had given her so much. And when this was all over, when everything was as it should be, she would spend the rest of her life with the love of her life and their two precious daughters.

Kathleen could think of no greater joy.

She gave him a nod of assurance and a brilliant smile of love. She wished this was for real. Wished that Sophia and Violet, who had stolen her heart the first moment they'd screamed, "Eudora!" could be here. But that was for later, when this nightmare was over.

For now, she smiled brilliantly and said, "We're set."

Though his smile was one of love and approval, she noted his eyes glittered with determination. His arm wrapped around her waist as he turned her to face the man dressed as a minister. The man, Simon Bonner, was a former special forces soldier who was as fully prepared as the rest of them to do what needed to be done.

There would be no surprises for anyone except for their prey.

"Dearly beloved. We are gathered here to unite this man and this woman in holy—"

A noise came from behind them. Not looking at each other, an arm wrapped around each other's waist, Kathleen and Eli turned as one.

Ivy Roane stood on the top step of the stairway, only a few feet away from them. Though her nose was swollen and slightly crooked, one eye was bruised and her mouth puffy from a busted lip, she somehow still managed to be beautiful. But her eyes had a dark coldness that told of the ugliness of this woman's soul. She had come here to kill and would destroy anyone who got in her way. A gun, steady in her hand, was pointed directly at Kathleen.

Okay, so far, so good. Even while nerves jittered and jumped inside her, Kathleen was relieved they wouldn't have to wait any longer for this final showdown.

Though she felt fury at the woman's arrogance, Kathleen fought to show only mild amusement. "I guess what they say is true about a bad penny always showing up."

Ivy gave an indolent lift of her shoulder. "I've got a job to do."

"Tenacious, aren't we? Do you honestly believe you can kill all of us and get away?"

The arch of an elegant brow said she believed she was far from being defeated. "It'll be like shooting fish in a barrel."

"You've tried several times, and you've failed each time," Eli said. "If you survive this and get away, you might want to consider another line of work. You obviously suck at this one."

While Kathleen knew that Eli wanted to keep Ivy's attention on him, insulting a killer was a risk. An injured one with a grudge made it even more dangerous.

"When your body is filled with bullets and sinking to the bottom of the ocean, you'll think different, Mr. Slater."

With her arm still around Eli, it was easy enough for Kathleen to slide out the nine-millimeter that he had hidden in the small of his back. In half a second, she was armed and pointing the gun at Ivy.

Ivy gave what might have been an approving nod. "Quite a bit more moxie than your sister. Poor Alice was so malleable. So easily led. So weak."

"Pissing me off is not the wisest course of action, Ivy. I could just shoot you."

"Perhaps. But you don't have the killer instinct."

"Unlike you."

"Yes," Ivy said softly, silver-gray eyes gleaming with pride. "Unlike me."

Kathleen wanted this woman to pay. Not just for what she had done to Alice, but for all the lives she had destroyed . Seeing her behind bars for the rest of her life would be sufficient.

Keeping Ivy's attention on Eli and herself, Kathleen said, "So what's your plan?"

"You will die, of course."

"Did you really think we wouldn't be prepared?" With an arrogant smugness designed to take her off guard and piss her off, Eli said, "You've been had, Ivy."

Showing that she really wasn't at her best, Ivy moved her head slightly, obviously just now noticing the six men surrounding her. Eli's four bodyguards, along with his brother Jonah and now Simon Bonner, were all armed, their weapons pointed directly at Ivy's head. She didn't stand a chance.

An ugly twisted grin briefly marred her beauty, and then she began to back toward the railing. "Touché, Mr. Slater. You won this round."

"Where do you think you're going?" Eli asked.

They were three stories up, and though Kathleen knew a fall into the water might not kill the woman, she would never survive in the open ocean, miles from land.

"It's much too crowded." Boosting herself up on the railing, Ivy gave a salute. "Until next time."

Anticipating her move, Kathleen sprang forward the instant Ivy fell backward and caught the woman by the wrist. They both plunged toward the water.

Sure that she and Ivy were both about to plummet to their deaths, Kathleen's breath caught in her throat when strong hands wrapped around her ankle. She looked up to see Eli holding her.

His eyes glimmering with a fierce determination, he shouted, "Let her go, Kat!"

"No. I can haul her back up, Eli. Help me. She has to pay."

"Let me go!" Ivy screamed and tugged hard.

This woman had killed Alice. Had tried to kill the man she loved. No way in hell was she going to let the bitch die this easily.

"Dammit, Kathleen. You have to let her go. I can't hold you both."

Bringing up the gun she still held in her hand, Ivy pointed it at Kathleen's head. "Let me go, bitch."

Pop!

For an instant, Kathleen wondered if Ivy had taken the shot and she just didn't feel it yet. Then she saw the woman's face, the blank, shocked look in her eyes that said she knew she'd lost.

"Drop her, Kat," Eli gritted out. "Now, dammit."

Kathleen opened her hands and watched Ivy tumble into the ocean, immediately swallowed up in a massive swell of water.

Pulling her up, Eli wrapped his arms around Kathleen and held her tight. She couldn't tell who was trembling the most. They held each other for several long moments. She knew there were people around them, scrambling to see if they could find Ivy Roane's body. She didn't care. She just wanted to stay in Eli's arms forever.

"It's over," she whispered. "It's really, finally, truly over."

Eli's hands cupped her face, and he kissed her softly, sweetly. "I love you, Kathleen Callahan. Now. Forever."

Her voice ragged with emotion, she said softly, "And I love you, Eli Slater. Now. Forever."

"Still want to marry me?"

"If possible, more than ever."

He gave her the beautiful, sexy smile she so loved. "Then let's go have a real wedding."

EPILOGUE

The lake house was the perfect place for a honeymoon. If anyone wondered why two children and a housekeeper had accompanied them, no one asked.

Sprawled in a chair, Eli smiled at the sound of his girls giggling. Kathleen sat in the middle of the floor, Violet on one side, Sophia on the other. They had played outside all morning. When it had started raining, they'd moved the fun indoors. Soon, Teresa would come for them, feed them lunch, and settle them down for a nap. Then he had nap plans of his own with his beautiful, sexy wife.

The last two weeks had been both exhausting and exhilarating. With both William Johnson and Ivy Roane out of the way, the fear was behind them. Explaining everything to the authorities in both France and the US had taken some time and diplomacy. Thankfully, with all the documentation, along with his and Justice's influence, the matter had been settled to everyone's satisfaction.

It hadn't been a happy ending for everyone. His mother was suffering from extreme guilt. She admitted that she'd given Phillippa their address in France so her friend could send a package of his mother's favorite cosmetics she hadn't been able to find in

France. Phillippa had been found beaten and bloodied in her hall closet. Why Ivy had left the woman alive would always be a mystery. The elderly woman was still in the hospital, recovering. Even though he hated that Phillippa had suffered, he was glad that his mother had taken it upon herself to care for her. It was time for Eleanor Slater to come out of hiding. She would never recover if she continued to dwell on the past.

Jonah was gone again. Eli had known he wouldn't hang around. He had an agenda and a mission. Nothing was going to stop him until he identified and destroyed the man who'd killed his fiancée. Eli understood his need but couldn't help but worry.

His sister, Lacey, had surprised him by declaring her intention to return to college and get a degree in psychology, claiming the need to try to figure out how the Slaters got so screwed up in the first place. He knew she hadn't been joking.

He'd seen Justice only once, and that had been at the small wedding reception Kennedy and Nick had thrown him and Kathleen when they'd arrived back in the States. Though Eli knew the man was relieved that Irelyn had had nothing to do with the murders or attempts on Eli's and Kathleen's lives, there was a lingering sadness in his demeanor. No matter how much he tried to hide it, his friend missed Irelyn Raine and needed her back in his life. Whether that would ever happen was anyone's guess.

How it came to be that Irelyn and Ivy looked like identical twins had yet to be answered. He'd questioned Justice about it and in return had gotten one of his famous blank looks. What Justice wanted people to know, he obliged. When he didn't, not even the devil himself could pry the information from him.

"Well, now, it's time for lunch for you two," Teresa announced from the doorway. "I've got peanut butter and jelly sandwiches all ready for you."

Jumping up, the girls gave quick kisses to Kathleen and then ran out the door.

Before leaving, Teresa gave him a twinkling smile. "I'll put them down for their nap and then occupy them for the rest of the afternoon. And perhaps tonight, too. If need be."

"Thank you, Teresa. Not only are you a jewel, you're also a very perceptive woman."

"Oh, Mr. Eli." Blushing slightly, she closed the door behind her.

Eli sat up and glanced over at his wife. "Care for a nap before lunch, my love?"

Gracefully getting to her feet, Kathleen Slater, the most beautiful woman in the world, replied softly, "My vote is a nap before and after lunch."

"You have a voracious appetite."

"Only for you, Mr. Slater. Only for you."

"Is that right, Mrs. Slater? Then perhaps an appetizer would be in order beforehand."

Kathleen placed one knee on either side of Eli's legs, straddling him. Her heart was so full she felt as if it might burst. Here was the joy she had longed for, never believing the possibility existed. After all the sadness, the heartache, and tears, this one man, with his determination, his good heart, had changed her life.

"Thank you, Eli."

"For what?"

"For interfering in my life."

His chest rumbled with laughter. "From anyone else that would sound like an insult, but I know what you mean. And believe it or not, it wasn't interfering so much as a necessity."

Kathleen nodded. "Because you wanted me to guard Sophia and Violet."

"No. That really never crossed my mind until I started getting the emails."

"Then why?"

"I didn't have a reasonable explanation for it then. Still don't. All I knew was the moment I saw you, I knew I had to have you in my life." His expression was both vulnerable and resolute as he added, "I can be quite ruthless in getting what I want."

Tears sprang to her eyes, and she whispered against his mouth, "Thank you for being ruthless, my love."

"My pleasure." His smile decidedly predatory, Eli proceeded to show her just how tenderly ruthless he could be.

Thank you for reading *Whatever It Takes, A Grey Justice Novel*. I sincerely hope you enjoyed it.

1. This book is lendable. Share it with a friend who would enjoy a dark and steamy romantic suspense.
2. Please consider writing a review at your favorite online retailer.
3. Be sure to sign up for my newsletter at http://christyreece. com to learn about upcoming books.
4. Follow me on Facebook at https://www.facebook.com/ AuthorChristyReece and on Twitter at http://www. twitter.com/christyreece

OTHER BOOKS BY CHRISTY REECE

Grey Justice Series

Nothing To Lose, A Grey Justice Novel

LCR Elite Series

Running On Empty, An LCR Elite Novel

Chance Encounter, An LCR Elite Novel

Last Chance Rescue Series

Rescue Me, A Last Chance Rescue Novel

Return To Me, A Last Chance Rescue Novel

Run To Me, A Last Chance Rescue Novel

No Chance, A Last Chance Rescue Novel

Second Chance, A Last Chance Rescue Novel

Last Chance, A Last Chance Rescue Novel

Sweet Justice, A Last Chance Rescue Novel

Sweet Revenge, A Last Chance Rescue Novel

Sweet Reward, A Last Chance Rescue Novel

Chances Are, A Last Chance Rescue Novel

Wildefire Series
Writing as Ella Grace

Midnight Secrets, A Wildefire Novel

Midnight Lies, A Wildefire Novel

Midnight Shadows, A Wildefire Novel

ACKNOWLEDGEMENTS:

Special thanks to the following people for helping make this book possible:

My husband, for his continued love and support, as well as numerous moments of comic relief.

My mom, who always listens with extreme patience, even though she's heard me complain about the same thing for every book I've written. Mom, 'these characters are driving me crazy' has got to be getting pretty stale by now. Love you!

My Aunt Billie and Uncle Marlin, for once again opening their home on the river to me.

Joyce Lamb, for her copyediting, fabulous suggestions, and delightful sense of humor.

Tricia Schmitt (Pickyme) for her beautiful cover art.

Marie Force's eBook Formatting Fairies for their professionalism and extreme patience.

Anne Woodall, my first reader, who always goes above and beyond, the extra mile, then one more mile, too, because she's just that awesome.

My beta readers, for reading so quickly and your great advice.

My proofreaders, for all the great catches you guys made. Special shout out to Linda for that 'one' awesome save.

The Reece's Readers street team, for their support, encouragement, and for spreading the word!

And a very special thank you to all my readers, for your patience and support. The encouraging emails and messages you've sent were so very much appreciated

ABOUT THE AUTHOR

Christy Reece is the award winning and New York Times Bestselling author of dark and sexy romantic suspense. She lives in Alabama with her husband, three precocious canines, an incredibly curious cat, one shy turtle, and a super cute flying squirrel.

Christy also writes steamy, southern suspense under the pen name Ella Grace.

You can contact her at <u>Christy@christyreece.com</u>

Praise for Christy Reece novels:

"*The type of book you will pick up and NEVER want to put down again.*" Coffee Time Romance and More

"Romantic suspense has a major new star!" *Romantic Times Magazine*

"Sizzling romance and fraught suspense fill the pages as the novel races toward its intensely riveting conclusion." *Publishers Weekly, Starred Review*

"*Flat-out scary, and I loved every minute of it!*" The Romance Reader's Connection

"*A brilliantly plotted book. Her main characters are vulnerable yet strong, and even the villains are written with skillful and delicate brush strokes haunting your mind long after the book is done.*" Fresh Fiction

"*A passionate and vivacious thrill-ride! ... I feel like I've been on an epic journey after finishing it.... Exquisite.*" Joyfully Reviewed